DATE DUE	BORROWER'S NAME	ROOM NUMBER

THE LOOKING GLASS BOOK OF STORIES

LOOKING GLASS LIBRARY

THE LOOKING GLASS BOOK OF STORIES

Edited by Hart Day Leavitt

LOOKING GLASS LIBRARY
Distributed by Random House
New York

Library of Congress Catalog Card Number: 60-9021

Manufactured in the United States of America by the Colonial Press Inc., Clinton, Massachusetts

Published in New York by Random House, Young Books, Inc.

Contents

SYMBOLIC STORIES

PURE ENTERTAINMENT

STRANGE PIECES

PART FUN, PART SYMBOL

HART DAY LEAVITT

Introduction

This book was not made up after asking young people what they like to read. It was put together after several young teen-agers asked where they could buy a book with such stories in it.

I had been reading these stories aloud to a group of eighth- and ninth-grade students, and my main reasons were that I just like the stories, and that I suspected my listeners had never heard anything like them.

It was true. Most of these young readers had been brought up on fiction that was too simple-minded, or too easily moralistic, or too conventional. They assumed that the only other kind of imaginative writing was what they saw in the fantastic images of science fiction.

They seemed to believe that there were only two kinds of literature: wildly fantastic, and utterly mundane. That the two might be joined was so strange that some of them thought it was not fair.

"Gee," said one boy, "I didn't think you were supposed to write good stories about things like THAT!" He had just read "The Hour of Letdown," which is based partly on a famous and not altogether proper joke.

Or else they were bewildered.

Imagine watching children frighten a ghost, or fighting fifty-one dragons, or seeing a musician conduct his orchestra with his tail, or meeting the devil in an oak tree.

That is the basis of these stories. . . . Just imagine!

It may be an entertaining game, as in Frank Stockton's sequel to "The Lady or the Tiger?" or it may be a dangerous game, as in Richard Connell's story, or it may be a secret and serious game, as in Conrad Aiken's tale of a young boy's imagination.

One thing it won't be is obvious moralizing and preaching, for no such stories have been included. Too many young people have been misled into believing that literature is not good unless it teaches a lesson. There are very few lessons here except those indirect ones that reveal the essence of style, humor, character and humanity.

I do hope that these qualities will, by surprising and challenging young readers, enable them to rise above the deadening influence of too much realism and practicality, which are erroneously supposed to be typical of an age of science. Great scientists have indulged in a great deal of nonsense before arriving at their great discoveries, so that there is a spiritual kinship between their wild imaginings and the disregard of no-nonsense which characterizes many of these stories.

SYMBOLIC
STORIES

MICHAEL FESSIER

That's What Happened to Me

I have done things and had things happen to me and nobody knows about it. So I am writing about it so that people will know. Although there are a lot of things I could tell about, I will just tell about the jumping because that is the most important. It gave me the biggest thrill. I mean high jumping, standing and running. You probably never heard of a standing high jumper but that's what I was. I was the greatest jumper ever was.

I was going to high school and I wasn't on any team. I couldn't be because I had to work for a drugstore and wash bottles and deliver medicine and sweep the floor. So I couldn't go out for any of the teams because the job started soon's school was over. I used to crab to the fellows about how old man Patch made me wash so many bottles and so they got to calling me Bottles Barton and I didn't like it. They'd call me Bottles in front of the girls and the girls'd giggle.

Once I poked one of the fellows for calling me Bottles. He was a big fellow and he played on the football team and I wouldn't have hit him because I was little and couldn't fight very well. But he called me Bottles before Anna Louise Daniels and she laughed and I was so mad I didn't know whether I wanted to hit her or the football player but finally I hit him. He caught my arm and threw me down and sat on me and pulled my nose.

"Look, Anna Louise," he said, "it stretches."

He pulled my nose again and Anna Louise put her arms around herself and jumped up and down and laughed and then I knew that it was her I should have taken the first poke at. I was more mad at her than the football player although it was him pulling my nose and sitting on me.

The next day I met Anna Louise in the hall going to ancient history class and she was with a couple of other girls and I tried to go past without them noticing me. I don't know why but I had a funny feeling like as if somebody was going to throw a rock at me or something. Anna Louise looked at me and giggled.

"Hello, old rubbernose," she said.

The girls giggled and I hurried down the hall and felt sick and mad and kind of like I was running away from a fight, although nobody'd expect me to fight a girl. And so they called me Bottles sometimes and Rubbernose other times and always whoever was near would laugh. They didn't think it was funny because Jimmy Wilkins was called Scrubby or Jack Harris was called Doodles. But they thought it was funny I was called Rubbernose and Bottles and they never got tired of laughing. It was a new joke every time.

Scrubby pitched for the baseball team and Doodles was quarterback of the football team.

I could have pitched for the baseball team or played quarterback on the football team. I could have pitched no-hit games and I could have made touchdowns from my own ten-yard line. I know I could. I had it all figured out. I went over how I'd throw the ball and how the batter'd miss and it was easy. I figured out how to run and dodge and straight-arm and that was easy too. But I didn't get the chance because I had to go right to Patch's Drugstore after school was out.

Old man Patch was a pretty good guy but his wife she was nothing but a crab. I'd wash bottles and old man Patch he would look at them and not say anything. But Mrs. Patch, old lady Patch, she would look at the bottles and wrinkle her nose and make me wash half of them over again. When I swept up at night she'd always find some corner I'd missed and she'd bawl me out. She was fat and her hair was all straggly and I wondered why in the deuce old man Patch ever married her, although I guess maybe she didn't look so awful when she was a girl. She couldn't have been very pretty though.

They lived in back of the drugstore and when people came in at noon or at six o'clock either old man or old lady Patch'd come out still chewing their food and look at the customer and swallow and then ask him what he wanted.

I studied salesmanship at high school and I figured this wasn't very good for business and I wanted to tell them but I never did.

One of the fellows at school was in waiting for a prescription and he saw me working at some of the things I did at the drugstore. So when another fellow asked me what I did this fellow he laughed and said, "Old Bottles! Why, he rates at that store. Yes, he does! He rates like an Armenian's helper."

That's about the way I did rate but I was planning on how I'd someday own a real, modern drugstore and run the Patches out of business so I didn't mind so much.

What I did mind was Anna Louise at school. She was the daughter of a doctor and she thought she was big people and maybe she was but she wasn't any better'n me. Maybe my clothes weren't so good but that was only temporary. I planned on having twenty suits someday.

I wanted to go up to her and say, "Look here, Anna Louise, you're not so much. Your father isn't a millionaire and someday I'm going to be one. I'm going to have a million dollars and twenty suits of clothes." But I never did.

After she laughed at me and started calling me Rubbernose, I began planning on doing things to make her realize I wasn't what she thought I was. That's how the jumping came about.

It was the day before the track meet and everybody

was talking about whether or not our school could win. They figured we'd have to win the high jump and pole vault to do it.

"Lord, if we only had old Heck Hansen back!" said Goobers MacMartin. "He'd outjump those Fairfield birds two inches in the high and a foot in the pole vault."

"Yeah," somebody else said, "but we haven't got Heck Hansen. What we got is pretty good but not good enough. Wish we had a jumper."

"We sure need one," I said.

There was a group of them all talking, boys and girls, and I was sort of on the outside listening.

"Who let you in?" Goobers asked me.

Frank Shay grabbed me by the arm and dragged me into the center of the circle.

"The very man we've been looking for," he said. "Yessir. Old Bottles Rubber-nose Barton. He can win the jumping events for us."

"Come on, Bottles," they said. "Save the day for us. Be a good old Rubbernose."

Anna Louise was one who laughed the most and it was the third time I'd wanted to pop her on the nose.

I went away from there and didn't turn back when they laughed and called and whistled at me.

"She'd be surprised if I did," I said.

I kept thinking this over and pretty soon I said, "Well, maybe you could."

Then when I was sweeping the drugstore floor I all of a sudden said, "I can!"

"You can what?" Mrs. Patch asked me.

"Nothing," I said.

"You can hurry about sweeping the floor, that's what you can do," she said.

There was a big crowd out for the track meet and we were tied when I went up to our coach. It was just time for the jumping to start.

"What the hell you doing in a track suit?" he asked me.

"I'm going to save the day for Brinkley," I said. "I'm going to jump."

"No, you aren't," he said. "You run along and start a marble game with some other kid."

I looked him in the eye and I spoke in a cold, level tone of voice.

"Mr. Smith," I said, "the track meet depends on the high jump and the pole vault and unless I am entered we will lose those two events and the meet. I can win and I am willing to do it for Brinkley. Do you want to win the meet?"

He looked amazed.

"Where have you been all the time?" he asked. "You talk like you've got something on the ball."

I didn't say anything, I just smiled.

The crowd all rushed over to the jumping pits and I took my time going over. When everybody had jumped but me the coach turned and said, "Come on now, Barton, let's see what you can do."

"Not yet," I said.

"What do you mean?" he asked.

"I'll wait until the last man has been eliminated," I said. "Then I'll jump."

The crowd laughed but I just stared coldly at them. The coach tried to persuade me to jump but I wouldn't change my mind.

"I stake everything on one jump," I said. "Have faith in me."

He looked at me and shook his head and said, "Have it your own way."

They started the bar a little over four feet and pretty soon it was creeping up toward five feet and a half. That's always been a pretty good distance for high school jumpers. When the bar reached five feet seven inches all our men except one was eliminated. Two from Fairfield were still in the event. They put the bar at five feet nine inches and one man from Fairfield made it. Our man tried hard but he scraped the bar and knocked it off.

The crowd started yelling, thinking Fairfield had won the event.

"Wait a minute," I yelled. "I haven't jumped yet."

The judges looked at their lists and saw it was so. Maybe you think it was against the rules for them to allow me to skip my turn but anyway that's the way it was.

"You can't make that mark," one of the judges said. "Why try? You're not warmed up."

"Never mind," I said.

I walked up close to the jumping standard and stood there.

"Go ahead and jump," one of the judges said.

"I will," I said.

"Well, don't stand there," he said. "Come on back here so's you can get a run at it."

"I don't want any run at the bar," I said. "I'll jump from here."

The judge yelled at the coach and told him to take me out on account of I was crazy.

I swung my arms in back of me and sprung up and down a second and then I jumped over the bar with inches to spare. When I came down it was so silent I could hear my footsteps as I walked across the sawdust pit. The judge that'd crabbed at me just stood and looked. His eyes were bugged out and his mouth hung open.

"Good Lord!" he said. "Almighty most loving Lord!"

Our coach came up and he stood beside the judge and they both looked the same, bug-eyed.

"Did you see that?" the coach asked. "Tell me you didn't. Please do. I'd rather lose this track meet than my mind."

The judge turned slowly and looked at him.

"Good Lord!" he said, "there's two of us."

All of a sudden everybody started yelling and the fellows near me pounded me on the back and tried to shake my hand. I smiled and brushed them aside and walked over to the judge.

"What's the high school record for this state?" I asked.

"Five feet, eleven inches," he said.

"Put her at six," I said.

They put the bar at six and I gathered myself together and gave a heave and went over the bar like I was floating. It was easy. Well, that just knocked the wind out of everybody. They'd thought I couldn't do anything and there I'd broken the state record for the high jump without a running start.

The crowd surrounded me and tried to shake my hand and the coach and judge got off to one side and reached out and pinched each other's cheek and looked at the bar and shook their heads. Frank Shay grabbed my hand and wrung it and said, "Gosh, Bottles, I was just kidding the other day. I didn't know you were such a ring-tailed wonder. Say, Bottles, we're having a frat dance tonight. Will you come?"

"You know what you can do with your frat," I said. "I don't approve of them. They're undemocratic."

A lot of the fellows that'd made fun of me before crowded around and acted as if I'd been their friend all along.

When Anna Louise crowded through the gang and said, "Oh, you're marvelous!" I just smiled at her and said, "Do you think so?" and walked away. She tagged around after me but I talked mostly with two other girls.

They didn't usually have a public address system at our track meets but they started using one then.

"Ladies and gentlemen," the announcer said, "you have just witnessed a record-breaking performance by Bottles Barton—."

He went on like that telling them what an astonishing thing I'd done and it came to me I didn't mind being called Bottles any more. In fact, I kind of liked it.

Mr. and Mrs. Patch came up and Mrs. Patch tried to

kiss me but I wouldn't let her. Old man Patch shook my hand.

"You've made our drugstore famous," he said. "From now on you're a clerk. No more bottle washing."

"We'll make him a partner," old lady Patch said.

"No, you won't," I said. "I think I'll go over to the McManus Pharmacy."

Then they called the pole vault and I did like I'd done before. I wouldn't jump until our men'd been eliminated. The bar was at eleven feet.

"It's your turn," our coach told me. "Ever use a pole before?"

"Oh, sure," I told him.

He gave me a pole and the crowd cleared away and grew silent. Everyone was watching me.

I threw the pole down and smiled at the crowd. The coach yelled for me to pick up the pole and jump. I picked it up and threw it ten feet away from me. Everybody gasped. Then I took a short run and went over the bar at eleven feet. It was simple.

This time the coach and the judge took pins and poked them in one another's cheeks. The coach grabbed me and said, "When I wake up I'm going to be so mad at you I'm going to give you the beating of your life."

Anna Louise came up and held my arm and said, "Oh, Bottles, you're so wonderful! I've always thought so. Please forgive me for calling you Rubbernose. I want you to come to our party tonight."

"All right," I said, "I'll forgive you but don't you call me Rubbernose again."

They moved the bar up again and the fellow from Fairfield couldn't make it. I took a short run and went over. I did it so easy it came to me I could fly if I wanted to but I decided not to try it on account of people wouldn't think it so wonderful if a fellow that could fly jumped eleven feet without a pole. I'd won the track meet for Brinkley High and the students all came down out of the stand and put me on their shoulders and paraded me around and around the track. A lot of fellows were waving papers at me asking me to sign them and get $1000 a week as a professional jumper. I signed one which threw in an automobile.

That's what I did once and nobody knows about it, so I am writing about it so people will know.

JAMES THURBER

The Secret Life of Walter Mitty

"We're going through!" The Commander's voice was like thin ice breaking. He wore his full-dress uniform, with the heavily braided white cap pulled down rakishly over one cold gray eye. "We can't make it, sir. It's spoiling for a hurricane, if you ask me." "I'm not asking you, Lieutenant Berg," said the Commander. "Throw on the power light! Rev her up to 8,500! We're going through!" The pounding of the cylinders increased: ta-pocketa-pocketa-pocketa-*pocketa-pocketa.* The Commander stared at the ice forming on the pilot window. He walked over and twisted a row of complicated dials. "Switch on No. 8 auxiliary!" he shouted. "Switch on No. 8 auxiliary!" repeated Lieutenant Berg. "Full strength in No. 3 turret!" shouted the Commander. "Full strength in No. 3 turret!"

The crew, bending to their various tasks in the huge, hurtling eight-engined Navy hydroplane, looked at each other and grinned. "The Old Man'll get us through," they said to one another. "The Old Man ain't afraid of Hell!" . . .

"Not so fast! You're driving too fast!" said Mrs. Mitty. "What are you driving so fast for?"

"Hmm?" said Walter Mitty. He looked at his wife, in the seat beside him, with shocked astonishment. She seemed grossly unfamiliar, like a strange woman who had yelled at him in a crowd. "You were up to fifty-five," she said. "You know I don't like to go more than forty. You were up to fifty-five." Walter Mitty drove on toward Waterbury in silence, the roaring of the SN202 through the worst storm in twenty years of Navy flying fading in the remote, intimate airways of his mind. "You're tensed up again," said Mrs. Mitty. "It's one of your days. I wish you'd let Dr. Renshaw look you over."

Walter Mitty stopped the car in front of the building where his wife went to have her hair done. "Remember to get those overshoes while I'm having my hair done," she said. "I don't need overshoes," said Mitty. She put her mirror back into her bag. "We've been all through that," she said, getting out of the car. "You're not a young man any longer." He raced the engine a little. "Why don't you wear your gloves? Have you lost your gloves?" Walter Mitty reached in a pocket and brought out the gloves. He put them on, but after she had turned and gone into the building and he had driven on to a red light, he took them off again. "Pick it up, brother!"

snapped a cop as the light changed, and Mitty hastily pulled on his gloves and lurched ahead. He drove around the streets aimlessly for a time, and then he drove past the hospital on his way to the parking lot.

. . . "It's the millionaire banker, Wellington McMillan," said the pretty nurse. "Yes?" said Walter Mitty, removing his gloves slowly. "Who has the case?" "Dr. Renshaw and Dr. Benbow, but there are two specialists here, Dr. Remington from New York and Mr. Pritchard-Mitford from London. He flew over." A door opened down a long, cool corridor and Dr. Renshaw came out. He looked distraught and haggard. "Hello, Mitty," he said. "We're having the devil's own time with McMillan, the millionaire banker and close personal friend of Roosevelt. Obstreosis of the ductal tract. Tertiary. Wish you'd take a look at him." "Glad to," said Mitty.

In the operating room there were whispered introductions: "Dr. Remington, Dr. Mitty. Mr. Pritchard-Mitford, Dr. Mitty." "I've read your book on streptothricosis," said Pritchard-Mitford, shaking hands. "A brilliant performance, sir." "Thank you," said Walter Mitty. "Didn't know you were in the States, Mitty," grumbled Remington. "Coals to Newcastle, bringing Mitford and me up here for a tertiary." "You are very kind," said Mitty. A huge, complicated machine, connected to the operating table, with many tubes and wires, began at this moment to go pocketa-pocketa-pocketa. "The new anesthetizer is giving way!" shouted an interne. "There is no one in the East who knows how to fix it!" "Quiet, man!" said Mitty, in a low, cool voice. He sprang to the machine, which was now going pocketa-pocketa-queep-pocketa-queep. He began fingering delicately a row of glistening dials. "Give me a fountain pen!" he snapped. Someone handed him a fountain pen. He pulled a faulty piston out of the machine and inserted the pen in its place. "That will hold for ten minutes," he said. "Get on with the operation." A nurse hurried over and whispered to Renshaw, and Mitty saw the man turn pale. "Coreopsis has set in," said Renshaw nervously. "If you would take over, Mitty?" Mitty looked at him and at the craven figure of Benbow, who drank, and at the grave, uncertain faces of the two great specialists. "If you wish," he said. They slipped a white gown on him; he adjusted a mask and drew on thin gloves; nurses handed him shining . . .

"Back it up, Mac! Look out for that Buick!" Walter Mitty jammed on the brakes. "Wrong lane, Mac," said the parking-lot attendant, looking at Mitty closely. "Gee. Yeh," muttered Mitty. He began cautiously to back out of the lane marked "Exit Only." "Leave her sit there," said the attendant. "I'll put her away." Mitty got out of the car. "Hey, better leave the key." "Oh," said Mitty, handing the man the ignition key. The attendant vaulted into the car, backed it up with insolent skill, and put it where it belonged.

They're so damn cocky, thought Walter Mitty, walking along Main Street; they think they know everything. Once he had tried to take his chains off, outside New Milford, and he had got them wound around the axles. A man had had to come out in a wrecking car and unwind them, a young, grinning garageman. Since then Mrs. Mitty always made him drive to a garage to have the chains taken off. The next time, he thought, I'll wear my right arm in a sling; they won't grin at me then. I'll have my right arm in a sling and they'll see I couldn't possibly take the chains off myself. He kicked at the slush on the sidewalk. "Overshoes," he said to himself, and he began looking for a shoe store.

When he came out into the street again, with the overshoes in a box under his arm, Walter Mitty began to wonder what the other thing was his wife had told him to get. She had told him twice, before they set out from their house for Waterbury. In a way he hated these weekly trips to town—he was always getting something wrong. Kleenex, he thought, Squibb's, razor blades? No. Toothpaste, toothbrush, bicarbonate, carborundum, initiative and referendum? He gave it up. But she would remember it. "Where's the what's-its-name?" she would ask. "Don't tell me you forgot the what's-its-name." A newsboy went by shouting something about the Waterbury trial.

. . . "Perhaps this will refresh your memory." The District Attorney suddenly thrust a heavy automatic at the quiet figure on the witness stand. "Have you ever seen this before?" Walter Mitty took the gun and examined it expertly. "This is my Webley-Vickers 50.80," he said calmly. An excited buzz ran around the courtroom. The judge rapped for order. "You are a crack shot with any sort of firearms, I believe?" said the District Attorney, insinuatingly. "Objection!" shouted Mitty's attorney. "We have shown that the defendant could not have fired the shot. We have shown that he wore his right arm in a sling on the night of the fourteenth of July." Walter Mitty raised his hand briefly and the bickering attorneys were stilled. "With any known make of gun," he said evenly, "I could have killed Gregory Fitzhurst at three hundred feet *with my left hand*." Pandemonium broke loose in the courtroom. A woman's scream rose above the bedlam and suddenly a lovely, dark-haired girl was in Walter Mitty's arms. The District Attorney struck at her savagely. Without rising from his chair, Mitty let the man have it on the point of the chin. "You miserable cur!" . . .

"Puppy biscuit," said Walter Mitty. He stopped walking and the buildings of Waterbury rose up out of the misty courtroom and surrounded him again. A woman who was passing laughed. "He said 'Puppy biscuit,'" she said to her companion. "That man said 'Puppy biscuit' to himself." Walter Mitty hurried on. He went into an A. & P., not the first one he came to but a smaller one farther up the street. "I want some biscuit for small, young dogs," he said to the clerk. "Any special brand, sir?" The greatest pistol shot in the world thought a moment. "It says 'Puppies Bark for It' on the box," said Walter Mitty.

His wife would be through at the hairdresser's in fifteen minutes, Mitty saw in looking at his watch, unless they had trouble drying it; sometimes they had trouble drying it. She didn't like to get to the hotel first; she would want him to be there waiting for her as usual. He found a big leather chair in the lobby, facing a window, and he put the overshoes and the puppy biscuit on the floor beside it. He picked up an old copy of *Liberty* and sank down into the chair. "Can Germany Conquer the World Through the Air?" Walter Mitty looked at the pictures of bombing planes and of ruined streets.

. . . "The cannonading has got the wind up in young Raleigh, sir," said the sergeant. Captain Mitty looked up at him through tousled hair. "Get him to bed," he said wearily. "With the others. I'll fly alone." "But you can't, sir," said the sergeant anxiously. "It takes two men to handle that bomber and the Archies are pounding hell out of the air. Von Richtman's circus is between here and Saulier." "Somebody's got to get that ammunition dump," said Mitty. "I'm going over. Spot of brandy?" He poured a drink for the sergeant and one for himself. War thundered and whined around the dugout and battered at the door. There was a rending of wood and splinters flew through the room. "A bit of a near thing," said Captain Mitty carelessly. "The box barrage is closing in," said the sergeant. "We only live once, Sergeant," said Mitty, with his faint, fleeting smile. "Or do we?" he poured another brandy and tossed it off. "I never see a man could hold his brandy like you, sir," said the sergeant. "Begging your pardon, sir." Captain Mitty stood up and strapped on his huge Webley-Vickers automatic. "It's forty kilometers through hell, sir," said the sergeant. Mitty finished one last brandy. "After all," he said softly, "what isn't?" The pounding of the cannon increased;

there was the rat-tat-tatting of machine guns, and from somewhere came the menacing pocketa-pocketa-pocketa of the new flame-throwers. Walter Mitty walked to the door of the dugout humming "Auprès de Ma Blonde." He turned and waved to the sergeant. "Cheerio!" he said. . . .

Something struck his shoulder. "I've been looking all over this hotel for you," said Mrs. Mitty. "Why do you have to hide in this old chair? How did you expect me to find you?" "Things close in," said Walter Mitty vaguely. "What?" Mrs. Mitty said. "Did you get the what's-its-name? The puppy biscuit? What's in that box?" "Overshoes," said Mitty. "Couldn't you have put them on in the store?" "I was thinking," said Walter Mitty. "Does it ever occur to you that I am sometimes thinking?" She looked at him. "I'm going to take your temperature when I get you home," she said.

They went out through the revolving doors that made a faintly derisive whistling sound when you pushed them. It was two blocks to the parking lot. At the drugstore on the corner she said, "Wait here for me. I forgot something. I won't be a minute." She was more than a minute. Walter Mitty lighted a cigarette. It began to rain, rain with sleet in it. He stood up against the wall of the drugstore, smoking. . . . He put his shoulders back and his heels together. "To hell with the handkerchief," said Walter Mitty scornfully. He took one last drag on his cigarette and snapped it away. Then, with that faint, fleeting smile playing about his lips, he faced the firing squad; erect and motionless, proud and disdainful, Walter Mitty the Undefeated, inscrutable to the last.

HEYWOOD BROUN

The Fifty-First Dragon

Of all the pupils at the knight school Gawaine le Cœur-Hardy was among the least promising. He was tall and sturdy, but his instructors soon discovered that he lacked spirit. He would hide in the woods when the jousting class was called, although his companions and members of the faculty sought to appeal to his better nature by shouting to him to come out and break his neck like a man. Even when they told him that the lances were padded, the horses no more than ponies and the field unusually soft for late autumn, Gawaine refused to grow enthusiastic. The Headmaster and the Assistant Professor of Pleasaunce were discussing the case one spring afternoon and the Assistant Professor could see no remedy but expulsion.

"No," said the Headmaster, as he looked out at the purple hills which ringed the school, "I think I'll train him to slay dragons."

"He might be killed," objected the Assistant Professor.

"So he might," replied the Headmaster brightly, but he added, more soberly, "we must consider the greater good. We are responsible for the formation of this lad's character."

"Are the dragons particularly bad this year?" interrupted the Assistant Professor. This was characteristic. He always seemed restive when the head of the school began to talk ethics and the ideals of the institution.

"I've never known them worse," replied the Headmaster. "Up in the hills to the south last week they killed a number of peasants, two cows and a prize pig. And if this dry spell holds there's no telling when they may start a forest fire simply by breathing around indiscriminately."

"Would any refund on the tuition fee be necessary in case of an accident to young Cœur-Hardy?"

"No," the principal answered, judicially, "that's all covered in the contract. But as a matter of fact he won't be killed. Before I send him up in the hills I'm going to give him a magic word."

"That's a good idea," said the Professor. "Sometimes they work wonders."

From that day on Gawaine specialized in dragons. His course included both theory and practice. In the morning there were long lectures on the history, anatomy, manners and customs of dragons. Gawaine did not distinguish himself in these studies. He had a marvelously versatile gift for forgetting things. In the afternoon he showed to better advantage, for then he would go down to the South Meadow and practice with a battle-ax. In this exercise he was truly impressive, for he had enormous strength as well as speed and grace. He even developed a deceptive display of ferocity. Old alumni say that it was a thrilling sight to see Gawaine charging across the field toward the dummy paper dragon which had been set up for his practice. As he ran he would brandish his ax and shout "A murrain on thee!" or some other vivid bit of campus slang. It never took him more than one stroke to behead the dummy dragon.

Gradually his task was made more difficult. Paper gave way to papier-mâché and finally to wood, but even the toughest of these dummy dragons had no terrors for Gawaine. One sweep of the ax always did the business. There were those who said that when the practice was protracted until dusk and the dragons threw long, fantastic shadows across the meadow Gawaine did not charge so impetuously nor shout so loudly. It is possible there was malice in this charge. At any rate, the Headmaster decided by the end of June that it was time for the test. Only the night before a dragon had come close to the school grounds and had eaten some of the lettuce from the garden. The faculty decided that Gawaine was ready. They gave him a diploma and a new battle-ax and the Headmaster summoned him to a private conference.

"Sit down," said the Headmaster. "Have a cigarette."

Gawaine hesitated.

"Oh, I know it's against the rules," said the Headmaster. "But after all, you have received your preliminary degree. You are no longer a boy. You are a man. Tomorrow you will go out into the world, the great world of achievement."

Gawaine took a cigarette. The Headmaster offered him a match, but he produced one of his own and began to puff away with a dexterity which quite amazed the principal.

"Here you have learned the theories of life," continued the Headmaster, resuming the thread of his discourse, "but after all, life is not a matter of theories. Life is a matter of facts. It calls on the young and the old alike to face these facts, even though they are hard and sometimes unpleasant. Your problem, for example, is to slay dragons."

"They say that those dragons down in the south wood are five hundred feet long," ventured Gawaine, timorously.

"Stuff and nonsense!" said the Headmaster. "The curate saw one last week from the top of Arthur's Hill. The dragon was sunning himself down in the valley. The curate didn't have an opportunity to look at him very long because he felt it was his duty to hurry back to make a report to me. He said the monster, or shall I say, the big lizard?—wasn't an inch over two hundred feet. But the size has nothing at all to do with it. You'll find the big ones even easier than the little ones. They're far slower on their feet and less aggressive, I'm told. Besides, before you go I'm going to equip you in such fashion that you need have no fear of all the dragons in the world."

"I'd like an enchanted cap," said Gawaine.

"What's that?" answered the Headmaster, testily.

"A cap to make me disappear," explained Gawaine.

The Headmaster laughed indulgently. "You mustn't believe all those old wives' stories," he said. "There isn't any such thing. A cap to make you disappear, indeed! What would you do with it? You haven't even appeared yet. Why, my boy, you could walk from here to London, and nobody would so much as look at you. You're nobody. You couldn't be more invisible than that."

Gawaine seemed dangerously close to a relapse into his old habit of whimpering. The Headmaster reassured him: "Don't worry; I'll give you something much better than an enchanted cap. I'm going to give you a magic word. All you have to do is to repeat this magic charm once and no dragon can possibly harm a hair of your head. You can cut off his head at your leisure."

He took a heavy book from the shelf behind his desk and began to run through it. "Sometimes," he said, "the charm is a whole phrase or even a sentence. I might, for instance, give you 'To make the'— No, that might not do. I think a single word would be best for dragons."

"A short word," suggested Gawaine.

"It can't be too short or it wouldn't be potent. There isn't so much hurry as all that. Here's a splendid magic word: 'Rumplesnitz.' Do you think you can learn that?"

Gawaine tried and in an hour or so he seemed to have the word well in hand. Again and again he interrupted the lesson to inquire, "And if I say 'Rumplesnitz' the dragon can't possibly hurt me?" And always the Headmaster replied, "If you only say 'Rumplesnitz,' you are perfectly safe."

Toward morning Gawaine seemed resigned to his career. At daybreak the Headmaster saw him to the edge of the forest and pointed him to the direction in which he should proceed. About a mile away to the southwest a cloud of steam hovered over an open meadow in the woods and the Headmaster assured Gawaine that under the steam he would find a dragon. Gawaine went forward slowly. He wondered whether it would be best to approach the dragon on the run as he did in his practice in the South Meadow or to walk slowly toward him, shouting "Rumplesnitz" all the way.

The problem was decided for him. No sooner had he come to the fringe of the meadow than the dragon spied him and began to charge. It was a large dragon and yet it seemed decidedly aggressive in spite of the Headmaster's statement to the contrary. As the dragon charged it released huge clouds of hissing steam through its nostrils. It was almost as if a gigantic teapot had gone mad. The dragon came forward so fast and Gawaine was so frightened that he had time to say "Rumplesnitz" only once. As he said it, he swung his battle-ax and off popped the head of the dragon. Gawaine had to admit that it was even easier to kill a real dragon than a wooden one if only you said "Rumplesnitz."

Gawaine brought the ears home and a small section of the tail. His schoolmates and the faculty made much of him, but the Headmaster wisely kept him from being spoiled by insisting that he go on with his work. Every clear day Gawaine rose at dawn and went out to kill dragons. The Headmaster kept him at home when it rained, because he said the woods were damp and unhealthy at such times and that he didn't want the boy to run needless risks. Few good days passed in which Gawaine failed to get a dragon. On one particularly fortunate day he killed three, a husband and wife and a visiting relative. Gradually he developed a technique. Pupils who sometimes watched him from the hilltops a long way off said that he often allowed the dragon to come within a few feet before he said "Rumplesnitz." He came to say it with a mocking sneer. Occasionally he did stunts. Once when an excursion party from London was watching him he went into action with his right hand tied behind his back. The dragon's head came off just as easily.

As Gawaine's record of killings mounted higher the Headmaster found it impossible to keep him completely in hand. He fell into the habit of stealing out at night and engaging in long drinking bouts at the village tavern. It was after such a debauch that he rose a little before dawn one fine August morning and started out after his fiftieth dragon. His head was heavy and his mind sluggish. He was heavy in other respects as well, for he had adopted the somewhat vulgar practice of wearing his medals, ribbons and all, when he went out dragon hunting. The decorations began on his chest and ran all the way down to his abdomen. They must have weighed at least eight pounds.

Gawaine found a dragon in the same meadow where he had killed the first one. It was a fair-sized dragon, but evidently an old one. Its face was wrinkled and Gawaine thought he had never seen so hideous a countenance. Much to the lad's disgust, the monster refused to charge and Gawaine was obliged to walk toward him. He whistled as he went. The dragon regarded him hopelessly, but craftily. Of course it had heard of Gawaine. Even when the lad raised his battle-ax the dragon made no move. It knew that there was no salvation in the quickest thrust of the head, for it had been informed that this hunter was protected by an enchantment. It merely waited, hoping something would turn up. Gawaine raised the battle-ax and suddenly lowered it again. He had grown very pale and he trembled violently. The dragon suspected a trick. "What's the matter?" it asked, with false solicitude.

"I've forgotten the magic word," stammered Gawaine.

"What a pity," said the dragon. "So that was the secret. It doesn't seem quite sporting to me, all this magic stuff, you know. Not cricket, as we used to say when I was a little dragon; but after all, that's a matter of opinion."

Gawaine was so helpless with terror that the dragon's confidence rose immeasurably and it could not resist the temptation to show off a bit.

"Could I possibly be of any assistance?" it asked. "What's the first letter of the magic word?"

"It begins with an 'r,'" said Gawaine weakly.

"Let's see," mused the dragon, "that doesn't tell us much, does it? What sort of a word is this? Is it an epithet, do you think?"

Gawaine could do no more than nod.

"Why, of course," exclaimed the dragon, "reactionary Republican."

Gawaine shook his head.

"Well, then," said the dragon, "we'd better get down to business. Will you surrender?"

With the suggestion of a compromise Gawaine mustered up enough courage to speak.

"What will you do if I surrender?" he asked.

"Why, I'll eat you," said the dragon.

"And if I don't surrender?"

"I'll eat you just the same."

"Then it doesn't make any difference, does it?" moaned Gawaine.

"It does to me," said the dragon with a smile. "I'd rather you didn't surrender. You'd taste much better if you didn't."

The dragon waited for a long time for Gawaine to ask "Why?" but the boy was too frightened to speak. At last the dragon had to give the explanation without his cue line. "You see," he said, "if you don't surrender you'll taste better because you'll die game."

This was an old and ancient trick of the dragon's. By means of some such quip he was accustomed to paralyze his victims with laughter and then to destroy them. Gawaine was sufficiently paralyzed as it was, but laughter had no part in his helplessness. With the last word of the joke the dragon drew back his head and struck. In that second there flashed into the mind of Gawaine the magic word "Rumplesnitz," but there was no time to say it. There was time only to strike and, without a word, Gawaine met the onrush of the dragon with a full swing. He put all his back and shoulders into it. The impact was terrific and the head of the dragon flew away almost a hundred yards and landed in a thicket.

Gawaine did not remain frightened very long after the death of the dragon. His mood was one of wonder. He was enormously puzzled. He cut off the ears of the monster almost in a trance. Again and again he thought to himself, "I didn't say 'Rumplesnitz'!" He was sure of that and yet there was no question that he had killed the dragon. In fact, he had never killed one so utterly. Never before had he driven a head for anything like the same distance. Twenty-five yards was perhaps his best previous record. All the way back to the knight school he kept rumbling about in his mind seeking an explanation for what had occurred. He went to the Headmaster immediately and after closing the door told him what had happened. "I didn't say 'Rumplesnitz,'" he explained with great earnestness.

The Headmaster laughed. "I'm glad you've found out," he said. "It makes you ever so much more of a hero. Don't you see that? Now you know that it was you who killed all these dragons and not that foolish little word 'Rumplesnitz.' "

Gawaine frowned. "Then it wasn't a magic word after all?" he asked.

"Of course not," said the Headmaster, "you ought to be too old for such foolishness. There isn't any such thing as a magic word."

"But you told me it was magic," protested Gawaine. "You said it was magic and now you say it isn't."

"It wasn't magic in a literal sense," answered the Headmaster, "but it was much more wonderful than that. The word gave you confidence. It took away your fears. If I hadn't told you that you might have been killed the very first time. It was your battle-ax did the trick."

Gawaine surprised the Headmaster by his attitude. He was obviously distressed by the explanation. He interrupted a long philosophic and ethical discourse by the Headmaster with, "If I hadn't of hit 'em all mighty hard and fast any one of 'em might have crushed me like a, like a——" He fumbled for a word.

"Egg shell," suggested the Headmaster.

"Like a egg shell," assented Gawaine, and he said it many times. All through the evening meal people who sat near him heard him muttering, "Like a egg shell, like a egg shell."

The next day was clear, but Gawaine did not get up at dawn. Indeed, it was almost noon when the Headmaster found him cowering in bed, with the clothes pulled over his head. The principal called the Assistant Professor of Pleasaunce, and together they dragged the boy toward the forest.

"He'll be all right as soon as he gets a couple more dragons under his belt," explained the Headmaster.

The Assistant Professor of Pleasaunce agreed. "It would be a shame to stop such a fine run," he said. "Why, counting that one yesterday, he's killed fifty dragons."

They pushed the boy into a thicket above which hung a meager cloud of steam. It was obviously quite a small dragon. But Gawaine did not come back that night or the next. In fact, he never came back. Some weeks afterward brave spirits from the school explored the thicket, but they could find nothing to remind them of Gawaine except the metal part of his medals. Even the ribbons had been devoured.

The Headmaster and the Assistant Professor of Pleasaunce agreed that it would be just as well not to tell the school how Gawaine had achieved his record and still less how he came to die. They held that it might have a bad effect on school spirit. Accordingly, Gawaine has lived in the memory of the school as its greatest hero. No visitor succeeds in leaving the building today without seeing a great shield which hangs on the wall of the dining hall. Fifty pairs of dragons' ears are mounted upon the shield and underneath in gilt letters is "Gawaine le Cœur-Hardy," followed by the simple inscription, "He killed fifty dragons." The record has never been equaled.

[redacted]

JOHN COLLIER

The Chaser

Alan Austen, as nervous as a kitten, went up certain dark and creaky stairs in the neighborhood of Pell Street, and peered about for a long time on the dim landing before he found the name he wanted written obscurely on one of the doors.

He pushed open this door, as he had been told to do, and found himself in a tiny room, which contained no furniture but a plain kitchen table, a rocking-chair, and an ordinary chair. On one of the dirty buff-colored walls were a couple of shelves, containing in all perhaps a dozen bottles and jars.

An old man sat in the rocking-chair, reading a newspaper. Alan, without a word, handed him the card he had been given. "Sit down, Mr. Austen," said the old man very politely. "I am glad to make your acquaintance."

"Is it true," asked Alan, "that you have a certain mixture that has—er—quite extraordinary effects?"

"My dear sir," replied the old man, "my stock in trade is not very large—I don't deal in laxatives and teething mixtures—but such as it is, it is varied. I think nothing I sell has effects which could be precisely described as ordinary."

"Well, the fact is—" began Alan.

"Here, for example," interrupted the old man, reaching for a bottle from the shelf. "Here is a liquid as colorless as water, almost tasteless, quite imperceptible in coffee, milk, wine, or any other beverage. It is also quite imperceptible to any known method of autopsy."

"Do you mean it is a poison?" cried Alan, very much horrified.

"Call it a glove-cleaner if you like," said the old man indifferently. "Maybe it will clean gloves. I have never tried. One might call it a life-cleaner. Lives need cleaning sometimes."

"I want nothing of that sort," said Alan.

"Probably it is just as well," said the old man. "Do you know the price of this? For one teaspoonful, which is sufficient, I ask five thousand dollars. Never less. Not a penny less."

"I hope all your mixtures are not as expensive," said Alan apprehensively.

"Oh dear, no," said the old man. "It would be no good charging that sort of price for a love potion, for example. Young people who need a love potion very seldom have five thousand dollars. Otherwise they would not need a love potion."

"I am glad to hear that," said Alan.

"I look at it like this," said the old man. "Please a customer with one article, and he will come back when he needs another. Even if it *is* more costly. He will save up for it, if necessary."

"So," said Alan, "you really do sell love potions?"

"If I did not sell love potions," said the old man, reaching for another bottle, "I should not have mentioned the other matter to you. It is only when one is in a position to oblige that one can afford to be so confidential."

"And these potions," said Alan. "They are not just—just—er——"

"Oh, no," said the old man. "Their effects are permanent, and extend far beyond casual impulse. But they include it. Bountifully, insistently. Everlastingly."

"Dear me!" said Alan, attempting a look of scientific detachment. "How very interesting!"

"But consider the spiritual side," said the old man.

"I do, indeed," said Alan.

"For indifference," said the old man, "they substitute devotion. For scorn, adoration. Give one tiny measure of this to the young lady—its flavor is imperceptible in orange juice, soup, or cocktails—and however gay and giddy she is, she will change altogether. She will want nothing but solitude, and you."

"I can hardly believe it," said Alan. "She is so fond of parties."

"She will not like them any more," said the old man. "She will be afraid of the pretty girls you may meet."

"She will actually be jealous?" cried Alan in a rapture. "Of me?"

"Yes, she will want to be everything to you."

"She is, already. Only she doesn't care about it."

"She will, when she has taken this. She will care intensely. You will be her sole interest in life."

"Wonderful!" cried Alan.

"She will want to know all you do," said the old man. "All that has happened to you during the day. Every word of it. She will want to know what you are thinking about, why you smile suddenly, why you are looking sad."

"That is love!" cried Alan.

"Yes," said the old man. "How carefully she will look after you! She will never allow you to be tired, to sit in a draught, to neglect your food. If you are an hour late, she will be terrified. She will think you are killed, or that some siren has caught you."

"I can hardly imagine Diana like that!" cried Alan, overwhelmed with joy.

"You will not have to use your imagination," said the old man. "And, by the way, since there are always sirens, if by any chance you *should*, later on, slip a little, you need not worry. She will forgive you, in the end. She will be terribly hurt, of course, but she will forgive you—in the end."

"That will not happen," said Alan fervently.

"Of course not," said the old man. "But, if it did, you

need not worry. She would never divorce you. Oh, no! And, of course, she herself will never give you the least, the very least, grounds for—uneasiness."

"And how much," said Alan, "is this wonderful mixture?"

"It is not as dear," said the old man, "as the glove-cleaner, or life-cleaner, as I sometimes call it. No. That is five thousand dollars, never a penny less. One has to be older than you are, to indulge in that sort of thing. One has to save up for it."

"But the love potion?" said Alan.

"Oh, that," said the old man, opening the drawer in the kitchen table, and taking out a tiny, rather dirty-looking phial. "That is just a dollar."

"I can't tell you how grateful I am," said Alan, watching him fill it.

"I like to oblige," said the old man. "Then customers come back, later in life, when they are rather better off, and want more expensive things. Here you are. You will find it very effective."

"Thank you again," said Alan. "Good-by."

"*Au revoir,*" said the old man.

ROBERT M. COATES

The Law

The first intimation that things were getting out of hand came one early-fall evening in the late nineteen-forties. What happened, simply, was that between seven and nine o'clock on that evening the Triborough Bridge had the heaviest concentration of outbound traffic in its entire history.

This was odd, for it was a weekday evening (to be precise, a Wednesday), and though the weather was agreeably mild and clear, with a moon that was close enough to being full to lure a certain number of motorists out of the city, these facts alone were not enough to explain the phenomenon. No other bridge or main highway was affected, and though the two preceding nights had been equally balmy and moonlit, on both of these the bridge traffic had run close to normal.

The bridge personnel, at any rate, was caught entirely unprepared. A main artery of traffic, like the Triborough, operates under fairly predictable conditions. Motor travel, like most other large-scale human activities, obeys the Law of Averages—that great, ancient rule that states that the actions of people in the mass will always follow consistent patterns—and on the basis of past experience it had always been possible to foretell, almost to the last digit, the number of cars that would cross the bridge at any given hour of the day or night. In this case, though, all rules were broken.

The hours from seven till nearly midnight are normally quiet ones on the bridge. But on that night it was as if all the motorists in the city, or at any rate a staggering proportion of them, had conspired together to upset tradition. Beginning almost exactly at seven o'clock, cars poured onto the bridge in such numbers and with such rapidity that the staff at the toll booths was overwhelmed almost from the start. It was soon apparent that this was no momentary congestion, and as it became more and more obvious that the traffic jam promised to be one of truly monumental proportions, added details of police were rushed to the scene to help handle it.

Cars streamed in from all directions—from the Bronx approach and the Manhattan one, from 125th Street and the East River Drive. (At the peak of the crush, about eight-fifteen, observers on the bridge reported that the drive was a solid line of car headlights as far south as the bend at Eighty-ninth Street, while the congestion cross-town in Manhattan disrupted traffic as far west as Amsterdam Avenue.) And perhaps the most confusing thing about the whole manifestation was that there seemed to be no reason for it.

Now and then, as the harried toll-booth attendants made change for the seemingly endless stream of cars, they would question the occupants, and it soon became clear that the very participants in the monstrous tieup were as ignorant of its cause as anyone else was. A report made by Sergeant Alfonse O'Toole, who commanded the detail in charge of the Bronx approach, is typical. "I kept askin' them," he said, "'Is there night football somewhere that we don't know about? Is it the races you're goin' to?' But the funny thing was half the time they'd be askin' *me*. 'What's the crowd for, Mac?' they would say. And I'd just look at them. There was one guy I mind, in a Ford convertible with a girl in the seat beside him, and when he asked me, I said to him, 'Hell, you're *in* the crowd, ain't you?' I said. 'What brings *you* here?' And the dummy just looked at me. 'Me?' he says. 'I just come out for a drive in the moonlight. But if I'd known there'd be a crowd like this . . .' he says. And then he asks me, 'Is there any place I can turn around and get out of this?'" As the *Herald Tribune* summed things up in its story next morning, it "just looked as if everybody in Manhattan who owned a motorcar had decided to drive out on Long Island that evening."

The incident was unusual enough to make all the front pages next morning, and because of this, many similar events, which might otherwise have gone unnoticed, received attention. The proprietor of the Aramis Theatre, on Eighth Avenue, reported that on several nights in the recent past his auditorium had been practically empty, while on others it had been jammed to suffocation. Lunchroom owners noted that increasingly their patrons were developing a habit of making runs on specific items; one day it would be the roast shoulder of veal with pan gravy that was ordered almost exclusively, while the next everyone would be taking the Vienna loaf, and the roast veal went begging. A man who ran a small notions store in Bayside revealed that over a period of four days two hundred and seventy-four successive customers had entered his shop and asked for a spool of pink thread.

These were news items that would ordinarily have gone into the papers as fillers or in the sections reserved for oddities. Now, however, they seemed to have a more serious significance. It was apparent at last that something decidedly strange was happening to people's habits, and it was as unsettling as those occasional moments on excursion boats when the passengers are moved, all at once, to rush to one side or the other of the vessel. It was not till one day in December when, almost incredibly, the Twentieth Century Limited left New York for Chicago with just three passengers aboard that business leaders discovered how disastrous the new trend could be, too.

Until then, the New York Central, for instance, could

operate confidently on the assumption that although there might be several thousand men in New York who had business relations in Chicago, on any single day no more—and no less—than some hundreds of them would have occasion to go there. The play producer could be sure that his patronage would sort itself out and that roughly as many persons would want to see the performance on Thursday as there had been on Tuesday or Wednesday. Now they couldn't be sure of anything. The Law of Averages had gone by the board, and if the effect on business promised to be catastrophic, it was also singularly unnerving for the general customer.

The lady starting downtown for a day of shopping, for example, could never be sure whether she would find Macy's department store a seething mob of other shoppers or a wilderness of empty, echoing aisles and unoccupied salesgirls. And the uncertainty produced a strange sort of jitteriness in the individual when faced with any impulse to action. "Shall we do it or shan't we?" people kept asking themselves, knowing that if they did do it, it might turn out that thousands of other individuals had decided similarly; knowing, too, that if they *didn't*, they might miss the one glorious chance of all chances to have Jones Beach, say, practically to themselves. Business languished, and a sort of desperate uncertainty rode everyone.

At this juncture, it was inevitable that Congress should be called on for action. In fact, Congress called on itself, and it must be said that it rose nobly to the occasion.

A committee was appointed, drawn from both Houses and headed by Senator J. Wing Slooper (R.), of Indiana, and though after considerable investigation the committee was forced reluctantly to conclude that there was no evidence of Communist instigation, the unconscious subversiveness of the people's present conduct was obvious at a glance. The problem was what to do about it. You can't indict a whole nation, particularly on such vague grounds as these were. But, as Senator Slooper boldly pointed out, "You can control it," and in the end a system of reëducation and reform was decided upon, designed to lead people back to—again we quote Senator Slooper—"the basic regularities, the homely averageness of the American way of life."

In the course of the committee's investigations, it had been discovered, to everyone's dismay, that the Law of Averages had never been incorporated into the body of federal jurisprudence, and though the upholders of States' Rights rebelled violently, the oversight was at once corrected, both by Constitutional amendment and by a law—the Hills-Slooper Act—implementing it. According to the Act, people were *required* to be average, and, as the simplest way of assuring it, they were divided alphabetically and their permissible activities catalogued accordingly. Thus, by the plan, a person whose name began with "G," "N," or "U," for example, could attend the theatre only on Tuesdays, and he could go to baseball games only on Thursdays, whereas his visits to a haberdashery were confined to the hours between ten o'clock and noon on Mondays.

The law, of course, had its disadvantages. It had a crippling effect on theatre parties, among other social functions, and the cost of enforcing it was unbelievably heavy. In the end, too, so many amendments had to be added to it—such as the one permitting gentlemen to take their fiancées (if accredited) along with them to various events and functions no matter what letter the said fiancées names began with—that the courts were frequently at a loss to interpret it when confronted with violations.

In its way, though, the law did serve its purpose, for it did induce—rather mechanically, it is true, but still adequately—a return to that average existence that Senator Slooper desired. All, indeed, would have been well if a year or so later disquieting reports had not begun to seep in from the backwoods. It seemed that there, in what had hitherto been considered to be marginal areas, a strange wave of prosperity was making itself felt. Tennessee mountaineers were buying Packard convertibles, and Sears, Roebuck reported that in the Ozarks their sales of luxury items had gone up nine hundred per cent. In the scrub sections of Vermont, men who formerly had barely been able to scratch a living from their rock-strewn acres were now sending their daughters to Europe and ordering expensive cigars from New York. It appeared that the Law of Diminishing Returns was going haywire, too.

WILLIAM CARLOS WILLIAMS

The Use of Force

They were new patients to me, all I had was the name, Olson. Please come down as soon as you can, my daughter is very sick.

When I arrived I was met by the mother, a big startled looking woman, very clean and apologetic who merely said, Is this the doctor? and let me in. In the back, she added. You must excuse us, doctor, we have her in the kitchen where it is warm. It is very damp here sometimes.

The child was fully dressed and sitting on her father's lap near the kitchen table. He tried to get up, but I motioned for him not to bother, took off my overcoat and started to look things over. I could see that they were all very nervous, eyeing me up and down distrustfully. As often, in such cases, they weren't telling me more than they had to, it was up to me to tell them; that's why they were spending three dollars on me.

The child was fairly eating me up with her cold, steady eyes, and no expression to her face whatever. She did not move and seemed, inwardly, quiet; an unusually attractive little thing, and as strong as a heifer in appearance. But her face was flushed, she was breathing rapidly, and I realized that she had a high fever. She had magnificent blonde hair, in profusion. One of those picture children often reproduced in advertising leaflets and the photogravure sections of the Sunday papers.

She's had a fever for three days, began the father and we don't know what it comes from. My wife has given her things, you know, like people do, but it don't do no good. And there's been a lot of sickness around. So we tho't you'd better look her over and tell us what is the matter.

As doctors often do I took a trial shot at it as a point of departure. Has she had a sore throat?

Both parents answered me together, No . . . No, she says her throat don't hurt her.

Does your throat hurt you? added the mother to the child. But the little girl's expression didn't change nor did she move her eyes from my face.

Have you looked?

I tried to, said the mother, but I couldn't see.

As it happens we had been having a number of cases of diphtheria in the school to which this child went during that month and we were all, quite apparently, thinking of that, though no one had as yet spoken of the thing.

Well, I said, suppose we take a look at the throat first. I smiled in my best professional manner and asking for the child's first name I said, come on, Mathilda, open your mouth and let's take a look at your throat.

Nothing doing.

Aw, come on, I coaxed, just open your mouth wide and let me take a look. Look, I said opening both hands wide, I haven't anything in my hands. Just open up and let me see.

Such a nice man, put in the mother. Look how kind he is to you. Come on, do what he tells you to. He won't hurt you.

At that I ground my teeth in disgust. If only they wouldn't use the word "hurt" I might be able to get somewhere. But I did not allow myself to be hurried or disturbed but speaking quietly and slowly I approached the child again.

As I moved my chair a little nearer suddenly with one catlike movement both her hands clawed instinctively for my eyes and she almost reached them too. In fact she knocked my glasses flying and they fell, though unbroken, several feet away from me on the kitchen floor.

Both the mother and father almost turned themselves inside out in embarrassment and apology. You bad girl, said the mother, taking her and shaking her by one arm. Look what you've done. The nice man . . .

For heaven's sake, I broke in. Don't call me a nice man

to her. I'm here to look at her throat on the chance that she might have diphtheria and possibly die of it. But that's nothing to her. Look here, I said to the child, we're going to look at your throat. You're old enough to understand what I'm saying. Will you open it now by yourself or shall we have to open it for you?

Not a move. Even her expression hadn't changed. Her breaths however were coming faster and faster. Then the battle began. I had to do it. I had to have a throat culture for her own protection. But first I told the parents that it was entirely up to them. I explained the danger but said that I would not insist on a throat examination so long as they would take the responsibility.

If you don't do what the doctor says you'll have to go to the hospital, the mother admonished her severely.

Oh yeah? I had to smile to myself. After all, I had already fallen in love with the savage brat, the parents were contemptible to me. In the ensuing struggle they grew more and more abject, crushed, exhausted while she surely rose to magnificent heights of insane fury of effort bred of her terror of me.

The father tried his best, and he was a big man but the fact that she was his daughter, his shame at her behavior and his dread of hurting her made him release her just at the critical times when I had almost achieved success, till I wanted to kill him. But his dread also that she might have diphtheria made him tell me to go on, go on though he himself was almost fainting, while the mother moved back and forth behind us raising and lowering her hands in an agony of apprehension.

Put her in front of you on your lap, I ordered, and hold both her wrists.

But as soon as he did the child let out a scream. Don't, you're hurting me. Let go of my hands. Let them go I tell you. Then she shrieked terrifyingly, hysterically. Stop it! Stop it! You're killing me!

Do you think she can stand it, doctor! said the mother.

You get out, said the husband to his wife. Do you want her to die of diphtheria?

Come on now, hold her, I said.

Then I grasped the child's head with my left hand and tried to get the wooden tongue depressor between her teeth. She fought, with clenched teeth, desperately! But now I also had grown furious—at a child. I tried to hold myself down but I couldn't. I know how to expose a throat for inspection. And I did my best. When finally I got the wooden spatula behind the last teeth and just the point of it into the mouth cavity, she opened up for an instant but before I could see anything she came down again and gripping the wooden blade between her molars she reduced it to splinters before I could get it out again.

Aren't you ashamed, the mother yelled at her. Aren't you ashamed to act like that in front of the doctor?

Get me a smooth-handled spoon of some sort, I told the mother. We're going through with this. The child's mouth was already bleeding. Her tongue was cut and she was screaming in wild hysterical shrieks. Perhaps I should have desisted and come back in an hour or more. No doubt it would have been better. But I have seen at least two children lying dead in bed of neglect in such cases, and feeling that I must get a diagnosis now or never I went at it again. But the worst of it was that I too had got beyond reason. I could have torn the child apart in my own fury and enjoyed it. It was a pleasure to attack her. My face was burning with it.

The damned little brat must be protected against her own idiocy, one says to one's self at such times. Others must be protected against her. It is a social necessity. And all these things are true. But a blind fury, a feeling of adult shame, bred of a longing for muscular release are the operatives. One goes on to the end.

In a final unreasoning assault I overpowered the child's neck and jaws. I forced the heavy silver spoon back of her teeth and down her throat till she gagged. And there it was—both tonsils covered with membrane. She had fought valiantly to keep me from knowing her secret. She had been hiding that sore throat for three days at least and lying to her parents in order to escape just such an outcome as this.

Now truly she was furious. She had been on the defensive before but now she attacked. Tried to get off her father's lap and fly at me while tears of defeat blinded her eyes.

PURE ENTERTAIN-MENT

E. B. WHITE

The Hour of Letdown

When the man came in, carrying the machine, most of us looked up from our drinks, because we had never seen anything like it before. The man set the thing down on top of the bar near the beerpulls. It took up an ungodly amount of room and you could see the bartender didn't like it any too well, having this big, ugly-looking gadget parked right there.

"Two rye-and-water," the man said.

The bartender went on puddling an Old-Fashioned that he was working on, but he was obviously turning over the request in his mind.

"You want a double?" he asked, after a bit.

"No," said the man. "Two rye-and-water, please." He

stared straight at the bartender, not exactly unfriendly but on the other hand not affirmatively friendly.

Many years of catering to the kind of people that come into saloons had provided the bartender with an adjustable mind. Nevertheless, he did not adjust readily to this fellow, and he did not like the machine—that was sure. He picked up a live cigarette that was idling on the edge of the cash register, took a drag out of it, and returned it thoughtfully. Then he poured two shots of rye whiskey, drew two glasses of water, and shoved the drinks in front of the man. People were watching. When something a little out of the ordinary takes place at a bar, the sense of it spreads quickly all along the line and pulls the customers together.

The man gave no sign of being the center of attention. He laid a five-dollar bill down on the bar. Then he drank one of the ryes and chased it with water. He picked up the other rye, opened a small vent in the machine (it was like an oil cup) and poured the whiskey in, and then poured the water in.

The bartender watched grimly. "Not funny," he said in an even voice. "And furthermore, your companion takes up too much room. Why'n you put it over on that bench by the door, make more room here."

"There's plenty of room for everyone here," replied the man.

"I ain't amused," said the bartender. "Put the goddam thing over near the door like I say. Nobody will touch it."

The man smiled. "You should have seen it this afternoon," he said. "It was magnificent. Today was the third day of the tournament. Imagine it—three days of continuous brainwork! And against the top players in the country, too. Early in the game it gained an advantage; then for two hours it exploited the advantage brilliantly, ending with the opponent's king backed in a corner. The sudden capture of a knight, the neutralization of a bishop, and it was all over. You know how much money it won, all told, in three days of playing chess?"

"How much?" asked the bartender.

"Five thousand dollars," said the man. "Now it wants to let down, wants to get a little drunk."

The bartender ran his towel vaguely over some wet spots. "Take it somewheres else and get it drunk there!" he said firmly. "I got enough troubles."

The man shook his head and smiled. "No, we like it here." He pointed at the empty glasses. "Do this again, will you, please?"

The bartender slowly shook his head. He seemed dazed but dogged. "You stow the things away," he ordered. "I'm not ladling out whiskey for jokestersmiths."

" 'Jokesmiths,' " said the machine. "The word is 'jokesmiths.' "

A few feet down the bar, a customer who was on his third highball seemed ready to participate in this conversation to which we had all been listening so attentively. He was a middle-aged man. His necktie was pulled down away from his collar, and he had eased the collar by unbuttoning it. He had pretty nearly finished his third drink, and the alcohol tended to make him throw his support in with the underprivileged and the thirsty.

"If the machine wants another drink, give it another drink," he said to the bartender. "Let's not have haggling."

The fellow with the machine turned to his new-found friend and gravely raised his hand to his temple, giving him a salute of gratitude and fellowship. He addressed his next remark to him, as though deliberately snubbing the bartender.

"You know how it is when you're all fagged out mentally, how you want a drink?"

"Certainly do," replied the friend. "Most natural thing in the world."

There was a stir all along the bar, some seeming to side with the bartender, others with the machine group. A tall, gloomy man standing next to me spoke up.

"Another whiskey sour, Bill," he said. "And go easy on the lemon juice."

"Picric acid," said the machine, sullenly. "They don't use lemon juice in these places."

"That does it!" said the bartender, smacking his hand on the bar. "Will you put that thing away or else beat it out of here. I ain't in the mood, I tell you. I got this saloon to run and I don't want lip from a mechanical brain or whatever the hell you've got there."

The man ignored this ultimatum. He addressed his friend, whose glass was now empty.

"It's not just that it's all tuckered out after three days of chess," he said amiably. "You know another reason it wants a drink?"

"No," said the friend. "Why?"

"It cheated," said the man.

At this remark, the machine chuckled. One of its arms dipped slightly, and a light glowed in a dial.

The friend frowned. He looked as though his dignity had been hurt, as though his trust had been misplaced. "Nobody can cheat at chess," he said. "Simpossible. In chess, everything is open and above the board. The nature of the game of chess is such that cheating is impossible."

"That's what I used to think, too," said the man. "But there *is* a way."

"Well, it doesn't surprise me any," put in the bartender. "The first time I laid my eyes on that crummy thing I spotted it for a crook."

"Two rye-and-water," said the man.

"You can't have the whiskey," said the bartender. He glared at the mechanical brain. "How do I know it ain't drunk already?"

"That's simple. Ask it something," said the man.

The customers shifted and stared into the mirror. We were all in this thing now, up to our necks. We waited. It was the bartender's move.

"Ask it what? Such as?" said the bartender.

"Makes no difference. Pick a couple big figures, ask it to multiply them together. You couldn't multiply big figures together if you were drunk, could you?"

The machine shook slightly, as though making internal preparations.

"Ten thousand eight hundred and sixty-two, multiply

it by ninety-nine," said the bartender, viciously. We could tell that he was throwing in the two nines to make it hard.

The machine flickered. One of its tubes spat, and a hand changed position, jerkily.

"One million seventy-five thousand three hundred and thirty-eight," said the machine.

Not a glass was raised all along the bar. People just stared gloomily into the mirror; some of us studied our own faces, others took carom shots at the man and the machine.

Finally, a youngish, mathematically minded customer got out a piece of paper and a pencil and went into retirement. "It works out," he reported, after some minutes of calculating. "You can't say the machine is drunk!"

Everyone now glared at the bartender. Reluctantly he poured two shots of rye, drew two glasses of water. The man drank his drink. Then he fed the machine its drink. The machine's light grew fainter. One of its cranky little arms wilted.

For a while the saloon simmered along like a ship at sea in calm weather. Every one of us seemed to be trying to digest the situation, with the help of liquor. Quite a few glasses were refilled. Most of us sought help in the mirror—the court of last appeal.

The fellow with the unbuttoned collar settled his score. He walked stiffly over and stood between the man and the machine. He put one arm around the man, the other arm around the machine. "Let's get out of here and go to a good place," he said.

The machine glowed slightly. It seemed to be a little drunk now.

"All right," said the man. "That suits me fine. I've got my car outside."

He settled for the drinks and put down a tip. Quietly and a trifle uncertainly he tucked the machine under his arm, and he and his companion of the night walked to the door and out into the street.

The bartender stared fixedly, then resumed his light housekeeping. "So he's got his car outside," he said, with heavy sarcasm. "Now isn't that nice!"

A customer at the end of the bar near the door left his drink, stepped to the window, parted the curtains, and looked out. He watched for a moment, then returned to his place and addressed the bartender. "It's even nicer than you think," he said. "It's a Cadillac. And which one of the three of them d'ya think is doing the driving?"

SAKI (H. H. MUNRO)

The Open Window

"My aunt will be down presently, Mr. Nuttel," said a very self-possessed young lady of fifteen; "in the meantime you must try and put up with me."

Framton Nuttel endeavoured to say the correct something which should duly flatter the niece of the moment without unduly discounting the aunt that was to come. Privately he doubted more than ever whether these formal visits on a succession of total strangers would do much towards helping the nerve cure which he was supposed to be undergoing.

"I know how it will be," his sister had said when he was preparing to migrate to this rural retreat; "you will bury yourself down there and not speak to a living soul, and your nerves will be worse than ever from moping.

From *The Short Stories of Saki* by H. H. Munro. Reprinted by permission of The Viking Press, Inc.

I shall just give you letters of introduction to all the people I know there. Some of them, as far as I can remember, were quite nice."

Framton wondered whether Mrs. Sappleton, the lady to whom he was presenting one of the letters of introduction, came into the nice division.

"Do you know many of the people round here?" asked the niece, when she judged that they had had sufficient silent communion.

"Hardly a soul," said Framton. "My sister was staying here, at the rectory, you know, some four years ago, and she gave me letters of introduction to some of the people here."

He made the last statement in a tone of distinct regret.

"Then you know practically nothing about my aunt?" pursued the self-possessed young lady.

"Only her name and address," admitted the caller. He was wondering whether Mrs. Sappleton was in the married or widowed state. An undefinable something about the room seemed to suggest masculine habitation.

"Her great tragedy happened just three years ago," said the child; "that would be since your sister's time."

"Her tragedy?" asked Framton; somehow in this restful country spot tragedies seemed out of place.

"You may wonder why we keep that window wide open on an October afternoon," said the niece, indicating a large French window that opened on to a lawn.

"It is quite warm for the time of the year," said Framton; "but has that window got anything to do with the tragedy?"

"Out through that window, three years ago to a day, her husband and her two young brothers went off for their day's shooting. They never came back. In crossing the moor to their favourite snipe-shooting ground they were all three engulfed in a treacherous piece of bog. It had been that dreadful wet summer, you know, and places that were safe in other years gave way suddenly without warning. Their bodies were never recovered. That was the dreadful part of it." Here the child's voice lost its self-possessed note and became falteringly human. "Poor aunt always thinks that they will come back some day, they and the little brown spaniel that was lost with them, and walk in at that window just as they used to do. That is why the window is kept open every evening till it is quite dusk. Poor dear aunt, she has often told me how they went out, her husband with his white waterproof coat over his arm, and Ronnie, her youngest brother, singing, 'Bertie, why do you bound?' as he always did to tease her, because she said it got on her nerves. Do you know, sometimes on still, quiet evenings like this, I almost get a creepy feeling that they will all walk in through that window——"

She broke off with a little shudder. It was a relief to Framton when the aunt bustled into the room with a whirl of apologies for being late in making her appearance.

"I hope Vera has been amusing you?" she said.

"She has been very interesting," said Framton.

"I hope you don't mind the open window," said Mrs. Sappleton briskly; "my husband and brothers will be home directly from shooting, and they always come in this way. They've been out for snipe in the marshes to-day, so they'll make a fine mess over my poor carpets. So like you menfolk, isn't it?"

She rattled on cheerfully about the shooting and the scarcity of birds, and the prospects for duck in the winter. To Framton it was all purely horrible. He made a desperate but only partially successful effort to turn the talk on to a less ghastly topic; he was conscious that his hostess was giving him only a fragment of her attention, and her eyes were constantly straying past him to the open window and the lawn beyond. It was certainly an unfortunate coincidence that he should have paid his visit on this tragic anniversary.

"The doctors agree in ordering me complete rest, an absence of mental excitement, and avoidance of anything in the nature of violent physical exercise," announced Framton, who laboured under the tolerably wide-spread delusion that total strangers and chance acquaintances are hungry for the least detail of one's ailments and infirmities, their cause and cure. "On the matter of diet they are not so much in agreement," he continued.

"No?" said Mrs. Sappleton, in a voice which only replaced a yawn at the last moment. Then she suddenly brightened into alert attention—but not to what Framton was saying.

"Here they are at last!" she cried. "Just in time for tea, and don't they look as if they were muddy up to the eyes!"

Framton shivered slightly and turned towards the niece with a look intended to convey sympathetic comprehension. The child was staring out through the open window with dazed horror in her eyes. In a chill shock of nameless fear Framton swung round in his seat and looked in the same direction.

In the deepening twilight three figures were walking across the lawn towards the window; they all carried guns under their arms, and one of them was additionally burdened with a white coat hung over his shoulders. A tired brown spaniel kept close at their heels. Noiselessly they neared the house, and then a hoarse young voice chanted out of the dusk: "I said, Bertie, why do you bound?"

Framton grabbed wildly at his stick and hat; the hall-door, the gravel-drive, and the front gate were dimly noted stages in his headlong retreat. A cyclist coming along the road had to run into the hedge to avoid imminent collision.

"Here we are, my dear," said the bearer of the white mackintosh, coming in through the window; "fairly muddy, but most of it's dry. Who was that who bolted out as we came up?"

"A most extraordinary man, a Mr. Nuttel," said Mrs. Sappleton; "could only talk about his illnesses, and dashed off without a word of good-bye or apology when you arrived. One would think he had seen a ghost."

"I expect it was the spaniel," said the niece calmly; "he told me he had a horror of dogs. He was once hunted into a cemetery somewhere on the banks of the Ganges by a pack of pariah dogs, and had to spend the night in a newly dug grave with the creatures snarling and grinning and foaming just above him. Enough to make any one lose their nerve."

Romance at short notice was her speciality.

ROBERT ARTHUR

Satan and Sam Shay

I am told that sin has somewhat declined since Satan met Sam Shay. I cannot vouch for this, but they say that production has definitely fallen off since that evening when Sam Shay won three wagers from the Devil. And this is the tale of it.

Sam Shay, you'll understand, was a bold rascal with Irish blood in his veins, though Yankee-born and -bred. Six feet he stood, with wide shoulders and a grin and dark hair with a touch of curl to it. Looking at his hands and his brawn, you'd hardly have guessed he'd never done an honest day's labor in his life. But it was true. For Sam was a gambling man, and since he was a boy, matching coppers or playing odd and even with his fellows, every penny passing through his fingers had been

Reprinted by permission of the author.

the fruit of wagering. And he was now approaching his thirtieth year.

Do not think to his discredit, however, that Sam Shay was a flinty-hearted professional betting only on things that were sure or at odds much tipped in his favor. He bet not mathematically but by intuition, and the betting was as important as the winning. Were you to have given him the money he would not have taken it; there would have been no savor to it. He must win it by his wits to enjoy it, and he could find fun in losing a good wager, too.

So it was a sad thing to Sam that the one girl of his heart, Shannon Malloy, should be dead set against gambling. But the late Malloy had squandered all his earnings in just such divertissements as Sam Shay enjoyed, and the Widow Malloy had brought her daughter up most strictly to abjure men who loved the sound of rolling dice, the riffle of the cards or the quickening of the pulse that comes as the horses turn into the home stretch and stream for the finish line.

In the early days of their acquaintance, Shannon Malloy, who was small, with dark eyes that held a glow in their depths, had overlooked Sam's failing, feeling that Sam would mend his ways for love of her. And indeed Sam promised. But he could no more live without betting than he could without eating—less, for he could go a day without food undistressed, but in twenty years no sun had set without his making a wager of some kind, however small, just to keep his hand in.

Frequently, therefore, Sam Shay found himself in disgrace, while Shannon, more in sorrow than in anger, pleaded with him. And each time Sam once again promised to reform, knowing in his heart that once again he would fail. Inevitably, then, there came the time when Shannon, putting aside the veils that love cast upon her vision, saw with sad clarity that Sam Shay was Sam Shay and naught would alter him. She loved him, but her convictions were as adamant. So she gave him back the ring she had accepted from him when his resolves had been less tarnished.

"I'm sorry, Sam," she had said, this very evening, and her words rang knell-like in Sam's ears now as he strode homeward through the soft evening dusk that lay across the park. "I'm sorry," and her voice had broken. "But today I heard your name spoken. By some men. And they were saying you are a born gambler who could make three bets with Satan and win them all. And if that is true, I can't marry you."

And Sam, knowing that only some force far stronger than himself could turn him from his wagering, took the ring and went with only one backward glance. That glance showed him Shannon Malloy weeping but resolute, and he was as proud of her resolution as disconsolate that she should feel so strongly about his little weakness.

The ring was in his pocket and his fingers touched it sadly as he walked. It was a circlet cold to the touch, a metal zero that summed the total of his chances for having Shannon Malloy to wife. The twilight lay upon the park, and it was queerly hushed, as if something was impending. But, lost in his thoughts, he strode along taking no notice.

It was as he came abreast an ancient oak that the shadow of the tree, athwart the sidewalk, with great unexpectedness solidified into a pillar of blackness church-steeple high, which condensed swiftly into a smallish individual with flowing white locks and a benign countenance.

The individual who had so unconventionally placed himself in Sam's path was clad in garments of sober cut, an old-fashioned cape slung over his shoulders and a soft dark hat upon his white hair. He smiled with innocent engagingness at Samuel Shay, and spoke in a voice both mild and friendly.

"Good evening, Sam," he said, as one might to an acquaintance not seen in a great while. "I'll bet you don't know who I am."

But Sam Shay, his right hand gripping the stout thorn stick he liked to carry about with him, was not to be trapped. He had seen the shadow of an oak tree change into a man, and this, to say the least, was unusual.

"Why," he proclaimed boldly, "I have a hundred dollars in my pocket, and I'll lay it against one that you are Satan."

Satan—for Sam's intuition had not failed him—let an expression of displeasure cross the benign countenance he had assumed for this visit. For he too had heard the report Shannon Malloy had quoted to Sam—that he could make three bets with Satan and win them all. And, his curiosity aroused, the Devil had come to test Sam's prowess, for he was fond of gambling, though a bad loser.

But the expression was gone in an instant and the gentle smile resumed its place. The old gentleman reached beneath his cloak and brought out a wallet which bulged pleasingly, although it was of a leather whose appearance Sam did not care for.

"That may be, Sam," Satan replied genially. "And if I am, I owe you a dollar. But I have another hundred here says you can't prove it."

And he waited, well pleased, for this was a wager that had stumped many eminent philosophers in centuries past. But Sam Shay was a man of action, not of words.

"Taken," he agreed at once, and raised his thorn stick above his head. "I'll just bash you a time or two over the pate. If you're an honest citizen I'll take your wallet, and if you're Satan I'll win the wager. For you could not let a mortal man trounce you so and still look yourself in the eye—an accomplishment quite individually yours. So——"

And Sam brought the stick down in a whistling blow.

A sulphurous sheet of flame cracked out from the heart of the oak tree, and the thorn stick was riven into a thousand splinters that hissed away through the air. A strong pain shot up Sam's arm, a tingling, numbing sensation that extended to the shoulder. But, rubbing his wrist, he was well satisfied.

Not so Satan. In his anger the little old gentleman had shot upward until he loomed twelve feet high now, and looked far more terrifying than benign.

"You win, Sam Shay," Satan told him sourly. "But there's a third bet yet to come." Which Sam knew to be true, for on any such occasion as this when the Devil showed himself to a mortal, the unhappy man must win three wagers from him to go free. "And this time we'll increase the stakes. Your soul against the contents of this wallet that you can't win from me again."

Sam did not hesitate. For he must wager, whether he would or not.

"Taken," he answered. "But I must name the bet, since you named the others and it is my turn now."

Satan it was who hesitated, but right and logic were with Sam, so he nodded.

"Name it, then," he directed, and his voice was like grumbling thunder beyond the skyline.

"Why, as to that," Sam told him with an impudent grin, "I am betting you do not intend for me to win this wager."

Hardly were the words out of his mouth before Satan, in uncontrolled rage, had shot up to a tremendous height, his black cloak flowing from him like night itself draping over the city. For Sam had caught him neatly. If he responded that he did intend for Sam to win, then Sam perforce must go free. And if he responded that he had not so intended, then Sam won anyway.

Glaring down from his great height, Satan directed an awful gaze upon Sam Shay.

"This is an ill night's work you have done!" he cried, in a voice that shook with rage, so that the skyscrapers nearby trembled a bit, and the next day's papers carried an item concerning a small earthquake. "Hear me well, Sam Shay! From this moment onward, never shall you win another wager! All the forces of hell will be marshalled to prevent you."

Then, while Sam still gaped upward in dismay, the great figure faded from sight. A vast blast of hot air fanned past Sam, singeing the leaves of the nearest trees. He heard a distant clanging sound, as of a metal gate closing. After that all was quiet as it had been before.

Sam Shay stood in thought for several minutes, and then realized he still was fingering the ring Shannon Malloy had returned to him. He laughed, in something of relief.

"Glory!" he said aloud. "I've been standing here dreaming, while my mind wandered. If I'm to have nightmares, I'd best have them in bed."

And he hurried homeward, stopping by the way only long enough to buy the next day's racing form.

By morning Sam had half forgotten his queer bemusement of the evening before. But that Shannon had dismissed him and returned his ring he remembered all too well. The bit of gold seemed heavy in his pocket as the weight that lay on his heart, so that he set about choosing his wagers for the day's racing with a gloomy mind.

It was perhaps this gloom that made it harder than was customary for him to make a choice. Usually his intuition made quick decision. But today he labored long, and was only half satisfied when he had finished marking down his picks.

Then, having breakfasted, with Shannon Malloy's face coming betwixt him and his coffee, he rode out to the track. Today he desired action, crowds, noise, excitement to take his mind off Shannon's rejection of him. So that the pushing throngs about the mutuel windows, the crowd murmur that rose to a shrill ululation as the horses burst from the barrier, the heart-tightening sensation as they turned into the home stretch all fitted well into his mood.

And he was feeling better when, his tickets tucked inside his pocket, he stood with the rest and watched the leaders in the first swing 'round the turn. He was well pleased to note his choice to the fore by half a dozen lengths, when something happened. Perhaps the nag put its hoof into a pocket in the track. Perhaps it broke stride, or merely tired. At all events it faltered, slowed as though the Devil himself had it by the tail—now why had that precise comparison flashed across his mind then, Sam Shay wondered—and was beaten to the finish by a neck.

Sam tore up his tickets and scattered them to the breeze. He was not distressed. There were six races yet to come, and his pockets were well filled with money.

But when in the second his pick threw its jockey rounding the three-quarter pole and in the lead, and when in the third a saddle girth broke just as the jockey was lifting his mount for a winning surge, Sam Shay began to whistle a bit beneath his breath.

It was queer. It was decidedly queer, and he did not like it in the least. And when in the fourth, just as it was in the clear, his choice swerved and cut across the nag behind it, thus being disqualified, Sam's whistle grew more tuneless. He sniffed, and sniffed again. Yes, it was there—the faintest whiff of sulphur somewhere about. In a most meditative mood Sam purchased a single two-dollar ticket for the fifth.

The ticket, as he had been unhappily convinced would be the case, proved a poor investment, his horse throwing a shoe at the far turn and pulling up last, limping badly.

Sam's whistle dropped until it was quite inaudible. He made his way toward the paddock and stood close as they led the winded horses out. As his choice passed he sniffed, strongly. And this time there was the slightest touch of brimstone mixed with the smell of sulphur.

Walking with a slow pace that did not in any way reflect the churning of his thoughts, Sam Shay returned to the grandstand and in the minutes before the next race was run reflected fast and furiously. Already his pockets, so thickly lined but an hour before, were well-nigh empty. And apprehension was beginning to sit, a tiny cloud, on Sam's brow.

This time he bought no ticket. But he sought out an individual with whom he had had dealings, and stood beside him as the race was run. The ponies were streaming around the three-quarter pole and into the stretch, with forty lengths and half a dozen horses separating the first nag from the last, when Sam spoke suddenly.

"Ten dollars," said he to his acquaintance, "to a dime that Seven doesn't win."

The bookie gave him an odd glance. For Seven was the trailer, forty lengths behind and losing distance steadily. Any mortal eye could see she couldn't win, and it came to him Sam might be daft.

"Twenty dollars!" said Samuel Shay. "To a five-cent piece!"

They were odds not to be resisted, and the bookie nodded.

"Taken!" he agreed, and the words were scarce out of his mouth before Seven put on a burst of speed. She seemed to rise into the air with the very rapidity of her motion. Her legs churned. And she whisked forward so fast her astonished jockey was but an ace from being blown out of the saddle by the very rush of air. Closing the gap in a manner quite unbelievable, she came up to the leaders and, with a scant yard to the finish, shot ahead to win.

The crowd was too dazed even to roar. The judges gathered at once in frowning conference. But nothing amiss with Seven's equipment could be found—no electric batteries or other illegal contrivances—so at last her number was posted.

Sam Shay paid over the twenty dollars, while his acquaintance goggled at him. He would have asked questions, but Sam was in no mood for conversation. He moved away and sought a seat. There he pondered.

There could no longer be any doubt. His dream of the evening before had been no dream. It was Satan himself he had met face to face in the park, and Satan was having his vengeance for being bested. Sam could not call to mind the name of any other man in history who had outwitted the Devil without ruing it, and it was plain he was not to be the exception.

Wagering was Sam's life and livelihood, as Satan had well known. And if Sam was never to win another bet —— He swallowed hard at the thought. Not only would he have lost Shannon Malloy for naught, but he would even be forced to the indignity of earning his living by the strength of his hands, he who had lived by his wits so pleasantly for so long.

It was a sobering reflection. But for the moment no helpful scheme would come. Just before the warning bell for the last race of the day, however, Sam rose with alacrity. He counted his money. Aside from carfare back to town, he had just fourteen dollars upon him. Seven two-dollar tickets—and in the last there was a field of seven!

Sam chuckled and bought seven tickets to win, one on each of the entries. Then, feeling somewhat set up, he found a position of vantage. Now, he said beneath his breath, let's see the Devil himself keep you from having a winning ticket this time, Samuel Shay! And complacently he watched his seven horses get off to a good start.

The race proceeded normally toward the half, and then to the three-quarters, with nothing untoward come about. Sam chuckled some more, for if he cashed a ticket on this race then Satan had been bested again, and his curse on Sam's wagering broken.

But the chuckle came too soon. As the seven turned into the stretch, into a sky that had been cerulean blue leaped a storm cloud purple and black. From the cloud a bolt of lightning sped downward, in a blinding flash, to strike among the branches of an ancient elm which stood beside the grandstand near the finish line. A horrid thunderclap deafened the throng. The elm tottered. Then it toppled and fell across the track, so that the seven jockeys were just able to pull up their mounts in time to avoid plunging into it.

And as sudden as it had come, the storm cloud was gone.

But obviously there could be no winner of the last race. The perplexed and shaken stewards hurriedly declared it no race, and announced that all bets would be refunded. Sam received his money back—but that was not winning. And with the bills thrust into his coat he gloomily returned to his lodgings to devote more thought to this matter. For it was plain the Devil had meant what he had said—Sam would never win another wager. And with all the myriad hosts of hell arrayed against him, Sam did not see what he could do about it.

But the Shays were never a quitter stock. Though Beelzebub and all his myrmidons opposed him, Sam was of no mind to turn to honest labor without giving the Devil a run for his money. So in the days that followed, Sam, with dogged resolution, did not cease his efforts to make a wager he could win. And his endeavors were a source of some concern in hell.

It was on an afternoon two weeks perhaps after the fateful meeting between Satan and Sam Shay that the Devil recalled the matter to his mind and pressed a button summoning his chief lieutenant to make report. Whisking from his private laboratory, where he was engaged in a delicate experiment leading toward the creation of a brand new and improved form of sin, his head assistant covered seven million miles in no time at all and deposited himself in Satan's presence, still scorching from the speed at which he had come.

The Devil, seated behind a desk of basalt, frowned upon him.

"I wish," he stated, "to know if my orders concerning the mortal y-clept Sam Shay have been carried out."

"To the letter, Infernal Highness," his lieutenant replied, with a slight air of reserve.

"He has not won a wager since I pronounced my curse upon him?"

"Not of the most inconsequential kind."

"He is thoroughly miserable?"

"Completely so."

"He is in such despair he might even commit suicide, and so place himself in our hands?"

The other was silent. Satan's voice took on sharpness.

"He is *not* in despair?"

"He is in a very low frame of mind indeed," his chief assistant replied with reluctance. "But there is no notion of suicide in his mind. He is defiant. And troublesome in the extreme, I must add."

"Troublesome?" The three-billion-bulb chandelier overhead rattled. "How can a mere mortal be troublesome to the hosts of hell? Kindly explain yourself."

The tips of his lieutenant's bat wings quivered with inward nervousness, and absently he plucked a loose scale from his chest. But summoning his resolution, he answered.

"He is a persistent mortal, this Sam Shay," he replied humbly. "Although your infernal curse has been passed upon him, he refuses to be convinced he cannot evade it. He is constantly scheming to get around the fiat by means of trickery and verbal quibbling. And I have had to assign a good many of my best and most resourceful workers to keep a twenty-four-hour watch on Sam Shay to see he does not succeed. Let me explain.

"Last week, having already tried some hundreds of wagers of various kinds, he offered to bet an acquaintance it would not rain before noon. The wager was the merest quibble of a bet, for it then lacked but ten seconds of the hour, the sun was shining in a cloudless sky, and in addition the Weather Bureau had actually predicted storm.

"Sam Shay, however, got his gamble accepted by promising to spend double his winnings, if he won, on strong drink for his companion. A completely specious wager if ever one was made. Nevertheless, had it not rained before the hour of noon, technically he would have been the winner of a bet, and so the letter of your hellish curse would have been violated.

"So, upon the notice of merest seconds, I had to call two hundred and eighty workers away from urgent duty in Proselytizing, to borrow on an instant's notice another hundred from Punishment, to take a score of my best laboratory technicians off Research, and rush them all to the spot. Between them they managed to divert a storm that was raging over Ohio and scheduled to cause a flood estimated to produce for us a job-lot of a hundred and eighty souls, whisking it to cover New England within the time-limit.

"But the affair caused widespread comment, threw us off schedule and has disrupted my entire force, due to the necessity for keeping a large emergency squad upon twenty-four-hour duty in constant readiness for any other such calls. And there have been dozens of them. Simply dozens!"

A drop of sweat rolled down the unhappy demon's brow, dissolving in steam.

"That's only a sample," he said earnestly. "This Sam Shay has scores of such tricks up his sleeves. Only yesterday he was attempting to win a wager at the race track, and his efforts kept us busy the entire afternoon. In the fifth race he made such a complicated series of bets as to the relative positions in which the various horses would finish that my most trusted aide completely lost track of them. He had to call on me personally at the last moment, and since one of the wagers was that the race itself wouldn't be finished, the only solution I could hit upon in time was to have all the horses finish in a dead heat, save for the one Sam Shay had bet upon to win.

"This one, in order to confound the fellow, I was forced to remove entirely from the race and set down in Australia, so that none of Shay's various stipulations concerning it could come true. But the talk caused by a seven-horse dead heat, together with the complete disappearance of one of the beasts and its jockey, caused a considerable stir.

"Taken in conjunction with the storm I had to arrange, and a number of similar matters, it has started a religious revival. People are flocking into the churches, undoing some of our best work. So, Your Infernal Highness, if only we could overlook one or two of Sam Shay's more difficult wagers, it would make things much easier to——"

The crash of Satan's hooves upon the adamantine tiling cut him short.

"Never! I have put my curse upon this Shay! It must be carried out to the letter. 'Tend to it!"

"Yes, Prince of Evil," his head assistant squeaked, and being a prudent demon hurled himself away and across the seven million miles of space to his laboratory so swiftly that he struck with such force at the other end he was lame for a month. And never again did he dare mention the matter.

But of all this Sam Shay had no inkling. He was immersed in his own problems. Having failed in every wager he had made, however difficult to lose, he was in a depressed state of mind.

His resources were coming to an end. There were but a few dollars left in his pockets and none in his bank account. Shannon Malloy refused to see him. He had not won a wager since the night he had met the Devil, and he was so low in his mind that several times he had caught himself glancing through the Help Wanted sections of the papers.

Upon this particular day he was so sunk in despair that it was the middle of the afternoon, and he had not once tried the Devil's mettle to see if this time he could slip a winning wager past the demonic forces on watchful guard all about him. It was a day cut and tailored to his mood. The sky was lowering gray and rain whipped down out of the north as if each drop had personal anger against the earth upon which it struck. And Sam Shay sat in his room, staring out at the storm, as close to despair as it had ever been his misfortune to come.

At last he bestirred himself; it was not in the blood of a Shay to sit thus forever wrapped in gray gloom. He found his hat and ulster, and with heavy step made his way out and down the street to a cozy bar and grill.

Ensconced in a corner where a fireplace glowed he found Tim Malloy, who was by way of being Shannon's brother, a round, merry little man who was the merrier because a mug of dark stood upon the table before him. Tim Malloy greeted him with words of cheer and Sam sat himself down, answering as nearly in kind as he might. He ordered himself a mug of dark too, and made inquiry concerning Shannon.

"Why, as to that," Tim Malloy said, draining off half his mug, "sometimes of a night I hear her crying behind her locked door. And——" he drained off the rest of his dark "—she never did that before she gave you back your ring, Sam."

"Have another," Sam invited, feeling, suddenly, somewhat heartened. "Then mayhap she might take back the ring if I asked her, you think?" he asked, hope in his tone.

Tim Malloy accepted the dark, but after dipping into it shook his head, a mustache of foam on his lip.

"Never while you're a betting man, Sam, and that'll be forever," he said, "unless some wondrous force stronger than she is makes her do it. Not though she's unhappy the rest of her life from sending you away."

Sam sighed.

"Would it make any difference if she knew I lost all the wagers I make now?" he asked.

"Not so much as a pin-point of difference," Tim Malloy answered. "Not so much as a pin-point. To change the subject, how long will it keep raining, would you say?"

"All day, I suppose," Sam said, in a gloom again. "And all night too. I've no doubt. Though I could stop it raining in five minutes if I'd a mind to."

"Could you so?" Tim Malloy said, interested. "Let's see how it goes, Sam. Just for curiosity's sake."

Sam Shay shrugged.

"Bet me a dollar it'll stop raining within five minutes," he said. "And I'll bet the same it'll not. But since it'll be costing me a dollar to show, you must promise to spend it back again treating me."

"Fair's fair," Tim Malloy answered prompt. "And I promise. Then, Sam, I bet you a dollar it'll stop raining inside five minutes."

Lackadaisically Sam accepted and they laid their wagers out upon the table. And sure enough, within the five minutes the storm clouds overhead abruptly whisked away. The blue sky appeared, the sun shone, and it was as if the storm had never been.

"Now that's a curious thing, Sam," Tim Malloy said, eyes wide, as he ordered up more dark. "And if you could do that any time you wished, your fortune would be made."

"Oh, I can do it," Sam sighed, disinterested. "Fair to storm and storm to fair, I need but wager on it to make it come the opposite of my bet. For that matter, any event I make a gamble on will come out the opposite, be it what it may. It's a curse laid upon me, Tim."

"Is it now?" said Tim Malloy, and his eyes grew wider. "And by whom would the curse be laid, Sam Shay?"

Sam leaned forward and whispered in his ear, and Tim Malloy's eyes bade fair to start from their sockets.

"Draw in a deep breath," Sam said, nodding. "Sniff hard, Tim. You'll see."

Tim Malloy sniffed long and deep, and awe crept upon his features.

"Sulphur!" he whispered. "Sulphur and brimstone!"

Sam but nodded and went on drinking his dark. Tim Malloy, though, stretched out a hand and put it upon his arm.

"Sam," he said, voice hoarse, "you have never heard that there's people willing to pay good money to insure the weather'll be as they want it upon a certain day? Have you never heard of insuring against storms, Sam, and against accidents, sickness, twins and such misfortunes? And insuring isn't really betting. It's but a business—a legitimate, money-making business."

Sam stopped drinking his dark. He put his mug upon the table with a bang, and upon his face there came a look.

"So it is," he said, struck by the sudden thought. "So it is!"

"Sam," Tim Malloy said, emotion in his tone, "let us take but a single example. This Sunday coming the Loyal Sons of Saint Patrick parade. Suppose, then, the Loyal Sons said to you, 'Sam, we want to insure it does not storm this Sunday coming. Here's twenty dollars insurance money against rain. If it storms, now, you must pay us five hundred, but if it's fair, you keep the twenty.'

"And then suppose, Sam, you came to me and, 'Tim,' you'd say, 'I want to make a bet. And the bet is one dollar against another dollar that this Sunday coming it will rain.' Whereupon I'd say to you, 'Sam, I accept the wager. One dollar to one dollar that it does not rain this Sunday coming.'

"And as you are doomed to lose your gamble, it does not rain; you keep the twenty dollars paid you by the Loyal Sons, and your profit, Sam, your fair profit on a straightforward business deal which no one could call gambling would be——"

"Nineteen dollars!" Sam said, much moved. "Nineteen dollars profit, Tim, and no wager involved. And you say there are many people wanting such insurance?"

"Thousands of them," said Tim Malloy. "Thousands upon thousands of them. And there's no reason why you shouldn't insure them against anything they wish—seeing as you're backed, one might say, by all the resources of a tremendous big firm."

Sam Shay stood up, and in his eyes there was a light.

"Tim," he said, in a voice that rang, "here is twenty dollars. Rent me an office and have a sign painted saying Samuel Shay, Insurance. The biggest sign that can be managed. And here, Tim, is a dollar. That dollar I bet you Shannon will not say 'yes' to me a moment hence when I call upon her. Do you take the wager?"

"I take it, Sam," agreed Tim Malloy, but already Sam was striding out, and in scarce a minute was standing in the Malloy living room, large and masterful, while Shannon, who had tried to hold the door shut against him, stared at him with blazing eyes.

"Sam Shay," she cried hotly, "I won't see you!"

"You cannot help seeing me," Sam replied with tenderness, "for I am standing here before you."

"Then I won't look at you!" cried Shannon, and shut her eyes.

"In that case you must take the consequences," said Sam, and stepping forward, kissed her so that Shannon's eyes flew open again.

"Sam Shay," she exclaimed, "I——"

"I'll bet a dollar," Sam interrupted her, "you're going to say you hate me."

It was indeed what Shannon had been about to say, but now some perverse demon seemed to seize her tongue.

"I'm not!" she denied. "I was going to say I love you." And having said it, she stared at Sam as if she could not believe her ears.

"Then, Shannon, darling," Sam Shay asked, "will you take back my ring and marry me? And I'll bet another dollar you're going to say no."

And "no" it was that Shannon tried to say. But once again it was as if a contrary devil had her tongue.

"Indeed I'm not," she declared, to her own consternation. "For I say yes, and I will."

With which Sam swept her into his arms and kissed her again, so soundly she had no more time to wonder at the way her tongue had twisted. Indeed, she was forced to believe it was some strange power in Sam himself that had drawn the words from her. And on this point Sam wisely refrained from ever correcting her.

Thus they were married, and at this moment Sam Shay's insurance business is prospering beyond belief.

Money is flowing in from all sides, and being a prudent man Sam has arranged his affairs in excellent order. He has wagered with Tim Malloy, his junior partner, that he and Shannon will not live in good health to be ninety-nine each, while Tim has wagered they will. Sam has likewise bet that he and Shannon will be desperately unhappy, Tim gambling to the contrary. Finally Sam has gambled that they will not have ten fine, strapping, children, six boys and four girls, and Tim has placed his money that they will.

So sin continues to decline as Sam's business grows, and Sam himself sleeps soundly of nights. And if there is sometimes the faintest smell of brimstone and sulphur about the house, as though from much coming and going of harassed demons, no one in the household minds it, not even Dion, youngest of the ten young Shays.

OSCAR WILDE

The Canterville Ghost

I

When Mr. Hiram B. Otis, the American Minister, bought Canterville Chase, every one told him he was doing a very foolish thing, as there was no doubt at all that the place was haunted. Indeed, Lord Canterville himself, who was a man of the most punctilious honour, had felt it his duty to mention the fact to Mr. Otis when they came to discuss terms.

"We have not cared to live in the place ourselves," said Lord Canterville, "since my grand-aunt, the Dowager Duchess of Bolton, was frightened into a fit, from which she never really recovered, by two skeleton hands being placed on her shoulders as she was dressing for dinner, and I feel bound to tell you, Mr. Otis, that the ghost has been seen by several living members of my family, as well as by the rector of the parish, the Rev. Augustus Dampier, who is a Fellow of King's College, Cambridge. After the unfortunate accident to the Duchess, none of our younger servants would stay with us, and Lady Canterville often got very little sleep at night, in consequence of the mysterious noises that came from the corridor and the library."

"My lord," answered the Minister, "I will take the furniture and the ghost at a valuation. I come from a modern country, where we have everything that money can buy; and with all our spry young fellows painting the Old World red, and carrying off your best actresses and prima donnas, I reckon that if there were such a thing as a ghost in Europe, we'd have it at home in a very short time in one of our public museums, or on the road as a show."

"I fear that the ghost exists," said Lord Canterville, smiling, "though it may have resisted the overtures of your enterprising impresarios. It has been well known for three centuries, since 1584 in fact, and always makes its appearance before the death of any member of our family."

"Well, so does the family doctor for that matter, Lord Canterville. But there is no such thing, sir, as a ghost, and I guess the laws of Nature are not going to be suspended for the British aristocracy."

"You are certainly very natural in America," answered Lord Canterville, who did not quite understand Mr. Otis's last observation, "and if you don't mind a ghost in the house, it is all right. Only you must remember I warned you."

A few weeks after this, the purchase was completed, and at the close of the season the Minister and his family went down to Canterville Chase. Mrs. Otis, who, as Miss Lucretia R. Tappan, of West 53rd Street, had been a celebrated New York belle, was now a very handsome, middle-aged woman, with fine eyes, and a superb profile. Many American ladies on leaving their native land adopt an appearance of chronic ill-health, under the impression that it is a form of European refinement, but Mrs. Otis had never fallen into this error. She had a magnificent constitution, and a really wonderful amount of animal spirits. Indeed, in many respects, she was quite English, and was an excellent example of the fact that we have really everything in common with America nowadays, except, of course, language. Her eldest son, christened Washington by his parents in a moment of patriotism, which he never ceased to regret, was a fair-haired, rather good-looking young man, who had qualified himself for American diplomacy by leading the German at the Newport Casino for three successive seasons, and even in London was well known as an excellent dancer. Gardenias and the peerage were his only weaknesses. Otherwise he was extremely sensible. Miss Virginia E. Otis was a little girl of fifteen, lithe and lovely as a fawn, and with a fine freedom in her large blue eyes. She was a wonderful amazon, and had once raced old Lord Bilton on her pony twice round the park, winning by a length and a half, just in front of the Achilles statue, to the huge delight of the young Duke of Cheshire, who proposed for her on the spot, and was sent back to Eton that very night by his guardians, in floods of tears. After Virginia came the twins, who were usually called "The Stars and Stripes," as they were always getting swished. They were delightful boys, and with the exception of the worthy Minister the only true republicans of the family.

As Canterville Chase is seven miles from Ascot, the nearest railway station, Mr. Otis had telegraphed for a waggonette to meet them, and they started on their drive in high spirits. It was a lovely July evening, and the air was delicate with the scent of the pinewoods. Now and then they heard a wood pigeon brooding over its own sweet voice, or saw, deep in the rustling fern, the burnished breast of the pheasant. Little squirrels peered at them from the beech-trees as they went by, and the rabbits scudded away through the brushwood and over the mossy knolls, with their white tails in the air. As they entered the avenue of Canterville Chase, however, the sky became suddenly overcast with clouds, a curious stillness seemed to hold the atmosphere, a great flight of rooks passed silently over their heads, and, before they reached the house, some big drops of rain had fallen.

Standing on the steps to receive them was an old woman, neatly dressed in black silk, with a white cap and apron. This was Mrs. Umney, the housekeeper, whom Mrs. Otis, at Lady Canterville's earnest request, had consented to keep on in her former position. She made them each a low curtsey as they alighted, and said in a quaint, old-fashioned manner, "I bid you welcome to

Canterville Chase." Following her, they passed through the fine Tudor hall into the library, a long, low room, panelled in black oak, at the end of which was a large stained-glass window. Here they found tea laid out for them, and, after taking off their wraps, they sat down and began to look round, while Mrs. Umney waited on them.

Suddenly Mrs. Otis caught sight of a dull red stain on the floor just by the fireplace and, quite unconscious of what it really signified, said to Mrs. Umney, "I am afraid something has been spilt there."

"Yes, madam," replied the old housekeeper in a low voice, "blood has been spilt on that spot."

"How horrid," cried Mrs. Otis; "I don't at all care for blood-stains in a sitting-room. It must be removed at once."

The old woman smiled, and answered in the same low, mysterious voice, "It is the blood of Lady Eleanore de Canterville, who was murdered on that very spot by her own hushand, Sir Simon de Canterville, in 1575. Sir Simon survived her nine years, and disappeared suddenly under very mysterious circumstances. His body has never been discovered, but his guilty spirit still haunts the Chase. The blood-stain has been much admired by tourists and others, and cannot be removed."

"That is all nonsense," cried Washington Otis; "Pinkerton's Champion Stain Remover and Paragon Detergent will clean it up in no time," and before the terrified housekeeper could interfere he had fallen upon his knees, and was rapidly scouring the floor with a small stick of what looked like a black cosmetic. In a few moments no trace of the blood-stain could be seen.

"I knew Pinkerton would do it," he exlaimed triumphantly, as he looked round at his admiring family; but no sooner had he said these words than a terrible flash of lightning lit up the sombre room, a fearful peal of thunder made them all start to their feet, and Mrs. Umney fainted.

"What a monstrous climate!" said the American Minister calmly, as he lit a long cheroot. "I guess the old country is so over-populated that they have not enough decent weather for everybody. I have always been of opinion that emigration is the only thing for England."

"My dear Hiram," cried Mrs. Otis, "what can we do with a woman who faints?"

"Charge it to her like breakages," answered the Minister; "she won't faint after that"; and in a few moments Mrs. Umney certainly came to. There was no doubt, however, that she was extremely upset, and she sternly warned Mr. Otis to beware of some trouble coming to the house.

"I have seen things with my own eyes, sir," she said, "that would make any Christian's hair stand on end, and many and many a night I have not closed my eyes in sleep for the awful things that are done here." Mr. Otis, however, and his wife warmly assured the honest soul that they were not afraid of ghosts, and, after invoking the blessings of Providence on her new master and making arrangements for an increase of salary, the old housekeeper tottered off to her own room.

II

The storm raged fiercely all that night, but nothing of particular note occurred. The next morning, however, when they came down to breakfast, they found the terrible stain of blood once again on the floor. "I don't think it can be the fault of the Paragon Detergent," said Washington, "for I have tried it with everything. It must be the ghost." He accordingly rubbed out the stain a second time, but the second morning it appeared again. The third morning also it was there, though the library had been locked up at night by Mr. Otis himself, and the key carried upstairs. The whole family were now quite interested; Mr. Otis began to suspect that he had been too dogmatic in his denial of the existence of ghosts, Mrs. Otis expressed her intention of joining the Psychical Society, and Washington prepared a long letter to Messrs. Myers and Podmore on the subject of the Permanence of Sanguineous Stains when Connected with Crime. That night all doubts about the objective existence of phantasmata were removed for ever.

The day had been warm and sunny; and, in the cool of the evening, the whole family went out for a drive. They did not return home till nine o'clock, when they had a light supper. The conversation in no way turned upon ghosts, so there were not even those primary conditions of receptive expectation which so often precede the presentation of psychical phenomena. The subjects discussed, as I have since learned from Mr. Otis, were merely such as form the ordinary conversation of cultured Americans of the better class, such as the immense superiority of Miss Fanny Davenport over Sarah Bernhardt as an actress; the difficulty of obtaining green corn, buckwheat cakes, and hominy, even in the best English houses; the importance of Boston in the development of the world-soul; the advantages of the baggage check system in railway travelling; and the sweetness of the New York accent as compared to the London drawl. No mention at all was made of the supernatural, nor was Sir Simon de Canterville alluded to in any way. At eleven o'clock the family retired, and by half-past all the lights were out. Some time after, Mr. Otis was awakened by a curious noise in the corridor, outside his room. It sounded like the clank of metal, and seemed to be coming nearer every moment. He got up at once, and struck a match, and looked at the time. It was exactly one o'clock. He was quite calm, and felt his pulse, which was not at all feverish. The strange noise still continued, and with it he heard distinctly the sound of footsteps. He put on his slippers, took a small oblong phial out of his dressing-case, and opened the door. Right in front of him he saw, in the wan moonlight, an old man of terrible aspect. His eyes were as red burning coals; long grey hair fell over his shoulders in matted coils; his garments, which were of antique cut, were soiled and ragged, and from his wrists and ankles hung heavy manacles and rusty gyves.

"My dear sir," said Mr. Otis, "I really must insist on your oiling those chains, and have brought you for that purpose a small bottle of the Tammany Rising Sun Lubricator. It is said to be completely efficacious upon one application, and there are several testimonials to that effect on the wrapper from some of our most eminent native divines. I shall leave it here for you by the bedroom candles, and will be happy to supply you with more should you require it." With these words the United States Minister laid the bottle down on a marble table, and, closing his door, retired to rest.

For a moment the Canterville ghost stood quite motionless in natural indignation; then, dashing the bottle violently upon the polished floor, he fled down the corridor, uttering hollow groans, and emitting a ghastly green light. Just, however, as he reached the top of the great oak staircase, a door was flung open, two little white-robed figures appeared, and a large pillow whizzed past his head! There was evidently no time to be lost, so hastily adopting the Fourth Dimension of Space as a means of escape, he vanished through the wainscoting, and the house became quite quiet.

On reaching a small secret chamber in the left wing, he leaned up against a moonbeam to recover his breath, and began to try and realise his position. Never, in a brilliant and uninterrupted career of three hundred years, had he been so grossly insulted. He thought of the Dowager Duchess, whom he had frightened into a fit as she stood before the glass in her lace and diamonds; of the four housemaids, who had gone off into hysterics when he merely grinned at them through the curtains of one of the spare bedrooms; of the rector of the parish, whose candle he had blown out as he was coming late one night from the library, and who had been under the care of Sir William Gull ever since, a perfect martyr to nervous disorders; and of old Madame de Tremouillac, who, having wakened up one morning early and seen a skeleton seated in an armchair by the fire reading her diary, had been confined to her bed for six weeks with an attack of brain fever, and, on her recovery, had become reconciled to the Church, and broken off her connection with that notorious sceptic Monsieur de Voltaire. He remembered the terrible night when the wicked Lord Canterville was found choking in his dressing-room, with the knave of diamonds halfway down his throat, and confessed, just before he died, that he had cheated Charles James Fox out of £50,000 at Crockford's by means of that very card, and swore that the ghost had made him swallow it. All his great achievements came back to him again, from the butler who had shot himself in the pantry because he had seen a green hand tapping at the window pane, to the beautiful Lady Stutfield, who was always obliged to wear a black velvet band round her throat to hide the mark of five fingers burnt upon her white skin, and who drowned herself at last in the carp-pond at the end of the King's Walk. With the enthusiastic egotism of the true artist he went over his most celebrated performances, and smiled bitterly to himself as he recalled to mind his last appearance as "Red Ruben, or the Strangled Babe," his *début* as "Gaunt Gibeon, the Blood-sucker of Bexley Moor," and the *furore* he had excited one lovely June evening by merely playing ninepins with his own bones upon the lawn-tennis ground.

And after all this, some wretched modern Americans were to come and offer him the Rising Sun Lubricator, and throw pillows at his head! It was quite unbearable. Besides, no ghosts in history had ever been treated in this manner. Accordingly, he determined to have vengeance, and remained till daylight in an attitude of deep thought.

III

The next morning when the Otis family met at breakfast, they discussed the ghost at some length. The United States Minister was naturally a little annoyed to find that his present had not been accepted. "I have no wish," he said, "to do the ghost any personal injury, and I must say that, considering the length of time he has been in the house, I don't think it is at all polite to throw pillows at him"—a very just remark, at which, I am sorry to say, the twins burst into shouts of laughter. "Upon the other hand," he continued, "if he really declines to use the Rising Sun Lubricator, we shall have to take his chains from him. It would be quite impossible to sleep, with such a noise going on outside the bedrooms."

For the rest of the week, however, they were undisturbed, the only thing that excited any attention being the continual renewal of the blood-stain on the library floor. This certainly was very strange, as the door was always locked at night by Mr. Otis, and the windows kept closely barred. The chameleon-like colour, also, of the stain excited a good deal of comment. Some mornings it was a dull (almost Indian) red, then it would be vermilion, then a rich purple, and once when they came down for family prayers, according to the simple rites of the Free American Reformed Episcopalian Church, they found it a bright emerald-green. These kaleidoscopic changes naturally amused the party very much, and bets on the subject were freely made every evening. The only person who did not enter the joke was little Virginia, who, for some unexplained reason, was always a good deal distressed at the sight of the blood-stain, and very nearly cried the morning it was emerald-green.

The second appearance of the ghost was on Sunday night. Shortly after they had gone to bed they were suddenly alarmed by a fearful crash in the hall. Rushing downstairs, they found that a large suit of old armour had become detached from its stand, and had fallen on the floor, while, seated in a high-backed chair, was the Canterville ghost, rubbing his knees with an expression of acute agony on his face. The twins, having brought their pea-shooters with them, at once discharged two pellets on him, with that accuracy of aim which can only be attained by long and careful practice on a writing-master, while the United States Minister covered him with his revolver, and called upon him, in accordance with Californian etiquette, to hold up his hands! The ghost started up with a wild shriek of rage, and swept through them like a mist, extinguishing Washington Otis's candle as he passed, and so leaving them all in total darkness. On reaching the top of the staircase he recovered himself, and determined to give his celebrated peal of demoniac laughter. This he had on more than one occasion found extremely useful. It was said to have turned Lord Raker's wig grey in a single night, and had certainly made three of Lady Canterville's French governesses give warning before their month was up. He accordingly laughed his most horrible laugh, till the old vaulted roof rang and rang again, but hardly had the fearful echo died away when a door opened, and Mrs. Otis came out in a light blue dressing-gown. "I am afraid you are far from well," she said, "and have brought you a bottle of Dr. Dobell's tincture. If it is indigestion, you will find it a most excellent remedy." The ghost glared at her in fury, and began at once to make preparations for turning himself into a large black log, an accomplishment for which he was justly renowned, and to which the family doctor always attributed the permanent idiocy of Lord Canterville's uncle, the Hon. Thomas Horton. The sound of approaching footsteps, however, made him hesitate in his fell purpose, so he contented himself with becoming faintly phosphorescent, and vanished with a deep churchyard groan, just as the twins had come up to him.

On reaching his room he entirely broke down, and became a prey to the most violent agitation. The vulgarity of the twins, and the gross materialism of Mrs. Otis, were naturally extremely annoying, but what really distressed him most was that he had been unable to wear the suit of mail. He had hoped that even modern Americans would be thrilled by the sight of a Spectre in Armour, if for no more sensible reason, at least out of respect for their national poet Longfellow, over whose graceful and attractive poetry he himself had whiled away many a weary hour when the Cantervilles were up in town. Besides, it was his own suit. He had worn it with great success at the Kenilworth tournament, and been highly complimented on it by no less a person than the Virgin Queen herself. Yet when he had put it on, he had been completely overpowered by the weight of the huge breastplate and steel casque, and had fallen heavily on the stone pavement, barking both his knees severely, and bruising the knuckles of his right hand.

For some days after this he was extremely ill, and hardly stirred out of his room at all, except to keep the blood-stain in proper repair. However, by taking great care of himself, he recovered, and resolved to make a third attempt to frighten the United States Minister and his family. He selected Friday, the seventeenth of August, for his appearance, and spent most of that day in looking over his wardrobe, ultimately deciding in favour of a large slouched hat with a red feather, a winding-sheet frilled at the wrists and neck, and a rusty dagger. Towards evening a violent storm of rain came on, and the wind was so high that all the windows and doors in the old house shook and rattled. In fact, it was just such weather as he loved. His plan of action was this. He was to make his way quietly to Washington Otis's room, gibber at him from the foot of the bed, and stab himself three times in the throat to the sound of slow music. He bore Washington a special grudge, being quite aware that it was he who was in the habit of removing the famous Canterville blood-stain, by means of Pinkerton's Paragon Detergent. Having reduced the reckless and foolhardy youth to a condition of abject terror, he was then to proceed to the room occupied by the United States Minister and his wife, and there to place a clammy hand on Mrs. Otis's forehead, while he hissed into her trembling husband's ear the awful secrets of the charnel-house. With regard to little Virginia, he had not quite made up his mind. She had never insulted him in any way, and was pretty and gentle. A few hollow groans from the wardrobe, he thought, would be more than sufficient, or, if that failed to wake her, he might grabble at the counterpane with palsy-twitching fingers. As for the twins, he was quite determined to teach them a lesson. The first thing to be done was, of course, to sit upon their chests, so as to produce the stifling sensation of nightmare. Then, as their beds were quite close to each other, to stand between them in the form of a green, icy-cold corpse, till they became paralysed with fear, and finally, to throw off the winding-sheet, and crawl round the room, with white bleached bones and one rolling eyeball, in the character of "Dumb Daniel, or the Suicide's Skeleton," a *rôle* in which he had on more than one occasion produced a great effect, and which he considered quite equal to his famous part of "Martin the Maniac, or the Masked Mystery."

At half-past ten he heard the family going to bed. For some time he was disturbed by wild shrieks of laughter from the twins, who, with the light-hearted gaiety of schoolboys, were evidently amusing themselves before they retired to rest, but at a quarter past eleven all was still, and, as midnight sounded, he sallied forth. The owl beat against the window panes, the raven croaked from the old yew-tree, and the wind wandered moaning round the house like a lost soul; but the Otis family slept unconscious of their doom, and high above the rain and storm he could hear the steady snoring of the Minister for the United States. He stepped stealthily out of the wainscoting, with an evil smile on his cruel, wrinkled mouth, and the moon hid her face in a cloud as he stole past the great oriel window, where his own arms and those of his murdered wife were blazoned in azure and gold. On and on he glided, like an evil shadow, the very darkness seeming to loathe him as he passed. Once he thought he heard something call, and stopped; but it was only the baying of a dog, from the Red Farm, and he went on, muttering strange sixteenth-century curses, and ever and anon brandishing the rusty dagger in the midnight air. Finally he reached the corner of the passage that led to luckless Washington's room. For a moment he paused there, the wind blowing his long grey locks about his head, and twisting into grotesque and fantastic folds the nameless horror of the dead man's shroud. Then the clock struck the quarter, and he felt the time was come. He chuckled to himself, and turned the corner; but no sooner had he done so, than, with a piteous wail of terror, he fell back, and hid his blanched face in his long, bony hands. Right in front of him was standing a horrible spectre, motionless as a carven image, and monstrous as a madman's dream! It's head was bald and burnished; its face round, and fat, and white; and hideous laughter seemed to have writhed its features into an eternal grin. From the eyes streamed rays of scarlet light, the mouth was a wide well of fire, and a hideous garment, like to his own, swathed with its silent snows the Titan form. On its breast was a placard with strange writing in antique characters, some scroll of shame it seemed, some record of wild sins, some awful calendar of crime, and, with its right hand, it bore aloft a falchion of gleaming steel.

Never having seen a ghost before, he naturally was terribly frightened, and, after a second hasty glance at the awful phantom, he fled back to his room, tripping up in his long winding-sheet as he sped down the corridor, and finally dropping the rusty dagger into the Minister's jack-boots, where it was found in the morning by the butler. Once in the privacy of his own apartment, he flung himself down on a small pallet-bed, and hid his face under the clothes. After a time, however, the brave old Canterville spirit asserted itself, and he determined to go and speak to the other ghost as soon as it was daylight. Accordingly, just as the dawn was touching the hills with silver, he returned towards the spot where he had first laid eyes on the grisly phantom, feeling that, after all, two ghosts were better than one, and that, by the aid of his new friend, he might safely grapple with the twins. On reaching the spot, however, a terrible sight met his gaze. Something had evidently happened to the spectre, for the light had entirely faded from its hollow eyes, the gleaming falchion had fallen from its hand, and it was leaning up against the wall in a strained and uncomfortable attitude. He rushed forward and seized it in his arms, when, to his horror, the head slipped off and rolled on the floor, the body assumed a recumbent posture, and he found himself clasping a white dimity bed-curtain, with a sweeping-brush, a kitchen cleaver, and a hollow turnip lying at his feet! Unable to understand this curious transformation, he clutched the placard with feverish haste, and there, in the grey morning light, he read these fearful words:—

Ye Otis Ghoste
Ye Onlie True and Original Spook
Beware of Ye Imitationes
All others are Counterfeite

The whole thing flashed across him. He had been tricked, foiled, and outwitted! The old Canterville look came into his eyes; he ground his toothless gums together; and, raising his withered hands high above his head, swore, according to the picturesque phraseology of the antique school, that when Chanticleer had sounded twice his merry horn, deeds of blood would be wrought, and Murder walk abroad with silent feet.

Hardly had he finished this awful oath when, from the red-tiled roof of a distant homestead, a cock crew. He laughed a long, low, bitter laugh, and waited. Hour after hour he waited, but the cock, for some strange reason, did not crow again. Finally, at half-past seven, the arrival of the housemaids made him give up his fearful vigil, and he stalked back to his room, thinking of his vain hope and baffled purpose. There he consulted several books of ancient chivalry, of which he was exceedingly fond, and found that, on every occasion on which his oath had been used, Chanticleer had always crowed a second time. "Perdition seize the naughty fowl," he muttered; "I have seen the day when, with my stout spear, I would have run him through the gorge, and made him crow for me an 'twere in death!" He then retired to a comfortable lead coffin, and stayed there till evening.

IV

The next day the ghost was very weak and tired. The terrible excitement of the last four weeks was beginning to have its effect. His nerves were completely shattered, and he started at the slightest noise. For five days he kept his room, and at last made up his mind to give up the point of the blood-stain on the library floor. If the Otis family did not want it, they clearly did not deserve it. They were evidently people on a low, material plane of existence, and quite incapable of appreciating the symbolic value of sensuous phenomena. The question of phantasmic apparitions, and the development of astral bodies, was of course quite a different matter, and really not under his control. It was his solemn duty to appear in the corridor once a week, and to gibber from the large oriel window on the first and third Wednesday in every month, and he did not see how he could honourably escape from his obligations. It is quite true that his life had been very evil, but, upon the other hand, he was most conscientious in all things connected with the supernatural. For the next three Saturdays, accordingly, he traversed the corridor as usual between midnight and three o'clock, taking every possible precaution against being either heard or seen. He removed his boots, trod as lightly as possible on the old worm-eaten boards, wore a large black velvet cloak, and was careful to use the Rising Sun Lubricator for oiling his chains. I am bound to acknowledge that it was with a good deal of difficulty that he brought himself to adopt this last mode of protection. However, one night, while the family were at dinner, he slipped into Mr. Otis's bedroom and carried off the bottle. He felt a little humiliated at first, but afterwards was sensible enough to see that there was a great deal to be said for the invention, and, to a certain degree, it served his purpose. Still, in spite of everything, he was not left unmolested. Strings were continually being stretched across the corridor, over which he tripped in the dark, and on one occasion, while dressed for the part of "Black Isaac, or the Huntsman of Hogley Woods," he met with a severe fall, through treading on a butter-slide, which the twins had constructed from the entrance of the Tapestry Chamber to the top of the oak staircase. This last insult so enraged him that he resolved to make one final effort to assert his dignity and social position, and determined to visit the insolent young Etonians the next night in his celebrated character of "Reckless Rupert, or the Headless Earl."

He had not appeared in this disguise for more than

seventy years; in fact, not since he had so frightened pretty Lady Barbara Modish by means of it, that she suddenly broke off her engagement with the present Lord Canterville's grandfather, and ran away to Gretna Green with handsome Jack Castleton, declaring that nothing in the world would induce her to marry into a family that allowed such a horrible phantom to walk up and down the terrace at twilight. Poor Jack was afterwards shot in a duel by Lord Canterville on Wandsworth Common, and Lady Barbara died of a broken heart at Tunbridge Wells before the year was out, so, in every way, it had been a great success. It was, however, an extremely difficult "make-up," if I may use such a theatrical expression in connection with one of the greatest mysteries of the supernatural, or, to employ a more scientific term, the higher-natural world, and it took him fully three hours to make his preparations. At last everything was ready, and he was very pleased with his appearance. The big leather riding-boots that went with the dress were just a little too large for him, and he could only find one of the two horse-pistols, but, on the whole, he was quite satisfied, and at a quarter past one he glided out of the wainscoting and crept down the corridor. On reaching the room occupied by the twins, which I should mention was called the Blue Bed Chamber, on account of the colour of its hangings, he found the door just ajar. Wishing to make an effective entrance, he flung it wide open, when a heavy jug of water fell right down on him, wetting him to the skin, and just missing his left shoulder by a couple of inches. At the same moment he heard stifled shrieks of laughter proceeding from the four-post bed. The shock to his nervous system was so great that he fled back to his room as hard as he could go, and the next day he was laid up with a severe cold. The only thing that at all consoled him in the whole affair was the fact that he had not brought his head with him, for, had he done so, the consequences might have been very serious.

He now gave up all hope of ever frightening this rude American family, and contented himself, as a rule, with creeping about the passages in list slippers, with a thick red muffler round his throat for fear of draughts, and a small arquebuse, in case he should be attacked by the twins. The final blow he received occurred on the nineteenth of September. He had gone downstairs to the great entrance-hall, feeling sure that there, at any rate, he would be quite unmolested, and was amusing himself by making satirical remarks on the large Saroni photographs of the United States Minister and his wife, which had now taken the place of the Canterville family pictures. He was simply but neatly clad in a long shroud, spotted with churchyard mould, had tied up his jaw with a strip of yellow linen, and carried a small lantern and a sexton's spade. In fact, he was dressed for the character of "Jonas the Graveless, or the Corpse-Snatcher of Chertsey Barn," one of his most remarkable impersonations, and one which the Cantervilles had every reason to remember, as it was the real origin of their quarrel with their neighbour, Lord Rufford. It was about a quarter past two o'clock in the morning, and, as far as he could ascertain, no one was stirring. As he was strolling towards the library, however, to see if there were any traces left of the blood-stain, suddenly there leaped out on him from a dark corner two figures, who waved their arms wildly above their heads, and shrieked out "BOO!" in his ear.

Seized with a panic, which, under the circumstances, was only natural, he rushed for the staircase, but found Washington Otis waiting for him there with the big garden-syringe; and being thus hemmed in by his enemies on every side, and driven almost to bay, he vanished into the great iron stove, which, fortunately for him, was not lit, and had to make his way home through the flues and chimneys, arriving at his own room in a terrible state of dirt, disorder, and despair.

After this he was not seen again on any nocturnal expedition. The twins lay in wait for him on several occasions, and strewed the passages with nutshells every night to the great annoyance of their parents and the servants, but it was of no avail. It was quite evident that his feelings were so wounded that he would not appear. Mr. Otis consequently resumed his great work on the history of the Democratic Party, on which he had been engaged for some years; Mrs. Otis organized a wonderful clambake, which amazed the whole county; the boys took to lacrosse, euchre, poker, and other American national games; and Virginia rode about the lanes on her pony, accompanied by the young Duke of Cheshire, who had come to spend the last week of his holidays at Canterville Chase. It was generally assumed that the ghost had gone away, and, in fact, Mr. Otis wrote a letter to that effect to Lord Canterville, who, in reply, expressed his great pleasure at the news, and sent his best congratulations to the Minister's worthy wife.

The Otises, however, were deceived, for the ghost was still in the house, and though now almost an invalid, was by no means ready to let matters rest, particularly as he heard that among the guests was the young Duke of Cheshire, whose grand-uncle, Lord Francis Stilton, had once bet a hundred guineas with Colonel Carbury that he would play dice with the Canterville ghost, and was found the next morning lying on the floor of the cardroom in such a helpless paralytic state, that though he lived on to a great age, he was never able to say anything again but "Double Sixes." The story was well known at the time, though, of course, out of respect to the feelings of the two noble families, every attempt was made to hush it up; and a full account of all the circumstances connected with it will be found in the third volume of Lord Tattle's *Recollections of the Prince Regent and his Friends*. The ghost, then, was naturally very anxious to show that he had not lost his influence over the Stiltons, with whom, indeed, he was distantly connected, his own first cousin having been married *en secondes noces* to the Sieur de Bulkeley, from whom, as every one knows, the Dukes of Cheshire are lineally descended. Accordingly, he made arrangements for appearing to Virginia's little lover in his celebrated impersonation of "The Vampire Monk, or the Bloodless Benedictine," a performance so horrible that when old

Lady Startup saw it, which she did on one fatal New Year's Eve, in the year 1764, she went off into the most piercing shrieks, which culminated in violent apoplexy, and died in three days, after disinheriting the Cantervilles, who were her nearest relations, and leaving all her money to her London apothecary. At the last moment, however, his terror of the twins prevented his leaving his room, and the little Duke slept in peace under the great feathered canopy in the Royal Bedchamber, and dreamed of Virginia.

V

A few days after this, Virginia and her curly-haired cavalier went out riding on Brockley meadows, where she tore her habit so badly in getting through a hedge, that, on their return home, she made up her mind to go up by the back staircase so as not to be seen. As she was running past the Tapestry Chamber, the door of which happened to be open, she fancied she saw some one inside, and thinking it was her mother's maid, who sometimes used to bring her work there, looked in to ask her to mend her habit. To her immense surprise, however, it was the Canterville Ghost himself! He was sitting by the window, watching the ruined gold of the yellowing trees fly through the air, and the red leaves dancing madly down the long avenue. His head was leaning on his hand, and his whole attitude was one of extreme depression. Indeed, so forlorn, and so much out of repair did he look, that little Virginia, whose first idea had been to run away and lock herself in her room, was filled with pity, and determined to try and comfort him. So light was her footfall, and so deep his melancholy, that he was not aware of her presence till she spoke to him.

"I am so sorry for you," she said, "but my brothers are going back to Eton to-morrow and then, if you behave yourself, no one will annoy you."

"It is absurd asking me to behave myself," he answered, looking round in astonishment at the pretty little girl who had ventured to address him, "quite absurd. I must rattle my chains, and groan through keyholes, and walk about at night, if that is what you mean. It is my only reason for existing."

"It is no reason at all for existing, and you know you have been very wicked. Mrs. Umney told us, the first day we arrived here, that you had killed your wife."

"Well, I quite admit it," said the ghost petulantly, "but it was a purely family matter, and concerned no one else."

"It is very wrong to kill any one," said Virginia, who at times had a sweet Puritan gravity, caught from some old New England ancestor.

"Oh, I hate the cheap severity of abstract ethics! My wife was very plain, never had my ruffs properly starched, and knew nothing about cookery. Why, there was a buck I had shot in Hogley Woods, a magnificent pricket, and do you know how she had it sent up to table? However, it is no matter now, for it is all over, and I don't think it was very nice of her brothers to starve me to death, though I did kill her."

"Starve you to death? Oh, Mr. Ghost, I mean Sir Simon, are you hungry? I have a sandwich in my case. Would you like it?"

"No, thank you, I never eat anything now; but it is very kind of you, all the same, and you are much nicer than the rest of your horrid, rude, vulgar, dishonest family."

"Stop!" cried Virginia, stamping her foot, "it is you who are rude, and horrid, and vulgar, and as for dishonesty, you know you stole the paints out of my box to try and furbish up that ridiculous blood-stain in the library. First you took all my reds, including the vermilion, and I couldn't do any more sunsets; then you took the emerald-green and the chrome-yellow, and finally I had nothing left but indigo and Chinese white, and could only do moonlight scenes, which are always depressing to look at, and not at all easy to paint. I never told on you, though I was very much annoyed, and it was most ridiculous, the whole thing; for who ever heard of emerald-green blood?"

"Well, really," said the ghost, rather meekly, "what was I to do? It is a very difficult thing to get real blood nowadays, and, as your brother began it all with his Paragon Detergent, I certainly saw no reason why I should not have your paints. As for colour, that is always a matter of taste: the Cantervilles have blue blood, for instance, the very bluest in England; but I know you Americans don't care for things of this kind."

"You know nothing about it, and the best thing you can do is to emigrate and improve your mind. My father will be only too happy to give you a free passage, and though there is a heavy duty on spirits of every kind, there will be no difficulty about the Custom House, as the officers are all Democrats. Once in New York, you are sure to be a great success. I know lots of people there who would give a hundred thousand dollars to have a grandfather, and much more than that to have a family ghost."

"I don't think I should like America."

"I suppose because we have no ruins and no curiosities," said Virginia satirically.

"No ruins! no curiosities!" answered the ghost; "you have your navy and your manners."

"Good evening; I will go and ask papa to get the twins an extra week's holiday."

"Please don't go, Miss Virginia," he cried; "I am so lonely and so unhappy, and I really don't know what to do. I want to go to sleep and I cannot."

"That's quite absurd! You have merely to go to bed and blow out the candle. It is very difficult sometimes to keep awake, especially at church, but there is no difficulty at all about sleeping. Why, even babies know how to do that, and they are not very clever."

"I have not slept for three hundred years," he said sadly, and Virginia's beautiful blue eyes opened in wonder; "for three hundred years I have not slept, and I am so tired."

Virginia grew quite grave, and her little lips trembled like rose-leaves. She came towards him, and kneeling down at his side, looked up into his old withered face.

"Poor, poor ghost," she murmured; "have you no place where you can sleep?"

"Far away beyond the pinewoods," he answered, in a low dreamy voice, "there is a little garden. There the grass grows long and deep, there are the great white stars of the hemlock flower, there the nightingale sings all night long. All night long he sings, and the cold, crystal moon looks down, and the yew-tree spreads out its giant arms over the sleepers."

Virginia's eyes grew dim with tears, and she hid her face in her hands.

"You mean the Garden of Death," she whispered.

"Yes, Death. Death must be so beautiful. To lie in the soft brown earth, with the grasses waving above one's head, and listen to silence. To have no yesterday, and no tomorrow. To forget time, to forgive life, to be at peace. You can help me. You can open for me the portals of Death's house, for Love is always with you, and Love is stronger than Death is."

Virginia trembled, a cold shudder ran through her, and for a few moments there was silence. She felt as if she was in a terrible dream.

Then the ghost spoke again, and his voice sounded like the sighing of the wind.

"Have you ever read the old prophecy on the library window?"

"Oh, often," cried the little girl, looking up; "I know it quite well. It is painted in curious black letters, and it is difficult to read. There are only six lines:

"'When a golden girl can win
Prayer from out the lips of sin,
When the barren almond bears,
And a little child gives away its tears,
Then shall all the house be still
And peace come to Canterville.'

"But I don't know what they mean."

"They mean," he said sadly, "that you must weep with me for my sins, because I have no tears, and pray with me for my soul, because I have no faith, and then, if you have always been sweet, and good, and gentle, the Angel of Death will have mercy on me. You will see fearful shapes in darkness, and wicked voices will whisper in your ear, but they will not harm you, for against the purity of a little child the powers of Hell cannot prevail."

Virginia made no answer, and the ghost wrung his hands in wild despair as he looked down at her bowed golden head. Suddenly she stood up, very pale, and with a strange light in her eyes. "I am not afraid," she said firmly, "and I will ask the Angel to have mercy on you."

He rose from his seat with a faint cry of joy, and taking her hand bent over it with old-fashioned grace and kissed it. His fingers were as cold as ice, and his lips burned like fire, but Virginia did not falter, as he led her across the dusky room. On the faded green tapestry were broidered little huntsmen. They blew their tasselled horns and with their tiny hands waved to her to go back. "Go back! little Virginia," they cried, "go back!" but the ghost clutched her hand more tightly, and she shut her eyes against them. Horrible animals with lizard tails, and goggle eyes, blinked at her from the carven chimney-piece, and murmured "Beware! little Virginia, beware! We may never see you again," but the ghost glided on more swiftly, and Virginia did not listen. When they reached the end of the room he stopped, and muttered some words she could not understand. She opened her eyes, and saw the wall slowly fading away like a mist, and a great black cavern in front of her. A bitter cold wind swept round them, and she felt something pulling at her dress. "Quick, quick," cried the ghost, "or it will be too late," and, in a moment, the wainscoting had closed behind them, and the Tapestry Chamber was empty.

VI

About ten minutes later, the bell rang for tea, and, as Virginia did not come down, Mrs. Otis sent up one of the footmen to tell her. After a little time he returned and said that he could not find Miss Virginia anywhere. As she was in the habit of going out to the garden every evening to get flowers for the dinner-table, Mrs. Otis was not at all alarmed at first, but when six o'clock struck, and Virginia did not appear, she became really agitated, and sent the boys out to look for her, while she herself and Mr. Otis searched every room in the house. At half-past six the boys came back and said that they could find no trace of their sister anywhere. They were all now in the greatest state of excitement, and did not know what to do, when Mr. Otis suddenly remembered that, some few days before, he had given a band of gypsies permission to camp in the park. He accordingly at once set off for Blackfell Hollow, where he knew they were, accompanied by his eldest son and two of the farm-servants. The little Duke of Cheshire, who was perfectly frantic with anxiety, begged hard to be allowed to go too, but Mr. Otis would not allow him, as he was afraid there might be a scuffle. On arriving at the spot, however, he found that the gypsies had gone, and it was evident that their departure had been rather sudden, as the fire was still burning, and some plates were lying on the grass. Having sent off Washington and the two men to scour the district, he ran home, and dispatched telegrams to all the police inspectors in the county, telling them to look out for a little girl who had been kidnapped by tramps or gypsies. He then ordered his horse to be brought round, and, after insisting on his wife and the three boys sitting down to dinner, rode off down the Ascot Road with a groom. He had hardly, however, gone a couple of miles when he heard somebody galloping after him, and, looking round, saw the little Duke coming up on his pony, with his face very flushed and no hat. "I'm awfully sorry, Mr. Otis," gasped out the boy, "but I can't eat any dinner as long as Virginia is lost. Please, don't be angry with me; if you had let us be engaged last year, there would never have been all this trouble. You won't send me back, will you? I can't go! I won't go!"

The Minister could not help smiling at the handsome young scapegrace, and was a good deal touched at his devotion to Virginia, so leaning down from his horse, he patted him kindly on the shoulders, and said, "Well, Cecil, if you won't go back I suppose you must come with me, but I must get you a hat at Ascot."

"Oh, bother my hat! I want Virginia!" cried the little Duke, laughing, and they galloped on to the railway station. There Mr. Otis inquired of the station-master if any one answering the description of Virginia had been seen on the platform, but could get no news of her. The station-master, however, wired up and down the line, and assured him that a strict watch would be kept for her, and, after having bought a hat for the little Duke from a linen-draper, who was just putting up his shutters, Mr. Otis rode off to Bexley, a village about four miles away, which he was told was a well-known haunt of the gypsies, as there was a large common next to it. Here they roused up the rural policeman, but could get no information from him, and, after riding all over the common, they turned their horses' heads homewards, and reached the Chase about eleven o'clock, dead-tired and almost heart-broken. They found Washington and the twins waiting for them at the gate-house with lanterns, as the avenue was very dark. Not the slightest trace of Virginia had been discovered. The gypsies had been caught on Brockley meadows, but she was not with them, and they had explained their sudden departure by saying that they had mistaken the date of Chorton Fair, and had gone off in a hurry for fear they might be late. Indeed, they had been quite distressed at hearing of Virginia's disappearance, as they were very grateful to Mr. Otis for having allowed them to camp in his park, and four of their number had stayed behind to help in the search. The carp-pond had been dragged, and the whole Chase thoroughly gone over, but without any result. It was evident that, for that night at any rate, Virginia was lost to them; and it was in a state of the deepest depression that Mr. Otis and the boys walked up to the house, the groom following behind with the two horses and the pony. In the hall they found a group of frightened servants, and lying on a sofa in the library was poor Mrs. Otis, almost out of her mind with terror and anxiety, and having her forehead bathed with eau-de-cologne by the old housekeeper. Mr. Otis at once insisted on her having something to eat, and ordered up supper for the whole party. It was a melancholy meal, as hardly any one spoke, and even the twins were awestruck and subdued, as they were very fond of their sister. When they had finished, Mr. Otis, in spite of the entreaties of the little Duke, ordered them all to bed, saying that nothing more could be done that night, and that he would telegraph in the morning to Scotland Yard for some detectives to be sent down immediately. Just as they were passing out of the dining-room, midnight began to boom from the clock tower, and when the last stroke sounded they heard a crash and a sudden shrill cry; a dreadful peal of thunder shook the house, a strain of unearthly music floated through the air, a panel at the top of the staircase flew back with a loud noise, and out on the landing, looking very pale and white, with a little casket in her hand, stepped Virginia. In a moment they had all rushed up to her. Mrs. Otis clasped her passionately in her arms, the Duke smothered her with violent kisses, and the twins executed a wild war-dance round the group.

"Good heavens! child, where have you been?" said Mr. Otis, rather angrily, thinking that she had been playing some foolish trick on them. "Cecil and I have been riding all over the country looking for you, and your mother has been frightened to death. You must never play these practical jokes any more."

"Except on the ghost! except on the ghost!" shrieked the twins, as they capered about.

"My own darling, thank God you are found; you must never leave my side again," murmured Mrs. Otis, as she kissed the trembling child, and smoothed the tangled gold of her hair.

"Papa," said Virginia quietly, "I have been with the ghost. He is dead, and you must come and see him. He had been very wicked, but he was really sorry for all that he had done, and he gave me this box of beautiful jewels before he died."

The whole family gazed at her in mute amazement, but she was quite grave and serious; and, turning round, she led them through the opening in the wainscoting down a narrow secret corridor, Washington following with a lighted candle, which he had caught up from the table. Finally, they came to a great oak door, studded with rusty nails. When Virginia touched it, it swung back on its heavy hinges, and they found themselves in a little low room, with a vaulted ceiling, and one tiny grated window. Imbedded in the wall was a huge iron ring, and chained to it was a gaunt skeleton, that was stretched out at full length on the stone floor, and seemed to be trying to grasp with its long fleshless fingers an old-fashioned trencher and ewer, that were placed just out of its reach. The jug had evidently been once filled with water, as it was covered inside with green mould. There was nothing on the trencher but a pile of dust. Virginia knelt down beside the skeleton, and, holding her little hands together, began to pray silently, while the rest of the party looked on in wonder at the terrible tragedy whose secret was now disclosed to them.

"Hallo!" suddenly exclaimed one of the twins, who had been looking out of the window to try and discover in what wing of the house the room was situated. "Hallo! The old withered almond tree has blossomed. I can see the flowers plainly in the moonlight."

"God has forgiven him," said Virginia gravely, as she rose to her feet, and a beautiful light seemed to illumine her face.

"What an angel you are!" cried the young Duke, and he put his arm round her neck and kissed her.

VII

Four days after these curious incidents a funeral started from Canterville Chase at about eleven o'clock at night. The hearse was drawn by eight black horses, each of which carried on its head a great tuft of nodding ostrich-plumes, and the leaden coffin was covered by a rich purple pall, on which was embroidered in gold the Canterville coat-of-arms. By the side of the hearse and the coaches walked the servants with lighted torches, and the whole procession was wonderfully impressive. Lord Canterville was the chief mourner, having come up specially from Wales to attend the funeral, and sat in the first carriage along with little Virginia. Then came the United States Minister and his wife, then Washington and the three boys, and in the last carriage was Mrs. Umney. It was generally felt that, as she had been frightened by the ghost for more than fifty years of her life, she had a right to see the last of him. A deep grave had been dug in the corner of the churchyard, just under the old yew-tree, and the service was read in the most impressive manner by the Rev. Augustus Dampier. When the ceremony was over, the servants, according to an old custom observed in the Canterville family, extinguished their torches, and, as the coffin was being lowered into the grave, Virginia stepped forward and laid on it a large cross made of white and pink almond-blossoms. As she did so, the moon came out from behind a cloud, and flooded with its silent silver the little churchyard, and from a distant copse a nightingale began to sing. She thought of the ghost's description of the Garden of Death, her eyes became dim with tears, and she hardly spoke a word during the drive home.

The next morning, before Lord Canterville went up

to town, Mr. Otis had an interview with him on the subject of the jewels the ghost had given to Virginia. They were perfectly magnificent, especially a certain ruby necklace with old Venetian setting, which was really a superb specimen of sixteenth-century work, and their value was so great that Mr. Otis felt considerable scruples about allowing his daughter to accept them.

"My lord," he said, "I know that in this country mortmain is held to apply to trinkets as well as to land, and it is quite clear to me that these jewels are, or should be, heirlooms in your family. I must beg you, accordingly, to take them to London with you, and to regard them simply as a portion of your property which has been restored to you under certain strange conditions. As for my daughter, she is merely a child, and has as yet, I am glad to say, but little interest in such appurtenances of idle luxury. I am also informed by Mrs. Otis, who, I may say, is no mean authority upon Art—having had the privilege of spending several winters in Boston when she was a girl—that these gems are of great monetary worth, and if offered for sale would fetch a tall price. Under these circumstances, Lord Canterville, I feel sure that you will recognize how impossible it would be for me to allow them to remain in the possession of any member of my family; and, indeed, all such vain gauds and toys, however suitable or necessary to the dignity of the British aristocracy, would be completely out of place among those who have been brought up on the severe, and I believe immortal, principles of republican simplicity. Perhaps I should mention that Virginia is very anxious that you should allow her to retain the box as a memento of your unfortunate but misguided ancestor. As it is extremely old, and consequently a good deal out of repair, you may perhaps think fit to comply with her request. For my own part, I confess I am a good deal surprised to find a child of mine expressing sympathy with mediaevalism in any form, and can only account for it by the fact that Virginia was born in one of your London suburbs shortly after Mrs. Otis had returned from a trip to Athens."

Lord Canterville listened very gravely to the worthy Minister's speech, pulling his grey moustache now and then to hide an involuntary smile, and when Mr. Otis had ended, he shook him cordially by the hand, and said, "My dear sir, your charming little daughter rendered my unlucky ancestor, Sir Simon, a very important service, and I and my family are much indebted to her for her marvellous courage and pluck. The jewels are clearly hers, and, egad, I believe that if I were heartless enough to take them from her, the wicked old fellow would be out of his grave in a fortnight, leading me the devil of a life. As for their being heirlooms, nothing is an heirloom that is not mentioned in a will or legal document, and the existence of these jewels has been quite unknown. I assure you I have no more claim on them than your butler, and when Miss Virginia grows up I daresay she will be pleased to have pretty things to wear. Besides, you forget, Mr. Otis, that you took the furniture and the ghost at a valuation, and anything that belonged to the ghost passed at once into your possession, as, whatever activity Sir Simon may have shown in the corridor at night, in point of law he was really dead, and you acquired his property by purchase."

Mr. Otis was a good deal distressed at Lord Canterville's refusal, and begged him to reconsider his decision, but the good-natured peer was quite firm, and finally induced the Minister to allow his daughter to retain the present the ghost had given her, and when, in the spring of 1890, the young Duchess of Cheshire was presented at the Queen's first drawing-room on the occasion of her marriage, her jewels were the universal theme of admiration. For Virginia received the coronet, which is the reward of all good little American girls, and was married to her boy-lover as soon as he came of age. They were both so charming, and they loved each other so much, that every one was delighted at the match, except the old Marchioness of Dumblton, who had tried to catch the Duke for one of her seven unmarried daughters, and had given no less than three expensive dinner-parties for that purpose, and, strange to say, Mr. Otis himself. Mr. Otis was extremely fond of the young Duke personally, but, theoretically, he objected to titles, and, to use his own words, "was not without apprehension lest, amid the enervating influences of a pleasure-loving aristocracy, the true principles of republican simplicity should be forgotten." His objections, however, were completely overruled, and I believe that when he walked up the aisle of St. George's, Hanover Square, with his daughter leaning on his arm, there was not a prouder man in the whole length and breadth of England.

The Duke and Duchess, after the honeymoon was over, went down to Canterville Chase, and on the day after their arrival they walked over in the afternoon to the lonely churchyard by the pinewoods. There had been a great deal of difficulty at first about the inscription on Sir Simon's tombstone, but finally it had been decided to engrave on it simply the initials of the old gentleman's name, and the verse from the library window. The Duchess had brought with her some lovely roses, which she strewed upon the grave, and after they had stood by it for some time they strolled into the ruined chancel of the old abbey. There the Duchess sat down on a fallen pillar, while her husband lay at her feet smoking a cigarette and looking up at her beautiful eyes. Suddenly he threw his cigarette away, took hold of her hand, and said to her, "Virginia, a wife should have no secrets from her husband."

"Dear Cecil! I have no secrets from you."

"Yes, you have," he answered, smiling, "you have never told me what happened to you when you were locked up with the ghost."

"I have never told any one, Cecil," said Virginia gravely.

"I know that, but you might tell me."

"Please don't ask me, Cecil, I cannot tell you. Poor Sir Simon! I owe him a great deal. Yes, don't laugh, Cecil, I really do. He made me see what Life is, and what Death signifies, and why Love is stronger than both."

The Duke rose and kissed his wife lovingly.

"You can have your secret as long as I have your heart," he murmured.

"You have always had that, Cecil."

"And you will tell our children some day, won't you?"

Virginia blushed.

STEPHEN VINCENT BENÉT

The King of the Cats

"But, my *dear,*" said Mrs. Culverin, with a tiny gasp, "you can't actually mean—a *tail!*"

Mrs. Dingle nodded impressively. "Exactly. I've seen him. Twice. Paris, of course, and then, a command appearance at Rome—we were in the Royal box. He conducted—my dear, you've never heard such effects from an orchestra—and, my dear," she hesitated slightly, "he conducted *with it.*"

"How perfectly, fascinatingly too horrid for words!" said Mrs. Culverin in a dazed but greedy voice. "We *must* have him to dinner as soon as he comes over—he is coming over, isn't he?"

"The twelfth," said Mrs. Dingle with a gleam in her

eyes. "The New Symphony people have asked him to be guest-conductor for three special concerts—I do hope you can dine with *us* some night while he's here—he'll be very busy, of course—but he's promised to give us what time he can spare——"

"Oh, thank you, dear," said Mrs. Culverin, abstractedly, her last raid upon Mrs. Dingle's pet British novelist still fresh in her mind. "You're always so delightfully hospitable—but you mustn't wear yourself out—the rest of us must do *our* part—I know Henry and myself would be only too glad to——"

"That's very sweet of you, darling." Mrs. Dingle also remembered the larceny of the British novelist. "But we're just going to give Monsieur Tibault—sweet name, isn't it! They say he's descended from the Tybalt in 'Romeo and Juliet' and that's why he doesn't like Shakespeare—we're just going to give Monsieur Tibault the simplest sort of time—a little reception after his first concert, perhaps. He hates," she looked around the table, "large, mixed parties. And then, of course, his—er—little idiosyncrasy——" She coughed delicately. "It makes him feel a trifle shy with strangers."

"But I don't understand yet, Aunt Emily," said Tommy Brooks, Mrs. Dingle's nephew. "Do you really mean this Tibault bozo has a tail? Like a monkey and everything?"

"Tommy dear," said Mrs. Culverin, crushingly, "in the first place Monsieur Tibault is not a bozo—he is a very distinguished musician—the finest conductor in Europe. And in the second place——"

"He has." Mrs. Dingle was firm. "He has a tail. He conducts with it."

"Oh, but honestly!" said Tommy, his ears pinkening. "I mean—of course, if you say so, Aunt Emily, I'm sure he has—but still, it sounds pretty steep, if you know what I mean! How about it, Professor Tatto?"

Professor Tatto cleared his throat. "Tck," he said, putting his fingertips together cautiously, "I shall be very anxious to see this Monsieur Tibault. For myself, I have never observed a genuine specimen of *homo caudatus*, so I should be inclined to doubt, and yet . . . In the Middle Ages, for instance, the belief in men—er—tailed or with caudal appendages of some sort, was both widespread and, as far as we can gather, well founded. As late as the Eighteenth Century, a Dutch sea-captain with some character for veracity recounts the discovery of a pair of such creatures in the island of Formosa. They were in a low state of civilization, I believe, but the appendages in question were quite distinct. And in 1860, Dr. Grimbrook, the English surgeon, claims to have treated no less than three African natives with short but evident tails—though his testimony rests upon his unsupported word. After all, the thing is not impossible, though doubtless unusual. Web feet—rudimentary gills—these occur with some frequency. The appendix we have with us always. The chain of our descent from the apelike form is by no means complete. For that matter," he beamed around the table, "what can we call the last few vertebrae of the normal spine but the beginnings of a concealed and rudimentary tail? Oh, yes—yes—it's possible—quite—that in an extraordinary case—a reversion of type—a survival—though, of course——"

"I told you so," said Mrs. Dingle triumphantly. "*Isn't* it fascinating? Isn't it, Princess?"

The Princess Vivrakanarda's eyes, blue as a field of larkspur, fathomless as the centre of heaven, rested lightly for a moment on Mrs. Dingle's excited countenance.

"Ve-ry fascinating," she said, in a voice like stroked, golden velvet. "I should like—I should like ve-ry much to meet this Monsieur Tibault."

"Well, *I* hope he breaks his neck!" said Tommy Brooks, under his breath—but nobody ever paid much attention to Tommy.

Nevertheless as the time for M. Tibault's arrival in these States drew nearer and nearer, people in general began to wonder whether the Princess had spoken quite truthfully—for there was no doubt of the fact that, up till then, she had been the unique sensation of the season—and you know what social lions and lionesses are.

It was if you remember, a Siamese season, and genuine Siamese were at quite as much of a premium as Russian accents had been in the quaint old days when the Chauve-Souris was a novelty. The Siamese Art Theatre, imported at terrific expense, was playing to packed houses. "Gushuptzgu," an epic novel of Siamese farm life, in nineteen closely-printed volumes, had just been awarded the Nobel prize. Prominent pet-and-newt dealers reported no cessation in the appalling demand for Siamese cats. And upon the crest of this wave of interest in things Siamese, the Princess Vivrakanarda poised with the elegant nonchalance of a Hawaiian water-baby upon its surfboard. She was indispensable. She was incomparable. She was everywhere.

Youthful, enormously wealthy, allied on one hand to the Royal Family of Siam and on the other to the Cabots (and yet with the first eighteen of her twenty-one years shrouded from speculation in a golden zone of mystery), the mingling of races in her had produced an exotic beauty as distinguished as it was strange. She moved with a feline, effortless grace, and her skin was as if it had been gently powdered with tiny grains of the purest gold—yet the blueness of her eyes, set just a trifle slantingly, was as pure and startling as the sea on the rocks of Maine. Her brown hair fell to her knees—she had been offered extraordinary sums by the Master Barbers' Protective Association to have it shingled. Straight as a waterfall tumbling over brown rocks, it had a vague perfume of sandalwood and suave spices and held tints of rust and the sun. She did not talk very much—but then she did not have to—her voice had an odd, small, melodious huskiness that haunted the mind. She lived alone and was reputed to be very lazy—at least it was known that she slept during most of the day—but at night she bloomed like a moonflower and a depth came into her eyes.

It was no wonder that Tommy Brooks fell in love with her. The wonder was that she let him. There was nothing exotic or distinguished about Tommy—he was just one of those pleasant, normal young men who seem created to carry on the bond business by reading the newspapers in the University Club during most of the day, and can always be relied upon at night to fill an unexpected hole in a dinner-party. It is true that the Princess could hardly be said to do more than tolerate any of her suitors—no one had ever seen those aloofly arrogant eyes enliven at the entrance of any male. But she seemed to be able to tolerate Tommy a little more than the rest—and that young man's infatuated day-dreams were beginning to be beset by smart solitaires and imaginary apartments on Park Avenue, when the famous M. Tibault conducted his first concert at Carnegie Hall.

Tommy Brooks sat beside the Princess. The eyes he turned upon her were eyes of longing and love, but her face was as impassive as a mask, and the only remark she made during the preliminary bustlings was that there seemed to be a number of people in the audience. But Tommy was relieved, if anything, to find her even a little more aloof than usual, for, ever since Mrs. Culverin's dinner-party, a vague disquiet as to the possible impression which this Tibault creature might make upon her had been growing in his mind. It shows his devotion that he was present at all. To a man whose simple Princetonian nature found in "Just a Little Love, a Little Kiss," the quintessence of musical art, the average symphony was a positive torture, and he looked forward to the evening's programme itself with a grim, brave smile.

"Ssh!" said Mrs. Dingle, breathlessly. "He's coming!" It seemed to the startled Tommy as if he were suddenly back in the trenches under a heavy barrage, as M. Tibault made his entrance to a perfect bombardment of applause.

Then the enthusiastic noise was sliced off in the middle and a gasp took its place—a vast, windy sigh, as if every person in that multitude had suddenly said, "Ah." For the papers had not lied about him. The tail was there.

They called him theatric—but how well he understood the uses of theatricalism! Dressed in unrelieved black from head to foot (the black dress-shirt had been a special token of Mussolini's esteem), he did not walk on; he strolled, leisurely, easily, aloofly, the famous tail curled nonchalantly about one wrist—a suave, black panther lounging through a summer garden with that little mysterious weave of the head that panthers have when they pad behind bars—the glittering darkness of his eyes unmoved by any surprise or elation. He nodded, twice, in regal acknowledgment, as the clapping reached an apogee of frenzy. To Tommy there was something dreadfully reminiscent of the Princess in the way he nodded. Then he turned to his orchestra.

A second and louder gasp went up from the audience at this point, for, as he turned, the tip of that incredible tail twined with dainty carelessness into some hidden pocket and produced a black baton. But Tommy did not even notice. He was looking at the Princess instead.

She had not even bothered to clap, at first, but now—— He had never seen her moved like this, never. She was not applauding, her hands were clenched in her lap, but her whole body was rigid, rigid as a steel bar, and the blue flowers of her eyes were bent upon the figure of M. Tibault in a terrible concentration. The pose of her entire figure was so still and intense that for an instant Tommy had the lunatic idea that any moment she might leap from her seat beside him as lightly as a moth, and land, with no sound, at M. Tibault's side to—yes—to rub her proud head against his coat in worship. Even Mrs. Dingle would notice in a moment.

"Princess——" he said, in a horrified whisper, "Princess——"

Slowly the tenseness of her body relaxed, her eyes veiled again, she grew calm.

"Yes, Tommy?" she said, in her usual voice, but there was still something about her . . .

"Nothing, only—oh, hang—he's starting!" said Tommy, as M. Tibault, his hands loosely clasped before him, turned and *faced* the audience. His eyes dropped, his tail switched once impressively, then gave three little preliminary taps with his baton on the floor.

Seldom has Gluck's overture to "Iphigenie in Aulis" received such an ovation. But it was not until the Eighth Symphony that the hysteria of the audience reached its climax. Never before had the New Symphony played so superbly—and certainly never before had it been led with such genius. Three prominent conductors in the audience were sobbing with the despairing admiration of envious children toward the close, and one at least was heard to offer wildly ten thousand dollars to a well-known facial surgeon there present for a shred of evidence that tails of some variety could by any stretch of science be grafted upon a normally decaudate form. There was no doubt about it—no mortal hand and arm, be they ever so dexterous, could combine the delicate elan and powerful grace displayed in every gesture of M. Tibault's tail.

A sable staff, it dominated the brasses like a flicker of black lightning; an ebon, elusive whip, it drew the last exquisite breath of melody from the woodwinds and ruled the stormy strings like a magician's rod. M. Tibault bowed and bowed again—roar after roar of frenzied admiration shook the hall to its foundations—and when he finally staggered, exhausted, from the platform, the president of the Wednesday Sonata Club was only restrained by force from flinging her ninety-thousand-dollar string of pearls after him in an excess of aesthetic appreciation. New York had come and seen—and New York was conquered. Mrs. Dingle was immediately besieged by reporters, and Tommy Brooks looked forward to the "little party" at which he was to meet the new hero of the hour with feelings only a little less lugubrious than those that would have come to him just before taking his seat in the electric chair.

The meeting between his Princess and M. Tibault was worse and better than he expected. Better because, after all, they did not say much to each other—and worse because it seemed to him, somehow, that some curious kinship of mind between them made words unnecessary. They were certainly the most distinguished-looking couple in the room, as he bent over her hand. "So darlingly foreign, both of them, and yet so different," babbled Mrs. Dingle—but Tommy couldn't agree.

They were different, yes—the dark, lithe stranger with the bizarre appendage tucked carelessly in his pocket, and the blue-eyed, brown-haired girl. But that difference only accentuated what they had in common—something in the way they moved, in the suavity of their gestures, in the set of their eyes. Something deeper, even, than race. He tried to puzzle it out—then, looking around at the others, he had a flash of revelation. It was as if that couple were foreign, indeed—not only to New York but to all common humanity. As if they were polite guests from a different star.

Tommy did not have a very happy evening, on the whole. But his mind worked slowly, and it was not until much later that the mad suspicion came upon him in full force.

Perhaps he is not to be blamed for his lack of immediate comprehension. The next few weeks were weeks of bewildered misery for him. It was not that the Princess's attitude toward him had changed—she was just as tolerant of him as before, but M. Tibault was always there. He had a faculty of appearing, as out of thin air—he walked, for all his height, as lightly as a butterfly—and Tommy grew to hate that faintest shuffle on the carpet that announced his presence.

And then, hang it all, the man was so smooth, so infernally, unrufflably smooth! He was never out of temper, never embarrassed. He treated Tommy with the extreme of urbanity, and yet his eyes mocked, deep-down, and Tommy could do nothing. And, gradually, the Princess became more and more drawn to this stranger, in a soundless communion that found little need for speech—and that, too, Tommy saw and hated, and that, too, he could not mend.

He began to be haunted not only by M. Tibault in the flesh, but by M. Tibault in the spirit. He slept badly, and when he slept, he dreamed—of M. Tibault, a man no longer, but a shadow, a spectre, the limber ghost of an animal whose words came purringly between sharp little pointed teeth. There was certainly something odd about the whole shape of the fellow—his fluid ease, the mould of his head, even the cut of his fingernails—but just what it was escaped Tommy's intensest cogitation. And when he did put his finger on it at length, at first he refused to believe.

A pair of petty incidents decided him, finally, against all reason. He had gone to Mrs. Dingle's, one winter afternoon, hoping to find the Princess. She was out with his aunt, but was expected back for tea, and he wandered idly into the library to wait. He was just about to switch on the lights, for the library was always dark even in summer, when he heard a sound of light breathing that seemed to come from the leather couch in the corner. He approached it cautiously and dimly made out the form of M. Tibault, curled up on the couch, peacefully asleep.

The sight annoyed Tommy so that he swore under his breath and was back near the door on his way out, when the feeling we all know and hate, the feeling that eyes we cannot see are watching us, arrested him. He turned back—M. Tibault had not moved a muscle of his body to all appearance—but his eyes were open now. And those eyes were black and human no longer. They were green—Tommy could have sworn it—and he could have sworn that they had no bottom and gleamed like little emeralds in the dark: It only lasted a moment, for Tommy pressed the light-button automatically—and there was M. Tibault, his normal self, yawning a little but urbanely apologetic, but it gave Tommy time to think. Nor did what happened a trifle later increase his peace of mind.

They had lit a fire and were talking in front of it—by now Tommy hated M. Tibault so thoroughly that he felt that odd yearning for his company that often occurs in such cases. M. Tibault was telling some anecdote and Tommy was hating him worse than ever for basking with such obvious enjoyment in the heat of the flames and the ripple of his own voice.

Then they heard the street-door open, and M. Tibault jumped up—and jumping, caught one sock on a sharp corner of the brass fire-rail and tore it open in a jagged flap. Tommy looked down mechanically at the tear—a second's glance, but enough—for M. Tibault, for the first time in Tommy's experience, lost his temper completely. He swore violently in some spitting, foreign tongue—his face distorted suddenly—he clapped his hand over his sock. Then, glaring furiously at Tommy, he fairly sprang from the room, and Tommy could hear him scaling the stairs in long, agile bounds.

Tommy sank into a chair, careless for once of the fact that he heard the Princess's light laugh in the hall. He didn't want to see the Princess. He didn't want to see anybody. There had been something revealed when M. Tibault had torn that hole in his sock—and it was not the skin of a man. Tommy had caught a glimpse of—black plush. Black velvet. And then had come M. Tibault's sudden explosion of fury. Good *Lord*—did the man wear black velvet stockings under his ordinary socks? Or could he—could he—but here Tommy held his fevered head in his hands.

He went to Professor Tatto that evening with a series of hypothetical questions, but as he did not dare confide his real suspicions to the Professor, the hypothetical answers he received served only to confuse him the more. Then he thought of Billy Strange. Billy was a good sort, and his mind had a turn for the bizarre. Billy might be able to help.

He couldn't get hold of Billy for three days and lived through the interval in a fever of impatience. But finally they had dinner together at Billy's apartment, where his queer books were, and Tommy was able to blurt out the whole disordered jumble of his suspicions.

Billy listened without interrupting until Tommy was quite through. Then he pulled at his pipe. "But, my dear *man*——" he said, protestingly.

"Oh, I know—I know——" said Tommy, and waved his hands, "I know I'm crazy—you needn't tell me that—but I tell you, the man's a cat all the same—no, I don't see how he could be, but he is—why, hang it, in the first place, everybody knows he's got a tail!"

"Even so," said Billy, puffing. "Oh, my dear Tommy, I don't doubt you saw, or think you saw, everything you say. But, even so——" He shook his head.

"But what about those other birds, werewolves and things?" said Tommy.

Billy looked dubious. "We-ll," he admitted, "you've got me there, of course. At least—a tailed man *is* possible. And the yarns about werewolves go back far enough, so that—well, I wouldn't say there aren't or haven't been werewolves—but then I'm willing to believe more things than most people. But a were-cat—or a man that's a cat and a cat that's a man—honestly, Tommy——"

"If I don't get some real advice I'll go clean off my hinge. For Heaven's sake, tell me something to *do!*"

"Lemme think," said Billy. "First, you're pizen-sure this man is——"

"A cat. Yeah," and Tommy nodded violently.

"Check. And second—if it doesn't hurt your feelings, Tommy—you're afraid this girl you're in love with has—er—at least a streak of—felinity—in her—and so she's drawn to him?"

"Oh, Lord, Billy, if I only knew!"

"Well—er—suppose she really is, too, you know—would you still be keen on her?"

"I'd marry her if she turned into a dragon every Wednesday!" said Tommy, fervently.

Billy smiled. "H'm," he said, "then the obvious thing to do is to get rid of this M. Tibault. Lemme think."

He thought about two pipes full, while Tommy sat on pins and needles. Then, finally, he burst out laughing.

"What's so darn funny?" said Tommy, aggrievedly.

"Nothing, Tommy, only I've just thought of a stunt—something so blooming crazy—but if he is—h'm—what you think he is—it *might* work——" And, going to the bookcase, he took down a book.

"If you think you're going to quiet my nerves by reading me a bedtime story——"

"Shut up, Tommy, and listen to this—if you really want to get rid of your feline friend."

"What is it?"

"Book of Agnes Repplier's. About cats. Listen.

" 'There is also a Scandinavian version of the ever famous story which Sir Walter Scott told to Washington Irving, which Monk Lewis told to Shelley and which, in one form or another, we find embodied in the folklore of every land'—now, Tommy, pay attention—'the story of the traveller who saw within a ruined abbey a procession of cats lowering into a grave a little coffin with a crown upon it. Filled with horror, he hastened from the spot; but when he had reached his destination, he could not forbear relating to a friend the wonder he had seen. Scarcely had the tale been told when his friend's cat, who lay curled up tranquilly by the fire, sprang to its feet, cried out, "Then I am the King of the Cats!" and disappeared in a flash up the chimney.'

"Well?" said Billy, shutting the book.

"By gum!" said Tommy, staring. "By gum! Do you think there's a chance?"

"*I* think we're both in the booby-hatch. But if you want to try it——"

"Try it! I'll spring it on him the next time I see him. But—listen—I can't make it a ruined abbey——"

"Oh, use your imagination! Make it Central Park—anywhere. Tell it as if it happened to you—seeing the funeral procession and all that. You can lead into it somehow—let's see—some general line—oh, yes—'Strange, isn't it, how fact so often copies fiction. Why, only yesterday——' See?"

"Strange, isn't it, how fact so often copies fiction," repeated Tommy dutifully. "Why, only yesterday——"

"I happened to be strolling through Central Park when I saw something very odd."

"I happened to be strolling through—here, gimme that book!" said Tommy, "I want to learn the rest of it by heart!"

Mrs. Dingle's farewell dinner to the famous Monsieur Tibault, on the occasion of his departure for his Western tour, was looked forward to with the greatest expectations. Not only would everybody be there, including the Princess Vivrakanarda, but Mrs. Dingle, a hinter if there ever was one, had let it be known that at this dinner an announcement of very unusual interest to Society might be made. So everyone, for once, was almost on time, except for Tommy. He was at least fifteen minutes early, for he wanted to have speech with his aunt alone. Unfortunately, however, he had hardly taken off his overcoat when she was whispering some news in his ear so rapidly that he found it difficult to understand a word of it.

"And you mustn't breathe it to a soul!" she ended, beaming. "That is, not before the announcement—I think we'll have *that* with the salad—people never pay very much attention to salad——"

"Breathe what, Aunt Emily?" said Tommy, confused.

"The Princess, darling—the dear Princess and Monsieur Tibault—they just got engaged this afternoon, dear things! Isn't it *fascinating?*"

"Yeah," said Tommy, and started to walk blindly through the nearest door. His aunt restrained him.

"Not there, dear—not in the library. You can congratulate them later. They're just having a sweet little moment alone there now——" And she turned away to harry the butler, leaving Tommy stunned.

But his chin came up after a moment. He wasn't beaten yet.

"Strange, isn't it, how often fact copies fiction?" he repeated to himself in dull mnemonics, and, as he did so, he shook his fist at the library door.

Mrs. Dingle was wrong, as usual. The Princess and M. Tibault were not in the library—they were in the conservatory, as Tommy discovered when he wandered aimlessly past the glass doors.

He didn't mean to look, and after a second he turned away. But that second was enough.

Tibault was seated in a chair and she was crouched on a stool at his side, while his hand, softly, smoothly, stroked her brown hair. Black cat and Siamese kitten. Her face was hidden from Tommy, but he could see Tibault's face. And he could hear.

They were not talking, but there was a sound between them. A warm and contented sound like the murmur of giant bees in a hollow tree—a golden, musical rumble, deep-throated, that came from Tibault's lips and was answered by hers—a golden purr.

Tommy found himself back in the drawing-room, shaking hands with Mrs. Culverin, who said, frankly, that she had seldom seen him look so pale.

The first two courses of the dinner passed Tommy like dreams, but Mrs. Dingle's cellar was notable, and by the middle of the meat course, he began to come to himself. He had only one resolve now.

For the next few moments he tried desperately to break into the conversation, but Mrs. Dingle was talking, and even Gabriel will have a time interrupting Mrs. Dingle. At last, though, she paused for breath and Tommy saw his chance.

"Speaking of that," said Tommy, piercingly, without knowing in the least what he was referring to, "Speaking of that——"

"As I was saying," said Professor Tatto. But Tommy would not yield. The plates were being taken away. It was time for salad.

"Speaking of that," he said again, so loudly and strangely that Mrs. Culverin jumped and an awkward hush fell over the table. "Strange, isn't it, how often fact copies fiction?" There, he was started. His voice rose even higher. "Why, only today I was strolling through——" and, word for word, he repeated his lesson. He could see Tibault's eyes glowing at him, as he described the funeral. He could see the Princess, tense.

He could not have said what he had expected might happen when he came to the end; but it was not bored silence, everywhere, to be followed by Mrs. Dingle's acrid, "Well, Tommy, is that *quite* all?"

He slumped back in his chair, sick at heart. He was a fool and his last resource had failed. Dimly he heard his aunt's voice, saying, "Well, then——" and realized that she was about to make the fatal announcement.

But just then Monsieur Tibault spoke.

"One moment, Mrs. Dingle," he said, with extreme politeness, and she was silent. He turned to Tommy.

"You are—positive I suppose, of what you saw this afternoon, Brooks?" he said, in tones of light mockery.

"Absolutely," said Tommy sullenly. "Do you think I'd——"

"Oh, no, no, no," Monsieur Tibault waved the implication aside, "but—such an interesting story—one likes to be sure of the details—and, of course, you *are* sure—*quite* sure—that the kind of crown you describe was on the coffin?"

"Of course," said Tommy, wondering, "but——"

"Then I'm the King of the Cats!" cried Monsieur Tibault in a voice of thunder, and, even as he cried it, the houselights blinked—there was the soft thud of an explosion that seemed muffled in cotton-wool from the minstrel gallery—and the scene was lit for a second by an obliterating and painful burst of light that vanished in an instant and was succeeded by heavy, blinding clouds of white, pungent smoke.

"Oh, those *horrid* photographers," came Mrs. Dingle's voice in a melodious wail. "I *told* them not to take the flashlight picture till dinner was over, and now they've taken it *just* as I was nibbling lettuce!"

Someone tittered a little nervously. Someone coughed. Then, gradually the veils of smoke dislimned and the green-and-black spots in front of Tommy's eyes died away.

They were blinking at each other like people who have just come out of a cave into brilliant sun. Even yet their eyes stung with the fierceness of that abrupt illumination and Tommy found it hard to make out the faces across the table from him.

Mrs. Dingle took command of the half-blinded company with her accustomed poise. She rose, glass in hand. "And now, dear friends," she said in a clear voice, "I'm sure all of us are very happy to——" Then she stopped, open-mouthed, an expression of incredulous horror on her features. The lifted glass began to spill its contents on the tablecloth in a little stream of amber. As she spoke, she had turned directly to Monsieur Tibault's place at the table—and Monsieur Tibault was no longer there.

Some say there was a bursting flash of fire that disappeared up the chimney—some say it was a giant cat that leaped through the window at a bound, without breaking the glass. Professor Tatto puts it down to a mysterious chemical disturbance operating only over M. Tibault's chair. The butler, who is pious, believes the devil in person flew away with him, and Mrs. Dingle hesitates between witchcraft and a malicious ectoplasm dematerializing on the wrong cosmic plane. But be that as it may, one thing is certain—in the instant of fictive darkness which followed the glare of the flashlight, Monsieur Tibault, the great conductor, disappeared forever from mortal sight, tail and all.

Mrs. Culverin swears he was an international burglar and that she was just about to unmask him, when he slipped away under cover of the flashlight smoke, but no one else who sat at that historic dinner-table believes her. No, there are no sound explanations, but Tommy thinks he knows, and he will never be able to pass a cat again without wondering.

Mrs. Tommy is quite of her husband's mind regarding cats—she was Gretchen Woolwine, of Chicago—for Tommy told her his whole story, and while she doesn't believe a great deal of it, there is no doubt in her heart that one person concerned in the affair was a *perfect* cat. Doubtless it would have been more romantic to relate how Tommy's daring finally won him his Princess—but, unfortunately, it would not be veracious. For the Princess Vivrakanarda, also, is with us no longer. Her nerves, shattered by the spectacular denouement of Mrs.

Dingle's dinner, required a sea-voyage, and from that voyage she has never returned to America.

Of course, there are the usual stories—one hears of her, a nun in a Siamese convent, or a masked dancer at Le Jardin de ma Soeur—one hears that she has been murdered in Patagonia or married in Trebizond—but, as far as can be ascertained, not one of these gaudy fables has the slightest basis of fact. I believe that Tommy, in his heart of hearts, is quite convinced that the sea-voyage was only a pretext, and that by some unheard-of means, she has managed to rejoin the formidable Monsieur Tibault, wherever in the world of the visible or the invisible he may be—in fact, that in some ruined city or subterranean palace they reign together now, King and Queen of all the mysterious Kingdom of Cats. But that, of course, is quite impossible.

JULIUS FAST

My Friend Merton

Before he got out of the car, Lefty peeled ten bills off his roll and handed them to me. The bills were fifties and hundreds.

"Look, Rocky," he said. "Take this and blow. It should hold you for a month. Get out of town. This place is too hot for us."

I said, "Hell, Lefty, where'll I go?"

"Get into the country." Lefty shrugged. "Rent an old house. Take it easy, but stay away from the city. Remember Chaney and Spike."

I remembered Chaney and Spike. It had cost me a hundred bucks for calla lilies. They had a swell funeral. I said, "Okay, Lefty."

He climbed out of the car and shook my hand. "It was

Reprinted by permission of the author.

a pleasure working with you, Rocky. You are an artist." Then he was gone into the rain.

I pushed out of the city and headed west. I kept thinking of Chaney and Spike, not that I grudged them the hundred, only——

Four days later, I hit Evanstown, and it was still raining. I looked up the nearest real estate office and leaned on the bell. A seedy little guy took my hat and coat, and led me into his office.

"I'm Mr. Driscoll," he apologized.

I said that was all right, and I explained what I wanted. A nice, little house, maybe four or five rooms and far away from anyone else. He thought it over for a minute and then said, of course, what I wanted was the Barton place.

I said, if it was okay with him it was okay with me, and he should give me the key and tell me how to get there.

"Don't you even want to see it, Mr.—er . . . ?" he asked.

"Smith," I said. "And if the house is good enough for you, Mr. Driscoll, then it's good enough for me. Give me the key and tell me how to get there, and where's the nearest liquor store?"

Uncertainly he handed me the key and a written set of directions and pointed out the liquor store down the street. The last I saw of him, he was shaking his head and holding the bill I gave him up to the light.

I picked up a week's supply of bologna and bread in a delicatessen, and then a case of Scotch in the liquor store. The road out to the Barton place looked like a bridle path, but the house itself wasn't bad. It was a tight little brick job, and had a built-in bar in the cellar. There wasn't any liquor, but I arranged my Scotch on the shelf, and poured myself a good, stiff drink. Then I had a bologna sandwich and crawled into bed. All in all, the place was okay.

I woke up again about four o'clock in the morning, and it was still raining. I could hear the drops on the roof. Trying to fall asleep, I had a feeling that something was wrong. I got out of bed and slipped into my bathrobe. Then I opened the bedroom door and looked downstairs. There was a light in the cellar. The door was open, and I could see the reflection on the stairs. At first I thought I had left it like that; then I heard the singing, and I knew someone was down there. I slipped my judiciary into the bathrobe pocket, and tiptoed down.

Whoever was singing had one lousy voice. Every time he hit a high note, I flinched. He had his back to me, and he was sitting in front of the bar in a deep easy chair. He was waving a highball in one hand in time to the music.

I said, "Okay, Bud. What's up?"

He turned around in his chair and squinted at me. It made me uneasy to realize that I could see through his face. He just wasn't solid. Waving one hand at me, he murmured, "Boo," in a weak voice. Then he hiccoughed.

I walked over to the bar and faced him, keeping my hand in my pocket around the automatic. "What are you doing here?" I asked.

He blinked once or twice and then waved his hand again. "Boo," he repeated. "Boo!"

I said, "Okay, cut the clowning and start talking."

He bit his lip, and then he looked at the rest of his drink. With a sigh he finished it and then handed me the glass. "Would you mind mixing me a Scotch and soda?"

Then as I put down the glass, he hiccoughed again and added, "Without the soda."

I poured out the drink, thoughtfully keeping one eye on him. The guy had nerve. "How come I can see through you?" I asked.

"I'm probably a bit tight," he said. Then, as I looked blank, he added, "I'm a ghost."

I swallowed. "Ghost?"

"Yes. You know, ectoplasm and all of that——"

I poured a drink for myself and gulped it down. The guy wasn't kidding, I could see that.

He looked at his glass regretfully and sighed again. "I don't suppose you were scared?"

"No." I leaned against the bar and looked at him. He was a little guy with sandy-colored hair and watery eyes. I waved my hand at the bottle. "How come all this? I don't get it. I thought you guys ran around in sheets and scared the hell out of people. What's the setup?"

He sipped his drink. "Do you think a sheet would help? I mean, could I frighten you if I wore one?" he asked hopefully, his voice wistful.

"No." I shook my head. "You're not the type."

He sighed again and finished his drink. I filled both

our glasses. "That's the trouble," he said. "I'm not the type. Lord knows, I've tried—but somehow——"

"Maybe if you laid off the booze?"

"No. It's not because I drink, I drink because of that."

I leaned forward. "Say that again."

He put his glass down and blinked at me. "It's not because of that, it's that because of it—that is, because of that, it is—am I making myself clear?"

"Uh, uh." I filled his glass again. "Maybe you need another drink?"

"Maybe I do." He looked up at me, and a tear rolled down his cheek. "You're so nice to me."

I put down my glass and picked up the bottle instead. I was beginning to feel good. "Not at all," I protested, "not at all."

He wagged his head at me slowly. "Oh yes, you're good to me. Very good. People don't understand me, people don't know what it's like to have to haunt night after night with no one to thank them, with no one to understand." He reached out his hand, and I gave him the rest of the bottle. "And it's not that I don't try; Lord knows, I'm eager . . . I just can't make a go of it."

He looked up at me, and the tears were rolling down his face. "You understand, don't you? You're different."

I said, "Sure, sure." I took another bottle from behind the bar and opened it. The ghost leaned forward eagerly.

"What's your name, Rocky?" he asked.

I said, "Rocky." Then I looked up at him. "How did you know?"

He waved one hand carelessly. "I guess I'm psychic. I can't help knowing things."

"Come again?"

"Psychic. I read minds."

I said, "Yeah. I seen a guy do that at Coney Island once. What else can you do?"

He hiccoughed gently and snapped his fingers. One-half of him disappeared. He snapped them again, and very slowly the rest of him faded. Only the glass was left, sort of hanging in the air.

I leaned forward. "Hey, where are you?"

His voice came from the chair, sort of blurred. "Right here."

"How about the drink? Can you make that go, too?"

I heard him snapping his fingers, but the glass still hung in the air. Then he faded back into view, shaking his head.

I said, "What's wrong?"

He put the drink down. "I must be just a little bit tight. Liquor inhibits me. I can't really express myself. But you'll see, when I'm sober, Rocky, I can make anything vanish."

"And bring it back later?"

He looked hurt. "Of course!"

I was getting an idea. "Look," I said. "What's your name?"

"Merton."

"Well, stick around, Merton. You and I got a lot in common—a lot." I took another slug from the bottle. Merton beamed at me.

"I certainly will, Rocky. I'll—I'll—why, I'll haunt you. How splendid. I'll haunt you, Rocky."

I said, "Yeah. That'll be ducky. You haunt me, Merton, and boy, will we have fun!" I opened another bottle and lifted it. "A toast, Merton. To you and me, partners."

That was the last thing I remember that night, except for one hazy recollection of Merton and me draped over the bar harmonizing on "The Road to Mandalay." I must have gotten up to my room and into bed, because I woke up there the next morning completely undressed except for my shoes.

My head felt like a balloon caught in a hurricane, so I steadied it with a stiff Scotch. Then I sat down to think things over. I didn't think too much about Merton. It made me feel uneasy. I just accepted him as he was. What really got me going was the possibility of Merton as a money maker. I threw on some clothes and went down to the kitchen to fix myself a bite to eat.

Merton was there before me wrapping a half dozen ice cubes up in a towel. I cut myself some bologna and bread and started to think.

"How would you like a little extra money, Merton?" I asked tentatively.

Merton winced. "Don't talk so loud," he groaned. "My head feels like something the dog buried last week. Where did you hide the rest of the Scotch?"

"Under my bed. Look, Merton, I've got a little proposition."

"After I have a drink, please." He left the room and I heard him climbing the stairs. When he came back, he looked much happier and a good deal more transparent. Standing in the door he beamed at me.

"My friend, Rocky!"

"Sure, sure I'm your friend, Merton," I said. "Now look, here's the setup." I led him to a seat and explained the thing carefully. He nodded solemnly and repeated what I told him. He had it down pat, but I felt worried. After all, Lefty had said to lay low.

I pulled my car up in front of the house, and I started to get behind the wheel. But Merton caught my arm.

"Let me drive, Rocky."

I said, "No. You've had too much to drink, Merton. I'll drive."

He drew himself up with an injured air. "If I'm not sober enough to drive, Rocky, I'm not sober enough to rob a bank."

I said, "Okay, you win. But be careful."

It was about five miles from the house to town, and most of the way was along a rough, dirt road. When we finally pulled on to the State Highway, Merton let the car out. I watched the needle hit eighty; then I leaned towards him. "Slow down," I told him. "You'll get us both killed."

He turned to me and giggled. "Don't be silly. Nothing can happen to me."

We were on the left side of the road, and a car was racing towards us. I grabbed the wheel, and we shot past with an inch to spare. I heard a shrill whine behind us. Merton stepped on the gas, and the needle crept up to eighty. I knew the car couldn't hold out.

I shouted, "Stop! You damned fool," and Merton stepped on the brake. My head cracked against the windshield, and for a few minutes I couldn't see. When my eyes cleared, I caught sight of Merton, or what was left of Merton, slowly becoming invisible. I swallowed, and then the cop on the motorcycle pulled up in front of me.

"I know," he said, "your Aunt Annie was dyin'." Then he saw where I was sitting. "What are you doing there?" he asked.

I said, "Look, Officer. I wasn't driving."

"Hell no, you were flying."

I smiled weakly and tried to slide over behind the wheel, but Merton was still sitting there. I heard him giggle, and he whispered, "I'm still with you, Rocky."

I said, "Get the hell out of there!" and the cop's eyes narrowed.

"What's that?"

I smiled weakly. "Must have fell out of here."

"What?"

"My driver's license." I pulled out my wallet.

He was writing out a ticket. I said, "Look, Officer, let's not be hasty."

He looked at the speedometer pointedly. "No, let's not."

I took hold of Merton's arm. "I can explain everything."

Merton pulled himself loose. "Let go of the arm, you chump!" he hissed.

The cop looked at me. "Chump?"

I said, "Oh, nuts. Give me the ticket and let's get it over with."

"Yeah, we have a bank to rob before noon," Merton added.

"A wise guy!" The cop put his pad away. "I think I'll run you in instead."

"Now look, Officer . . ." I started to say, when Merton cut in.

"Let's see you do it, you big palooka!"

The cop shut his mouth with a click. "That clinches it," he said between his teeth. "Ninety miles an hour, and you've got nerve enough to talk back. Come on, follow me."

He turned towards his motorcycle, and Merton called out, "It's a democracy, isn't it? We got rights; it's a free country." Then I clapped my hand over his mouth.

The cop started his motor and called back. "It's a free country, but not where you're going. And stop changing your voice!"

I was blazing mad when I came up before the judge, and that didn't help matters. He leaned back and pressed his fingertips together.

"You've heard of speed limits?"

I said, "All right, cut the comedy. What's the fine?" I took my wallet out.

"Fifty dollars." His voice was very soft.

I counted out the bills and handed them to the clerk. The judge closed his eyes. "And thirty days."

They gave me a nice cell, it had a western exposure,

and I could watch the sunsets from my window. The first night I won ten bucks from the warden in gin rummy, and I settled for a bottle of Scotch. Things began to look better; after all, I was after a rest.

Then Merton came back. I was playing solitaire on my cot, when one of the red tens picked itself up and settled on a red jack. I murmured, "Red on black, stupid," and I started to lift it off. Then my hand stopped in the air. I gulped and looked around. A glass of Scotch was floating lazily about four feet from the floor.

I stood up slowly, and the glass backed away.

"Come out and let me see you," I muttered. "Come out, you anemic excuse for a ghost—come out and let me tear your arms off!"

The glass backed up against the wall.

"Now don't get excited, Rocky. It won't do you any good to hurt me."

I sat down on the bed and used a few four-letter words. Merton laughed uneasily. "You didn't think I'd desert you, Rocky?"

"I had my hopes!" I said bitterly.

Merton finished his drink and emptied the rest of my Scotch into his glass. While he was doing it, his arms and head came into view. He waved the glass dramatically. I could see he was stewed again.

"Desert my bosom pal—not me, not Merton."

I growled, "Either appear or disappear."

He looked hurt. "You don't understand my ectoplasmic limitations."

"Ectoplasmic, hell! What do you want?"

"I got you into thish, and I'll get you out. Trusht me, Rocky."

I walked over to the bars and yelled, "Warden!" The warden came over to the cell door and looked in.

"No more gin rummy, Rocky," he said soothingly. "The judge doesn't like it."

I said, "Get that graveyard monstrosity out of here." I turned around, but Merton was gone. Only the glass remained, suspended in the air.

The warden's eyes narrowed. "Magic, huh? So you're one of them amateur magicians. So that's where my ten bucks went."

"Oh, what's the use." I sat down on my bed, and the warden walked away. Merton's arms came back into view, then his head. He looked at me reproachfully.

"And I tried to help you, Rocky." He snapped his fingers and a keyring and keys faded into view. I sat up on the bed.

"Are those . . . ?"

"Uh, uh. Now aren't you sorry?"

I grabbed at the keys, but Merton snatched them away. "First you gotta promise."

"What?"

He tried to look casual, but it didn't quite come off. "Oh, nothing much."

"What?"

"Look, Rocky. I like you. You're the first real friend I've had."

"Get that out of your head," I said bitterly. "I'm no friend of yours."

"You're a real friend," he insisted, "your hard exterior doesn't fool me a bit."

"It convinces me," I muttered.

"Beneath that hard exterior beats a heart of gold."

I said, "Yeah, next week, East Lynne. What are you driving at?"

"Rocky, I want to be your pal. Promise me I can haunt you always, and I'll give you the keys."

"Always? Are you nuts? I'd rather be in stir."

A tear rolled out of the corner of his eye and splashed into the Scotch. "Then for a year, Rocky."

"Not even for a minute. Beat it!"

"A month?"

"Scram!"

He finished his drink and threw the keys on the bed, "Well, I tried. The spirit was willing, but the flesh was weak. So long, Rocky . . . take the key, anyway."

I began to feel sorry for the guy. "Come on," I muttered. "At least we can have a drink together."

His eyes lit up. "Where?"

"At the nearest bar, if I can get out of this joint." I tried each of the keys, and the fourth one fitted. The door swung open noiselessly, and I grabbed the empty Scotch bottle and tiptoed out. The warden was sitting at a desk at the end of the corridor, his back to me.

Merton hiccoughed gently, and the warden lifted his head. I flattened myself against the wall and held my breath. After a moment, the warden leaned forward, and I exhaled deeply. I stole down the corridor till I was directly behind him, then I pressed the neck of the bottle into the small of his back.

"Don't move, warden. I've got you covered."

He lifted his hands slowly. "Now what did you want to do that for, Rocky? Weren't you happy?"

I said, "Get up and walk to my cell. Keep your back to me." Backing away, I put down the bottle. The warden marched to the cell in front of me, and I called out, "Merton!"

He materialized behind the desk, but his head was missing. "Did you call me, Rocky?"

"Yeah. Tie the warden's arms and legs. Lie down on my cot, warden. You can gag him, too, Merton."

"What'll I use for rope?"

"Tear up a sheet."

The warden sat down on the cot, and Merton stepped in front of him. The warden took one look, then he fell back on the bed with his eyes closed. Merton was surprised.

"I must be a sight."

"It's only your hair, dearie. Tie him up, anyway."

We got out of the building without any trouble. On the way down, Merton got back his head, but lost both legs. He smiled at me apologetically.

"I lose control when I get a little high."

It was dark out, and I could see the neon lights of a bar at the corner. We stopped in there. It was empty except for one drunk and the bartender.

"Two Scotches," I said.

The drunk put down his glass and stared at Merton's legs, or at where Merton's legs should have been. Then he looked at me and blinked.

"He ain't got no legs."

I said, "Nah, he lost them in the war."

The drunk nodded, "Oh, I see." He picked up his glass and staggered over to the table.

The bartender brought our drinks, and I gulped mine down and ordered another.

The drunk caught my eye. "How does he stand?"

"He holds himself up."

"Oh, I see."

Merton turned around and looked at the drunk solemnly. "Hold your tongue, inebriate, or I'll frighten you out of your pants."

The drunk stuck his under lip out. "Gettin' tough, eh?"

Merton's head vanished, and he waved his arms. "Boooo!"

The drunk screamed and fell under the table. The bartender came over to us shaking his head. "You'll have to get out unless the gentleman puts his head back. I don't like no trouble."

I took Merton's arm and put a dollar down on the bar. "Okay, bud. Come on, Merton."

"That's another dime you owe me."

I threw a quarter to him, "Keep the change."

"Thanks." He sounded sarcastic. I got Merton outside, and the night air seemed to sober him up. His head came back and most of his legs. We started walking down the street.

Merton said, "Where're you going, Rocky?"

"To the railway station and as far from this burg as I can get." I hailed a passing taxi and climbed in. Merton got in next to me.

"You can drop me off at the graveyard," he murmured. The taxi driver said, "Where to, Mister?" And I had an idea. A sucker never learns.

I said, "You know where the bank is?"

"The trust company?"

"No, the savings bank."

"You want to go there?"

"I'm going to the house around the corner from the bank."

"Oh." He started the car. "You mean the Bakers. Nice folks. You know them? My son, Benny, goes out with Rose Anne. She's the youngest kid. A nice girl, but a little wild."

Merton groaned. "Spare us the background, just drive us there." He leaned back and turned to me happily. "Do I guess right, Rocky? Are you going to rob the B-A-N-K?"

The taxi almost collided with a traffic stanchion, and I shoved my elbow into Merton's ribs. The taxi driver pulled over to the curb.

"This is the place. That's fifty cents, Mister." He looked at Merton nervously. I paid him, and we waited till he drove out of sight. Then we hurried around the corner to the bank.

I said, "Look, Merton. I'll wait out here. You get inside and do your stuff. But, remember, make the money invisible."

Merton blinked and looked at me in surprise. "Aren't you coming in, too?"

"No, I'll keep watch outside."

Merton looked around longingly. I saw that Scotch and soda expression in his eyes. "I think I'm scared, Rocky."

"What of it? What have you got to lose?" I put my arm around his shoulders. "Besides, I'll buy you a drink; I'll buy you a case."

That clinched it. Merton started up the steps, but before he reached the top, he just faded away into thin air. I lit a cigarette and leaned against the lamppost. Now if I could only ditch Merton, get hold of my car again and blow, things would be all right. Just then a taxi pulled up at the curb, and I stepped back into the shadows. It was the same driver who had just dropped Merton and me. A cop was sitting alongside him.

I turned around and started walking. The cop's voice stopped me. "Wait up, bub."

I turned around and tried to keep my hand from shaking. This cop was a stranger.

"What's up?"

I tried to smile. " 'Up?' Sorry, Officer, I'm just waiting here for a friend."

The cop turned to the taxi driver. "This the guy?"

The taxi driver nodded. "Yeah, he had a friend with him."

I said, "See, that's the friend I'm waiting for."

The cop squinted at me suspiciously. "What's this about robbin' a bank?"

I started to laugh. "My God! Can't a fellow kid around in this burg? What is this, the Gestapo?"

The cop grinned and scratched his head. "Does sound sort of screwy, but you can't be too careful."

"Hell, no. You can't." I wiped the sweat off my forehead and stuck out my hand. "Be seein' you, Officer."

Then Merton came down the steps.

He materialized about halfway down, his arms full of green banknotes. Some of them were falling on the steps behind him. He dumped them into my arms and waved a whiskey bottle in the air.

"Look what I found in the cashier's drawer. It's rye, but what the hell—a drink's a drink."

They gave me a cell with an eastern exposure this time, but that's all right, because I'm raising nasturtiums in a window box, and they need the morning sun. I've got maybe ten years with good behavior, and I'm very happy. The warden still plays gin rummy with me, but not for keeps. Merton disappeared the night I was arrested, and I haven't seen him since, thank God!

The only thing that worries me is the warden's whiskey. He claims that it evaporates faster than he can drink it. It's probably one of the guards . . . still . . .

H. C. BUNNER

Zenobia's Infidelity

Dr. Tibbitt stood on the porch of Mrs. Pennypepper's boarding house, and looked up and down the deserted Main Street of Sagawaug with a contented smile, the while he buttoned his driving gloves. The little doctor had good cause to be content with himself and with everything else—with his growing practice, with his comfortable boarding house, with his own good looks, with his neat attire, and with the world in general. He could not but be content with Sagawaug, for there never was a prettier country town. The doctor looked across the street and picked out the very house that he proposed to buy when the one remaining desire of his soul was gratified. It was a house with a hip roof and with a long garden running down to the river.

There was no one in the house today, but there was no one in any of the houses. Not even a pair of round bare arms was visible among the clothes that waved in the August breeze in every backyard. It was circus day in Sagawaug.

The doctor was climbing into his gig when a yell startled him. A freckled boy with saucer eyes dashed around the corner.

"Doctor!" he gasped, "come quick! The circus got afire an' the trick elephant's most roasted!"

"Don't be silly, Johnny," said the doctor, reprovingly.

"Hope to die—honest Injun—cross my breast!" said the boy. The doctor knew the sacredness of this juvenile oath.

"Get in here with me," he said, "and if I find you're trying to be funny, I'll drop you in the river."

As they drove toward the outskirts of the town, Johnny told his tale.

"Now," he began, "the folks was all out of the tent after the show was over, and one of the circus men, he went to the oil barrel in the green wagon with Dan'l in the Lion's Den onto the outside of it, an' he took in a candle an' left it there, and fust thing the barrel busted, an' he wasn't hurted a bit, but the trick elephant she was burned awful, an' the ringtailed baboon, he was so scared he had a fit. Say, did you know baboons had fits?"

When they reached the circus grounds, they found a crowd around a small side-show tent. A strong odor of burnt leather confirmed Johnny's story. Dr. Tibbitt pushed his way through the throng, and gazed upon the huge beast, lying on her side on the grass, her broad shoulder charred and quivering. Her bulk expanded and contracted with spasms of agony, and from time to time she uttered a moaning sound. On her head was a structure of red cloth, about the size of a bushel basket, apparently intended to look like a British soldier's forage cap. This was secured by a strap that went under her chin—if an elephant has a chin. This scarlet cheese box every now and then slipped down over her eye, and the faithful animal patiently, in all her anguish, adjusted it with her prehensile trunk.

By her side stood her keeper and the proprietor of the show, a large man with a dyed mustache, a wrinkled face, and hair oiled and frizzed. These two bewailed their loss alternately.

"The boss elephant in the business!" cried the showman. "Barnum never had no trick elephant like Zenobia. And them lynes and Dan'l was painted in new before I took the road this season. Oh, there's been a hoodoo on me since I showed ag'inst the Sunday-school picnic!"

"That there elephant's been like my own child," groaned the keeper, "or my own wife, I may say."

The doctor had been carefully examining his patient.

"If there is any analogy——" he began.

"Neuralogy!" snorted the indignant showman; "'tain't neuralogy, you jay pill box, she's *cooked!*"

"If there is any analogy," repeated Dr. Tibbitt, flushing a little, "between her case and that of a human being, I think I can save your elephant. Get me a barrel of linseed oil, and drive these people away."

The doctor's orders were obeyed with eager submission. He took off his coat and went to work. He had never doctored an elephant, and the job interested him. At the end of an hour, Zenobia's sufferings were somewhat alleviated. She lay on her side, chained tightly to the ground, and swaddled in bandages. Her groans had ceased.

"I'll call tomorrow at noon," said the doctor—"good gracious, what's that?" Zenobia's trunk was playing around his waistband.

"She wants to shake hands with you," her keeper explained. "She's a lady, she is, and she knows you done her good."

"I'd rather not have anything of the sort," said the doctor, decisively.

When Dr. Tibbitt called at twelve on the morrow, he found Zenobia's tent nearly roped in, an amphitheater of circus benches constructed around her, and this amphitheater packed with people.

"Got a quarter apiece from them jays," whispered the showman, "jest to see you dress them wownds." Subsequently the showman relieved his mind to a casual acquaintance. "He's got a heart like a gunflint, that doctor," he said, "made me turn out every one of them jays and give 'em their money back before he'd lay a hand on Zenobia."

But if the doctor suppressed the clinic, neither he nor the showman suffered. From dawn till dusk people came from miles around to stare a quarter's worth at the burnt elephant. Once in a while, as a rare treat, the keeper lifted a corner of her bandages, and revealed the seared flesh. The show went off in a day or two, leaving Zenobia to recover at leisure; and as it wandered westward, it did an increased business simply because it had had a burnt trick elephant. Such, dear friends, is the human mind.

The doctor fared even better. The fame of his new case spread far and wide. People seemed to think that if he could cure an elephant he could cure anything. He was called into consultation in neighboring towns. Women in robust health imagined ailments, so as to send for him and ask him shuddering questions about "that *wretched* animal." The trustees of the orphan asylum made him staff physician—in this case the doctor thought he could trace a connection of ideas, in which children and a circus were naturally associated. And the local newspaper called him a *savant*.

He called every day upon Zenobia, who greeted him with trumpetings of joyful welcome. She also desired to shake hands with him, and her keeper had to sit on her head and hold her trunk to repress the familiarity. In two weeks she was cured, except for extensive and permanent scars, and she waited only for a favorable opportunity to rejoin the circus.

The doctor had got his fee in advance.

Upon a sunny afternoon in the last of August, Dr. Tibbitt jogged slowly toward Sagawaug in his neat little gig. He had been to Pelion, the next town, to call upon Miss Minetta Bunker, the young lady whom he desired to install in the house with the garden running down to the river. He had found her starting out for a drive in Tom Matson's dogcart. Now, the doctor feared no foe, in medicine or in love; but when a young woman is inscrutable as to the state of her affections, when the richest young man in the county is devoting himself to her, and when the young lady's mother is backing the rich man, a young country doctor may well feel perplexed and anxious over his chance of the prize.

The doctor was so troubled, indeed, that he paid no heed to a heavy, repeated thud behind him, on the macadamized road. His gentle little mare heard it, though, and began to curvet and prance. The doctor was pulling her in, and calming her with a "soo—soo—down, girl, down!" when he interrupted himself to shout, "Great Cæsar! Get off me!"

Something like a yard of rubber hose had come in through the side of the buggy, and was rubbing itself against his face. He looked around, and the cold sweat stood out on him as he saw Zenobia, her chain dragging from her hind foot, her red cap a-cock on her head, trotting along by the side of his vehicle, snorting with joy, and evidently bent on lavishing her pliant, serpentine, but leathery caresses upon his person.

His fear vanished in a moment. The animal's intentions were certainly pacific, to put it mildly. He reflected that if he could keep his horse ahead of her, he could toll her around the block and back toward her tent. He had hardly guessed, as yet, the depth of the impression which he had made upon Zenobia's heart, which must have been a large organ, if the size of her ears was any indication—according to the popular theory.

The doctor tolled his elephant around the block without further misadventure, and they started up the road toward Zenobia's tent, Zenobia caressing her benefactor while shudders of antipathy ran over his frame. In a few minutes the keeper hove in sight. Zenobia saw him first, blew a shrill blast on her trumpet, close to the doctor's ear, bolted through a snake fence, lumbered across a turnip field, and disappeared in a patch of woods, leaving the doctor to quiet his excited horse and to face the keeper, who advanced with rage in his eye.

"What do you mean, you cuss," he began, "weaning a man's elephant's affections away from him? You ain't got no more morals than a Turk, you ain't. That elephant an' me has been side-partners for fourteen years, an' here you come between us."

"I don't want your confounded elephant," roared the doctor. "Why don't you keep it chained up?"

"She busted her chain to git after you," replied the keeper.

"Oh, I seen you two lally-gaggin' all along the road. I knowed you wa'n't no good the first time I set eyes on yer, a-sayin' hoodoo words over the poor dumb beast."

The doctor resolved to banish "analogy" from his vocabulary.

The next morning, about four o'clock, Dr. Tibbitt awoke with a troubled mind. He had driven home after midnight from a late call, and he had had an uneasy fancy that he saw a great shadowy bulk ambling along in the mist-hid fields by the roadside. He jumped out of bed and went to the window. Below him, completely covering Mrs. Pennypepper's nasturtium bed, her prehensile trunk ravaging the early chrysanthemums, stood Zenobia, swaying to and fro, the dew glistening on her seamed sides beneath the early morning sunlight. The doctor hastily dressed himself and slipped downstairs and out, to meet this Frankenstein's-monster of affection.

There was but one thing to do. Zenobia would follow him wherever he went—she rushed madly through Mrs. Pennypepper's roses to greet him—and his only course was to lead her out of the town before people began to get up, and to detain her in some remote meadow until he could get her keeper to come for her and secure her by force or stratagem. He set off by the least frequented streets, and he experienced a pang of horror as he remembered that his way led him past the house of his one professional rival in Sagawaug. Suppose Dr. Pettengill should be coming home or going out as he passed!

The doctor found a secluded pasture, near the woods that encircled the town, and there he sat him down, in the corner of a snake fence, to wait until some farmer or market gardener should pass by, to carry his message to the keeper. He had another message to send, too. He had several cases that must be attended to at once. Unless he could get away from his pachydermatous familiar, Dr.

Pettengill must care for his cases that morning. It was hard—but what was he to do?

Zenobia stood by his side, dividing her attention between the caresses she bestowed on him and the care she was obliged to take of her red cap, which was not tightly strapped on, and slipped in various directions at every movement of her gigantic head. She was unmistakably happy. From time to time she trumpeted cheerily. She plucked up tufts of grass, and offered them to the doctor. He refused them, and she ate them herself. Once he took a daisy from her, absent-mindedly, and she was so greatly pleased that she smashed his hat in her endeavors to pet him. The doctor was a kind-hearted man. He had to admit that Zenobia meant well. He patted her trunk, and made matters worse. Her elephantine ecstasy came near being the death of him.

Still the farmer came not, nor the market gardener. Dr. Tibbitt began to believe that he had chosen a meadow that was *too* secluded. At last two boys appeared. After they had stared at him and at Zenobia for half an hour, one of them agreed to produce Dr. Pettengill and Zenobia's keeper for fifty cents. Dr. Pettengill was the first to arrive. He refused to come nearer than the farthest limit of the pasture.

"Hello, doctor," he called out, "hear you've been seeing elephants. Want me to take your cases? Guess I can. Got a half hour free. Brought some bromide down for you, if you'd like to try it."

To judge from his face, Zenobia was invisible. But his

presence alarmed that sensitive animal. She crowded up close to the fence, and every time she flicked her skin to shake off the flies she endangered the equilibrium of the doctor, who was sitting on the top rail, for dignity's sake. He shouted his directions to his colleague, who shouted back professional criticisms.

"Salicylate of soda for that old woman? What's the matter with salicylate of cinchonidia? Don't want to kill her before you get out of this swamp, do you?"

Dr. Tibbitt was not a profane man, but at this moment he could not restrain himself.

"*Damn you!*" he said, with such vigor that the elephant gave a convulsive start. The doctor felt his seat depart from under him—he was going—going into space for a brief moment, and then he scrambled up out of the soft mud of the cow-wallow back of the fence on which he had been sitting. Zenobia had backed against the fence.

The keeper arrived soon after. He had only reached the meadow when Zenobia lifted her trunk in the air, emitted a mirthful toot, and struck out for the woods with the picturesque and cumbersome gallop of a mastodon pup.

"Dern *you*," said the keeper to Dr. Tibbitt, who was trying to fasten his collar, which had broken loose in his fall; "if the boys was here, and I hollered 'Hey, Rube!'—there wouldn't be enough left of yer to spread a plaster fer a baby's bile!"

The doctor made himself look as decent as the situation allowed, and then he marched toward the town with the light of a firm resolve illuminating his face. The literature of his childhood had come to his aid. He remembered the unkind tailor who pricked the elephant's trunk. It seemed to him that the tailor was a rather good fellow.

"If that elephant's disease is gratitude," thought the doctor, "I'll give her an antidote."

He went to the drug store, and, as he went, he pulled out a blank pad and wrote down a prescription, from mere force of habit. It read thus:

PESSELS & MORTON,

DRUGGISTS,

Commercial Block, Main Street, Sagawaug.

PRESCRIPTIONS CAREFULLY COMPOUNDED.

℞ Calcium sul ℥ij

Calcis chl ℥xvj

Capsicum pulv ℥i

M et ft. Bol.

Sig. Take at once.

Tibbitt

When the druggist looked at it, he was taken short of breath.

"What's this?" he asked—"a bombshell?"

"Put it up," said the doctor, "and don't talk so much." He lingered nervously on the druggist's steps, looking up and down the street. He had sent a boy to order the stableman to harness his gig. By and by, the druggist put his head out of the door.

"I've got some asafetida pills," he said, "that are kind o' tired, and half a pound of whale-oil soap that's higher 'n Haman——"

"Put 'em in!" said the doctor, grimly, as he saw Zenobia coming in sight far down the street.

She came up while the doctor was waiting for the bolus. Twenty-three boys were watching them, although it was only seven o'clock in the morning.

"Down, Zenobia!" said the doctor, thoughtlessly, as he might have addressed a dog. He was talking with the druggist, and Zenobia was patting his ear with her trunk. Zenobia sank to her knees. The doctor did not notice her. She folded her trunk about him, lifted him to her back, rose with a heave and a sway to her feet, and started up the road. The boys cheered. The doctor got off on the end of an elm-branch. His descent was watched from nineteen second-story windows.

His gig came to meet him at last, and he entered it and drove rapidly out of town, with Zenobia trotting contentedly behind him. As soon as he had passed Deacon Burgee's house, he drew rein, and Zenobia approached, while his perspiring mare stood on her hind legs.

"Zenobia—pill!" said the doctor.

As she had often done in her late illness, Zenobia opened her mouth at the word of command, and swallowed the infernal bolus. Then they started up again, and the doctor headed for Zenobia's tent.

But Zenobia's pace was sluggish. She had been dodging about the woods for two nights, and she was tired.

When the doctor whipped up, she seized the buggy by any convenient projection, and held it back. This damaged the buggy and frightened the horse; but it accomplished Zenobia's end. It was eleven o'clock before Jake Bumgardner's "Half-Way-House" loomed up white, afar down the dusty road, and the doctor knew that his roundabout way had at length brought him near to the field where the circus tent had been pitched. He drove on with a lighter heart in his bosom. He had not heard Zenobia behind him for some time. He did not know what had become of her, or what she was doing, but he learned later.

The doctor had compounded a pill well calculated to upset Zenobia's stomach. That it would likewise give her a consuming thirst he had not considered. But chemistry was doing its duty without regard to him. A thirst like a furnace burned within Zenobia. Capsicum and chloride of lime were doing their work. She gasped and groaned. She searched for water. She filled her trunk at a wayside trough and poured the contents into her mouth. Then she sucked up a puddle or two. Then she came to Bumgardner's, where a dozen kegs of lager beer and a keg of what passed at Bumgardner's for gin stood on the sidewalk. Zenobia's circus experience had taught her what a water barrel meant. She applied her knowledge. With her forefoot she deftly staved in the head of one keg after another, and with her trunk she drew up the beer and the gin, and delivered them to her stomach. If you think her taste at fault, remember the bolus.

Bumgardner rushed out and assailed her with a bung-starter. She turned upon him and squirted lager beer over him until he was covered with an iridescent lather of foam from head to foot. Then she finished the kegs and went on her way to overtake the doctor.

The doctor was speeding his mare merrily along, grateful for even a momentary relief from Zenobia's attentions, when, at one and the same time, he heard a heavy, uncertain thumping on the road behind him, and the quick patter of a trotter's hoofs on the road ahead of him. He glanced behind him first, and saw Zenobia. She swayed from side to side, more than was her wont. Her red cap was far down over her left eye. Her aspect was rakish, and her gait was unsteady. The doctor did not know it, but Zenobia was drunk.

Zenobia was sick, but intoxication dominated her sickness. Even sulphide of calcium withdrew courteously before the might of beer and gin. Rocking from side to side, reeling across the road and back, trumpeting in imbecile inexpressive tones, Zenobia advanced.

The doctor looked forward. Tom Matson sat in his dogcart, with Miss Bunker by his side. His horse had caught sight of Zenobia, and he was rearing high in air, and whinnying in terror. Before Tom could pull him down, he made a sudden break, overturned the dogcart, and flung Tom and Miss Minetta Bunker on a bank by the side of the road. It was a soft bank, well-grown with mint and stinging nettles, just above a creek. Tom had scarce landed before he was up and off, running hard across the fields.

Miss Minetta rose and looked at him with fire in her eyes.

"Well!" she said aloud, "I'd like mother to see you *now!*"

The doctor had jumped out of his gig and let his little mare go galloping up the road. He had his arm about Miss Minetta's waist when he turned to face his familiar demon—which may have accounted for the pluck in his face.

But Zenobia was a hundred yards down the road, and she was utterly incapable of getting any farther. She trumpeted once or twice, then she wavered like a reed in the wind; her legs weakened under her, and she sank on her side. Her red cap had slipped down, and she picked it up with her trunk, broke its band in a reckless swing that resembled the wave of jovial farewell, gave one titanic hiccup, and fell asleep by the roadside.

An hour later, Dr. Tibbitt was driving toward Pelion, with Miss Bunker by his side. His horse had been stopped at the tollgate. He was driving with one hand. Perhas he needed the other to show how they could have a summer-house in the garden that ran down to the river.

But it was evening when Zenobia awoke to find her keeper sitting on her head. He jabbed a cotton hook firmly and decisively into her ear, and led her homeward down the road lit by the golden sunset. That was the end of Zenobia's infidelity.

STEPHEN LEACOCK

A, B, and C—The Human Element in Mathematics

The student of arithmetic who has mastered the first four rules of his art and successfully striven with money sums and fractions finds himself confronted by an unbroken expanse of questions known as problems. These are short stories of adventure and industry with the end omitted, and though betraying a strong family resemblance, are not without a certain element of romance.

The characters in the plot of the problem are three people called A, B, and C; the form of the question is generally of this sort:

"A, B, and C do a certain piece of work. A can do as much work in one hour as B in two, or C in four. Find how long they work at it."

From *Literary Lapses*, published by Dodd, Mead & Company, Inc., 1910. Reprinted by permission of the publishers.

Or thus: "A, B, and C are employed to dig a ditch. A can dig as much in one hour as B can dig in two, and B can dig twice as fast as C. Find how long, etc., etc."

Or after this wise: "A lays a wager that he can walk faster than B or C. A can walk half as fast again as B, and C is only an indifferent walker. Find how far, and so forth."

The occupations of A, B, and C are many and varied. In the older arithmetics they contented themselves with doing a "certain piece of work." This statement of the case, however, was found too sly and mysterious, or possibly lacking in romantic charm. It became the fashion to define the job more clearly and to set them at walking matches, ditch-digging, regattas, and piling cordwood. At times, they became commercial and entered into partnership, having, with their old mystery, a "certain" capital. Above all they revel in motion. When they tire of walking matches, A rides on horseback, or borrows a bicycle and competes with his weaker-minded associates on foot. Now they race on locomotives; now they row; or again they become historical and engage stagecoaches; or at times they are aquatic and swim. If their occupation is actual work, they prefer to pump water into cisterns, two of which leak through holes in the bottom and one of which is water-tight. A, of course, has the good one; he also takes the bicycle, and the best locomotive, and the right of swimming with the current. Whatever they do they put money on it, being all three sports. A always wins.

In the early chapters of the arithmetic, their identity

is concealed under the names of John, William, and Henry, and they wrangle over the division of marbles. In algebra they are often called X, Y, Z. But these are only their Christian names, and they are really the same people.

Now to one who has followed the history of these men through countless pages of problems, watched them in their leisure hours dallying with cordwood, and seen their panting sides heave in the full frenzy of filling a cistern with a leak in it, they become something more than mere symbols. They appear as creatures of flesh and blood, living men with their own passions, ambitions, and aspirations like the rest of us.

A is full-blooded, hot-headed and strong-willed. It is he who proposes everything, challenges B to work, makes the bets, and bends the others to his will. He is a man of great physical strength and phenomenal endurance. He has been known to walk forty-eight hours at a stretch, and to pump ninety-six. His life is arduous and full of peril. A mistake in the working of a sum may keep him digging a fortnight without sleep. A repeating decimal in the answer might kill him.

B is a quiet, easy-going fellow, afraid of A and bullied by him, but very gentle and brotherly to little C, the weakling. He is quite in A's power, having lost all his money in bets.

Poor C is an undersized, frail man, with a plaintive face. Constant walking, digging, and pumping have broken his health and ruined his nervous system. His joyless life has driven him to drink and smoke more than is good for him, and his hand often shakes as he digs ditches. He has not the strength to work as the others do, in fact, as Hamlin Smith has said, "A can do more work in one hour than C in four."

The first time that ever I saw these men was one evening after a regatta. They had all been rowing in it, and it had transpired that A could row as much in one hour as B in two, or C in four. B and C had come in dead fagged and C was coughing badly. "Never mind, old fellow," I heard B say, "I'll fix you up on the sofa and get you some hot tea." Just then A came blustering in and shouted, "I say, you fellows, Hamlin Smith has shown me three cisterns in his garden and he says we can pump them until tomorrow night. I bet I can beat you both. Come on. You can pump in your rowing things, you know. Your cistern leaks a little, I think, C." I heard B growl that it was a dirty shame and that C was used up now, but they went and presently I could tell from the sound of the water that A was pumping four times as fast as C.

For years after that I used to see them constantly about the town and always busy. I never heard of any of them eating or sleeping. After that, owing to a long absence from home, I lost sight of them. On my return I was surprised to find A, B, and C no longer at their old tasks; on inquiry I heard that work in this line was now done by N, M, and O, and that some people were employing for algebraical jobs four foreigners called Alpha, Beta, Gamma, and Delta.

Now it chanced one day that I stumbled upon old D,

in the little garden in front of his cottage, hoeing in the sun. D is an aged laboring man who used occasionally to be called in to help A, B, and C. "Did I know 'em, sir?" he answered. "Why I knowed 'em ever since they was little fellows in brackets. Master A, he were a fine-hearted lad, sir, though I always said, give me Master B for kind-heartedness-like. Many's the job as we've been on together, sir, though I never did no racing nor aught of that, but just the plain labor, as you might say. I'm getting a bit too old and stiff for it nowadays, sir—just scratch about in the garden here and grow a bit of a logarithm, or raise a common denominator or two. But Mr. Euclid he uses me still for propositions, he do."

From the garrulous old man I learned the melancholy end of my former acquaintances. Soon after I left town, he told me, C had been ill. It seems that A and B had been rowing on the river for a wager, and C had been running on the bank and then sat in a draught. Of course the bank had refused the draught and C was taken ill. A and B came home and found C lying helpless in bed. A shook him roughly and said, "Get up, C, we're going to pile wood." C looked so worn and pitiful that B said, "Look here, A, I won't stand this, he isn't fit to pile wood tonight." C smiled feebly and said, "Perhaps I might pile a little if I sat up in bed." Then B, thoroughly alarmed, said, "See here, A, I'm going to fetch a doctor; he's dying." A flared up and answered, "You've got no money to fetch a doctor." "I'll reduce him to his lowest terms," B said firmly, "that'll fetch him." C's life might even then have been saved but they made a mistake about the medicine. It stood at the head of the bed on a bracket, and the nurse accidentally removed it from the bracket without changing the sign. After the fatal blunder C seems to have sunk rapidly. On the evening of the next day, it was clear, as the shadows deepened, that the end was near. I think that even A was affected at the last as he stood with bowed head, aimlessly offering to bet with the doctor on C's labored breathing. "A," whispered C, "I think I'm going fast." "How fast do you think you'll go, old man?" murmured A. "I don't know," said C, "but I'm going at any rate." The end came soon after that. C rallied for a moment and asked for a certain piece of work that he had left downstairs. A put it in his arms and he expired. As his soul sped heavenward, A watched its flight with melancholy admiration. B burst into a passionate flood of tears and sobbed, "Put away his little cistern and the rowing clothes he used to wear; I feel as if I could hardly ever dig again."—The funeral was plain and unostentatious. It differed in nothing from the ordinary, except that out of deference to sporting men, and mathematicians, A engaged two hearses. Both vehicles started at the same time, B driving the one which bore the sable parallelepipes containing the last remains of his ill-fated friend. A on the box of the empty hearse generously consented to a handicap of a hundred years, but arrived first at the cemetery by driving four times as fast as B. (Find the distance to the cemetery.) As the sarcophagus was lowered, the grave was surrounded by the broken figures of the first book of Euclid.

It was noticed that after the death of C, A became a

changed man. He lost interest in racing with B, and dug but languidly. He finally gave up his work and settled down to live on the interest of his bets.—B never recovered from the shock of C's death; his grief preyed upon his intellect and it became deranged. He grew moody and spoke only in monosyllables. His disease became rapidly aggravated, and he presently spoke in words whose spelling was regular and which presented no difficulty to the beginner. Realizing his precarious condition he voluntarily submitted to be incarcerated in an asylum, where he abjured mathematics and devoted himself to writing the History of the Swiss Family Robinson in words of one syllable.

SAKI (H. H. MUNRO)

Laura

"You are not really dying, are you?" asked Amanda.

"I have the doctor's permission to live till Tuesday," said Laura.

"But today is Saturday; this is serious!" gasped Amanda.

"I don't know about it being serious; it is certainly Saturday," said Laura.

"Death is always serious," said Amanda.

"I never said I was going to die. I am presumbly going to leave off being Laura, but I shall go on being something. An animal of some kind, I suppose. You see, when one hasn't been very good in the life one has just lived, one reincarnates in some lower organism. And I haven't been very good, when one comes to think of it. I've been petty and mean and vindictive and all that sort of thing when circumstances have seemed to warrant it."

"Circumstances never warrant that sort of thing," said Amanda hastily.

"If you don't mind my saying so," observed Laura, "Egbert is a circumstance that would warrant any amount of that sort of thing. You're married to him—that's different; you've sworn to love, honour, and endure him: I haven't."

"I don't see what's wrong with Egbert," protested Amanda.

"Oh, I dare say the wrongness has been on my part," admitted Laura dispassionately; "he has merely been the extenuating circumstance. He made a thin, peevish kind of fuss, for instance, when I took the collie puppies from the farm out for a run the other day."

"They chased his young broods of speckled Sussex and drove two sitting hens off their nests, besides running all over the flower beds. You know how devoted he is to his poultry and garden."

"Anyhow, he needn't have gone on about it for the entire evening and then have said, 'Let's say no more about it' just when I was beginning to enjoy the discussion. That's where one of my petty vindictive revenges came in," added Laura with an unrepentant chuckle; "I turned the entire family of speckled Sussex into his seedling shed the day after the puppy episode."

"How could you?" exclaimed Amanda.

"It came quite easy," said Laura; "two of the hens pretended to be laying at the time, but I was firm."

"And we thought it was an accident!"

"You see," resumed Laura, "I really *have* some grounds for supposing that my next incarnation will be in a lower organism. I shall be an animal of some kind. On the other hand, I haven't been a bad sort in my way, so I think I may count on being a nice animal, something elegant and lively, with a love of fun. An otter, perhaps."

"I can't imagine you as an otter," said Amanda.

"Well, I don't suppose you can imagine me as an angel, if it comes to that," said Laura.

Amanda was silent. She couldn't.

"Personally I think an otter life would be rather enjoyable," continued Laura; "salmon to eat all the year round, and the satisfaction of being able to fetch the trout in their own homes without having to wait for hours till they condescend to rise to the fly you've been dangling before them; and an elegant svelte figure—"

"Think of the otter hounds," interposed Amanda; "how dreadful to be hunted and harried and finally worried to death!"

"Rather fun with half the neighborhood looking on, and anyhow not worse than this Saturday-to-Tuesday business of dying by inches; and then I should go on into something else. If I had been a moderately good otter I suppose I should get back into human shape of some sort; probably something rather primitive—a little brown, unclothed Nubian boy, I should think."

"I wish you would be serious," sighed Amanda; "you really ought to be if you're only going to live till Tuesday."

As a matter of fact Laura died on Monday.

"So dreadfully upsetting," Amanda complained to her uncle-in-law, Sir Lulworth Quayne. "I've asked quite a lot of people down for golf and fishing, and the rhododendrons are just looking their best."

"Laura always was inconsiderate," said Sir Lulworth; "she was born during Goodwood week, with an Ambassador staying in the house who hated babies."

"She had the maddest kind of ideas," said Amanda; "do you know if there was any insanity in her family?"

"Insanity? No, I never heard of any. Her father lives in West Kensington, but I believe he's sane on all other subjects."

"She had an idea that she was going to be reincarnated as an otter," said Amanda.

"One meets with those ideas of reincarnation so frequently, even in the West," said Sir Lulworth, "that one can hardly set them down as being mad. And Laura was such an unaccountable person in this life that I should not like to lay down definite rules as to what she might be doing in an after state."

"You think she really might have passed into some animal form?" asked Amanda. She was one of those who shape their opinions rather readily from the standpoint of those around them.

Just then Egbert entered the breakfast-room, wearing an air of bereavement that Laura's demise would have been insufficient, in itself, to account for.

"Four of my speckled Sussex have been killed," he exclaimed; "the very four that were to go to the show on

Friday. One of them was dragged away and eaten right in the middle of that new carnation bed that I've been to such trouble and expense over. My best flower bed and my best fowls singled out for destruction; it almost seems as if the brute that did the deed had special knowledge how to be as devastating as possible in a short space of time."

"Was it a fox, do you think?" asked Amanda.

"Sounds more like a polecat," said Sir Lulworth.

"No," said Egbert, "there were marks of webbed feet all over the place, and we followed the tracks down to the stream at the bottom of the garden; evidently an otter."

Amanda looked quickly and furtively across at Sir Lulworth.

Egbert was too agitated to eat any breakfast, and went out to superintend the strengthening of the poultry yard defences.

"I think she might at least have waited till the funeral was over," said Amanda in a scandalized voice.

"It's her own funeral, you know," said Sir Lulworth; "it's a nice point in etiquette how far one ought to show respect to one's own mortal remains."

Disregard for mortuary convention was carried to further lengths next day; during the absence of the family at the funeral ceremony the remaining survivors of the speckled Sussex were massacred. The marauder's line of retreat seemed to have embraced most of the flower beds on the lawn, but the strawberry beds in the lower garden had also suffered.

"I shall get the otter hounds to come here at the earliest possible moment," said Egbert savagely.

"On no account! You can't dream of such a thing!" exclaimed Amanda. "I mean, it wouldn't do, so soon after a funeral in the house."

"It's a case of necessity," said Egbert; "once an otter takes to that sort of thing it won't stop."

"Perhaps it will go elsewhere now that there are no more fowls left," suggested Amanda.

"One would think you wanted to shield the beast," said Egbert.

"There's been so little water in the stream lately," objected Amanda; "it seems hardly sporting to hunt an animal when it has so little chance of taking refuge anywhere."

"Good gracious!" fumed Egbert, "I'm not thinking about sport. I want to have the animal killed as soon as possible."

Even Amanda's opposition weakened when, during church time on the following Sunday, the otter made its way into the house, raided half a salmon from the larder and worried it into scaly fragments on the Persian rug in Egbert's studio.

"We shall have it hiding under our beds and biting pieces out of our feet before long," said Egbert, and from what Amanda knew of this particular otter she felt that the possibility was not a remote one.

On the evening preceding the day fixed for the hunt Amanda spent a solitary hour walking by the banks of the stream, making what she imagined to be hound noises. It was charitably supposed by those who overheard her performance that she was practicing for farmyard imitations at the forthcoming village entertainment.

It was her friend and neighbour, Aurora Burret, who brought her news of the day's sport.

"Pity you weren't out; we had quite a good day. We found it at once, in the pool just below your garden."

"Did you—kill?" asked Amanda.

"Rather. A fine she-otter. Your husband got rather badly bitten in trying to 'tail it.' Poor beast, I felt quite sorry for it, it had such a human look in its eyes when it was killed. You'll call me silly, but do you know who the look reminded me of? My dear woman, what is the matter?"

When Amanda had recovered to a certain extent from her attack of nervous prostration Egbert took her to the Nile Valley to recuperate. Change of scene speedily brought about the desired recovery of health and mental balance. The escapades of an adventurous otter in search of a variation of diet were viewed in their proper light. Amanda's normally placid temperament reasserted itself. Even a hurricane of shouted curses, coming from her husband's dressing-room, in her husband's voice, but hardly in his usual vocabulary, failed to disturb her serenity as she made a leisurely toilet one evening in a Cairo hotel.

"What is the matter? What has happened?" she asked in amused curiosity.

"The little beast has thrown all my clean shirts into the bath! Wait till I catch you, you little——"

"What little beast?" asked Amanda, suppressing a

desire to laugh; Egbert's language was so hopelessly inadequate to express his outraged feelings.

"A little beast of a naked brown Nubian boy," spluttered Egbert.

And now Amanda is seriously ill.

MARK TWAIN

The Facts Concerning the Recent Carnival of Crime in Connecticut

I was feeling blithe, almost jocund. I put a match to my cigar, and just then the morning's mail was handed in. The first superscription I glanced at was in a handwriting that sent a thrill of pleasure through and through me. It was aunt Mary's; and she was the person I loved and honored most in all the world, outside of my own household. She had been my boyhood's idol; maturity, which is fatal to so many enchantments, had not been able to dislodge her from her pedestal; no, it had only justified her right to be there, and placed her dethronement permanently among the impossibilities. To show how strong her influence over me was, I will observe that long after everybody else's "*do*-stop-smoking" had ceased to affect me in the slightest degree, aunt Mary could still stir my torpid conscience into faint signs of life when she touched upon the matter. But all things have their limit, in this world. A happy day came at last, when even aunt Mary's words could no longer move me. I was not merely glad to see that day arrive; I was more than glad—I was grateful; for when its sun had set, the one alloy that was able to mar my enjoyment of my aunt's society was gone. The remainder of her stay with us that winter was in every way a delight. Of course she pleaded with me just as earnestly as ever, after that blessed day, to quit my pernicious habit, but to no purpose whatever; the moment she opened the subject I at once became calmly, peacefully, contentedly indifferent—absolutely, adamantinely indifferent. Consequently the closing weeks of that memorable visit melted away as pleasantly as a dream, they were so freighted, for me, with tranquil satisfaction. I could not have enjoyed my pet vice more if my gentle tormentor had been a smoker herself, and an advocate of the practice. Well, the sight of her handwriting reminded me that I was getting very hungry to see her again. I easily guessed what I should find in her letter. I opened it. Good! just as I expected; she was coming! Coming this very day, too, and by the morning train; I might expect her any moment.

I said to myself, "I am thoroughly happy and content, now. If my most pitiless enemy could appear before me at this moment, I would freely right any wrong I may have done him."

Straightway the door opened, and a shriveled, shabby

dwarf entered. He was not more than two feet high. He seemed to be about forty years old. Every feature and every inch of him was a trifle out of shape; and so, while one could not put his finger upon any particular part and say, "This is a conspicuous deformity," the spectator perceived that this little person was a deformity as a whole—a vague, general, evenly-blended, nicely-adjusted deformity. There was a fox-like cunning in the face and the sharp little eyes, and also alertness and malice. And yet, this vile bit of human rubbish seemed to bear a sort of remote and ill-defined resemblance to me! It was dully perceptible in the mean form, the countenance, and even the clothes, gestures, manner, and attitudes of the creature. He was a far-fetched, dim suggestion of a burlesque upon me, a caricature of me in little. One thing about him struck me forcibly, and most unpleasantly: he was covered all over with a fuzzy, greenish mold, such as one sometimes sees upon mildewed bread. The sight of it was nauseating.

He stepped along with a chipper air, and flung himself into a doll's chair in a very free and easy way, without waiting to be asked. He tossed his hat into the waste basket. He picked up my old chalk pipe from the floor, gave the stem a wipe or two on his knee, filled the bowl from the tobacco-box at his side, and said to me in a tone of pert command,—

"Gimme a match!"

I blushed to the roots of my hair; partly with indignation, but mainly because it somehow seemed to me that this whole performance was very like an exaggeration of conduct which I myself had sometimes been guilty of in my intercourse with familiar friends,—but never, never with strangers, I observed to myself. I wanted to kick the pygmy into the fire, but some incomprehensible sense of being legally and legitimately under his authority forced me to obey his order. He applied the match to the pipe, took a contemplative whiff or two, and remarked, in an irritatingly familiar way,—

"Seems to me it's devilish odd weather for this time of year."

I flushed again, and in anger and humiliation as before; for the language was hardly an exaggeration of some that I have uttered in my day, and moreover was delivered in a tone of voice and with an exasperating drawl that had the seeming of a deliberate travesty of my style. Now there is nothing I am quite so sensitive about as a mocking imitation of my drawling infirmity of speech. I spoke up sharply and said,—

"Look here, you miserable ash-cat! you will have to give a little more attention to your manners, or I will throw you out of the window!"

The manikin smiled a smile of malicious content and security, puffed a whiff of smoke contemptuously toward me, and said, with a still more elaborate drawl,—

"Come—go gently, now; don't put on *too* many airs with your betters."

This cool snub rasped me all over, but it seemed to subjugate me, too, for a moment. The pygmy contemplated me a while with his weasel eyes, and then said, in a peculiarly sneering way,—

"You turned a tramp away from your door this morning."

I said crustily,—

"Perhaps I did, perhaps I didn't. How do *you* know?"

"Well, I know. It isn't any matter *how* I know."

"Very well. Suppose I *did* turn a tramp away from the door—what of it?"

"Oh, nothing; nothing in particular. Only you lied to him."

"I *didn't!* That is, I"—

"Yes, but you did; you lied to him."

I felt a guilty pang,—in truth I had felt it forty times before that tramp had traveled a block from my door,—but still I resolved to make a show of feeling slandered; so I said,—

"This is a baseless impertinence. I said to the tramp"—

"There—wait. You were about to lie again. *I* know what you said to him. You said the cook was gone down town and there was nothing left from breakfast. Two lies. You knew the cook was behind the door, and plenty of provisions behind *her*."

This astonishing accuracy silenced me; and it filled me with wondering speculations, too, as to how this cub could have got his information. Of course he could have culled the conversation from the tramp, but by what sort of magic had he contrived to find out about the concealed cook? Now the dwarf spoke again:—

"It was rather pitiful, rather small, in you to refuse to read that poor young woman's manuscript the other day, and give her an opinion as to its literary value; and she had come so far, too, and *so* hopefully. Now *wasn't* it?"

I felt like a cur! And I had felt so every time the thing had recurred to my mind, I may as well confess. I flushed hotly and said,—

"Look here, have you nothing better to do than prowl around prying into other people's business? Did that girl tell you that?"

"Never mind whether she did or not. The main thing is, you did that contemptible thing. And you felt ashamed of it afterwards. Aha! you feel ashamed of it *now!*"

This with a sort of devilish glee. With fiery earnestness I responded,—

"I told that girl, in the kindest, gentlest way, that I could not consent to deliver judgment upon *any* one's manuscript, because an individual's verdict was worthless. It might underrate a work of high merit and lose it to the world, or it might overrate a trashy production and so open the way for its infliction upon the world. I said that the great public was the only tribunal competent to sit in judgment upon a literary effort, and therefore it must be best to lay it before that tribunal in the outset, since in the end it must stand or fall by that mighty court's decision anyway."

"Yes, you said all that. So you did, you juggling, small-souled shuffler! And yet when the happy hopefulness faded out of that poor girl's face, when you saw her furtively slip beneath her shawl the scroll she had so patiently and honestly scribbled at,—so ashamed of her darling now, so proud of it before,—when you saw the gladness go out of her eyes and the tears come there, when she crept away so humbly who had come so"—

"Oh, peace! peace! peace! Blister your merciless tongue, haven't all these thoughts tortured me enough, without *your* coming here to fetch them back again?"

Remorse! remorse! It seemed to me that it would eat the very heart out of me! And yet that small fiend only sat there leering at me with joy and contempt, and placidly chuckling. Presently he began to speak again. Every sentence was an accusation, and every accusation a truth. Every clause was freighted with sarcasm and derision, every slow-dropping word burned like vitriol. The dwarf reminded me of times when I had flown at my children in anger and punished them for faults which a little inquiry would have taught me that others, and not they, had committed. He reminded me of how I had disloyally allowed old friends to be traduced in my hearing, and been too craven to utter a word in their defense. He reminded me of many dishonest things which I had done; of many which I had procured to be done by children and other irresponsible persons; of some which I had planned, thought upon, and longed to do, and been kept from the performance by fear of consequences only. With exquisite cruelty he recalled to my mind, item by item, wrongs and unkindnesses I had inflicted and humiliations I had put upon friends since dead, "who died thinking of those injuries, maybe, and grieving over them," he added, by way of poison to the stab.

"For instance," said he, "take the case of your younger brother, when you two were boys together, many a long year ago. He always lovingly trusted in you with a fidelity that your manifold treacheries were not able to shake. He followed you about like a dog, content to suffer wrong and abuse if he might only be with you; patient under these injuries so long as it was your hand that inflicted them. The latest picture you have of him in health and strength must be such a comfort to you! You pledged your honor that if he would let you blindfold him no harm should come to him; and then, giggling and choking over the rare fun of the joke, you led him to a brook thinly glazed with ice, and pushed him in; and how you did laugh! Man, you will never forget the gentle, reproachful look he gave you as he struggled shivering out, if you live a thousand years! Oho! you see it now, you see it *now!*"

"Beast, I have seen it a million times, and shall see it a million more! and may you rot away piecemeal, and suffer till doomsday what I suffer now, for bringing it back to me again!"

The dwarf chuckled contentedly, and went on with his accusing history of my career. I dropped into a moody, vengeful state, and suffered in silence under the merciless lash. At last this remark of his gave me a sudden rouse:—

"Two months ago, on a Tuesday, you woke up, away in the night, and fell to thinking, with shame, about a peculiarly mean and pitiful act of yours toward a poor ignorant Indian in the wilds of the Rocky Mountains in the winter of eighteen hundred and"—

"Stop a moment, devil! Stop! Do you mean to tell

me that even my very *thoughts* are not hidden from you?"

"It seems to look like that. Didn't you think the thoughts I have just mentioned?"

"If I didn't, I wish I may never breathe again! Look here, friend—look me in the eye. Who *are* you?"

"Well, who do you think?"

"I think you are Satan himself. I think you are the devil."

"No."

"No? Then who *can* you be?"

"Would you really like to know?"

"*Indeed* I would."

"Well, I am your *Conscience!*"

In an instant I was in a blaze of joy and exultation. I sprang at the creature, roaring,—

"Curse you, I have wished a hundred million times that you were tangible, and that I could get my hands on your throat once! Oh, but I will wreak a deadly vengeance on"—

Folly! Lightning does not move more quickly than my Conscience did! He darted aloft so suddenly that in the moment my fingers clutched the empty air he was already perched on the top of the high bookcase, with his thumb at his nose in token of derision. I flung the poker at him, and missed. I fired the boot-jack. In a blind rage I flew from place to place, and snatched and hurled any missile that came handy; the storm of books, inkstands, and chunks of coal gloomed the air and beat about the manikin's perch relentlessly, but all to no purpose; the nimble figure dodged every shot; and not only that, but burst into a cackle of sarcastic and triumphant laughter as I sat down exhausted. While I puffed and gasped with fatigue and excitement, my Conscience talked to this effect:—

"My good slave, you are curiously witless—no, I mean characteristically so. In truth, you are always consistent, always yourself, always an ass. Otherwise it must have occurred to you that if you attempted this murder with a sad heart and a heavy conscience, I would droop under the burdening influence instantly. Fool, I should have weighed a ton, and could not have budged from the floor; but instead, you are so cheerfully anxious to kill me that your conscience is as light as a feather; hence I am away up here out of your reach. I can almost respect a mere ordinary sort of fool; but *you*—pah!"

I would have given anything, then, to be heavy-hearted, so that I could get this person down from there and take his life, but I could no more be heavy-hearted over such a desire than I could have sorrowed over its accomplishment. So I could only look longingly up at my master, and rave at the ill-luck that denied me a heavy conscience the one only time that I had ever wanted such a thing in my life. By and by I got to musing over the hour's strange adventure, and of course my human curiosity began to work. I set myself to framing in my mind some questions for this fiend to answer. Just then one of my boys entered, leaving the door open behind him, and exclaimed,—

"My! what *has* been going on, here! The book-case is all one riddle of"—

I sprang up in consternation, and shouted,—

"Out of this! Hurry! Jump! Fly! Shut the door! Quick, or my Conscience will get away!"

The door slammed to, and I locked it. I glanced up and was grateful, to the bottom of my heart, to see that my owner was still my prisoner. I said,—

"Hang you, I might have lost you! Children are the heedlessest creatures. But look here, friend, the boy did not seem to notice you at all; how is that?"

"For a very good reason. I am invisible to all but you."

I made mental note of that piece of information with a good deal of satisfaction. I could kill this miscreant now, if I got a chance, and no one would know it. But this very reflection made me so light-hearted that my Conscience could hardly keep his seat, but was like to float aloft toward the ceiling like a toy balloon. I said, presently,—

"Come, my Conscience, let us be friendly. Let us fly a flag of truce for a while. I am suffering to ask you some questions."

"Very well. Begin."

"Well, then, in the first place, why were you never visible to me before?"

"Because you never asked to see me before; that is, you never asked in the right spirit and the proper form before. You were just in the right spirit this time, and when you called for your most pitiless enemy I was that person by a very large majority, though you did not suspect it."

"Well, did that remark of mine turn you into flesh and blood?"

"No. It only made me visible to you. I am unsubstantial, just as other spirits are."

This remark prodded me with a sharp misgiving. If he was unsubstantial, how was I going to kill him? But I dissembled, and said persuasively,—

"Conscience, it isn't sociable of you to keep at such a distance. Come down and take another smoke."

This was answered with a look that was full of derision, and with this observation added:—

"Come where you can get at me and kill me? The invitation is declined with thanks."

"All right," said I to myself; "so it seems a spirit *can* be killed, after all; there will be one spirit lacking in this world, presently, or I lose my guess." Then I said aloud,—

"Friend"—

"There; wait a bit. I am not your friend, I am your enemy; I am not your equal, I am your master. Call me 'my lord,' if you please. You are too familiar."

"I don't like such titles. I am willing to call you *sir*. That is as far as"—

"We will have no argument about this. Just obey; that is all. Go on with your chatter."

"Very well, my lord,—since nothing but my lord will suit you,—I was going to ask you how long you will be visible to me?"

"Always!"

I broke out with strong indignation: "This is simply an outrage. That is what I think of it. You have dogged, and dogged, and *dogged* me, all the days of my life, invisible. That was misery enough; now to have such a looking thing as you tagging after me like another shadow all the rest of my days is an intolerable prospect. You have my opinion, my lord; make the most of it."

"My lad, there was never so pleased a conscience in this world as I was when you made me visible. It gives me an unconceivable advantage. *Now,* I can look you straight in the eye, and call you names, and leer at you, jeer at you, sneer at you; and *you* know what eloquence there is in visible gesture and expression, more especially when the effect is heightened by audible speech. I shall always address you henceforth in your o-w-n s-n-i-v-e-l-i-n-g d-r-a-w-l baby!"

I let fly with the coal-hod. No result. My lord said,—

"Come, come! Remember the flag of truce!"

"Ah, I forgot that. I will try to be civil; and *you* try it, too, for a novelty. The idea of a *civil* conscience! It is a good joke; an excellent joke. All the consciences *I* have ever heard of were nagging, badgering, fault-finding, execrable savages! Yes; and always in a sweat about some poor little insignificant trifle or other—destruction catch the lot of them, *I* say! I would trade mine for the small-pox and seven kinds of consumption, and be glad of the chance. Now tell me, why *is* it that a conscience can't haul a man over the coals once, for an offense, and then let him alone? Why is it that it wants to keep on pegging at him, day and night and night and day, week in and week out, forever and ever, about the same old thing? There is no sense in that, and no reason in it. I think a conscience that will act like that is meaner than the very dirt itself."

"Well, *we* like it; that suffices."

"Do you do it with the honest intent to improve a man?"

The question produced a sarcastic smile, and this reply:—

"No, sir. Excuse me. We do it simply because it is 'business.' It is our trade. The *purpose* of it *is* to improve the man, but *we* are merely disinterested agents. We are appointed by authority, and haven't anything to say in the matter. We obey orders and leave the consequences where they belong. But I am willing to admit this much: we *do* crowd the orders a trifle when we get a chance, which is most of the time. We enjoy it. We are instructed to remind a man a few times of an error; and I don't mind acknowledging that we try to give pretty good measure. And when we get hold of a man of a peculiarly sensitive nature, oh, but do we haze him! I have known consciences to come all the way from China and Russia to see a person of that kind put through his paces, on a special occasion. Why, I knew a man of that sort who had accidentally crippled a mulatto baby; the news went abroad, and I wish you may never commit another sin if the consciences didn't flock from all over the earth to enjoy the fun and help his master exercise him. That man walked the floor in torture for forty-eight hours, without eating or sleeping, and then blew his brains out. The child was perfectly well again in three weeks."

"Well, you are a precious crew, not to put it too strong.

I think I begin to see, now, why you have always been a trifle inconsistent with me. In your anxiety to get all the juice you can out of a sin, you make a man repent of it in three or four different ways. For instance, you found fault with me for lying to that tramp, and I suffered over that. But it was only yesterday that I told a tramp the square truth, to wit, that, it being regarded as bad citizenship to encourage vagrancy, I would give him nothing. What did you do *then?* Why, you made me say to myself, 'Ah, it would have been so much kinder and blameless to ease him off with a little white lie, and send him away feeling that if he could not have bread, the gentle treatment was at least something to be grateful for!' Well, I suffered all day about *that.* Three days before, I had fed a tramp, and fed him freely, supposing it a virtuous act. Straight off you said, 'Oh false citizen, to have fed a tramp!' and I suffered as usual. I gave a tramp work; you objected to it,—*after* the contract was made, of course; you never speak up beforehand. Next, I *refused* a tramp work; you objected to *that.* Next, I proposed to kill a tramp; you kept me awake all night, oozing remorse at every pore. Sure I was going to be right *this* time, I sent the next tramp away with my benediction; and I wish you may live as long as I do, if you didn't make me smart all night again because I didn't kill him. Is there *any* way of satisfying that malignant invention which is called a conscience?"

"Ha, ha! this is luxury! Go on!"

"But come, now, answer me that question. *Is* there any way?"

"Well, none that I propose to tell *you,* my son. Ass! I don't care *what* act you may turn your hand to, I can straightway whisper a word in your ear and make you think you have committed a dreadful meanness. It is my *business*—and my joy—to make you repent of *everything* you do. If I have fooled away any opportunities it was not intentional; I beg to assure you it was not intentional."

"Don't worry; you haven't missed a trick that *I* know of. I never did a thing in all my life, virtuous or otherwise, that I didn't repent of within twenty-four hours. In church last Sunday I listened to a charity sermon. My first impulse was to give three hundred and fifty dollars; I repented of that and reduced it a hundred; repented of that and reduced it another hundred; repented of that and reduced it another hundred; repented of that and reduced the remaining fifty to twenty-five; repented of that and came down to fifteen; repented of that and dropped to two dollars and a half; when the plate came around at last, I repented once more and contributed ten cents. Well, when I got home, I did wish to goodness I had that ten cents back again! You never *did* let me get through a charity sermon without having something to sweat about."

"Oh, and I never shall, I never shall. You can always depend on me."

"I think so. Many and many's the restless night I've wanted to take you by the neck. If I could only get hold of you now!"

"Yes, no doubt. But I am not an ass, I am only the saddle of an ass. But go on, go on. You entertain me more than I like to confess."

"I am glad of that. (You will not mind my lying a little, to keep in practice.) Look here; not to be too personal, I think you are about the shabbiest and most contemptible little shriveled-up reptile that can be imagined. I am grateful enough that you are invisible to other people, for I should die with shame to be seen with such a mildewed monkey of a conscience as *you* are. Now if you were five or six feet high, and"—

"Oh, come! who is to blame?"

"*I* don't know."

"Why, you are; nobody else."

"Confound you, I wasn't consulted about your personal appearance."

"I don't care, you had a good deal to do with it, nevertheless. When you were eight or nine years old, I was seven feet high and as pretty as a picture."

"I wish you had died young! So you have grown the wrong way, have you?"

"Some of us grow one way and some the other. You had a large conscience once; if you've a small conscience now, I reckon there are reasons for it. However, both of us are to blame, you and I. You see, you used to be conscientious about a great many things; morbidly so, I may say. It was a great many years ago. You probably do not remember it, now. Well, I took a great interest in my work, and I so enjoyed the anguish which certain pet sins of yours afflicted you with, that I kept pelting at you until I rather overdid the matter. You began to rebel.

Of course I began to lose ground, then, and shrivel a little,—diminish in stature, get moldy, and grow deformed. The more I weakened, the more stubbornly you fastened on to those particular sins; till at last the places on my person that represent those vices became as callous as shark skin. Take smoking, for instance. I played that card a little too long, and I lost. When people plead with you at this late day to quit that vice, that old callous place seems to enlarge and cover me all over like a shirt of mail. It exerts a mysterious, smothering effect; and presently I, your faithful hater, your devoted Conscience, go sound asleep! Sound? It is no name for it. I couldn't hear it thunder at such a time. You have some few other vices—perhaps eighty, or maybe ninety—that affect me in much the same way."

"This is flattering; you must be asleep a good part of your time."

"Yes, of late years. I should be asleep *all* the time, but for the help I get."

"Who helps you?"

"Other consciences. Whenever a person whose conscience I am acquainted with tries to plead with you about the vices you are callous to, I get my friend to give his client a pang concerning some villainy of his own, and that shuts off his meddling and starts him off to hunt personal consolation. My field of usefulness is about trimmed down to tramps, budding authoresses, and that line of goods, now; but don't you worry—I'll harry you on *them* while they last! Just you put your trust in me."

"I think I can. But if you had only been good enough

to mention these facts some thirty years ago, I should have turned my particular attention to sin, and I think that by this time I should not only have had you pretty permanently asleep on the entire list of human vices, but reduced to the size of a homeopathic pill, at that. That is about the style of conscience *I* am pining for. If I only had you shrunk down to a homeopathic pill, and I could get my hands on you, would I put you in a glass case for a keepsake? No, sir! I would give you to a yellow dog! That is where *you* ought to be—you and all your tribe. You are not fit to be in society, in my opinion. Now another question. Do you know a good many consciences in this section?"

"Plenty of them."

"I would give anything to see some of them! Could you bring them here? And would they be visible to me?"

"Certainly not."

"I suppose I ought to have known that, without asking. But no matter, you can describe them. Tell me about my neighbor Thompson's conscience, please."

"Very well. I know him intimately; have known him many years. I knew him when he was eleven feet high and of a faultless figure. But he is very rusty and tough and misshapen, now, and hardly ever interests himself about anything. As to his present size—well, he sleeps in a cigar box."

"Likely enough. There are few smaller, meaner men in this region than Hugh Thompson. Do you know Robinson's conscience?"

"Yes. He is a shade under four and a half feet high; used

to be a blond; is a brunette, now, but still shapely and comely."

"Well, Robinson is a good fellow. Do you know Tom Smith's conscience?"

"I have known him from childhood. He was thirteen inches high, and rather sluggish, when he was two years old—as nearly all of us are, at that age. He is thirty-seven feet high, now, and the stateliest figure in America. His legs are still racked with growing-pains, but he has a good time, nevertheless. Never sleeps. He is the most active and energetic member of the New England Conscience Club; is president of it. Night and day you can find him pegging away at Smith, panting with his labor, sleeves rolled up, countenance all alive with enjoyment. He has got his victim splendidly dragooned, now. He can make poor Smith imagine that the most innocent little thing he does is an odious sin; and then he sets to work and almost tortures the soul out of him about it."

"Smith is the noblest man in all this section, and the purest; and yet is always breaking his heart because he cannot be good! Only a conscience *could* find pleasure in heaping agony upon a spirit like that. Do you know my aunt Mary's conscience?"

"I have seen her at a distance, but am not acquainted with her. She lives in the open air altogether, because no door is large enough to admit her."

"I can believe that. Let me see. Do you know the conscience of that publisher who once stole some sketches of mine for a 'series' of his, and then left me to pay the law expenses I had to incur in order to choke him off?"

"Yes. He has a wide fame. He was exhibited, a month ago, with some other antiquities, for the benefit of a recent Member of the Cabinet's conscience, that was starving in exile. Tickets and fares were high, but I traveled for nothing by pretending to be the conscience of an editor, and got in for half price by representing myself to be the conscience of a clergyman. However, the publisher's conscience, which was to have been the main feature of the entertainment, was a failure—as an exhibition. He was there, but what of that? The management had provided a microscope with a magnifying power of only thirty thousand diameters, and so nobody got to see him, after all. There was great and general dissatisfaction, of course, but"—

Just here there was an eager footstep on the stair; I opened the door, and my aunt Mary burst into the room. It was a joyful meeting, and a cheery bombardment of questions and answers concerning family matters ensued. By and by my aunt said,—

"But I am going to abuse you a little now. You promised me, the day I saw you last, that you would look after the needs of the poor family around the corner as faithfully as I had done it myself. Well, I found out by accident that you failed of your promise. *Was* that right?"

In simple truth, I never had thought of that family a second time! And now such a splintering pang of guilt shot through me! I glanced up at my Conscience. Plainly, my heavy heart was affecting him. His body was drooping forward; he seemed about to fall from the book-case. My aunt continued:—

"And think how you have neglected my poor *protégée* at the almshouse, you dear hard-hearted promise-breaker!" I blushed scarlet, and my tongue was tied. As the sense of my guilty negligence waxed sharper and stronger, my Conscience began to sway heavily back and forth; and when my aunt, after a little pause, said in a grieved tone, "Since you never once went to see her, maybe it will not distress you now to know that that poor child died months ago, utterly friendless and forsaken!" My Conscience could no longer bear up under the weight of my sufferings, but tumbled headlong from his high perch and struck the floor with a dull, leaden thump. He lay there writhing with pain and quaking with apprehension, but straining every muscle in frantic efforts to get up. In a fever of expectancy I sprang to the door, locked it, placed my back against it, and bent a watchful gaze upon my struggling master. Already my fingers were itching to begin their murderous work.

"Oh, what *can* be the matter!" exclaimed my aunt, shrinking from me, and following with her frightened eyes the direction of mine. My breath was coming in short, quick gasps now, and my excitement was almost uncontrollable. My aunt cried out,—

"Oh, do not look so! You appall me! Oh, what can the matter be? What is it you see? Why do you stare so? Why do you work your fingers like that?"

"Peace, woman!" I said, in a hoarse whisper. "Look elsewhere; pay no attention to me; it is nothing—nothing. I am often this way. It will pass in a moment. It comes from smoking too much."

My injured lord was up, wild-eyed with terror, and trying to hobble toward the door. I could hardly breathe, I was so wrought up. My aunt wrung her hands and said,—

"Oh, I knew how it would be; I knew it would come to this at last! Oh, I implore you to crush out that fatal habit while it may yet be time! You must not, you shall not be deaf to my supplications longer!" My struggling Conscience showed sudden signs of weariness! "Oh, promise me you will throw off this hateful slavery of tobacco!" My Conscience began to reel drowsily, and grope with his hands—enchanting spectacle! "I beg you, I beseech you, I implore you! Your reason is deserting you! There is madness in your eye! It flames with frenzy! Oh, hear me, hear me, and be saved! See, I plead with you on my very knees!" As she sank before me my Conscience reeled again, and then drooped languidly to the floor, blinking toward me a last supplication for mercy, with heavy eyes. "Oh, promise, or you are lost! Promise, and be redeemed! Promise! Promise and live!" With a long-drawn sigh my conquered Conscience closed his eyes and fell fast asleep!

With an exultant shout I sprang past my aunt, and in an instant I had my lifelong foe by the throat. After so many years of waiting and longing, he was mime at last. I tore him to shreds and fragments. I rent the fragments to bits. I cast the bleeding rubbish into the fire, and drew into my nostrils the grateful incense of my burnt-offering. At last, and forever, my Conscience was dead!

I was a free man! I turned upon my poor aunt, who was almost petrified with terror, and shouted,—

"Out of this with your paupers, your charities, your reforms, your pestilent morals! You behold before you a man whose life-conflict is done, whose soul is at peace; a man whose heart is dead to sorrow, dead to suffering, dead to remorse; a man WITHOUT A CONSCIENCE! In my joy I spare you, though I could throttle you and never feel a pang! Fly!"

She fled. Since that day my life is all bliss. Bliss, unalloyed bliss. Nothing in all the world could persuade me to have a conscience again. I settled all my old outstanding scores, and began the world anew. I killed thirty-eight persons during the first two weeks—all of them on account of ancient grudges. I burned a dwelling that interrupted my view. I swindled a widow and some orphans out of their last cow, which is a very good one, though not thoroughbred, I believe. I have also committed scores of crimes, of various kinds, and have enjoyed my work exceedingly, whereas it would formerly have broken my heart and turned my hair gray, I have no doubt.

In conclusion I wish to state, by way of advertisement, that medical colleges desiring assorted tramps for scientific purposes, either by the gross, by cord measurement, or per ton, will do well to examine the lot in my cellar before purchasing elsewhere, as these were all selected and prepared by myself, and can be had at a low rate, because I wish to clear out my stock and get ready for the spring trade.

FRANK R. STOCKTON

The Lady or the Tiger?

In the very olden time, there lived a semi-barbaric king, whose ideas, though somewhat polished and sharpened by the progressiveness of distant Latin neighbors, were still large, florid, and untrammeled, as became the half of him which was barbaric. He was a man of exuberant fancy, and, withal, of an authority so irresistible that, at his will, he turned his varied fancies into facts. He was greatly given to self-communing, and when he and himself agreed upon anything, the thing was done. When every member of his domestic and political systems moved smoothly in its appointed course, his nature was bland and genial; but whenever there was a little hitch, and some of his orbs got out of their orbits, he was blander and more genial still, for nothing pleased him so much as to make the crooked straight, and crush down uneven places.

Among the borrowed notions by which his barbarism had become semified was that of the public arena, in which, by exhibitions of manly and beastly valor, the minds of his subjects were refined and cultured.

But even here the exuberant and barbaric fancy asserted itself. The arena of the king was built, not to give the people an opportunity of hearing the rhapsodies of dying gladiators, nor to enable them to view the inevitable conclusion of a conflict between religious opinions and hungry jaws, but for purposes far better adapted to widen and develop the mental energies of the people. This vast amphitheater, with its encircling galleries, its mysterious vaults, and its unseen passages, was an agent of poetic justice, in which crime was punished, or virtue rewarded, by the decrees of an impartial and incorruptible chance.

When a subject was accused of a crime of sufficient importance to interest the king, public notice was given that on an appointed day the fate of the accused person would be decided in the king's arena—a structure which well deserved its name; for, although its form and plan were borrowed from afar, its purpose emanated solely from the brain of this man, who, every barleycorn a king, knew no tradition to which he owed more allegiance than pleased his fancy, and who ingrafted on every adopted form of human thought and action the rich growth of his barbaric idealism.

When all the people had assembled in the galleries,

and the king, surrounded by his court, sat high up on his throne of royal state on one side of the arena, he gave a signal, a door beneath him opened, and the accused subject stepped out into the amphitheater. Directly opposite him, on the other side of the enclosed space, were two doors, exactly alike and side by side. It was the duty and the privilege of the person on trial to walk directly to these doors and open one of them. He could open either door he pleased. He was subject to no guidance or influence but that of the aforementioned impartial and incorruptible chance. If he opened the one, there came out of it a hungry tiger, the fiercest and most cruel that could be procured, which immediately sprang upon him, and tore him to pieces, as a punishment for his guilt. The moment that the case of the criminal was thus decided, doleful iron bells were clanged, great wails went up from the hired mourners posted on the outer rim of the arena, and the vast audience, with bowed heads and downcast hearts, wended slowly their homeward way, mourning greatly that one so young and fair, or so old and respected, should have merited so dire a fate.

But if the accused person opened the other door, there came forth from it a lady, the most suitable to his years and station that his Majesty could select among his fair subjects; and to this lady he was immediately married, as a reward of his innocence. It mattered not that he might already possess a wife and family, or that his affections might be engaged upon an object of his own selection. The king allowed no such subordinate arrangements to interfere with his great scheme of retribution and reward. The exercises, as in the other instance, took place immediately, and in the arena. Another door opened beneath the king, and a priest, followed by a band of choristers, and dancing maidens blowing joyous airs on golden horns and treading an epithalamic measure, advanced to where the pair stood side by side, and the wedding was promptly and cheerily solemnized. Then the gay brass bells rang forth their merry peals, the people shouted glad hurrahs, and the innocent man, preceded by children strewing flowers on his path, led his bride to his home.

This was the king's semi-barbaric method of administering justice. Its perfect fairness is obvious. The criminal could not know out of which door would come the lady. He opened either he pleased, without having the slightest idea whether, in the next instant, he was to be devoured or married. On some occasions the tiger came out of one door, and on some out of the other. The decisions of this tribunal were not only fair—they were positively determinate. The accused person was instantly punished if he found himself guilty, and if innocent he was rewarded on the spot, whether he liked it or not. There was no escape from the judgments of the king's arena.

The institution was a very popular one. When the people gathered together on one of the great trial days, they never knew whether they were to witness a bloody slaughter or a hilarious wedding. This element of uncertainty lent an interest to the occasion which it could not otherwise have attained. Thus the masses were entertained and pleased, and the thinking part of the community could bring no charge of unfairness against this plan; for did not the accused person have the whole matter in his own hands?

This semi-barbaric king had a daughter as blooming as his most florid fancies, and with a soul as fervent and imperious as his own. As is usual in such cases, she was the apple of his eye, and was loved by him above all humanity. Among his courtiers was a young man of that fineness of blood and lowness of station common to the conventional heroes of romance who love royal maidens. This royal maiden was well satisfied with her lover, for he was handsome and brave to a degree unsurpassed in all this kingdom, and she loved him with an ardor that had enough of barbarism in it to make it exceedingly warm and strong. This love affair moved on happily for many months, until, one day, the king happened to discover its existence. He did not hesitate nor waver in regard to his duty in the premises. The youth was immediately cast into prison, and a day was appointed for his trial in the king's arena. This, of course, was an especially important occasion, and his Majesty, as well as all the people, was greatly interested in the workings and development of this trial. Never before had such a case occurred—never before had a subject dared to love the daughter of a king. In after years such things became commonplace enough, but then they were, in no slight degree, novel and startling.

The tiger cages of the kingdom were searched for the

most savage and relentless beasts, from which the fiercest monster might be selected for the arena, and the ranks of maiden youth and beauty throughout the land were carefully surveyed by competent judges, in order that the young man might have a fitting bride in case fate did not determine for him a different destiny. Of course, everybody knew that the deed with which the accused was charged had been done. He had loved the princess, and neither he, she, nor any one else thought of denying the fact. But the king would not think of allowing any fact of this kind to interfere with the workings of the tribunal, in which he took such great delight and satisfaction. No matter how the affair turned out, the youth would be disposed of, and the king would take an esthetic pleasure in watching the course of events which would determine whether or not the young man had done wrong in allowing himself to love the princess.

The appointed day arrived. From far and near the people gathered, and thronged the great galleries of the arena, while crowds, unable to gain admittance, massed themselves against its outside walls. The king and his court were in their places, opposite the twin doors—those fateful portals, so terrible in their similarity!

All was ready. The signal was given. A door beneath the royal party opened, and the lover of the princess walked into the arena. Tall, beautiful, fair, his appearance was greeted with a low hum of admiration and anxiety. Half the audience had not known so grand a youth had lived among them. No wonder the princess loved him! What a terrible thing for him to be there!

As the youth advanced into the arena, he turned, as the custom was, to bow to the king. But he did not think at all of that royal personage; his eyes were fixed upon the princess, who sat to the right of her father. Had it not been for the moiety of barbarism in her nature, it is probable that lady would not have been there. But her intense and fervid soul would not allow her to be absent on an occasion in which she was so terribly interested. From the moment that the decree had gone forth that her lover should decide his fate in the king's arena, she had thought of nothing, night or day, but this great event and the various subjects connected with it. Possessed of more power, influence, and force of character than any one who had ever before been interested in such a case, she had done what no other person had done—she had possessed herself of the secret of the doors. She knew in which of the two rooms behind those doors stood the cage of the tiger, with its open front, and in which waited the lady. Through these thick doors, heavily curtained with skins on the inside, it was impossible that any noise or suggestion should come from within to the person who should approach to raise the latch of one of them. But gold, and the power of a woman's will, had brought the secret to the princess.

Not only did she know in which room stood the lady, ready to emerge, all blushing and radiant, should her door be opened, but she knew who the lady was. It was one of the fairest and loveliest of the damsels of the court who had been selected as the reward of the accused youth, should he be proved innocent of the crime of aspiring to one so far above him; and the princess hated her. Often had she seen, or imagined that she had seen, this fair creature throwing glances of admiration upon the person of her lover, and sometimes she thought these glances were perceived and even returned. Now and then she had seen them talking together. It was but for a moment or two, but much can be said in a brief space. It may have been on most unimportant topics, but how could she know that? The girl was lovely, but she had dared to raise her eyes to the loved one of the princess, and, with all the intensity of the savage blood transmitted to her through long lines of wholly barbaric ancestors, she hated the woman who blushed and trembled behind that silent door.

When her lover turned and looked at her, and his eye met hers as she sat there paler and whiter than any one in the vast ocean of anxious faces about her, he saw, by that power of quick perception which is given to those whose souls are one, that she knew behind which door crouched the tiger, and behind which stood the lady. He had expected her to know it. He understood her nature, and his soul was assured that she would never rest until she had made plain to herself this thing, hidden to all other lookers-on, even to the king. The only hope for the youth in which there was any element of certainty was based upon the success of the princess in discovering this mystery, and the moment he looked upon her, he saw she had succeeded.

Then it was that his quick and anxious glance asked the question, "Which?" It was as plain to her as if he shouted it from where he stood. There was not an instant to be lost. The question was asked in a flash; it must be answered in another.

Her right arm lay on the cushioned parapet before her. She raised her hand, and made a slight, quick movement toward the right. No one but her lover saw her. Every eye but his was fixed on the man in the arena.

He turned, and with a firm and rapid step he walked across the empty space. Every heart stopped beating, every breath was held, every eye was fixed immovably upon that man. Without the slightest hesitation, he went to the door on the right, and opened it.

Now, the point of the story is this: Did the tiger come out of that door, or did the lady?

The more we reflect upon this question, the harder it is to answer. It involves a study of the human heart which leads us through devious mazes of passion, out of which it is difficult to find our way. Think of it, fair reader, not as if the decision of the question depended upon yourself, but upon that hot-blooded, semi-barbaric princess, her soul at a white heat beneath the combined fires of despair and jealousy. She had lost him, but who should have him?

How often, in her waking hours and in her dreams, had she started in wild horror and covered her face with her hands as she thought of her lover opening the door on the other side of which waited the cruel fangs of the tiger!

But how much oftener had she seen him at the other

door! How in her grievous reveries had she gnashed her teeth and torn her hair when she saw his start of rapturous delight as he opened the door of the lady! How her soul had burned in agony when she had seen him rush to meet that woman, with her flushing cheek and sparkling eye of triumph; when she had seen him lead her forth, his whole frame kindled with the joy of recovered life; when she had heard the glad shouts from the multitude, and the wild ringing of the happy bells; when she had seen the priest, with his joyous followers, advance to the couple, and make them man and wife before her very eyes; and when she had seen them walk away together upon their path of flowers, followed by the tremendous shouts of the hilarious multitude, in which her one despairing shriek was lost and drowned!

Would it not be better for him to die at once, and go to wait for her in the blessed regions of semi-barbaric futurity?

And yet, that awful tiger, those shrieks, that blood!

Her decision had been indicated in an instant, but it had been made after days and nights of anguished deliberation. She had known she would be asked, she had decided what she would answer, and, without the slightest hesitation, she had moved her hand to the right.

The question of her decision is one not to be lightly considered, and it is not for me to presume to set up myself as the one person able to answer it. So I leave it with all of you: Which came out of the opened door—the lady or the tiger?

FRANK R. STOCKTON

The Discourager of Hesitancy

A CONTINUATION OF "THE LADY OR THE TIGER?"

It was nearly a year after the occurrence of that event in the arena of the semi-barbaric king, known as the incident of the lady or the tiger, that there came to the palace of this monarch a deputation of five strangers from a far country. These men, of venerable and dignified aspect and demeanor, were received by a high officer of the court, and to him they made known their errand.

"Most noble officer," said the speaker of the deputation, "it so happened that one of our countrymen was present here, in your capital city, on that momentous occasion when a young man who had dared to aspire to the hand of your king's daughter had been placed in the arena, in the midst of the assembled multitude, and ordered to open one of two doors, not knowing whether a ferocious tiger would spring out upon him, or a beauteous lady would advance, ready to become his bride. Our fellow-citizen who was then present was a man of supersensitive feelings, and at the moment when the youth was about to open the door he was so fearful lest he should behold a horrible spectacle that his nerves failed him, and he fled precipitately from the arena, and, mounting his camel, rode homeward as fast as he could go.

"We were all very much interested in the story which our countryman told us, and we were extremely sorry that he did not wait to see the end of the affair. We hoped, however, that in a few weeks some traveller from your city would come among us and bring us further news, but up to the day when we left our country no such traveller had arrived. At last it was determined that the only thing to be done was to send a deputation to this country, and ask the question: 'Which came out of the open door, the lady or the tiger?' "

When the high officer had heard the mission of this most respectable deputation, he led the five strangers into an inner room, where they were seated upon soft cushions, and where he ordered coffee, pipes, sherbet, and other semi-barbaric refreshments to be served to them. Then, taking his seat before them, he thus addressed the visitors:

"Most noble strangers, before answering the question you have come so far to ask, I will relate to you an incident which occurred not very long after that to which you have referred. It is well known in all regions hereabout that our great king is very fond of the presence of beautiful women about his court. All the ladies in waiting upon the queen and royal family are most lovely maidens, brought here from every part of the kingdom. The fame of this concourse of beauty, unequalled in any other royal court, has spread far and wide, and had it not been for the equally wide-spread fame of the systems of impetuous justice adopted by our king, many foreigners would doubtless have visited our court.

"But not very long ago there arrived here from a distant land a prince of distinguished appearance and undoubted rank. To such an one, of course, a royal audience was granted, and our king met him very graciously, and begged him to make known the object of his visit. Thereupon the prince informed his Royal Highness that, having heard of the superior beauty of the ladies of his court, he had come to ask permission to make one of them his wife.

"When our king heard this bold announcement, his face reddened, he turned uneasily on his throne, and we were all in dread lest some quick words of furious condemnation should leap from out his quivering lips. But by a mighty effort he controlled himself, and after a moment's silence he turned to the prince and said: 'Your request is granted. To-morrow at noon you shall wed one of the fairest damsels of our court.' Then turning to his officers, he said: 'Give orders that everything be prepared for a wedding in this palace at high noon to-morrow. Convey this royal prince to suitable apartments. Send to him tailors, bootmakers, hatters, jewellers, armorers, men of every craft whose services he may need.

Whatever he asks, provide. And let all be ready for the ceremony to-morrow.'

" 'But, your Majesty,' exclaimed the prince, 'before we make these preparations, I would like——'

" 'Say no more!' roared the king. 'My royal orders have been given, and nothing more is needed to be said. You have asked a boon. I granted it, and I will hear no more on the subject. Farewell, my prince, until to-morrow noon.'

"At this the king arose and left the audience chamber, while the prince was hurried away to the apartments selected for him. Here came to him tailors, hatters, jewellers, and every one who was needed to fit him out in grand attire for the wedding. But the mind of the prince was much troubled and perplexed.

" 'I do not understand,' he said to his attendants, 'this precipitancy of action. When am I to see the ladies, that I may choose among them? I wish opportunity, not only to gaze upon their forms and faces, but to become acquainted with their relative intellectual development.'

" 'We can tell you nothing,' was the answer. 'What our king thinks is right, that will he do. More than this we know not.'

" 'His Majesty's notions seem to be very peculiar,' said the prince, 'and, so far as I can see, they do not at all agree with mine.'

"At that moment an attendant whom the prince had not before noticed came and stood beside him. This was a broad-shouldered man of cheery aspect, who carried, its hilt in his right hand, and its broad back resting on his broad arm, an enormous cimeter, the upturned edge of which was keen and bright as any razor. Holding this formidable weapon as tenderly as though it had been a sleeping infant, this man drew closer to the prince and bowed.

" 'Who are you?' exclaimed his Highness, starting back at the sight of the frightful weapon.

" 'I,' said the other, with a courteous smile, 'am the Discourager of Hesitancy. When our king makes known his wishes to any one, a subject or visitor, whose disposition in some little points may be supposed not wholly to coincide with that of his Majesty, I am appointed to attend him closely, that, should he think of pausing in the path of obedience to the royal will he may look at me and proceed.'

"The prince looked at him, and proceeded to be measured for a coat.

"The tailors and shoemakers and hatters worked all night, and the next morning, when everything was ready, and the hour of noon was drawing nigh, the prince again anxiously inquired of his attendants when he might expect to be introduced to the ladies.

" 'The king will attend to that,' they said. 'We know nothing of the matter.'

" 'Your Highness,' said the Discourager of Hesitancy, approaching with a courtly bow, 'will observe the excellent quality of this edge.' And drawing a hair from his head, he dropped it upon the upturned edge of his cimeter, upon which it was cut in two at the moment of touching.

"The prince glanced, and turned upon his heel.

"Now came officers to conduct him to the grand hall of the palace, in which the ceremony was to be performed. Here the prince found the king seated on the throne, with his nobles, his courtiers, and his officers standing about him in magnificent array. The prince was led to a position in front of the king, to whom he made obeisance, and then said:

" 'Your Majesty, before I proceed further——'

"At this moment an attendant, who had approached with a long scarf of delicate silk, wound it about the lower part of the prince's face so quickly and adroitly that he was obliged to cease speaking. Then, with wonderful dexterity, the rest of the scarf was wound around the prince's head, so that he was completely blindfolded. Thereupon the attendant quickly made openings in the scarf over the mouth and ears, so that the prince might breathe and hear, and, fastening the ends of the scarf securely, he retired.

"The first impulse of the prince was to snatch the silken folds from his head and face, but, as he raised his hands to do so, he heard beside him the voice of the Discourager of Hesitancy, who gently whispered, 'I am here, your Highness.' And, with a shudder, the arms of the prince fell down by his side.

"Now before him he heard the voice of a priest, who had begun the marriage service in use in that semi-barbaric country. At his side he could hear a delicate rustle, which seemed to proceed from fabrics of soft silk. Gently putting forth his hand, he felt folds of such silk close beside him. Then came the voice of the priest requesting him to take the hand of the lady by his side; and reaching forth his right hand, the prince received within it another hand, so small, so soft, so delicately fashioned, and so delightful to the touch, that a thrill went through his being. Then, as was the custom of the country the priest first asked the lady would she have this man to be her husband; to which the answer gently came, in the sweetest voice he had ever heard: 'I will.'

"Then ran raptures rampant through the prince's blood. The touch, the tone, enchanted him. All the ladies of that court were beautiful, the Discourager was behind him, and through his parted scarf he boldly answered: 'Yes, I will.'

"Whereupon the priest pronounced them man and wife.

"Now the prince heard a little bustle about him, the long scarf was rapidly unrolled from his head, and he turned with a start, to gaze upon his bride. To his utter amazement, there was no one there. He stood alone. Unable on the instant to ask a question or say a word, he gazed blankly about him.

"Then our king arose from his throne, and came down, and took him by the hand.

" 'Where is my wife?' gasped the prince.

" 'She is here,' said the king, leading him to a curtain doorway at the side of the hall.

"The curtains were drawn aside, and the prince, entering, found himself in a long apartment, near the opposite wall of which stood a line of forty ladies, all dressed in rich attire, and each one apparently more beautiful than the rest.

"Waving his hand toward the line, the king said to the prince: 'There is your bride! Approach and lead her forth! But remember this: that if you attempt to take away one of the unmarried damsels of our court, your execution shall be instantaneous. Now, delay no longer. Step up and take your bride.'

"The prince, as in a dream, walked slowly along the line of ladies, and then walked slowly back again. Nothing could he see about any one of them to indicate that she was more of a bride than the others. Their dresses were all similar, they all blushed, they all looked up and then looked down. They all had charming little hands. Not one spoke a word. Not one lifted a finger to make a sign. It was evident that the orders given them had been very strict.

" 'Why this delay?' roared the king. 'If I had been married this day to one so fair as the lady who wedded you, I should not wait one second to claim her.'

"The bewildered prince walked again up and down the line. And this time there was a slight change in the countenances of two of the ladies. One of the fairest gently smiled as he passed her. Another, just as beautiful, slightly frowned.

" 'Now,' said the prince to himself, 'I am sure that it is one of those two ladies whom I have married. But which? One smiled. And would not any woman smile when she saw, in such a case, her husband coming toward her? Then again, on the other hand, would not any woman frown when she saw her husband come toward her and fail to claim her? Would she not knit her lovely brows? Would she not inwardly say, "It is I! Don't you know it? Don't you feel it? Come!" But if this woman had not been married, would she not frown when she saw the man looking at her? Would she not say inwardly, "Don't stop at me! It is the next but one. It is two ladies above. Go on!" Then again, the one who married me did not see my face. Would she not now smile if she thought me comely? But if I wedded the one who frowned, could she restrain her disapprobation if she did not like me? Smiles invite the approach of true love. A frown is a reproach to a tardy advance. A smile——'

" 'Now hear me!' loudly cried the king. 'In ten seconds, if you do not take the lady we have given you, she who has just been made your bride shall be your widow.'

"And, as the last word was uttered, the Discourager of Hesitancy stepped close behind the prince and whispered, 'I am here!'

"Now the prince could not hesitate an instant; he stepped forward and took one of the two ladies by the hand.

"Loud rang the bells, loud cheered the people, and the king came forward to congratulate the prince. He had taken his lawful bride.

"Now, then," said the high officer to the deputation of five strangers from a far country, "when you can decide among yourselves which lady the prince chose, the one who smiled or the one who frowned, then will I tell you which came out of the opened door, the lady or the tiger!"

At the latest accounts the five strangers had not yet decided.

STRANGE PIECES

RICHARD CONNELL

The Most Dangerous Game

"Off there to the right—somewhere—is a large island," said Whitney. "It's rather a mystery—"

"What island is it?" Rainsford asked.

"The old charts call it 'Ship-Trap Island,'" Whitney replied. "A suggestive name, isn't it? Sailors have a curious dread of the place. I don't know why. Some superstition—"

"Can't see it," remarked Rainsford, trying to peer through the dank tropical night that was palpable as it pressed its thick warm blackness in upon the yacht.

"You've good eyes," said Whitney, with a laugh, "and I've seen you pick off a moose moving in the brown fall bush at four hundred yards, but even you can't see four miles or so through a moonless Caribbean night."

"Not four yards," admitted Rainsford. "Ugh! It's like moist black velvet."

"It will be light enough in Rio," promised Whitney. "We should make it in a few days. I hope the jaguar guns have come from Purdey's. We should have some good hunting up the Amazon. Great sport, hunting."

"The best sport in the world," agreed Rainsford.

"For the hunter," amended Whitney. "Not for the jaguar."

"Don't talk rot, Whitney," said Rainsford. "You're a big-game hunter, not a philosopher. Who cares how a jaguar feels?"

"Perhaps the jaguar does," observed Whitney.

"Bah! They've no understanding."

"Even so, I rather think they understand one thing—fear. The fear of pain and the fear of death."

"Nonsense," laughed Rainsford. "This hot weather is making you soft, Whitney. Be a realist. The world is made up of two classes—the hunters and the hunted. Luckily, you and I are hunters. Do you think we've passed that island yet?"

"I can't tell in the dark. I hope so."

"Why?" asked Rainsford.

"The place has a reputation—a bad one."

"Cannibals?" suggested Rainsford.

"Hardly. Even cannibals wouldn't live in such a God-forsaken place. But it's gotten into sailor lore, somehow.

Didn't you notice that the crew's nerves seemed a bit jumpy today?"

"They were a bit strange, now you mention it. Even Captain Nielsen—"

"Yes, even that tough-minded old Swede, who'd go up to the devil himself and ask him for a light. Those fishy blue eyes held a look I never saw there before. All I could get out of him was: 'This place has an evil name among seafaring men, sir.' Then he said to me, very gravely: 'Don't you feel anything?'—as if the air about us was actually poisonous. Now, you mustn't laugh when I tell you this—I did feel something like a sudden chill.

"There was no breeze. The sea was as flat as a plate-glass window. We were drawing near the island then. What I felt was a—a mental chill; a sort of sudden dread."

"Pure imagination," said Rainsford. "One superstitious sailor can taint the whole ship's company with his fear."

"Maybe. But sometimes I think sailors have an extra sense that tells them when they are in danger. Sometimes I think evil is a tangible thing—with wave lengths, just as sound and light have. An evil place can, so to speak, broadcast vibrations of evil. Anyhow, I'm glad we're getting out of this zone. Well, I think I'll turn in now, Rainsford."

"I'm not sleepy," said Rainsford. "I'm going to smoke another pipe up on the afterdeck."

"Good night, then, Rainsford. See you at breakfast."

"Right. Good night, Whitney."

There was no sound in the night as Rainsford sat there, but the muffled throb of the engine that drove the yacht swiftly through the darkness, and the swish and ripple of the wash of the propeller.

Rainsford, reclining in a steamer chair, indolently puffed on his favorite brier. The sensuous drowsiness of the night was on him. "It's so dark," he thought, "that I could sleep without closing my eyes; the night would be my eyelids—"

An abrupt sound startled him. Off to the right he heard it, and his ears, expert in such matters, could not be mistaken. Again he heard the sound, and again. Somewhere, off in the blackness, someone had fired a gun three times.

Rainsford sprang up and moved quickly to the rail, mystified. He strained his eyes in the direction from which the reports had come, but it was like trying to see through a blanket. He leaped upon the rail and balanced himself there, to get greater elevation; his pipe, striking a rope, was knocked from his mouth. He lunged for it; a short, hoarse cry came from his lips as he realized he had reached too far and had lost his balance. The cry was pinched off short as the blood-warm waters of the Caribbean Sea closed over his head.

He struggled up to the surface and tried to cry out, but the wash from the speeding yacht slapped him in the face and the salt water in his open mouth made him gag and strangle. Desperately he struck out with strong strokes after the receding lights of the yacht, but he stopped before he had swum fifty feet. A certain cool-headedness had come to him; it was not the first time he had been in a tight place. There was a chance that his cries could be heard by someone aboard the yacht, but that chance was slender, and grew more slender as the yacht raced on. He wrestled himself out of his clothes, and shouted with all his power. The lights of the yacht became faint and ever-vanishing fireflies; then they were blotted out entirely by the night.

Rainsford remembered the shots. They had come from the right, and doggedly he swam in that direction, swimming with slow, deliberate strokes, conserving his strength. For a seemingly endless time he fought the sea. He began to count his strokes; he could do possibly a hundred more and then—

Rainsford heard a sound. It came out of the darkness, a high, screaming sound, the sound of an animal in an extremity of anguish and terror.

He did not recognize the animal that made the sound; he did not try to; with fresh vitality he swam toward the sound. He heard it again; then it was cut short by another noise, crisp, staccato.

"Pistol shot," muttered Rainsford, swimming on.

Ten minutes of determined effort brought another sound to his ears—the most welcome he had ever heard—the muttering and growling of the sea breaking on a rocky shore. He was almost on the rocks before he saw them; on a night less calm he would have been shattered against them. With his remaining strength he dragged himself from the swirling waters. Jagged crags appeared to jut up into the opaqueness; he forced himself upward, hand over hand. Gasping, his hands raw, he reached a flat place at the top. Dense jungle came down to the very edge of the cliffs. What perils that tangle of trees and underbrush might hold for him did not concern Rainsford just then. All he knew was that he was safe from his enemy, the sea, and that utter weariness was on him. He flung himself down at the jungle edge and tumbled headlong into the deepest sleep of his life.

When he opened his eyes he knew from the position of the sun that it was late in the afternoon. Sleep had given him new vigor; a sharp hunger was picking at him. He looked about him, almost cheerfully.

"Where there are pistol shots, there are men. Where there are men, there is food," he thought. But what kind of men, he wondered, in so forbidding a place? An unbroken front of snarled and ragged jungle fringed the shore.

He saw no sign of a trail through the closely knit web of weeds and trees; it was easier to go along the shore, and Rainsford floundered along by the water. Not far from where he had landed, he stopped.

Some wounded thing, by the evidence a large animal, had thrashed about in the underbrush; the jungle weeds were crushed down and the moss was lacerated; one patch of weeds was stained crimson. A small, glittering object not far away caught Rainsford's eye and he picked it up. It was an empty cartridge.

"A twenty-two," he remarked. "That's odd. It must have been a fairly large animal too. The hunter had his nerve with him to tackle it with a light gun. It's clear that the brute put up a fight. I suppose the first three shots I heard was when the hunter flushed his quarry and wounded it. The last shot was when he trailed it here and finished it."

He examined the ground closely and found what he had hoped to find—the print of hunting-boots. They pointed along the cliff in the direction he had been going. Eagerly he hurried along, now slipping on a rotten log or a loose stone, but making headway; night was beginning to settle down on the island.

Bleak darkness was blacking out the sea and jungle when Rainsford sighted the lights. He came upon them as he turned a crook in the coast line, and his first thought was that he had come upon a village, for there were many lights. But as he forged along he saw to his great astonishment that all the lights were in one enormous building—a lofty structure with pointed towers plunging upward into the gloom. His eyes made out the shadowy outlines of a palatial château; it was set on a high bluff, and on three sides of it cliffs dived down to where the sea licked greedy lips in the shadows.

"Mirage," thought Rainsford. But it was no mirage, he found, when he opened the tall spiked iron gate. The stone steps were real enough; the massive door with a leering gargoyle for a knocker was real enough; yet about it all hung an air of unreality.

He lifted the knocker, and it creaked up stiffly, as if it had never before been used. He let it fall, and it startled him with its booming loudness. He thought he heard steps within; the door remained closed. Again Rainsford lifted the heavy knocker, and let it fall. The door opened then, opened as suddenly as if it were on a spring, and Rainsford stood blinking in the river of glaring gold light that poured out. The first thing Rainsford's eyes discerned was the largest man Rainsford had ever seen —a gigantic creature, solidly made and black-bearded to the waist. In his hand the man held a long-barreled revolver, and he was pointing it straight at Rainsford's heart.

Out of the snarl of beard two small eyes regarded Rainsford.

"Don't be alarmed," said Rainsford, with a smile which he hoped was disarming. "I'm no robber. I fell off a yacht. My name is Sanger Rainsford of New York City."

The menacing look in the eyes did not change. The revolver pointed as rigidly as if the giant were a statue. He gave no sign that he understood Rainsford's words, or that he had even heard them. He was dressed in uniform, a black uniform trimmed with gray astrakhan.

"I'm Sanger Rainsford of New York," Rainsford began again. "I fell off a yacht. I am hungry."

The man's only answer was to raise with his thumb the hammer of his revolver. Then Rainsford saw the man's free hand go to his forehead in a military salute, and he saw him click his heels together and stand at attention. Another man was coming down the broad marble steps, an erect, slender man in evening clothes. He advanced to Rainsford and held out his hand.

In a cultivated voice marked by a slight accent that gave it added precision and deliberateness, he said: "It is a very great pleasure and honor to welcome Mr. Sanger Rainsford, the celebrated hunter, to my home."

Automatically Rainsford shook the man's hand.

"I've read your book about hunting snow leopards in Tibet, you see," explained the man. "I am General Zaroff."

Rainsford's first impression was that the man was singularly handsome; his second was that there was an original, almost bizarre quality about the general's face. He was a tall man past middle age, for his hair was a vivid white; but his thick eyebrows and pointed military mustache were as black as the night from which Rainsford had come. His eyes, too, were black and very bright. He had high cheekbones, a sharp-cut nose, a spare, dark face, the face of a man used to giving orders, the face of an aristocrat. Turning to the giant in uniform, the general made a sign. The giant put away his pistol, saluted, withdrew.

"Ivan is an incredibly strong fellow," remarked the general, "but he has the misfortune to be deaf and dumb. A simple fellow, but, I'm afraid, like all his race, a bit of a savage."

"Is he Russian?"

"He is a Cossack," said the general, and his smile showed red lips and pointed teeth. "So am I.

"Come," he said, "we shouldn't be chatting here. We can talk later. Now you want clothes, food, rest. You shall have them. This is a most restful spot."

Ivan had reappeared, and the general spoke to him with lips that moved but gave forth no sound.

"Follow Ivan, if you please, Mr. Rainsford," said the general. "I was about to have my dinner when you came. I'll wait for you. You'll find that my clothes will fit you, I think."

It was to a huge, beam-ceilinged bedroom with a canopied bed big enough for six men that Rainsford followed the silent giant. Ivan laid out an evening suit, and Rainsford, as he put it on, noticed that it came from a London tailor who ordinarily cut and sewed for none below the rank of duke.

The dining room to which Ivan conducted him was in many ways remarkable. There was a medieval magnificence about it; it suggested a baronial hall of feudal times with its oaken panels, its high ceiling, its vast refectory table where twoscore men could sit down to eat. About the hall were the mounted heads of many animals—lions, tigers, elephants, moose, bears; larger or more perfect specimens Rainsford had never seen. At the great table the general was sitting alone.

"You'll have a cocktail, Mr. Rainsford," he suggested. The cocktail was surpassingly good; and, Rainsford noted, the table appointments were of the finest—the linen, the crystal, the silver, the china.

They were eating *borsch*, the rich, red soup with whipped cream so dear to Russian palates. Half apologetically General Zaroff said: "We do our best to preserve the amenities of civilization here. Please forgive any lapses. We are well off the beaten track, you know. Do you think the champagne has suffered from its long ocean trip?"

"Not in the least," declared Rainsford. He was finding the general a most thoughtful and affable host, a true cosmopolite. But there was one small trait of the general's that made Rainsford uncomfortable. Whenever he looked up from his plate he found the general studying him, appraising him narrowly.

"Perhaps," said General Zaroff, "you were surprised that I recognized your name. You see, I read all books on hunting published in English, French, and Russian. I have but one passion in my life, Mr. Rainsford, and it is the hunt."

"You have some wonderful heads here," said Rainsford as he ate a particularly well cooked filet mignon. "That Cape buffalo is the largest I ever saw."

"Oh, that fellow. Yes, he was a monster."

"Did he charge you?"

"Hurled me against a tree," said the general. "Fractured my skull. But I got the brute."

"I've always thought," said Rainsford, "that the Cape buffalo is the most dangerous of all big game."

For a moment the general did not reply; he was smiling his curious red-lipped smile. Then he said slowly: "No. You are wrong, sir. The Cape buffalo is not the most dangerous big game." He sipped his wine. "Here in my preserve on this island," he said in the same slow tone, "I hunt more dangerous game."

Rainsford expressed his surprise. "Is there big game on this island?"

The general nodded. "The biggest."

"Really?"

"Oh, it isn't here naturally, of course. I have to stock the island."

"What have you imported, general?" Rainsford asked. "Tigers?"

The general smiled. "No," he said. "Hunting tigers ceased to interest me some years ago. I exhausted their possibilities, you see. No thrill left in tigers, no real danger. I live for danger, Mr. Rainsford."

The general took from his pocket a gold cigarette case and offered his guest a long black cigarette with a silver tip; it was perfumed and gave off a smell like incense.

"We will have some capital hunting, you and I," said the general. "I shall be most glad to have your society."

"But what game—" began Rainsford.

"I'll tell you," said the general. "You will be amused, I know. I think I may say, in all modesty, that I have done a rare thing. I have invented a new sensation. May I pour you another glass of port, Mr. Rainsford?"

"Thank you, general."

The general filled both glasses, and said: "God makes some men poets. Some He makes kings, some beggars. Me He made a hunter. My hand was made for the trigger, my father said. He was a very rich man with a quarter of a million acres in the Crimea, and he was an ardent sportsman. When I was only five years old he gave me a little gun, specially made in Moscow for me, to shoot sparrows with. When I shot some of his prize turkeys with it, he did not punish me; he complimented me on my marksmanship. I killed my first bear in the Caucasus when I was ten. My whole life has been one prolonged hunt. I went into the army—it was expected of noblemen's sons—and for a time commanded a division of Cossack cavalry, but my real interest was always the hunt. I have hunted every kind of game in every land. It would be impossible for me to tell you how many animals I have killed."

The general puffed at his cigarette.

"After the debacle in Russia I left the country, for it was imprudent for an officer of the Czar to stay there. Many noble Russians lost everything. I, luckily, had invested heavily in American securities, so I shall never have to open a tearoom in Monte Carlo or drive a taxi in Paris. Naturally, I continued to hunt—grizzlies in your Rockies, crocodiles in the Ganges, rhinoceroses in East Africa. It was in Africa that the Cape buffalo hit me and laid me up for six months. As soon as I recovered I started for the Amazon to hunt jaguars, for I had heard they were unusually cunning. They weren't." The Cossack sighed. "They were no match at all for a hunter with his wits about him, and a high-powered rifle. I was bitterly disappointed. I was lying in my tent with a splitting headache one night when a terrible thought pushed its way into my mind. Hunting was beginning to bore me! And hunting, remember, had been my life. I have heard that in America businessmen often go to pieces when they give up the business that has been their life."

"Yes, that's so," said Rainsford.

The general smiled. "I had no wish to go to pieces,"

he said. "I must do something. Now, mine is an analytical mind, Mr. Rainsford. Doubtless that is why I enjoy the problems of the chase."

"No doubt, General Zaroff."

"So," continued the general, "I asked myself why the hunt no longer fascinated me. You are much younger than I am, Mr. Rainsford, and have not hunted as much, but you perhaps can guess the answer."

"What was it?"

"Simply this: hunting had ceased to be what you call 'a sporting proposition.' It had become too easy. I always got my quarry. Always. There is no greater bore than perfection."

The general lit a fresh cigarette.

"No animal had a chance with me any more. That is no boast; it is a mathematical certainty. The animal had nothing but his legs and his instinct. Instinct is no match for reason. When I thought of this it was a tragic moment for me, I can tell you."

Rainsford leaned across the table, absorbed in what his host was saying.

"It came to me as an inspiration what I must do," the general went on.

"And that was?"

The general smiled the quiet smile of one who has faced an obstacle and surmounted it with success. "I had to invent a new animal to hunt," he said.

"A new animal? You're joking."

"Not at all," said the general. "I never joke about hunting. I needed a new animal. I found one. So I bought this island, built this house, and here I do my hunting. The island is perfect for my purposes—there are jungles with a maze of trails in them, hills, swamps—"

"But the animal, General Zaroff?"

"Oh," said the general, "it supplies me with the most exciting hunting in the world. No other hunting compares with it for an instant. Every day I hunt, and I never grow bored now, for I have a quarry with which I can match my wits."

Rainsford's bewilderment showed in his face.

"I wanted the ideal animal to hunt," explained the general. "So I said: 'what are the attributes of an ideal quarry?' And the answer was, of course: 'It must have courage, cunning, and, above all, it must be able to reason.' "

"But no animal can reason," objected Rainsford.

"My dear fellow," said the general, "there is one that can."

"But you can't mean—" gasped Rainsford.

"And why not?"

"I can't believe you are serious, General Zaroff. This is a grisly joke."

"Why should I not be serious? I am speaking of hunting."

"Hunting? Good God, General Zaroff, what you speak of is murder."

The general laughed with entire good nature. He regarded Rainsford quizzically. "I refuse to believe that so modern and civilized a young man as you seem to be harbors romantic ideas about the value of human life. Surely your experiences in the war—"

"Did not make me condone cold-blooded murder," finished Rainsford stiffly.

Laughter shook the general. "How extraordinarily droll you are!" he said. "One does not expect nowadays to find a young man of the educated class, even in America, with such a naïve, and, if I may say so, mid-Victorian point of view. It's like finding a snuffbox in a limousine. Ah, well, doubtless you had Puritan ancestors. So many Americans appear to have had. I'll wager you'll forget your notions when you go hunting with me. You've a genuine new thrill in store for you, Mr. Rainsford."

"Thank you, I'm a hunter, not a murderer."

"Dear me," said the general, quite unruffled, "again that unpleasant word. But I think I can show you that your scruples are quite ill founded."

"Yes?"

"Life is for the strong, to be lived by the strong, and, if needs be, taken by the strong. The weak of the world were put here to give the strong pleasure. I am strong. Why should I not use my gift? If I wish to hunt, why should I not? I hunt the scum of the earth—sailors from tramp ships—lascars, blacks, Chinese whites, mongrels—a thoroughbred horse or hound is worth more than a score of them."

"But they are men," said Rainsford hotly.

"Precisely," said the general. "That is why I use them. It gives me pleasure. They can reason, after a fashion. So they are dangerous."

"But where do you get them?"

The general's left eyelid fluttered down in a wink. "This island is called 'Ship-Trap,' " he answered. "Sometimes an angry god of the high seas sends them to me. Sometimes, when Providence is not so kind, I help Providence a bit. Come to the window with me."

Rainsford went to the window and looked out toward the sea.

"Watch! Out there!" exclaimed the general, pointing into the night. Rainsford's eyes saw only blackness, and then, as the general pressed a button, far out to sea Rainsford saw the flash of lights.

The general chuckled. "They indicate a channel," he said, "where there's none: giant rocks with razor edges crouch like a sea monster with wide-open jaws. They can crush a ship as easily as I crush this nut." He dropped a walnut on the hardwood floor and brought his heel grinding down on it. "Oh, yes," he said, casually, as if in answer to a question, "I have electricity. We try to be civilized here."

"Civilized? And you shoot down men?"

A trace of anger was in the general's black eyes, but it was there for but a second, and he said, in his most pleasant manner: "Dear me, what a righteous young man you are! I assure you I do not do the thing you suggest. That would be barbarous. I treat these visitors with every consideration. They get plenty of good food and exercise. They get into splendid physical condition. You shall see for yourself tomorrow."

"What do you mean?"

"We'll visit my training school," smiled the general. "It's in the cellar. I have about a dozen pupils down there now. They're from the Spanish bark San Lucar that had the bad luck to go on the rocks out there. A very inferior lot, I regret to say. Poor specimens and more accustomed to the deck than to the jungle."

He raised his hand, and Ivan, who served as waiter, brought thick Turkish coffee. Rainsford, with an effort, held his tongue in check.

"It's a game, you see," pursued the general blandly. "I suggest to one of them that we go hunting. I give him a supply of food and an excellent hunting knife. I give him three hours' start. I am to follow, armed only with a pistol of the smallest caliber and range. If my quarry eludes me for three whole days, he wins the game. If I find him"—the general smiled—"he loses."

"Suppose he refuses to be hunted?"

"Oh," said the general, "I give him his option, of course. He need not play that game if he doesn't wish to. If he does not wish to hunt, I turn him over to Ivan. Ivan once had the honor of serving as official knouter to the Great White Czar, and he has his own ideas of sport. Invariably, Mr. Rainsford, invariably they choose the hunt."

"And if they win?"

The smile on the general's face widened. "To date I have not lost," he said.

Then he added, hastily: "I don't wish you to think me a braggart, Mr. Rainsford. Many of them afford only the most elementary sort of problem. Occasionally I strike a Tartar. One almost did win. I eventually had to use the dogs."

"The dogs?"

"This way, please. I'll show you."

The general steered Rainsford to a window. The lights from the windows sent a flickering illumination that made grotesque patterns on the courtyard below, and Rainsford could see moving about there a dozen or so huge black shapes; as they turned toward him, their eyes glittered greenly.

"A rather good lot, I think," observed the general. "They are let out at seven every night. If anyone should try to get into my house—or out of it—something extremely regrettable would occur to him." He hummed a snatch of song from the Folies Bergère.

"And now," said the general, "I want to show you my new collection of heads. Will you come with me to the library?"

"I hope," said Rainsford, "that you will excuse me tonight, General Zaroff. I'm really not feeling at all well."

"Ah, indeed?" the general inquired solicitously. "Well, I suppose that's only natural, after your long swim. You need a good, restful night's sleep. Tomorrow you'll feel like a new man, I'll wager. Then we'll hunt, eh? I've one rather promising prospect—"

Rainsford was hurrying from the room.

"Sorry you can't go with me tonight," called the general. "I expect rather fair sport—a big, strong black. He looks resourceful— Well, good night, Mr. Rainsford; I hope you have a good night's rest."

The bed was good, and the pajamas of the softest silk, and he was tired in every fiber of his being, but nevertheless Rainsford could not quiet his brain with the opiate of sleep. He lay, eyes wide open. Once he thought he heard stealthy steps in the corridor outside his room. He sought to throw open the door; it would not open. He went to the window and looked out. His room was high up in one of the towers. The lights of the château were out now, and it was dark and silent, but there was a fragment of sallow moon, and by its wan light he could see, dimly, the courtyard; there, weaving in and out in the pattern of shadow, were black, noiseless forms; the hounds heard him at the window and looked up, expectantly, with their green eyes. Rainsford went back to the bed and lay down. By many methods he tried to put himself to sleep. He had achieved a doze when, just as morning began to come, he heard, far off in the jungle, the faint report of a pistol.

General Zaroff did not appear until luncheon. He was dressed faultlessly in the tweeds of a country squire. He was solicitous about the state of Rainsford's health.

"As for me," sighed the general, "I do not feel so well. I am worried, Mr. Rainsford. Last night I detected traces of my old complaint."

To Rainsford's questioning glance the general said: "Ennui. Boredom."

Then, taking a second helping of Crêpes Suzette, the general explained: "The hunting was not good last night. The fellow lost his head. He made a straight trail that offered no problems at all. That's the trouble with these sailors; they have dull brains to begin with, and they do not know how to get about in the woods. They do excessively stupid and obvious things. It's most annoying. Will you have another glass of Chablis, Mr. Rainsford?"

"General," said Rainsford firmly, "I wish to leave this island at once."

The general raised his thickets of eyebrows; he seemed hurt. "But, my dear fellow," the general protested, "you've only just come. You've had no hunting—"

"I wish to go today," said Rainsford. He saw the dead black eyes of the general on him, studying him. General Zaroff's face suddenly brightened.

He filled Rainsford's glass with venerable Chablis from a dusty bottle.

"Tonight," said the general, "we will hunt—you and I."

Rainsford shook his head. "No, general," he said. "I will not hunt."

The general shrugged his shoulders and delicately ate a hothouse grape. "As you wish, my friend," he said. "The choice rests entirely with you. But may I not venture to suggest that you will find my idea of sport more diverting than Ivan's?"

He nodded toward the corner to where the giant stood, scowling, his thick arms crossed on his hogshead of chest.

"You don't mean—" cried Rainsford.

"My dear fellow," said the general, "have I not told you I always mean what I say about hunting? This is really an inspiration. I drink to a foeman worthy of my steel—at last."

The general raised his glass, but Rainsford sat staring at him.

"You'll find this game worth playing," the general said enthusiastically. "Your brain against mine. Your woodcraft against mine. Your strength and stamina against mine. Outdoor chess! And the stake is not without value, eh?"

"And if I win—" began Rainsford huskily.

"I'll cheerfully acknowledge myself defeated if I do not find you by midnight of the third day," said General Zaroff. "My sloop will place you on the mainland near a town."

The general read what Rainsford was thinking.

"Oh, you can trust me," said the Cossack. "I will give you my word as a gentleman and a sportsman. Of course you, in turn, must agree to say nothing of your visit here."

"I'll agree to nothing of the kind," said Rainsford.

"Oh," said the general, "in that case— But why discuss that now? Three days hence we can discuss it over a bottle of Veuve Cliquot, unless—"

The general sipped his wine.

Then a businesslike air animated him. "Ivan," he said to Rainsford, "will supply you with hunting clothes, food, a knife. I suggest you wear moccasins; they leave a poorer trail. I suggest too that you avoid the big swamp in the southeast corner of the island. We call it Death Swamp. There's quicksand there. One foolish fellow tried it. The deplorable part of it was that Lazarus followed him. You can imagine my feelings, Mr. Rainsford. I loved Lazarus; he was the finest hound in my pack. Well, I must beg you to excuse me now. I always take a siesta after lunch. You'll hardly have time for a nap, I fear. You'll want to start, no doubt. I shall not follow till dusk. Hunting at night is so much more exciting than by day, don't you think? Au revoir, Mr. Rainsford, au revoir."

General Zaroff, with a deep, courtly bow, strolled from the room.

From another door came Ivan. Under one arm he carried khaki hunting clothes, a haversack of food, a leather sheath containing a long-bladed hunting knife; his right hand rested on a cocked revolver thrust in the crimson sash about his waist. . . .

Rainsford had fought his way through the bush for two hours. "I must keep my nerve. I must keep my nerve," he said through tight teeth.

He had not been entirely clear-headed when the château gates snapped shut behind him. His whole idea at first was to put distance between himself and General Zaroff, and, to this end, he had plunged along, spurred on by the sharp rowels of something very like panic. Now he had got a grip on himself, had stopped, and was taking stock of himself and the situation.

He saw that straight flight was futile; inevitably it would bring him face to face with the sea. He was in a picture with a frame of water, and his operations, clearly, must take place within that frame.

"I'll give him a trail to follow," muttered Rainsford, and he struck off from the rude path he had been following into the trackless wilderness. He executed a series of intricate loops; he doubled on his trail again and again, recalling all the lore of the fox hunt, and all the dodges of the fox. Night found him leg-weary, with hands and face lashed by the branches, on a thickly wooded ridge. He knew it would be insane to blunder on through the dark, even if he had the strength. His need for rest was imperative and he thought: "I have played the fox, now I must play the cat of the fable." A big tree with a thick trunk and outspread branches was near by, and, taking care to leave not the slightest mark, he climbed up into the crotch, and stretching out on one of the broad limbs, after a fashion, rested. Rest brought him new confidence and almost a feeling of security. Even so zealous a hunter as General Zaroff could not trace him there, he told himself; only the devil himself could follow that complicated trail through the jungle after dark. But, perhaps, the general was a devil—

An apprehensive night crawled slowly by like a wounded snake, and sleep did not visit Rainsford, although the silence of a dead world was on the jungle.

Toward morning when a dingy gray was varnishing the sky, the cry of some startled bird focused Rainsford's attention in that direction. Something was coming through the bush, coming slowly, carefully, coming by the same winding way Rainsford had come. He flattened himself down on the limb, and through a screen of leaves almost as thick as tapestry, he watched. The thing that was approaching was a man.

It was General Zaroff. He made his way along with his eyes fixed in utmost concentration on the ground before him. He paused, almost beneath the tree, dropped to his knees and studied the ground. Rainsford's impulse was to hurl himself down like a panther, but he saw that the general's right hand held something metallic—a small automatic pistol.

The hunter shook his head several times, as if he were puzzled. Then he straightened up and took from his case one of his black cigarettes; its pungent incenselike smoke floated up to Rainsford's nostrils.

Rainsford held his breath. The general's eyes had left the ground and were traveling inch by inch up the tree. Rainsford froze there, every muscle tensed for a spring. But the sharp eyes of the hunter stopped before they reached the limb where Rainsford lay; a smile spread over his brown face. Very deliberately he blew a smoke ring into the air; then he turned his back on the tree and walked carelessly away, back along the trail he had come. The swish of the underbrush against his hunting-boots grew fainter and fainter.

The pent-up air burst hotly from Rainsford's lungs.

His first thought made him feel sick and numb. The general could follow a trail through the woods at night; he could follow an extremely difficult trail; he must have uncanny powers; only by the merest chance had the Cossack failed to see his quarry.

Rainsford's second thought was even more terrible. It sent a shudder of cold horror through his whole being. Why had the general smiled? Why had he turned back?

Rainsford did not want to believe what his reason told him was true, but the truth was as evident as the sun that had by now pushed through the morning mists. The general was playing with him! The general was saving him for another day's sport! The Cossack was the cat; he was the mouse. Then it was that Rainsford knew the full meaning of terror.

"I will not lose my nerve. I will not."

He slid down from the tree, and struck off again into the woods. His face was set and he forced the machinery of his mind to function. Three hundred yards from his hiding-place he stopped where a huge dead tree leaned precariously on a smaller, living one. Throwing off his sack of food, Rainsford took his knife from its sheath and began to work with all his energy.

The job was finished at last, and he threw himself down behind a fallen log a hundred feet away. He did not have to wait long. The cat was coming again to play with the mouse.

Following the trail with the sureness of a bloodhound, came General Zaroff. Nothing escaped those searching black eyes, no crushed blade of grass, no bent twig, no mark, no matter how faint, in the moss. So intent was the Cossack on his stalking that he was upon the thing Rainsford had made before he saw it. His foot touched the protruding bough that was the trigger. Even as he touched it, the general sensed his danger and leaped back with the agility of an ape. But he was not quite quick enough; the dead tree, delicately adjusted to rest on the cut living one, crashed down and struck the general a glancing blow on the shoulder as it fell; but for his alertness, he must have been smashed beneath it. He staggered, but he did not fall; nor did he drop his revolver. He stood there, rubbing his injured shoulder, and Rainsford, with fear again gripping his heart, heard the general's mocking laugh ring through the jungle.

"Rainsford," called the general, "if you are within sound of my voice, as I suppose you are, let me congratulate you. Not many men know how to make a Malay man-catcher. Luckily, for me, I too have hunted in Malacca. You are proving interesting, Mr. Rainsford. I am going now to have my wound dressed; it's only a slight one. But I shall be back. I shall be back."

When the general, nursing his bruised shoulder, had gone, Rainsford took up his flight again. It was flight now, a desperate, hopeless flight, that carried him on for some hours. Dusk came, then darkness, and still he pressed on. The ground grew softer under his moccasins; the vegetation grew ranker, denser; insects bit him savagely. Then, as he stepped forward, his foot sank into the ooze. He tried to wrench it back, but the muck sucked viciously at his foot as if it were a giant leech. With a violent effort he tore his foot loose. He knew where he was now. Death Swamp and its quicksand.

His hands were tight closed as if his nerve were something tangible that someone in the darkness was trying to tear from his grip. The softness of the earth had given him an idea. He stepped back from the quicksand a dozen feet or so and, like some huge prehistoric beaver, he began to dig.

Rainsford had dug himself in in France when a second's delay meant death. That had been a placid pastime compared to his digging now. The pit grew deeper; when it was above his shoulders, he climbed out and from some hard saplings cut stakes and sharpened them to a fine point. These stakes he planted in the bottom of the pit with the points sticking up. With flying fingers he wove a rough carpet of weeds and branches and with it he covered the mouth of the pit. Then, wet with sweat and aching with tiredness, he crouched behind the stump of a lightning-charred tree.

He knew his pursuer was coming; he heard the padding sound of feet on the soft earth, and the night breeze brought him the perfume of the general's cigarette. It seemed to Rainsford that the general was coming with unusual swiftness; he was not feeling his way along, foot by foot. Rainsford, crouching there, could not see the general, nor could he see the pit. He lived a year in a minute. Then he felt an impulse to cry aloud with joy, for he heard the sharp crackle of the breaking branches as the cover of the pit gave way; he heard the sharp scream of pain as the pointed stakes found their mark. He leaped up from his place of concealment. Then he cowered back. Three feet from the pit a man was standing, with an electric torch in his hand.

"You've done well, Rainsford," the voice of the general called. "Your Burmese tiger pit has claimed one of my best dogs. Again you score. I think, Mr. Rainsford, I'll see what you can do against my whole pack. I'm going home for a rest now. Thank you for a most amusing evening."

At daybreak Rainsford, lying near the swamp, was awakened by a sound that made him know that he had new things to learn about fear. It was a distant sound, faint and wavering, but he knew it. It was the baying of a pack of hounds.

Rainsford knew he could do one of two things. He could stay where he was and wait. That was suicide. He could flee. That was postponing the inevitable. For a moment he stood there, thinking. An idea that held a wild chance came to him, and, tightening his belt, he headed away from the swamp. The baying of the hounds drew nearer, then still nearer, nearer, ever nearer. On a ridge Rainsford climbed a tree. Down a watercourse, not a quarter of a mile away, he could see the bush moving. Straining his eyes, he saw the lean figure of General Zaroff; just ahead of him Rainsford made out another figure whose wide shoulders surged through the tall jungle weeds; it was the giant Ivan, and he seemed pulled forward by some unseen force; Rainsford knew that Ivan must be holding the pack in leash.

They would be on him any minute now. His mind

worked frantically. He thought of a native trick he had learned in Uganda. He slid down the tree. He caught hold of a springy young sapling and to it he fastened his hunting knife, with the blade pointing down the trail; with a bit of wild grapevine he tied back the sapling. Then he ran for his life. The hounds raised their voices as they hit the fresh scent. Rainsford knew now how an animal at bay feels.

He had to stop to get his breath. The baying of the hounds stopped abruptly, and Rainsford's heart stopped too. They must have reached the knife.

He shinned excitedly up a tree and looked back. His pursuers had stopped. But the hope that was in Rainsford's brain when he climbed died, for he saw in the shallow valley that General Zaroff was still on his feet. But Ivan was not. The knife, driven by the recoil of the springing tree, had not wholly failed.

Rainsford had hardly tumbled to the ground when the pack took up the cry again.

"Nerve, nerve, nerve!" he panted, as he dashed along. A blue gap showed between the trees dead ahead. Ever nearer drew the hounds. Rainsford forced himself on toward that gap. He reached it. It was the shore of the sea. Across a cove he could see the gloomy gray stone of the château. Twenty feet below him the sea rumbled and hissed. Rainsford hesitated. He heard the hounds. Then he leaped far out into the sea. . . .

When the general and his pack reached the place by the sea, the Cossack stopped. For some minutes he stood regarding the blue-green expanse of water. He shrugged his shoulders. Then he sat down, took a drink of brandy from a silver flask, lit a perfumed cigarette, and hummed a bit from "Madame Butterfly."

General Zaroff had an exceedingly good dinner in his great paneled dining hall that evening. With it he had a bottle of Pol Roger and half a bottle of Chambertin. Two slight annoyances kept him from perfect enjoyment. One was the thought that it would be difficult to repla Ivan; the other was that his quarry had escaped him; course the American hadn't played the game—so thought the general as he tasted his after-dinner liqueur. In his library he read, to soothe himself, from the works of Marcus Aurelius. At ten he went up to his bedroom. He was deliciously tired, he said to himself, as he locked himself in. There was a little moonlight, so, before turning on his light, he went to the window and looked down at the courtyard. He could see the great hounds, and he called: "Better luck another time," to them. Then he switched on the light.

A man, who had been hiding in the curtains of the bed, was standing there.

"Rainsford!" screamed the general. "How in God's name did you get here?"

"Swam," said Rainsford. "I found it quicker than walking through the jungle."

The general sucked in his breath and smiled. "I congratulate you," he said. "You have won the game."

Rainsford did not smile. "I am still a beast at bay," he said, in a low, hoarse voice. "Get ready, General Zaroff."

The general made one of his deepest bows. "I see," he

said. "Splendid! One of us is to furnish a repast for the hounds. The other will sleep in this very excellent bed. On guard, Rainsford." . . .

He had never slept in a better bed, Rainsford decided.

FITZ-JAMES O'BRIEN

What Was It?

It is, I confess, with considerable diffidence that I approach the strange narrative which I am about to relate. The events which I purpose detailing are of so extraordinary a character that I am quite prepared to meet with an unusual amount of incredulity and scorn. I accept all such beforehand. I have, I trust, the literary courage to face unbelief. I have, after mature consideration, resolved to narrate, in as simple and straightforward a manner as I can compass, some facts that passed under my observation, in the month of July last, and which, in the annals of the mysteries of physical science, are wholly unparalleled.

I live at No. — Twenty-sixth Street, in New York. The house is in some respects a curious one. It has enjoyed for the last two years the reputation of being haunted.

It is a large and stately residence, surrounded by what was once a garden, but which is now only a green enclosure used for bleaching clothes. The dry basin of what has been a fountain, and a few fruit-trees, ragged and unpruned, indicate that this spot in past years was a pleasant, shady retreat, filled with fruits and flowers and the sweet murmur of waters.

The house is very spacious. A hall of noble size leads to a large spiral staircase winding through its center, while the various apartments are of imposing dimensions. It was built some fifteen or twenty years since by Mr. A——, the well-known New York merchant, who five years ago threw the commercial world into convulsions by a stupendous bank fraud. Mr. A——, as every one knows, escaped to Europe, and died not long after, of a broken heart. Almost immediately, after the news of his decease reached this country and was verified, the report spread in Twenty-sixth Street that No. — was haunted. Legal measures had dispossessed the widow of its former owner, and it was inhabited merely by a caretaker and his wife, placed there by the house agent into whose hands it had passed for the purpose of renting or sale. These people declared that they were troubled with unnatural noises. Doors were opened without any visible agency. The remnants of furniture scattered through the various rooms were, during the night, piled one upon the other by unknown hands. Invisible feet passed up and down the stairs in broad daylight, accompanied by the rustle of unseen silk dresses, and the gliding of viewless hands along the massive balusters.

The caretaker and his wife declared they would live there no longer. The house agent laughed, dismissed them, and put others in their place. The noises and supernatural manifestations continued. The neighborhood caught up the story, and the house remained untenanted for three years. Several persons negotiated for it; but, somehow, always before the bargain was closed they heard the unpleasant rumors, and declined to treat any further.

It was in this state of things that my landlady, who at that time kept a boarding-house in Bleecker Street, and who wished to move farther uptown, conceived the bold idea of renting No. —, Twenty-sixth Street. Happening to have in her house rather a plucky and philosophical set of boarders, she laid her scheme before us, stating candidly everything she had heard respecting the ghostly qualities of the establishment to which she wished to remove us. With the exception of two timid persons,—a sea-captain and a returned Californian, who immediately gave notice that they would leave,—all of Mrs. Moffat's guests declared that they would accompany her in her chivalric incursion into the abode of spirits.

Our removal was effected in the month of May, and we were charmed with our new residence. The portion of Twenty-sixth Street where our house is situated, between Seventh and Eighth Avenues, is one of the pleasantest localities in New York. The gardens back of the houses, running down nearly to the Hudson, form, in the summer-time, a perfect avenue of verdure. The air is pure and invigorating, sweeping, as it does, straight across the river from the Weehawken heights, and even the ragged garden which surrounded the house, although displaying on washing days rather too much clothesline, still gave us a piece of greensward to look at, and a cool retreat in the summer evenings, where we smoked our cigars in the dusk, and watched the fireflies flashing their dark-lanterns in the long grass.

Of course we had no sooner established ourselves at No. — than we began to expect ghosts. We absolutely awaited their advent with eagerness. Our dinner conversation was supernatural. One of the boarders, who had purchased Mrs. Crowe's "Night Side of Nature" for his own private delectation, was regarded as a public enemy by the entire household for not having bought twenty copies. The man led a life of supreme wretchedness while he was reading this volume. A system of espionage was established, of which he was the victim. If he incautiously laid the book down for an instant and left the room, it was immediately seized and read aloud in secret places to a select few. I found myself a person of immense importance, it having leaked out that I was tolerably well versed in the history of supernaturalism, and had once written a story, the foundation of which was a ghost. If a table or a wainscoat panel happened to warp when we were assembled in the large drawing-room, there was an instant silence, and every one was prepared for an immediate clanking of chains and a spectral form.

After a month of psychological excitement, it was with the utmost dissatisfaction that we were forced to acknowledge that nothing in the remotest degree approaching the supernatural had manifested itself. Once the black butler asseverated that his candle had been blown out by some invisible agency while he was undressing himself for the night; but as I had more than once discovered this colored gentleman in a condition when one candle must have appeared to him like two, I thought it possible that by going a step further in his potations, he might have reversed this phenomenon, and seen no candle at all where he ought to have beheld one.

Things were in this state when an accident took place so awful and inexplicable in its character that my reason fairly reels at the bare memory of the occurrence. It was the tenth of July. After dinner was over I repaired, with my friend Dr. Hammond, to the garden to smoke my evening pipe. Independent of certain mental sympathies which existed between the Doctor and myself, we were linked together by a vice. We both smoked opium. We knew each other's secret, and respected it. We enjoyed together that wonderful expansion of thought, that marvelous intensifying of the perceptive faculties, that boundless feeling of existence when we seem to have points of contact with the whole universe,—in short, that unimaginable spiritual bliss, which I would not surrender for a throne, and which I hope you, reader, will never—never taste.

Those hours of opium happiness which the Doctor and I spent together in secret were regulated with a scientific accuracy. We did not blindly smoke the drug of paradise, and leave our dreams to chance. While smoking, we carefully steered our conversation through the brightest and calmest channels of thought. We talked of the East, and endeavored to recall the magical panorama of its glowing scenery. We criticized the most sensuous poets,—those who painted life ruddy with health, brimming with passion, happy in the possession of youth and strength and beauty. If we talked of Shakespeare's "Tempest," we lingered over Ariel, and avoided Caliban. Like the Guebers, we turned our faces to the East, and saw only the sunny side of the world.

This skilful coloring of our train of thought produced in our subsequent visions a corresponding tone. The splendors of Arabian fairyland dyed our dreams. We paced the narrow strip of grass with the tread and port of kings. The song of the *rana arborea,* while he clung to the bark of the ragged plum-tree, sounded like the strains of divine musicians. Houses, walls and streets melted like rain clouds, and vistas of unimaginable glory stretched away before us. It was a rapturous companionship. We enjoyed the vast delight more perfectly because, even in our most ecstatic moments, we were conscious of each other's presence. Our pleasures, while individual, were still twin, vibrating and moving in musical accord.

On the evening in question, the tenth of July, the Doctor and myself drifted into an unusually metaphysical mood. We lit our large meerschaums, filled with fine Turkish tobacco, in the core of which burned a little black nut of opium, that, like the nut in the fairy-tale, held within its narrow limits wonders beyond the reach of kings; we paced to and fro, conversing. A strange perversity dominated the currents of our thought. They would *not* flow through the sunlit channels into which we strove to divert them. For some unaccountable reason, they constantly diverged into dark and lonesome beds, where a continual gloom brooded. It was in vain that, after our old fashion, we flung ourselves on the shores of the East, and talked of its gay bazaars, of the splendors of the time of Haroun, of harems and golden palaces. Black afreets continually arose from the depths of our talk, and expanded, like the one the fisherman released from the copper vessel, until they blotted everything bright from our vision. Insensibly, we yielded to the occult force that swayed us, and indulged in gloomy speculation. We had talked some time upon the proneness of the human mind to mysticism, and the almost universal love of the terrible, when Hammond suddenly said to me, "What do you consider to be the greatest element of terror?"

The question puzzled me. That many things were terrible, I knew. Stumbling over a corpse in the dark; beholding, as I once did, a woman floating down a deep and rapid river with wildly lifted arms, and awful, upturned face, uttering, as she drifted, shrieks that rent one's heart while we, spectators, stood frozen at a window which overhung the river at a height of sixty feet, unable to make the slightest effort to save her, but dumbly watching her last supreme agony and her disappearance. A shattered wreck, with no life visible, encountered floating listlessly on the ocean, is a terrible object, for it suggests a huge terror, the proportions of which are veiled. But it now struck me, for the first time, that there must be one great and ruling embodiment of fear,—a King of Terrors, to which all others must succumb. What might it be? To what train of circumstances would it owe its existence?

"I confess, Hammond," I replied to my friend, "I never considered the subject before. That there must be one Something more terrible than any other thing, I feel. I cannot attempt, however, even the most vague definition."

"I am somewhat like you, Harry," he answered. "I feel my capacity to experience a terror greater than anything yet conceived by the human mind;—something combining in fearful and unnatural amalgamation hitherto supposed incompatible elements. The calling of the voices in Brockden Brown's novel of 'Wieland' is awful; so is the picture of the Dweller of the Threshold, in Bulwer's 'Zanoni'; but," he added, shaking his head gloomily, "there is something more horrible still than those."

"Look here, Hammond," I rejoined, "let us drop this kind of talk, for Heaven's sake! We shall suffer for it, depend on it."

"I don't know what's the matter with me to-night," he replied, "but my brain is running upon all sorts of weird and awful thoughts. I feel as if I could write a story like Hoffmann, to-night, if I were only master of a literary style."

"Well, if we are going to be Hoffmannesque in our talk,

I'm off to bed. Opium and nightmares should never be brought together. How sultry it is! Good-night, Hammond."

"Good-night, Harry. Pleasant dreams to you."

"To you, gloomy wretch, afreets, ghouls and enchanters."

We parted, and each sought his respective chamber. I undressed quickly and got into bed, taking with me, according to my usual custom, a book, over which I generally read myself to sleep. I opened the volume as soon as I had laid my head upon the pillow, and instantly flung it to the other side of the room. It was Goudon's "History of Monsters,"—a curious French work, which I had lately imported from Paris, but which, in the state of mind I had then reached, was anything but an agreeable companion. I resolved to go to sleep at once; so, turning down my gas until nothing but a little blue point of light glimmered on the top of the tube, I composed myself to rest.

The room was in total darkness. The atom of gas that still remained alight did not illuminate a distance of three inches round the burner. I desperately drew my arm across my eyes, as if to shut out even the darkness, and tried to think of nothing. It was in vain. The confounded themes touched on by Hammond in the garden kept obtruding themselves on my brain. I battled against them. I erected ramparts of would-be blankness of intellect to keep them out. They still crowded upon me. While I was lying still as a corpse, hoping that by a perfect physical inaction I should hasten mental repose, an awful incident occurred. A Something dropped, as it seemed, from the ceiling, plumb upon my chest, and the next instant I felt two bony hands encircling my throat, endeavoring to choke me.

I am no coward, and am possessed of considerable physical strength. The suddenness of the attack, instead of stunning me, strung every nerve to its highest tension. My body acted from instinct, before my brain had time to realize the terrors of my position. In an instant I wound two muscular arms around the creature, and squeezed it, with all the strength of despair against my chest. In a few seconds the bony hands that had fastened on my throat loosened their hold, and I was free to breathe once more. Then commenced a struggle of awful intensity. Immersed in the most profound darkness, totally ignorant of the nature of the Thing by which I was so suddenly attacked, finding my grasp slipping every moment, by reason, it seemed to me, of the entire nakedness of my assailant, bitten with sharp teeth in the shoulder, neck, and chest, having every moment to protect my throat against a pair of sinewy, agile hands, which my utmost efforts could not confine,—these were a combination of circumstances to combat which required all the strength, skill, and courage that I possessed.

At last, after a silent, deadly, exhausting struggle, I got my assailant under by a series of incredible efforts of strength. Once pinned, with my knee on what I made out to be its chest, I knew that I was victor. I rested for a moment to breathe. I heard the creature beneath me panting in the darkness, and felt the violent throbbing of a heart. It was apparently as exhausted as I was! That was one comfort. At this moment I remembered that I usually placed under my pillow, before going to bed, a large yellow silk pocket handkerchief. I felt for it instantly; it was there. In a few seconds more I had, after a fashion, pinioned the creature's arms.

I now felt tolerably secure. There was nothing more to be done but to turn on the gas, and, having first seen what my midnight assailant was like, arouse the household. I will confess to being actuated by a certain pride in not giving the alarm before; I wished to make the capture alone and unaided.

Never losing my hold for an instant, I slipped from the bed to the floor, dragging my captive with me. I had but a few steps to make to reach the gasburner; these I made with the greatest caution, holding the creature in a grip like a vise. At last I got within arm's length of the tiny speck of blue light which told me where the gas-burner lay. Quick as lightning I released my grasp with one hand and let on the full flood of light. Then I turned to look at my captive.

I cannot even attempt to give any definition of my sensations the instant after I turned on the gas. I suppose I must have shrieked with terror, for in less than a minute afterward my room was crowded with the inmates of the house. I shudder now as I think of that awful moment. *I saw nothing!* Yes; I had one arm firmly clasped round a breathing, panting, corporeal shape, my other hand gripped with all its strength a throat as warm, as apparently fleshy, as my own; and yet, with this living substance in my grasp, with its body pressed against my own, and all in the bright glare of a large jet of gas, I absolutely beheld nothing! Not even an outline,—a vapor!

I do not, even at this hour, realize the situation in which I found myself. I cannot recall the astounding incident thoroughly. Imagination in vain tries to compass the awful paradox.

It breathed. I felt its warm breath upon my cheek. It struggled fiercely. It had hands. They clutched me. Its skin was smooth, like my own. There it lay, pressed close up against me, solid as stone,—and yet utterly invisible!

I wonder that I did not faint or go mad, on the instant. Some wonderful instinct must have sustained me; for, absolutely, in place of loosening my hold on the terrible Enigma, I seemed to gain an additional strength in my moment of horror, and tightened my grasp with such wonderful force that I felt the creature shivering with agony.

Just then Hammond entered my room at the head of the household. As soon as he beheld my face—which, I suppose, must have been an awful sight to look at—he hastened forward, crying, "Great heaven, Harry! What has happened?"

"Hammond! Hammond!" I cried, "come here. Oh, this is awful! I have been attacked in bed by something or other, which I have hold of; but I can't see it,—can't see it!"

Hammond, doubtless struck by the unfeigned horror

expressed in my countenance, made one or two steps forward with an anxious yet puzzled expression. A very audible titter burst from the remainder of my visitors. This suppressed laughter made me furious. To laugh at a human being in my position! It was the worst species of cruelty. *Now,* I can understand why the appearance of a man struggling violently, as it would seem, with an airy nothing, and calling for assistance against a vision, should have appeared ludicrous. *Then,* so great was my rage against the mocking crowd that had I the power I would have stricken them dead where they stood.

"Hammond! Hammond!" I cried again, despairingly, "for God's sake, come to me. I can hold the—the thing but a short while longer. It is overpowering me. Help me! Help me!"

"Harry," whispered Hammond, approaching me, "you have been smoking too much opium."

"I swear to you, Hammond, that this is no vision," I answered, in the same low tone. "Don't you see how it shakes my whole frame with its struggles? If you don't believe me, convince yourself. Feel it,—touch it."

Hammond advanced and laid his hand in the spot I indicated. A wild cry of horror burst from him. He had felt it!

In a moment he had discovered somewhere in my room a long piece of cord, and was the next instant winding it and knotting it about the body of the unseen being that I clasped in my arms.

"Harry," he said, in a hoarse, agitated voice, for,

though he preserved his presence of mind, he was deeply moved, "Harry, it's all safe now. You may let go, old fellow, if you're tired. The Thing can't move."

I was utterly exhausted, and I gladly loosed my hold.

Hammond stood holding the ends of the cord that bound the Invisible, twisted round his hand, while before him, self-supporting as it were, he beheld a rope laced and interlaced, and stretching tightly around a vacant space. I never saw a man look so thoroughly stricken with awe. Nevertheless his face expressed all the courage and determination which I knew him to possess. His lips, although white, were set firmly, and one could perceive at a glance, that, although stricken with fear, he was not daunted.

The confusion that ensued among the guests of the house who were witnesses of this extraordinary scene between Hammond and myself,—who beheld the pantomine of binding this struggling Something,—who, beheld me almost sinking from physical exhaustion when my task of jailer was over,—the confusion and terror that took possession of the bystanders, when they saw all this, was beyond description. The weaker ones fled from the apartment. The few who remained clustered near the door and could not be induced to approach Hammond and his Charge. Still incredulity broke out through their terror. They had not the courage to satisfy themselves, and yet they doubted. It was in vain that I begged of some of the men to come near and convince themselves by touch of the existence in that room of a living being which was invisible. They were incredulous, but did not dare to undeceive themselves. How could a solid, living, breathing body be invisible, they asked. My reply was this. I gave a sign to Hammond, and both of us—conquering our fearful repugnance to touch the invisible creature—lifted it from the ground, manacled as it was, and took it to my bed. Its weight was about that of a boy of fourteen.

"Now, my friends," I said, as Hammond and myself held the creature suspended over the bed, "I can give you self-evident proof that here is a solid, ponderable body, which, nevertheless, you cannot see. Be good enough to watch the surface of the bed attentively."

I was astonished at my own courage in treating this strange event so calmly; but I had recovered from my first terror, and felt a sort of scientific pride in the affair, which dominated every other feeling.

The eyes of the bystanders were immediately fixed on my bed. At a given signal Hammond and I let the creature fall. There was a dull sound of a heavy body alighting on a soft mass. The timbers of the bed creaked. A deep impression marked itself distinctly on the pillow, and on the bed itself. The crowd who witnessed this gave a low cry, and rushed from the room. Hammond and I were left alone with our Mystery.

We remained silent for some time, listening to the low, irregular breathing of the creature on the bed, and watching the rustle of the bedclothes as it impotently struggled to free itself from confinement. Then Hammond spoke.

"Harry, this is awful."

"Aye, awful."

"But not unaccountable."

"Not unaccountable. What do you mean? Such a thing has never occurred since the birth of the world. I know not what to think, Hammond. God grant that I am not mad, and that this is not an insane fantasy!"

"Let us reason a little, Harry. Here is a solid body which we touch, but which we cannot see. The fact is so unusual that it strikes us with terror. Is there no parallel, though, for such a phenomenon? Take a piece of pure glass. It is tangible and transparent. A certain chemical coarseness is all that prevents its being so entirely transparent as to be totally invisible. It is not *theoretically impossible,* mind you, to make a glass which shall not reflect a single ray of light,—a glass so pure and homogeneous in its atoms that the rays from the sun will pass through it as they do through the air, refracted but not reflected. We do not see the air, and yet we feel it."

"That's all very well, Hammond, but these are inanimate substances. Glass does not breathe, air does not breathe. *This* thing has a heart that palpitates,—a will that moves it,—lungs that play, and inspire and respire."

"You forget the phenomena of which we have so often heard of late," answered the Doctor, gravely. "At the meetings called 'spirit circles,' invisible hands have been thrust into the hands of those persons round the table,—warm, fleshly hands that seemed to pulsate with mortal life."

"What? Do you think, then, that this thing is—"

"I don't know what it is," was the solemn reply; "but

please the gods I will, with your assistance, thoroughly investigate it."

We watched together, smoking many pipes, all night long, by the bedside of the unearthly being that tossed and panted until it was apparently wearied out. Then we learned by the low, regular breathing that it slept.

The next morning the house was all astir. The boarders congregated on the landing outside my room, and Hammond and myself were lions. We had to answer a thousand questions as to the state of our extraordinary prisoner, for as yet not one person in the house except ourselves could be induced to set foot in the apartment.

The creature was awake. This was evidenced by the convulsive manner in which the bedclothes were moved in its efforts to escape. There was something truly terrible in beholding, as it were, those second-hand indications of the terrible writhings and agonized struggles for liberty which themselves were invisible.

Hammond and myself had racked our brains during the long night to discover some means by which we might realize the shape and general appearance of the Enigma. As well as we could make out by passing our hands over the creature's form, its outlines and lineaments were human. There was a mouth, a round, smooth head without hair; a nose, which, however, was little elevated above the cheeks; and its hands and feet felt like those of a boy. At first we thought of placing the being on a smooth surface and tracing its outlines with chalk, as shoemakers trace the outline of the foot. This plan was given up as being of no value. Such an outline would give not the slightest idea of its conformation.

A happy thought struck me. We would take a cast of it in plaster of Paris. This would give us the solid figure, and satisfy all our wishes. But how to do it? The movements of the creature would disturb the setting of the plastic covering, and distort the mold. Another thought. Why not give it chloroform? It had respiratory organs,—that was evident by its breathing. Once reduced to a state of insensibility, we could do with it what we would. Doctor X—— was sent for; and after the worthy physician had recovered from the first shock of amazement, he proceeded to administer the chloroform. In three minutes afterward we were enabled to remove the fetters from the creature's body, and a modeler was busily engaged in covering the invisible form with the moist clay. In five minutes more we had a mold, and before evening a rough facsimile of the Mystery. It was shaped like a man,—distorted, uncouth, and horrible, but still a man. It was small, not over four feet and some inches in height, and its limbs revealed a muscular development that was unparalleled. Its face surpassed in hideousness anything I had ever seen. Gustav Doré, or Callot, or Tony Johannot, never conceived anything so horrible. There is a face in one of the latter's illustrations to *Un voyage où il vous plaira,* which somewhat approaches the countenance of this creature, but does not equal it. It was the physiognomy of what I should fancy a ghoul might be. It looked as if it was capable of feeding on human flesh.

Having satisfied our curiosity, and bound every one in

the house to secrecy, it became a question what was to be done with our Enigma? It was impossible that we should keep such a horror in our house; it was equally impossible that such an awful being should be let loose upon the world. I confess that I would have gladly voted for the creature's destruction. But who would shoulder the responsibility? Who would undertake the execution of this horrible semblance of a human being? Day after day this question was deliberated gravely. The boarders all left the house. Mrs. Moffat was in despair, and threatened Hammond and myself with all sorts of legal penalties if we did not remove the Horror. Our answer was, "We will go if you like, but we decline taking this creature with us. Remove it yourself, if you please. It appeared in your house. On you the responsibility rests." To this there was, of course, no answer. Mrs. Moffat could not obtain for love or money a person who would even approach the Mystery.

The most singular part of the affair was that we were entirely ignorant of what the creature habitually fed on. Everything in the way of nutriment that we could think of was placed before it, but was never touched. It was awful to stand by, day after day, and see the clothes toss, and hear the hard breathing, and know that it was starving.

Ten, twelve days, a fortnight passed, and it still lived. The pulsations of the heart, however, were daily growing fainter, and had now nearly ceased. It was evident that the creature was dying for want of sustenance. While this terrible life-struggle was going on, I felt miserable. I could not sleep. Horrible as the creature was, it was pitiful to think of the pangs it was suffering.

At last it died. Hammond and I found it cold and stiff one morning in the bed. The heart had ceased to beat, the lungs to inspire. We hastened to bury it in the garden. It was a strange funeral, the dropping of that viewless corpse into the damp hole. The cast of its form I gave to Doctor X——, who keeps it in his museum in Tenth Street.

As I am on the eve of a long journey from which I may not return, I have drawn up this narrative of an event the most singular that has ever come to my knowledge.

EDGAR ALLAN POE

The Masque of the Red Death

The "Red Death" had long devastated the country. No pestilence had ever been so fatal, or so hideous. Blood was its Avator and its seal—the redness and the horror of blood. There were sharp pains, and sudden dizziness, and then profuse bleeding at the pores, with dissolution. The scarlet stains upon the body and especially upon the face of the victim, were the pest ban which shut him out from the aid and from the sympathy of his fellow-men. And the whole seizure, progress and termination of the disease, were the incidents of half an hour.

But the Prince Prospero was happy and dauntless and sagacious. When his dominions were half depopulated, he summoned to his presence a thousand hale and light-hearted friends from among the knights and dames of his court, and with these retired to the deep seclusion of one of his castellated abbeys. This was an extensive and magnificent structure, the creation of the prince's own eccentric yet august taste. A strong and lofty wall girdled it in. This wall had gates of iron. The courtiers, having entered, brought furnaces and massy hammers and welded the bolts. They resolved to leave means neither of ingress or egress to the sudden impulses of despair or of frenzy from within. The abbey was amply provisioned. With such precautions the courtiers might bid defiance to contagion. The external world could take care of itself. In the meantime it was folly to grieve, or to think. The prince had provided all the appliances of pleasure. There were buffoons, there were improvisatori, there were ballet-dancers, there were musicians, there was Beauty, there was wine. All these and security were within. Without was the "Red Death."

It was toward the close of the fifth or sixth month of his seclusion, and while the pestilence raged most furiously abroad, that the Prince Prospero entertained his thousand friends at a masked ball of the most unusual magnificence.

It was a voluptuous scene, that masquerade. But first let me tell of the rooms in which it was held. There were seven—an imperial suite. In many palaces, however, such suites form a long and straight vista, while the folding doors slide back nearly to the walls on either hand, so that the view of the whole extent is scarcely impeded. Here the case was very different; as might have been expected from the duke's love of the *bizarre*. The apartments were so irregularly disposed that the vision embraced but little more than one at a time. There was a sharp turn at every twenty or thirty yards, and at each turn a novel effect. To the right and left, in the middle of each wall, a tall and narrow Gothic window looked out upon a closed corridor which pursued the windings of the suite. These windows were of stained glass whose color varied in accordance with the prevailing hue of the decorations of the chamber into which it opened. That at the eastern extremity was hung, for example, in blue—and vividly blue were its windows. The second chamber was purple in its ornaments and tapestries, and here the panes were purple. The third was green throughout, and so were the casements. The fourth was furnished and lighted with orange—the fifth with white—the sixth with violet. The seventh apartment was closely shrouded in black velvet tapestries that hung all over the ceiling and down the walls, falling in heavy folds upon a carpet of the same material and hue. But in this chamber only, the color of the windows failed to correspond with the decorations. The panes here were scarlet—a deep blood color. Now in no one of the seven apartments was there any lamp or candelabrum, amid the profusion of golden ornaments that lay scattered to and fro or depended from the roof. There was no light of any kind emanating from lamp or candle within the suite of chambers. But in the corridors that followed the suite, there stood, opposite to each window, a heavy tripod, bearing a brazier of fire that projected its rays through the tinted glass and so glaringly illumined the room. And thus were produced a multitude of gaudy and fantastic appearances. But in the western or black chamber the effect of the fire-light that streamed upon the dark hangings through the blood-tinted panes, was ghastly in the extreme, and produced so wild a look upon the countenances of those who entered, that there were few of the company bold enough to set foot within its precincts at all.

It was in this apartment, also, that there stood against the western wall, a gigantic clock of ebony. Its pendulum swung to and fro with a dull, heavy, monotonous clang; and when the minute-hand made the circuit of the face, and the hour was to be stricken, there came from the brazen lungs of the clock a sound which was clear and loud and deep and exceedingly musical, but of so peculiar a note and emphasis that, at each lapse of an hour, the musicians of the orchestra were constrained to pause, momentarily, in their performance, to hearken to the sound; and thus the waltzers perforce ceased their evolutions; and there was a brief disconcert of the whole gay company; and, while the chimes of the clock yet rang, it was observed that the giddiest grew pale, and the more aged and sedate passed their hands over their brows as if in confused revery or meditation. But when the echoes had fully ceased, a light laughter at once pervaded the assembly; the musicians looked at each other and smiled as if at their own nervousness and folly, and made whispering vows, each to the other, that the next chiming of the clock should produce in them no similar emotion; and then, after the lapse of sixty minutes (which embrace three thousand and six hundred seconds of the Time that flies), there came yet another chiming of the clock, and then were the same disconcert and tremulousness and meditation as before.

But, in spite of these things, it was a gay and magnificent revel. The tastes of the duke were peculiar. He had a fine eye for colors and effects. He disregarded the *decora* of mere fashion. His plans were bold and fiery, and his conceptions glowed with barbaric lustre. There are some who would have thought him mad. His followers felt that he was not. It was necessary to hear and see and touch him to be *sure* that he was not.

He had directed, in great part, the movable embellishments of the seven chambers, upon occasion of this great *fête;* and it was his own guiding taste which had given character to the masqueraders. Be sure they were grotesque. There were much glare and glitter and piquancy and phantasm—much of what has been since seen in "Hernani." There were arabesque figures with unsuited limbs and appointments. There were delirious fancies such as the madman fashions. There was much of the beautiful, much of the wanton, much of the *bizarre*, something of the terrible, and not a little of that which might have excited disgust. To and fro in the seven chambers there stalked, in fact, a multitude of dreams. And these—the dreams—writhed in and about, taking hue from the rooms, and causing the wild music of the orchestra to seem as the echo of their steps. And, anon, there strikes the ebony clock which stands in the hall of the velvet. And then, for a moment, all is still, and all is silent save the voice of the clock. The dreams are stiff-frozen as they stand. But the echoes of the chime die away—they have endured but an instant—and a light, half-subdued laughter floats after them as they depart. And now again the music swells, and the dreams live, and writhe to and fro more merrily than ever, taking hue from the many tinted windows through which stream the rays from the tripods. But to the chamber which lies most westwardly of the seven, there are now none of the maskers who venture; for the night is waning away; and there flows a ruddier light through the blood-colored panes; and the blackness of the sable drapery appalls; and to him whose foot falls upon the sable carpet, there comes from the near clock of ebony a muffled peal more solemnly emphatic than any which reaches *their* ears who indulge in the more remote gayeties of the other apartments.

But these other apartments were densely crowded, and in them beat feverishly the heart of life. And the revel went whirlingly on, until at length there commenced the sounding of midnight upon the clock. And then the music ceased, as I have told; and the evolutions of the waltzers were quieted; and there was an uneasy cessation of all things as before. But now there were twelve strokes to be sounded by the bell of the clock; and thus it happened, perhaps, that before the last echoes of the last chime had utterly sunk into silence, there were many individuals in the crowd who had found leisure to become aware of the presence of a masked figure which had arrested the attention of no single individual before. And the rumor of this new presence having spread itself whisperingly around, there arose at length from the whole company, a buzz, or murmur, expressive of disapprobation and surprise—then, finally, of terror, of horror, and of disgust.

In an assembly of phantasms such as I have painted, it may well be supposed that no ordinary appearance could have excited such sensation. In truth the masquerade license of the night was nearly unlimited; but the figure in question had out-Heroded Herod, and gone beyond the bounds of even the prince's indefinite decorum. There are chords in the hearts of the most reckless which cannot be touched without emotion. Even with the utterly lost, to whom life and death are equally jests, there are matters of which no jest can be made. The whole company, indeed, seemed now deeply to feel that in the costume and bearing of the stranger neither wit nor propriety existed. The figure was tall and gaunt, and shrouded from head to foot in the habiliments of the grave. The mask which concealed the visage was made so nearly to resemble the countenance of a stiffened corpse that the closest scrutiny must have had difficulty in detecting the cheat. And yet all this might have been endured, if not approved, by the mad revellers around. But the mummer had gone so far as to assume the type of the "Red Death." His vesture was dabbled in *blood*—and his broad brow, with all the features of the face, was besprinkled with the scarlet horror.

When the eyes of Prince Prospero fell upon this spectral image (which with a slow and solemn movement, as if more fully to sustain its *rôle,* stalked to and fro among the waltzers) he was seen to be convulsed, in the first moment, with a strong shudder either of terror or distaste; but, in the next, his brow reddened with rage.

"Who dares?" he demanded hoarsely of the courtiers who stood near him—"who dares insult us with this blasphemous mockery? Seize him and unmask him—that we may know whom we have to hang at sunrise, from the battlements!"

It was in the eastern or blue chamber in which stood the Prince Prospero as he uttered these words. They rang throughout the seven rooms loudly and clearly—for the prince was a bold and robust man, and the music had become hushed at the waving of his hand.

It was in the blue room where stood the prince, with a group of pale courtiers by his side. At first, as he spoke, there was a slight rushing movement of this group in the direction of the intruder, who at the moment was also near at hand, and now, with deliberate and stately step, made closer approach to the speaker. But from a certain nameless awe with which the mad assumptions of the mummer had inspired the whole party, there were found none who put forth hand to seize him; so that, unimpeded, he passed within a yard of the prince's person; and, while the vast assembly, as if with one impulse, shrank from the centres of the room to the walls, he made his way uninterruptedly, but with the same solemn and measured step which had distinguished him from the first, through the blue chamber to the purple—through the purple to the green—through the green to the orange—through this again to the white—and even thence to the violet, ere a decided movement had been made to arrest him. It was then, however, that the Prince Prospero, maddening with rage and the shame of his own momentary cowardice, rushed hurriedly through the six chambers, while none followed him on account of a deadly terror that had seized upon all. He bore aloft a drawn dagger, and had approached, in rapid impetuosity, to within three or four feet of the retreating figure, when the latter, having attained the extremity of the velvet apartment, turned suddenly and confronted his pursuer. There was a sharp cry—and the dagger dropped gleaming upon the sable carpet, upon which, instantly afterwards, fell prostrate in death the Prince Prospero. Then, summoning the wild courage of despair, a throng of the revellers at once threw themselves into the black apartment, and, seizing the mummer, whose tall figure stood erect and motionless within the shadow of the ebony clock, gasped in unutterable horror at finding the grave-cerements and corpse-like mask which they handled with so violent a rudeness, untenanted by any tangible form.

And now was acknowledged the presence of the "Red Death." He had come like a thief in the night. And one by one dropped the revellers in the blood-bedewed halls of their revel, and died each in the despairing posture of his fall. And the life of the ebony clock went out with that of the last of the gay. And the flames of the tripods expired. And Darkness and Decay and the "Red Death" held illimitable dominion over all.

AMBROSE BIERCE

An Occurrence at Owl Creek Bridge

I

A man stood upon a railroad bridge in Northern Alabama, looking down into the swift waters twenty feet below. The man's hands were behind his back, the wrists bound with a cord. A rope loosely encircled his neck. It was attached to a stout cross-timber above his head, and the slack fell to the level of his knees. Some loose boards laid upon the sleepers supporting the metals of the railway supplied a footing for him and his executioners—two private soldiers of the Federal army, directed by a sergeant, who in civil life may have been a deputy sheriff. At a short remove upon the same temporary platform was an officer in the uniform of his rank, armed. He was a captain. A sentinel at each end of the bridge stood with his rifle in the position known as "support," that is to say, vertical in front of the left shoulder, the hammer resting on the forearm thrown straight across the chest—a formal and unnatural position, enforcing an erect carriage of the body. It did not appear to be the duty of these two men to know what was occurring at the center of the bridge; they merely blockaded the two ends of the foot-plank which traversed it.

Beyond one of the sentinels nobody was in sight; the railroad ran straight away into a forest for a hundred yards, then, curving, was lost to view. Doubtless there was an outpost further along. The other bank of the stream was open ground—a gentle acclivity crowned with a stockade of vertical tree-trunks, loopholed for rifles, with a single embrasure through which protruded the muzzle of a brass cannon commanding the bridge. Midway up the slope between the bridge and fort were the spectators—a single company of infantry in line, at "parade rest," the butts of the rifles on the ground, the barrels inclining slightly backward against the right shoulder, the hands crossed upon the stock. A lieutenant stood at the right of the line, the point of his sword upon the ground, his left hand resting upon his right. Excepting the group of four at the center of the bridge not a man moved. The company faced the bridge, staring stonily, motionless. The sentinels, facing the banks of the stream, might have been statues to adorn the bridge. The captain stood with folded arms, silent, observing the work of his subordinates, but making no sign. Death is a dignitary who, when he comes announced, is to be received with formal manifestations of respect, even by those most familiar with him. In the code of military etiquette silence and fixity are forms of deference.

The man who was engaged in being hanged was apparently about thirty-five years of age. He was a civilian, if one might judge from his dress, which was that of a planter. His features were good—a straight nose, firm mouth, broad forehead, from which his long, dark hair was combed straight back, falling behind his ears to the collar of his well-fitting frock coat. He wore a mustache and pointed beard, but no whiskers; his eyes were large and dark gray, and had a kindly expression which one would hardly have expected of one whose neck was in the hemp. Evidently this was no vulgar assassin. The liberal military code makes provision for hanging many kinds of people, and gentlemen are not excluded.

The preparations being complete, the two private soldiers stepped aside, and each drew away the plank upon which he had been standing. The sergeant turned to the captain, saluted, and placed himself immediately behind that officer, who in turn moved apart one pace. These movements left the condemned man and the sergeant standing on the two ends of the same plank, which spanned three of the cross-ties of the bridge. The end upon which the civilian stood almost, but not quite, reached a fourth. This plank had been held in place by the weight of the captain; it was now held by that of the sergeant. At a signal from the former the latter would step aside, the plank would tilt, and the condemned man go down between two ties. The arrangement commended itself to his judgment as simple and effective. His face had not been covered nor his eyes bandaged. He looked a moment at his "unsteadfast footing," then let his gaze wander to the swirling water of the stream racing madly beneath his feet. A piece of dancing driftwood caught his attention, and his eyes followed it down the current. How slowly it appeared to move! What a sluggish stream!

He closed his eyes in order to fix his last thoughts upon his wife and children. The water, touched to gold by the early sun, the brooding mists under the banks at some distance down the stream, the fort, the soldiers, the piece of drift—all had distracted him. And now he became conscious of a new disturbance. Striking through the thought of his dear ones was a sound he could neither ignore nor understand, a sharp, distinct, metallic percussion like the stroke of a blacksmith's hammer upon the anvil; it had the same ringing quality. He wondered what it was, and whether immeasurably distant or near by—it seemed both. Its recurrence was regular, but as slow as the tolling of a death-knell. He awaited each stroke with impatience and—he knew not why—apprehension. The intervals of silence grew progressively longer; the delays maddening. With their greater infrequency the sounds increased in strength and sharpness. They hurt his ear like the thrust of a knife; he feared he would shriek. What he heard was the ticking of his watch.

He unclosed his eyes and saw again the water below him. "If I could free my hands," he thought, "I might throw off the noose and spring into the stream. By diving, I could evade the bullets, and, swimming vigorously, reach the bank, take to the woods, and get away home. My home, thank God, is as yet outside their lines; my wife and little ones are still beyond the invaders' farthest advance."

As these thoughts, which have here to be set down in words, were flashed into the doomed man's brain rather than evolved from it, the captain nodded to the sergeant. The sergeant stepped aside.

II

Peyton Farquhar was a well-to-do planter, of an old and highly respected Alabama family. Being a slave-owner, and, like other slave-owners, a politician, he was naturally an original secessionist and ardently devoted to the Southern cause. Circumstances of an imperious nature which it is unnecessary to relate here had prevented him from taking service with the gallant army which had fought the disastrous campaigns ending with the fall of Corinth, and he chafed under the inglorious restraint, longing for the release of his energies, the larger life of the soldier, the opportunity for distinction. That opportunity, he felt, would come, as it comes to all in war-time. Meanwhile, he did what he could. No service was too humble for him to perform in aid of the South, no adventure too perilous for him to undertake if consistent with the character of a civilian who was at heart a soldier, and who in good faith and without too much qualification assented to at least a part of the frankly villainous dictum that all is fair in love and war.

One evening while Farquhar and his wife were sitting on a rustic bench near the entrance to his grounds, a gray-clad soldier rode up to the gate and asked for a drink of water. Mrs. Farquhar was only too happy to serve him with her own white hands. While she was gone to fetch the water, her husband approached the dusty horseman and inquired eagerly for news from the front.

"The Yanks are repairing the railroads," said the man, "and are getting ready for another advance. They have reached the Owl Creek Bridge, put it in order, and built a stockade on the other bank. The commandant has issued an order, which is posted everywhere, declaring that any civilian caught interfering with the railroad, its bridges, tunnels, or trains, will be summarily hanged. I saw the order."

"How far is it to the Owl Creek Bridge?" Farquhar asked.

"About thirty miles."

"Is there no force on this side of the creek?"

"Only a picket post half a mile out, on the railroad, and a single sentinel at this end of the bridge."

"Suppose a man—a civilian and student of hanging—should elude the picket post and perhaps get the better of the sentinel," said Farquhar, smiling, "what could he accomplish?"

The soldier reflected. "I was there a month ago," he replied. "I observed that the flood of last winter had lodged a great quantity of driftwood against the wooden pier at this end of the bridge. It is now dry, and would burn like tow."

The lady had now brought the water, which the soldier drank. He thanked her ceremoniously, bowed to her husband, and rode away. An hour later, after nightfall, he repassed the plantation, going northward in the direction from which he had come. He was a Federal scout.

III

As Peyton Farquhar fell straight downward through the bridge, he lost consciousness and was as one already dead. From this state he was awakened—ages later, it seemed to him—by the pain of a sharp pressure upon his throat, followed by a sense of suffocation. Keen, poignant agonies seemed to shoot from his neck downward through every fiber of his body and limbs. These pains seemed to flash along well-defined lines of ramification, and to beat with an inconceivably rapid periodicity. They seemed like streams of pulsating fire, heating him to an intolerable temperature. As to his head, he was conscious of nothing but a feeling of fulness—of congestion. These sensations were unaccompanied by thought. The intellectual part of his nature was already effaced; he had power only to feel, and feeling was torment. He was conscious of motion. Encompassed in a luminous cloud, of which he was now merely the fiery heart, without material substance, he swung through unthinkable arcs of oscillation, like a vast pendulum. Then all at once, with terrible suddenness, the light about him shot upward with the noise of a loud splash, a frightful roaring was in his ears, and all was cold and dark. The power of thought was restored; he knew that the rope had broken and he had fallen into the stream. There was no additional strangulation; the noose about his neck was already suffocating him, and kept the water from his lungs. To die hanging at the bottom of a river—the idea seemed to him ludicrous. He opened his eyes in the blackness and saw above him a gleam of light, but how distant, how inaccessible! He was still sinking, for the light became fainter and fainter until it was a mere glimmer. Then it began to grow and brighten, and he knew that he was rising toward the surface—knew it with reluctance, for he was now very comfortable. "To be hanged and drowned," he thought, "that is not so bad; but I do not wish to be shot. No; I will not be shot; that is not fair."

He was not conscious of an effort, but a sharp pain in his wrists apprized him that he was trying to free his hands. He gave the struggle his attention, as an idler might observe the feat of a juggler, without interest in the outcome. What splendid effort—what magnificent, what superhuman strength! Ah, that was a fine endeavor! Bravo! The cord fell away; his arms parted and floated upward, the hands dimly seen on each side in the growing light. He watched them with a new interest as first one and then the other pounced upon the noose at his neck. They tore it away and thrust it fiercely aside, its undulations resembling those of a water-snake. "Put it back!

Put it back!" He thought he shouted these words to his hands, for the undoing of the noose had been succeeded by the direst pang which he had yet experienced. His neck ached horribly; his brain was on fire; his heart, which had been fluttering faintly, gave a great leap, trying to force itself out of his mouth. His whole body was racked and wrenched with an insupportable anguish! But his disobedient hands gave no heed to the command. They beat the water vigorously with quick, downward strokes, forcing him to the surface. He felt his head emerge; his eyes were blinded by the sunlight; his chest expanded convulsively, and with a supreme and crowning agony his lungs engulfed a great draught of air, which instantly he expelled in a shriek!

He was now in full possession of his physical senses. They were, indeed, preternaturally keen and alert. Something in the awful disturbance of his organic system had so exalted and refined them that they made record of things never before perceived. He felt the ripples upon his face and heard their separate sounds as they struck. He looked at the forest on the bank of the stream, saw the individual trees, the leaves and the veining of each leaf—saw the very insects upon them, the locusts, the brilliant-bodied flies, the gray spiders stretching their webs from twig to twig. He noted the prismatic colors in all the dewdrops upon a million blades of grass. The humming of the gnats that danced above the eddies of the stream, the beating of the dragonflies' wings, the strokes of the waterspiders' legs, like oars which have lifted their boat—all these made audible music. A fish slid along beneath his eyes, and he heard the rush of its body parting the water.

He had come to the surface facing down the stream; in a moment the visible world seemed to wheel slowly round, himself the pivotal point, and he saw the bridge, the fort, the soldiers on the bridge, the captain, the sergeant, the two privates, his executioners. They were in silhouette against the blue sky. They shouted and gesticulated, pointing at him; the captain had drawn his pistol, but did not fire; the others were unarmed. Their movements were grotesque and horrible, their forms gigantic.

Suddenly he heard a sharp report, and something struck the water smartly within a few inches of his head, spattering his face with spray. He heard a second report, and saw one of the sentinels with his rifle at his shoulder, a light cloud of blue smoke rising from the muzzle. The man in the water saw the eye of the man on the bridge gazing into his own through the sights of the rifle. He observed that it was a gray eye, and remembered having read that gray eyes were keenest, and that all famous marksmen had them. Nevertheless, this one had missed.

A counter-swirl had caught Farquhar and turned him half round; he was again looking into the forest on the bank opposite the fort. The sound of a clear, high voice in a monotonous sing-song now rang out behind him and came across the water with a distinctness that pierced and subdued all other sounds, even the beating of the ripples in his ears. Although no soldier, he had frequented camps enough to know the dread significance of that deliberate, drawling, aspirated chant; the lieutenant on shore was taking a part in the morning's work. How coldly and pitilessly—with what an even, calm intonation, presaging and enforcing tranquillity in the men—with what accurately measured intervals fell those cruel words: "Attention, company. Shoulder arms. Ready. Aim. Fire!"

Farquhar dived—dived as deeply as he could. The water roared in his ears like the voice of Niagara, yet he heard the dulled thunder of the volley, and rising again toward the surface, met shining bits of metal, singularly flattened, oscillating slowly downward. Some of them touched him on the face and hands, then fell away, continuing their descent. One lodged between his collar and neck; it was uncomfortably warm, and he snatched it out.

As he rose to the surface, gasping for breath, he saw that he had been a long time under water; he was perceptibly farther down-stream—nearer to safety! The soldiers had almost finished reloading; the metal ramrods flashed all at once in the sunshine as they were drawn from the barrels, turned in the air, and thrust into their sockets. The two sentinels fired again, independently and ineffectually.

The hunted man saw all this over his shoulder; he was now swimming vigorously with the current. His brain was as energetic as his arms and legs; he thought with the rapidity of lightning.

"The officer," he reasoned, "will not make that martinet's error a second time. It is as easy to dodge a volley as a single shot. He has probably already given the command to fire at will. God help me, I cannot dodge them all!"

An appalling plash within two yards of him, followed by a loud rushing sound, diminuendo, which seemed to travel back through the air to the fort and died in an explosion which stirred the very river to its deeps. A rising sheet of water, which curved over him, fell down upon him, blinded him, strangled him. The cannon had taken a hand in the game. As he shook his head free from the commotion of the smitten water, he heard the deflected shot humming through the air ahead, and in an instant it was cracking and smashing the branches in the forest beyond.

"They will not do that again," he thought; "the next time they will use a charge of grape. I must keep my eye upon the gun; the smoke will apprize me—the report arrives too late; it lags behind the missile. It is a good gun."

Suddenly he felt himself whirled round and around—spinning like a top. The water, the banks, the forest, the now distant bridge, fort and men—all were commingled and blurred. Objects were represented by their colors only; circular horizontal streaks of color—that was all he saw. He had been caught in a vortex, and was being whirled on with a velocity of advance and gyration which made him giddy and sick. In a few moments he was flung upon the gravel at the foot of the left bank of the stream—the southern bank—and behind a projecting point which concealed him from his enemies. The sudden arrest of his motion, the abrasion of one of his hands on the gravel, restored him, and he wept with delight. He dug his fingers into the sand, threw it over himself in handfuls and audibly blessed it. It looked like gold, like diamonds, rubies, emeralds; he could think of nothing beautiful which it did not resemble. The trees upon the bank were giant garden plants; he noted a definite order in their arrangement, inhaled the fragrance of their blooms. A strange, roseate light shone through the spaces among their trunks, and the wind made in their branches the music of Æolian harps. He had no wish to perfect his escape, was content to remain in that enchanting spot until retaken.

A whizz and rattle of grapeshot among the branches high above his head roused him from his dream. The baffled cannoneer had fired him a random farewell. He sprung to his feet, rushed up the sloping bank, and plunged into the forest.

All that day he traveled, laying his course by the rounding sun. The forest seemed interminable; nowhere did he discover a break in it, not even a woodman's road. He had not known that he lived in so wild a region. There was something uncanny in the revelation.

By nightfall he was fatigued, footsore, famishing. The thought of his wife and children urged him on. At last he found a road which led him in what he knew to be the right direction. It was as wide and straight as a city street, yet it seemed untraveled. No fields bordered it, no dwelling anywhere. Not so much as the barking of a dog suggested human habitation. The black bodies of the great trees formed a straight wall on both sides, terminating on the horizon in a point, like a diagram in a lesson in perspective. Overhead, as he looked up through this rift in the wood, shone great golden stars looking unfamiliar and grouped in strange constellations. He was sure they were arranged in some order which had a secret and malign significance. The wood on either side was full of singular noises, among which—once, twice, and again—he distinctly heard whispers in an unknown tongue.

His neck was in pain, and lifting his hand to it, he found it horribly swollen. He knew that it had a circle of black where the rope had bruised it. His eyes felt congested; he could no longer close them. His tongue was swollen with thirst; he relieved its fever by thrusting it forward from between his teeth into the cool air. How softly the turf had carpeted the untraveled avenue! He could no longer feel the roadway beneath his feet!

Doubtless, despite his suffering, he fell asleep while walking, for now he sees another scene—perhaps he has merely recovered from a delirium. He stands at the gate of his own home. All is as he left it, and all bright and beautiful in the morning sunshine. He must have traveled the entire night. As he pushes open the gate and passes up the wide white walk, he sees a flutter of female garments; his wife, looking fresh and cool and sweet, steps down from the veranda to meet him. At the bottom of the steps she stands waiting, with a smile of ineffable joy, an attitude of matchless grace and dignity. Ah, how beautiful she is! He springs forward with extended arms.

As he is about to clasp her, he feels a stunning blow upon the back of the neck; a blinding white light blazes all about him, with a sound like the shock of a cannon—then all is darkness and silence!

Peyton Farquhar was dead; his body, with a broken neck, swung gently from side to side beneath the timbers of the Owl Creek Bridge.

WILBUR DANIEL STEELE

Footfalls

This is not an easy story; not a road for tender feet or for casual feet. Better the meadows. Let me warn you, it is as hard as that old man's soul and as sunless as his eyes. It has its inception in catastrophe, and its end in an almost incredible act of violence; between them it tells barely how one, long blind, can become also deaf and dumb.

He lived in one of those old Puritan sea towns where the strain has come down austere and moribund, so that his act would not be quite unbelievable. Except that the town is no longer Puritan and Yankee. It has been betrayed; it has become an outpost of the Portuguese islands.

This man, the blind cobbler himself, was Portuguese

from St. Michael, in the Western Islands, and his name was Boaz Negro.

He was happy. An unquenchable exuberance lived in him. When he arose in the morning he made vast, as it were uncontrollable, gestures with his stout arms. He came into his shop singing. His voice, strong and deep as the chest from which it emanated, rolled out through the doorway and along the street, and the fishermen, done with their morning work and lounging and smoking along the wharves, said, "Boaz is to work already." Then they came up to sit in the shop.

In that town a cobbler's shop is a club. One sees the interior always dimly thronged. They sit on the benches watching the artisan at his work for hours, and they talk about everything in the world. A cobbler is known by the company he keeps.

Boaz Negro kept young company. He would have nothing to do with the old. On his own head the gray hairs set thickly.

He had a grown son. But the benches in his shop were for the lusty and valiant young, men who could spend the night drinking, and then at three o'clock in the morning turn out in the rain and dark to pull at the weirs, sing songs, buffet one another among the slippery fish in the boat's bottom, and make loud jokes about the fundamental things, love and birth and death. Harkening to their boasts and strong prophecies his breast heaved and his heart beat faster. He was a large, full-blooded fellow, fashioned for exploits; the flame in his darkness burned higher even to hear of them.

It is scarcely conceivable how Boaz Negro could have come through this much of his life still possessed of that unquenchable and priceless exuberance; how he would sing in the dawn; how, simply listening to the recital of deeds in gale or brawl, he could easily forget himself, a blind man, tied to a shop and a last; easily make of himself a lusty young fellow breasting the sunlit and adventurous tide of life.

He had had a wife, whom he had loved. Fate, which had scourged him with the initial scourge of blindness, had seen fit to take his Angelina away. He had four sons. Three, one after another, had been removed, leaving only Manuel, the youngest. Recovering slowly, with agony, from each of these recurrent blows, his unquenchable exuberance had lived. And there was another thing quite as extraordinary. He had never done anything but work, and that sort of thing may kill the flame where an abrupt catastrophe fails. Work in the dark. Work, work, work! And accompanied by privation; an almost miserly scale of personal economy. Yes, indeed, he had "skinned his fingers," especially in the earlier years. When it tells most.

How he had worked! Not alone in the daytime, but also sometimes, when orders were heavy, far into the night. It was strange for one, passing along that deserted street at midnight, to hear issuing from the black shop of Boaz Negro the rhythmical tap-tap-tap of hammer on wooden peg.

Nor was that sound all: no man in town could get far past that shop in his nocturnal wandering unobserved.

No more than a dozen footfalls, and from the darkness Boaz's voice rolled forth, fraternal, stentorian, "Good-night, Antone!" "Good-night to you, Caleb Snow!"

To Boaz Negro it was still broad day.

Now, because of this, he was what might be called a substantial man. He owned his place, his shop, opening on the sidewalk, and behind it the dwelling-house with trellised galleries upstairs and down.

And there was always something for his son, a "piece for the pocket," a dollar-, five-, or even a ten-dollar bill if he had "got to have it." Manuel was a "good boy." Boaz not only said this; he felt that he was assured of it in his understanding, to the infinite peace of his heart.

It was curious that he should be ignorant only of the one nearest to him. Not because he was physically blind. Be certain he knew more of other men and of other men's sons than they or their neighbors did. More, that is to say, of their hearts and understandings, their idiosyncrasies, and their ultimate weight in the balance-pan of eternity.

His simple explanation of Manuel was that Manuel "wasn't too stout." To others he said this, and to himself. Manuel was not indeed too robust. How should he be vigorous when he never did anything to make him so? He never worked. Why should he work, when existence was provided for, and when there was always that "piece for the pocket"? Even a ten-dollar bill on a Saturday night! No, Manuel "wasn't too stout."

In the shop they let it go at that. The missteps and frailties of every one else in the world were canvassed there with the most shameless publicity. But Boaz Negro was a blind man, and in a sense their host. Those reckless, strong young fellows respected and loved him. It was allowed to stand at that. Manuel was a "good boy." Which did not prevent them, by the way, from joining later in the general condemnation of that father's laxity—"the ruination of the boy!"

"He should have put him to work, that's what."

"He should have said to Manuel, 'Look here, if you want a dollar, go earn it first.' "

As a matter of fact, only one man ever gave Boaz the advice direct. That was Campbell Wood. And Wood never sat in that shop.

In every small town there is one young man who is spoken of as "rising." As often as not he is not a native, but "from away."

In this town Campbell Wood was that man. He had come from another part of the state to take a place in the bank. He lived in the upper story of Boaz Negro's house, the ground floor now doing for Boaz and the meager remnant of his family. The old woman who came in to tidy up for the cobbler looked after Wood's rooms as well.

Dealing with Wood, one had first of all the sense of his incorruptibility. A little ruthless perhaps, as if one could imagine him, in defense of his integrity, cutting off his friend, cutting off his own hand, cutting off the very stream flowing out from the wellsprings of human kindness. An exaggeration, perhaps.

He was by long odds the most eligible young man in

town; good looking in a spare, ruddy, sandy-haired Scottish fashion; important, incorruptible, "rising." But he took good care of his heart. Precisely that; like a sharp-eyed duenna to his own heart. One felt that here was the man, if ever was the man, who held his destiny in his own hand. Failing, of course, some quite gratuitous and unforeseeable catastrophe.

Not that he was not human, or even incapable of laughter or passion. He was, in a way, immensely accessible. He never clapped one on the shoulder; on the other hand, he never failed to speak. Not even to Boaz.

Returning from the bank in the afternoon, he had always a word for the cobbler. Passing out again to supper at his boarding-place, he had another, about the weather, the prospects of rain. And if Boaz were at work in the dark when he returned from an evening at the Board of Trade, there was a "Good-night, Mr. Negro!"

On Boaz's part, his attitude toward his lodger was curious and paradoxical. He did not pretend to anything less than reverence for the young man's position; precisely on account of that position he was conscious toward Wood of a vague distrust. This was because he was an uneducated fellow.

To the uneducated the idea of large finance is as uncomfortable as the idea of the law. It must be said for Boaz that, responsive to Wood's unfailing civility, he fought against this sensation of dim and somehow shameful distrust. Nevertheless his whole parental soul was in arms that evening, when, returning from the bank and finding the shop empty of loungers, Wood paused a moment to propose the bit of advice already referred to.

"Haven't you ever thought of having Manuel learn the trade?"

A suspicion, a kind of presumption, lighted the fires of defense.

"Shoemaking," said Boaz, "is good enough for a blind man."

"Oh, I don't know. At least it's better than doing nothing at all."

Boaz's hammer was still. He sat silent, monumental. Outwardly. For once his unfailing response had failed him, "Manuel ain't too stout, you know." Perhaps it had become suddenly inadequate.

He hated Wood; he despised Wood; more than ever before, a hundredfold more, quite abruptly, he distrusted Wood.

How could a man say such things as Wood had said? And where Manuel himself might hear!

Where Manuel *had* heard! Boaz's other emotions—hatred and contempt and distrust—were overshadowed. Sitting in darkness, no sound had come to his ears, no footfall, no infinitesimal creaking of the floor-plank. Yet by some sixth uncanny sense of the blind he was aware that Manuel was standing in the dusk of the entry joining the shop to the house.

Boaz made a Herculean effort. The voice came out of his throat, harsh, bitter, and loud enough to have carried ten times the distance to his son's ears.

"Manuel is a good boy!"

"Yes—h'm—yes—I suppose so."

Wood shifted his weight. He seemed uncomfortable.

"Well. I'll be running along, I—ugh! Heavens!"

Something was happening. Boaz heard exclamations, breathings, the rustle of sleeve-cloth in large, frantic, and futile graspings—all without understanding. Immediately there was an impact on the floor, and with it the unmistakable clink of metal. Boaz even heard that the metal was minted, and that the coins were gold. He understood. A coin-sack, gripped not quite carefully enough for the moment under the other's overcoat, had shifted, slipped, escaped, and fallen.

And Manuel had heard!

It was a dreadful moment for Boaz, dreadful in its native sense, as full of dread. Why? It was a moment of horrid revelation, ruthless clarification. His son, his link with the departed Angelina, that "good boy"—Manuel, standing in the shadow of the entry, visible alone to the blind, had heard the clink of falling gold, and—*and Boaz wished that he had not!*

There, amazing, disconcerting, destroying, stood the sudden fact.

Sitting as impassive and monumental as ever, his strong, bleached hands at rest on his work, round drops of sweat came out on Boaz's forehead. He scarcely took the sense of what Wood was saying. Only fragments.

"Government money, understand—for the breakwater workings—huge—too many people know here, everywhere—don't trust the safe—tin safe—'Noah's Ark' —give you my word—Heavens, no!"

It boiled down to this—the money, more money than was good for that antiquated "Noah's Ark" at the bank—and whose contemplated sojourn there over night was public to too many minds—in short, Wood was not only incorruptible; he was canny. To what one of those minds, now, would it occur that he should take away that money bodily, under casual cover of his coat, to his own lodgings behind the cobbler-shop of Boaz Negro? For this one, this important night!

He was sorry the coin-sack had slipped, because he did not like to have the responsibility of secret sharer cast upon anyone, even upon Boaz, even by accident. On the other hand, how tremendously fortunate that it had been Boaz and not another. So far as that went, Wood had no more anxiety now than before. One incorruptible knows another.

"I'd trust you, Mr. Negro" (that was one of the fragments which came and stuck in the cobbler's brain), "as far as I would myself. As long as it's only you. I'm just going up here and throw it under the bed. Oh, yes, certainly."

Boaz ate no supper. For the first time in his life food was dry in his gullet. Even under those other successive crushing blows of Fate the full and generous habit of his functionings had carried on unabated; he had always eaten what was set before him. To-night, over his untouched plate, he watched Manuel with the sightless eyes, keeping track of his every mouthful, word, intonation, breath. What profit he expected to extract from this cat-like surveillance it is impossible to say.

When they arose from the supper-table Boaz made another Herculean effort.

"Manuel, you're a good boy!"

The formula had a quality of appeal, of despair, and of command.

"Manuel, you should be short of money, maybe. Look, what's this? A tenner? Well, there's a piece for the pocket; go and enjoy yourself."

He would have been frightened had Manuel, upsetting tradition, declined the offering. With the morbid contrariness of the human imagination, the boy's avid grasping gave him no comfort.

He went out into the shop, where it was already dark, drew to him his last, his tools, mallets, cutters, pegs, leather. And having prepared to work, he remained idle. He found himself listening.

It has been observed that the large phenomena of sunlight and darkness were nothing to Boaz Negro. A busy night was broad day. Yet there was a difference; he knew it with the blind man's eyes, the ears.

Day was a vast confusion, or rather a wide fabric, of sounds; great and little sounds all woven together, voices, footfalls, wheels, far-off whistles and foghorns, flies buzzing in the sun. Night was another thing. Still there were voices and footfalls, but rarer, emerging from the large, pure body of silence as definite, surprising, and yet familiar entities.

To-night there was an easterly wind, coming off the water and carrying the sound of waves. So far as other fugitive sounds were concerned it was the same as silence. The wind made little difference to the ears. It nullified, from one direction at least, the other two visual processes of the blind, the sense of touch and the sense of smell. It blew away from the shop, toward the living-house.

As has been said, Boaz found himself listening, scrutinizing with an extraordinary attention, this immense background of sound. He heard footfalls. The story of that night was written, for him, in footfalls.

He heard them moving about the house, the lower floor, prowling here, there, halting for long spaces, advancing, retreating softly on the planks. About this aimless, interminable perambulation there was something to twist the nerves, something led and at the same time driven like a succession of frail and indecisive charges.

Boaz lifted himself from his chair. All his impulse called him to make a stir, join battle, cast in the breach the reënforcement of his presence, authority, good will. He sank back again; his hands fell down. The curious impotence of the spectator held him.

He heard footfalls, too, on the upper floor, a little fainter, borne to the inner rather than the outer ear, along the solid causeway of partitions and floor, the legs of his chair, the bony framework of his body. Very faint indeed. Sinking back easily into the background of the wind. They, too, came and went, this room, that, to the passage, the stair-head, and away. About them, too, there was the same quality of being led and at the same time of being driven.

Time went by. In his darkness it seemed to Boaz that hours must have passed. He heard voices. Together with the footfalls, that abrupt, brief, and (in view of Wood's position) astounding interchange of sentences made up his history of the night. Wood must have opened the door at the head of the stair; by the sound of his voice he would be standing there, peering below perhaps; perhaps listening.

"What's wrong down there?" he called. "Why don't you go to bed?"

After a moment, came Manuel's voice, "Ain't sleepy."

"Neither am I. Look here, do you like to play cards?"

"What kind? Euchre! I like euchre all right. Or pitch."

"Well, what would you say to coming up and having a game of euchre then, Manuel? If you can't sleep?"

"That'd be all right."

The lower footfalls ascended to join the footfalls on the upper floor. There was the sound of a door closing.

Boaz sat still. In the gloom he might have been taken for a piece of furniture, of machinery, an extraordinary lay figure, perhaps, for the trying on of the boots he made. He seemed scarcely to breathe, only the sweat starting from his brow giving him an aspect of life.

He ought to have run, and leaped up that inner stair and pounded with his fists on that door. He seemed unable to move. At rare intervals feet passed on the sidewalk outside, just at his elbow, so to say, and yet somehow, to-night, immeasurably far away. Beyond the orbit of the moon. He heard Rugg, the policeman, noting the silence of the shop, muttering, "Boaz is to bed to-night," as he passed.

The wind increased. It poured against the shop with its deep, continuous sound of a river. Submerged in its body, Boaz caught the note of the town bell striking midnight.

Once more, after a long time, he heard footfalls. He heard them coming around the corner of the shop from the house, footfalls half swallowed by the wind, passing discreetly, without haste, retreating, merging step by step with the huge, incessant background of the wind.

Boaz's muscles tightened all over him. He had the impulse to start up, to fling open the door, shout into the night, "What are you doing? Stop there! Say! What are you doing and where are you going?"

And as before, the curious impotence of the spectator held him motionless. He had not stirred in his chair. And those footfalls, upon which hinged, as it were, that momentous decade of his life, were gone.

There was nothing to listen for now. Yet he continued to listen. Once or twice, half arousing himself, he drew toward him his unfinished work. And then relapsed into immobility.

As has been said, the wind, making little difference to the ears, made all the difference in the world with the sense of feeling and the sense of smell. From the one important direction of the house. That is how it could come about that Boaz Negro could sit, waiting and listening to nothing in the shop and remain ignorant of disaster until the alarm had gone and come back again, pounding, shouting, clanging.

"Fire!" he heard them bawling in the street. *"Fire! Fire!"*

Only slowly did he understand that the fire was in his own house.

There is nothing stiller in the world than the skeleton of a house in the dawn after a fire. It is as if everything living, positive, violent, had been completely drained in the one flaming act of violence, leaving nothing but negation till the end of time. It is worse than a tomb. A monstrous stillness! Even the footfalls of the searchers cannot disturb it, for they are separate and superficial. In its presence they are almost frivolous.

Half an hour after dawn the searchers found the body, if what was left from that consuming ordeal might be called a body. The discovery came as a shock. It seemed incredible that the occupant of that house, no cripple or invalid but an able man in the prime of youth, should not have awakened and made good his escape. It was the upper floor which had caught; the stairs had stood to the last. It was beyond calculation, even if he had been asleep!

And he had not been asleep. This second and infinitely more appalling discovery began to be known. Slowly. By a hint, a breath of rumor here; there an allusion, half taken back. The man, whose incinerated body still lay curled in its bed of cinders, had been dressed at the moment of disaster; even to the watch, the cuff-buttons, the studs, the very scarf-pin. Fully clothed to the last detail, precisely as those who had dealings at the bank might have seen Campbell Wood any week-day morning for the past eight months. A man does not sleep with his clothes on. The skull of the man had been broken, as if with a blunt instrument of iron. On the charred lacework of the floor lay the leg of an old andiron with which Boaz Negro and his Angelina had set up housekeeping in that new house.

It needed only Mr. Asa Whitelaw, coming up the street from the gaping "Noah's Ark" at the bank, to round out the scandalous circle of circumstance.

"Where is Manuel?"

Boaz Negro still sat in his shop, impassive, monumental, his thick, hairy arms resting on the arms of his chair. The tools and materials of his work remained scattered about him, as his irresolute gathering of the night before had left them. Into his eyes no change could come. He had lost his house, the visible monument of all those years of "skinning his fingers." It would seem that he had lost his son. And he had lost something incalculably precious—that hitherto unquenchable exuberance of the man.

"Where is Manuel?"

When he spoke his voice was unaccented and stale, like the voice of a man already dead.

"Yes, where is Manuel?"

He had answered them with their own question.

"When did you last see him?"

Neither he nor they seemed to take note of that profound irony. "At supper."

"Tell us, Boaz; you knew about this money?"

The cobbler nodded his head.

"And did Manuel?"

He might have taken sanctuary in a legal doubt. How did he know what Manuel knew? Precisely! As before, he nodded his head.

"After supper, Boaz, you were in the shop? But you heard something?"

He went on to tell them what he had heard: the footfalls, below and above, the extraordinary conversation which had broken for a moment the silence of the inner hall. The account was bare, the phrases monosyllabic. He reported only what had been registered on the sensitive tympanums of his ears, to the last whisper of footfalls stealing past the dark wall of the shop. Of all the formless tangle of thoughts, suspicions, interpretations, and the special and personal knowledge given to the blind which moved his brain, he said nothing.

He shut his lips there. He felt himself on the defensive. Just as he distrusted the higher ramifications of finance (his house had gone down uninsured), so before the rites and processes of that inscrutable creature, the Law, he felt himself menaced by the invisible and the unknown, helpless, oppressed; in an abject sense, skeptical.

"Keep clear of the Law!" they had told him in his youth. The monster his imagination summoned up then still stood beside him in his age.

Having exhausted his monosyllabic and superficial evidence, they could move him no farther. He became deaf and dumb. He sat before them, an image cast in some immensely heavy stuff, inanimate. His lack of visible emotion impressed them. Remembering his exuberance, it was only the stranger to see him unmoving and unmoved. Only once did they catch sight of something beyond. As they were preparing to leave he opened his mouth. What he said was like a swan-song to the years of his exuberant happiness. Even now there was no color of expression in his words, which sounded mechanical.

"Now I have lost everything. My house. My last son. Even my honor. You would not think I would like to live. But I go to live. I go to work. That *cachorra,* one day he shall come back again, in the dark night, to have a look. I shall go to show you all. That *cachorra!*"

(And from that time on, it was noted, he never referred to the fugitive by any other name than *cachorra,* which is a kind of dog. "That *cachorra!*" As if he had forfeited the relationship not only of the family, but of the very genus, the very race! "That *cachorra!*")

He pronounced this resolution without passion. When they assured him that the culprit would come back again indeed, much sooner than he expected, "with a rope around his neck," he shook his head slowly.

"No, you shall not catch that *cachorra* now. But one day——"

There was something about its very colorlessness which made it sound oracular. It was at least prophetic. They searched, laid their traps, proceeded with all their placards, descriptions, rewards, clues, trails. But on Manuel Negro they never laid their hands.

Months passed and became years. Boaz Negro did not rebuild his house. He might have done so, out of his earnings, for upon himself he spent scarcely anything, reverting to his old habit of an almost miserly economy. Yet perhaps it would have been harder after all. For his earnings were less and less. In that town a cobbler who sits in an empty shop is apt to want for trade. Folk take their boots to mend where they take their bodies to rest and their minds to be edified.

No longer did the walls of Boaz's shop resound to the boastful recollections of young men. Boaz had changed. He had become not only different, but opposite. A metaphor will do best. The spirit of Boaz Negro had been a mellowed hillside giving upon the open sea, the sun, the warm, wild winds from beyond the blue horizon. And covered with flowers, always hungry and thirsty for the sun and the fabulous wind-bright showers of rain. It had become an entrenched camp, lying silent, sullen, verdureless, under a gray sky. He stood solitary against the world. His approaches were closed. He was blind, and he was also deaf and dumb.

Against that what can young fellows do who wish for nothing but to rest themselves and talk about their friends and enemies? They had come and they had tried. They had raised their voices even higher than before. Their boasts had grown louder, more presumptuous, more preposterous, until, before the cold separation of that unmoving and as if contemptuous presence in the cobbler's chair, they burst of their own air, like toy balloons. And they went and left Boaz alone.

There was another thing which served, if not to keep them away, at least not to entice them back. That was the aspect of the place. It was not cheerful. It invited no one. In its way that fire-bitten ruin grew to be almost as great a scandal as the act itself had been. It was plainly an eyesore. A valuable property, on the town's main thoroughfare—and an eyesore! The neighboring owners protested.

Their protestations might as well have gone against a stone wall. The man was deaf and dumb. He had become, in a way, a kind of vegetable, for the quality of a vegetable is that, while it is endowed with life, it remains fixed in one spot. For years Boaz was scarcely seen to move foot out of that shop that was left him, a small, square, blistered promontory on the shores of ruin.

He must indeed have carried out some rudimentary sort of domestic program under the débris at the rear (he certainly did not sleep and eat in the shop). One or two lower rooms were left fairly intact. The outward aspect of the place was formless; it grew to be no more than a mound in time; the charred timbers, one or two still standing, lean and naked against the sky, lost their blackness and faded to a silvery gray. It would have seemed strange, had they not grown accustomed to the thought, to imagine that blind man, like a mole, or some slow slug, turning himself mysteriously in the depths of that gray mound—that time-silvered "eyesore."

When they saw him, however, he was in the shop. They opened the door to take in their work (when other cobblers turned them off), and they saw him seated in his chair in the half darkness, his whole person, legs, torso, neck, head, as motionless as the vegetable of which we have spoken—only his hands and his bare arms endowed with visible life. The gloom had bleached the skin to the color of damp ivory, and against the background of his immobility they moved with a certain amazing monstrousness, interminably. No, they were never still. One wondered what they could be at. Surely he could not have had enough work now to keep those insatiable hands so monstrously in motion. Even far into the night. Tap-tap-tap! Blows continuous and powerful. On what? On nothing? On the bare iron last? And for what purpose? To what conceivable end?

Well, one could imagine those arms, growing paler, also growing thicker and more formidable with that unceasing labor; the muscles feeding themselves omnivorously on their own waste, the cords toughening, the bone-tissues revitalizing themselves without end. One could imagine the whole aspiration of that mute and motionless man pouring itself out into those pallid arms, and the arms taking it up with a kind of blind greed. Storing it up. Against a day!

"That *cachorra!* One day——"

What were the thoughts of the man? What moved within that motionless cranium covered with long hair? Who can say? Behind everything, of course, stood that bitterness against the world—the blind world—blinder than he would ever be. And against "that *cachorra.*" But this was no longer a thought; it was the man.

Just as all muscular aspiration flowed into his arms, so

all the energies of his senses turned to his ears. The man had become, you might say, two arms and two ears. Can you imagine a man listening, intently, through the waking hours of nine years?

Listening to footfalls. Marking with a special emphasis of concentration the beginning, rise, full passage, falling away, and dying of the footfalls. By day, by night, winter and summer and winter again. Unraveling the skein of footfalls passing up and down the street!

For three years he wondered when they would come. For the next three he wondered if they would ever come. It was during the last three that a doubt began to trouble him. It gnawed at his huge moral strength. Like a hidden seepage of water, it undermined (in anticipation) his terrible resolution. It was a sign perhaps of age, a slipping away of the reckless infallibility of youth.

Supposing, after all, that his ears should fail him. Supposing they were capable of being tricked, without his being able to know it. Supposing that that *cachorra* should come and go, and he, Boaz, living in some vast delusion, some unrealized distortion of memory, should let him pass unknown. Supposing precisely this thing had already happened!

Or the other way around. What if he should hear the footfalls coming, even into the very shop itself? What, then, if he should strike? And what then, if it were not that *cachorra* after all? How many tens and hundreds of millions of people were there in the world? Was it possible for them all to have footfalls distinct and different?

Then they would take him and hang him. And that

cachorra might then come and go at his own will, undisturbed.

As he sat there sometimes the sweat rolled down his nose, cold as ruin.

Supposing!

Sometimes, quite suddenly, in broad day, in the booming silence of the night, he would start. Not outwardly. But beneath the pale integument of his skin all his muscles tightened and his nerves sang. His breathing stopped. It seemed almost as if his heart stopped.

What was it? Were these the feet, there, emerging faintly from the distance? Yes, there was something about them. Yes. Memory was in travail. Yes, yes, yes! No! The footfalls were already passing. They were gone, swallowed up already by time and space. Had that been that *cachorra*?

Nothing in his life had been so hard to meet as this insidious drain of distrust in his own powers; this sense of a traitor within the walls. His iron-gray hair had turned white. It was always this now, from the beginning of the day to the end of the night: how was he to know? How was he to be inevitably, unshakably, sure?

Curiously, after all his purgatory of doubts, he did know them. For a moment at least, when he heard them, he was unshakably sure.

It was on an evening of the winter holidays, the Portuguese festival of *Menin' Jesus*. Christ was born again in a hundred mangers on a hundred tiny altars; there was cake and wine; songs went shouting by to the accompaniment of mandolins and tramping feet. The wind blew cold under a clear sky. In all the houses there were lights; even in Boaz Negro's shop a lamp was lit just now, for a man had been in for a pair of boots which Boaz had patched. The man had gone out again. Boaz was thinking of blowing out the light. It meant nothing to him.

He leaned forward, judging the position of the lamp-chimney by the heat on his face, and puffed out his cheeks to blow. Then his cheeks collapsed suddenly, and he sat back again.

It was not odd that he had failed to hear the footfalls until they were actually within the door. A crowd of merrymakers was passing just then; their songs and tramping almost shook the shop.

Boaz sat back. Beneath his passive exterior his nerves thrummed; his muscles had grown as hard as wood. Yes! Yes! But no! He had heard nothing; no more than a single step, a single foot-pressure on the planks within the door. Dear God! He could not tell!

Going through the pain of an enormous effort, he opened his lips.

"What can I do for you?"

"Well, I—I don't know. To tell the truth——"

The voice was unfamiliar, but it might be assumed. Boaz held himself. His face remained blank, interrogating, slightly helpless.

"I am a little deaf," he said. "Come nearer."

The footfalls came halfway across the intervening floor, and there appeared to hesitate. The voice, too, had a note of uncertainty.

"I was just looking around. I have a pair of—well, you mend shoes?"

Boaz nodded his head. It was not in response to the words, for they meant nothing. What he had heard was the footfalls on the floor.

Now he was sure. As has been said, for a moment at least after he heard them he was unmistakably sure. The congestion of his muscles had passed. He was at peace.

The voice became audible once more. Before the massive preoccupation of the blind man it became still less certain of itself.

"Well, I haven't got the shoes with me. I was—just looking around."

It was amazing to Boaz, this miraculous sensation of peace.

"Wait!" Then bending his head as if listening to the winter wind, "It's cold to-night. You've left the door open. But wait!" Leaning down, his hand fell on a rope's end hanging by the chair. The gesture was one continuous, undeviating movement of the hand. No hesitation. No groping. How many hundreds, how many thousands of times, had his hand schooled itself in that gesture!

A single strong pull. With a little *bang* the front door had swung to and latched itself. Not only the front door. The other door, leading to the rear, had closed, too, and latched itself with a little *bang*. And leaning forward from his chair, Boaz blew out the light.

There was not a sound in the shop. Outside, feet continued to go by, ringing on the frozen road; voices were lifted; the wind hustled about the corners of the wooden shell with a continuous, shrill note of whistling. All of this outside, as on another planet. Within the blackness of the shop the complete silence persisted.

Boaz listened. Sitting on the edge of his chair, half-crouching, his head, with its long, unkempt, white hair, bent slightly to one side, he concentrated upon this chambered silence the full powers of his senses. He hardly breathed. The other person in that room could not be breathing at all, it seemed.

No, there was not a breath, not the stirring of a sole on wood, not the infinitesimal rustle of any fabric. It was as if in this utter stoppage of sound, even the blood had ceased to flow in the veins and arteries of that man, who was like a rat caught in a trap.

It was appalling even to Boaz; even to the cat. Listening became more than a labor. He began to have to fight against a growing impulse to shout out loud, to leap, sprawl forward without aim in that unstirred darkness—do something. Sweat rolled down from behind his ears, into his shirt-collar. He gripped the chair-arms. To keep quiet he sank his teeth into his lower lip. He would not! He would not!

And of a sudden he heard before him, in the center of the room, an outburst of breath, an outrush from lungs in the extremity of pain, thick, laborious, fearful. A coughing up of dammed air.

Pushing himself from the arms of the chair, Boaz leaped.

His fingers, passing swiftly through the air, closed on something. It was a sheaf of hair, bristly and thick. It was a man's beard.

On the road outside, up and down the street for a hundred yards, merry-making people turned to look at one another. With an abrupt cessation of laughter, of speech. Inquiringly. Even with an unconscious dilation of the pupils of their eyes.

"What was that?"

There had been a scream. There could be no doubt of that. A single, long-drawn note. Immensely high-pitched. Not as if it were human.

"What was that? Where'd it come from?"

Those nearest said it came from the cobbler-shop of Boaz Negro. They went and tried the door. It was closed; even locked, as if for the night. There was no light behind the window-shade. But Boaz would not have a light. They beat on the door. No answer.

But from where, then, had that prolonged, as if animal, note come?

They ran about, penetrating into the side lanes, interrogating, prying. Coming back at last, inevitably, to the neighborhood of Boaz Negro's shop.

The body lay on the floor at Boaz's feet, where it had tumbled down slowly after a moment from the spasmodic embrace of his arms; those ivory-colored arms which had beaten so long upon the bare surface of a last. Blows continuous and powerful. It seemed incredible. They were so weak now. They could not have lifted the hammer now.

But that beard! That bristly, thick, square beard of a stranger!

His hands remembered it. Standing with his shoulders fallen forward and his weak arms hanging down, Boaz began to shiver. The whole thing was incredible. What was on the floor there, upheld in the vast gulf of darkness, he could not see. Neither could he hear it; smell it. Nor (if he did not move his foot) could he feel it. What he did not hear, smell, or touch did not exist. It was not there. Incredible!

But that beard! All the accumulated doubtings of those years fell down upon him. After all, the thing he had been so fearful of in his weak imaginings had happened. He had killed a stranger. He, Boaz Negro, had murdered an innocent man!

And all on account of that beard. His deep panic made him light-headed. He began to confuse cause and effect. If it were not for that beard, it would have been that *cachorra*.

On this basis he began to reason with a crazy directness. And to act. He went and pried open the door into the entry. From a shelf he took down his razor. A big, heavy-heeled strop. His hands began to hurry. And the mug, half full of soap. And water. It would have to be cold water. But, after all, he thought (light-headedly), at this time of night——

Outside, they were at the shop again. The crowd's habit is to forget a thing quickly, once it is out of sight and hearing. But there had been something about that solitary cry which continued to bother them, even in memory. Where had it been? Where had it come from? And those who had stood nearest the cobbler-shop had heard it again. They were certain now, dead certain. They could swear!

In the end they broke down the door.

If Boaz heard them he gave no sign. An absorption as complete as it was monstrous wrapped him. Kneeling in the glare of the lantern they had brought, as impervious as his own shadow sprawling behind him, he continued to shave the dead man on the floor.

No one touched him. Their minds and imaginations were arrested by the gigantic proportions of the act. The unfathomable presumption of the act. As throwing murder in their faces to the tune of a jig in a barber-shop. It is a fact that none of them so much as thought of touching him. No less than all of them, together with all other men, shorn of their imaginations—that is to say, the expressionless and imperturbable creature of the Law —would be sufficient to touch that ghastly man.

On the other hand, they could not leave him alone. They could not go away. They watched. They saw the damp, lather-soaked beard of that victimized stranger falling away, stroke by stroke of the flashing, heavy razor. The dead denuded by the blind!

It was seen that Boaz was about to speak. It was something important he was about to utter; something, one would say, fatal. The words would not come all at once. They swelled his cheeks out. His razor was arrested. Lifting his face, he encircled the watchers with a gaze at once of imploration and of command. As if he could see them. As if he could read his answer in the expressions of their faces.

"Tell me one thing now. Is it that *cachorra?*"

For the first time those men in the room made sounds. They shuffled their feet. It was as if an uncontrollable impulse to ejaculation, laughter, derision, forbidden by the presence of death, had gone down into their bootsoles.

"Manuel?" one of them said. "You mean *Manuel?*"

Boaz laid the razor down on the floor beside its work. He got up from his knees slowly, as if his joints hurt. He sat down in his chair, rested his hands on the arms, and once more encircled the company with his sightless gaze.

"Not Manuel. Manuel was a good boy. But tell me now, is it that *cachorra?*"

Here was something out of their calculations; something for them, mentally, to chew on. Mystification is a good thing sometimes. It gives the brain a fillip, stirs memory, puts the gears of imagination into mesh. One man, an old, tobacco-chewing fellow, began to stare harder at the face on the floor. Something moved in his intellect.

"No, but look here now——"

He had even stopped chewing. But he was forestalled by another. "Say, now, if it don't look like that fellow Wood, himself. The bank fellow—that was burned—remember? Himself."

"That *cachorra* was not burned. Not that Wood. You fool."

Boaz spoke from his chair. They hardly knew his voice,

emerging from its long silence; it was so didactic and arid.

"That *cachorra* was not burned. It was my boy that was burned. It was that *cachorra* called my boy upstairs. That *cachorra* put his clothes on my boy, and he set my house on fire. I knew that all the time. Because when I heard those feet come out of my house and go away, I knew they were the feet of that *cachorra* from the bank. I did not know where he was going to. Something said to me—you better ask him where he is going to. But then I said, you are foolish. He had the money from the bank. I did not know. And then my house was on fire. No, it was not my boy that went away; it was that *cachorra* all the time. You fools! Did you think I was waiting for my own boy?

"Now I show you all," he said at the end. "And now I can get hanged."

No one ever touched Boaz Negro for that murder. For murder it was in the eyes and letter of the Law. The Law in a small town is sometimes a curious creature; it is sometimes blind only in one eye.

Their minds and imaginations in that town were arrested by the romantic proportions of the act. Simply, no one took it up. I believe the man, Wood, was understood to have died from heart-failure.

When they asked Boaz why he had not told what he knew as to the identity of that fugitive in the night, he seemed to find it hard to say exactly. How could a man of no education define for them his own but half-defined misgivings about the Law, his sense of oppression, constraint, and awe, of being on the defensive, even, in an abject way, his skepticism? About his wanting, come what might, to "keep clear of the Law"?

He did say this, "You would have laughed at me."

And this, "If I told folk it was Wood went away, then I say he would not dare come back again."

That was the last. Very shortly he began to refuse to talk about the thing at all. The act was completed. Like the creature of fable, it had consumed itself. Out of that old man's consciousness it had departed. Amazingly. Like a dream dreamed out.

Slowly at first, in a makeshift, piece-at-a-time, poor man's way, Boaz commenced to rebuild his house. That "eyesore" vanished.

And slowly at first, like the miracle of a green shoot pressing out from the dead earth, that priceless and unquenchable exuberance of the man was seen returning. Unquenchable, after all.

ANTON CHEKHOV

The Bet

I

It was a dark autumn night. The old banker was pacing from corner to corner of his study, recalling to his mind the party he gave in the autumn fifteen years before. There were many clever people at the party and much interesting conversation. They talked among other things of capital punishment. The guests, among them not a few scholars and journalists, for the most part disapproved of capital punishment. They found it obsolete as a means of punishment, unfitted to a Christian State and immoral. Some of them thought that capital punishment should be replaced universally by life-imprisonment.

"I don't agree with you," said the host. "I myself have experienced neither capital punishment nor life-imprisonment, but if one may judge *a priori,* then in my opinion capital punishment is more moral and more humane than imprisonment. Execution kills instantly, life-imprisonment kills by degrees. Who is the more humane executioner; one who kills you in a few seconds or one who draws the life out of you incessantly, for years?"

"They're both equally immoral," remarked one of the guests, "because their purpose is the same, to take away life. The State is not God. It has no right to take away that which it cannot give back, if it should so desire."

Among the company was a lawyer, a young man of about twenty-five. On being asked his opinion, he said:

"Capital punishment and life-imprisonment are equally immoral; but if I were offered the choice between them, I would certainly choose the second. It's better to live somehow than not to live at all."

There ensued a lively discussion. The banker, who was then younger and more nervous, suddenly lost his temper, banged his fist on the table, and turning to the young lawyer, cried out:

"It's a lie. I bet you two millions you wouldn't stick in a cell even for five years."

"If you mean it seriously," replied the lawyer, "then I bet I'll stay not five but fifteen."

"Fifteen! Done!" cried the banker. "Gentlemen, I stake two millions."

"Agreed. You stake two millions, I my freedom," said the lawyer.

So this wild, ridiculous bet came to pass. The banker, who at that time had too many millions to count, spoiled and capricious, was beside himself with rapture. During supper he said to the lawyer jokingly:

"Come to your senses, young man, before it's too late. Two millions are nothing to me, but you stand to lose three or four of the best years of your life. I say three or four, because you'll never stick it out any longer. Don't forget either, you unhappy man, that voluntary is much heavier than enforced imprisonment. The idea that you have the right to free yourself at any moment will poison the whole of your life in the cell. I pity you."

And now the banker, pacing from corner to corner, recalled all this and asked himself:

"Why did I make this bet? What's the good? The lawyer loses fifteen years of his life and I throw away two millions. Will it convince people that capital punishment is worse or better than imprisonment for life? No, no! All stuff and rubbish. On my part, it was the caprice of a well-fed man; on the lawyer's pure greed of gold."

He recollected further what happened after the evening party. It was decided that the lawyer must undergo his imprisonment under the strictest observation, in a garden wing of the banker's house. It was agreed that during the period he would be deprived of the right to cross the threshold, to see living people, to hear human voices, and to receive letters and newspapers. He was permitted to have a musical instrument, to read books, to write letters, to drink wine and smoke tobacco. By the agreement he could communicate, but only in silence, with the outside world through a little window specially constructed for this purpose. Everything necessary, books, music, wine, he could receive in any quantity by sending a note through the window. The agreement provided for all the minutest details, which made the confinement strictly solitary, and it obliged the lawyer to remain exactly fifteen years from twelve o'clock of November 14th, 1870, to twelve o'clock of November 14th, 1885. The least attempt on his part to violate the conditions, to escape if only for two minutes before the time, freed the banker from the obligation to pay him the two millions.

During the first year of imprisonment, the lawyer, as far as it was possible to judge from his short notes, suffered terribly from loneliness and boredom. From his wing day and night came the sound of the piano. He rejected wine and tobacco. "Wine," he wrote, "excites desires, and desires are the chief foes of a prisoner; besides, nothing is more boring than to drink good wine alone, and tobacco spoils the air in his room." During the first year the lawyer was sent books of a light character; novels with a complicated love interest, stories of crime and fantasy, comedies, and so on.

In the second year the piano was heard no longer and the lawyer asked only for classics. In the fifth year, music was heard again, and the prisoner asked for wine. Those who watched him said that during the whole of that year he was only eating, drinking, and lying on his bed. He yawned often and talked angrily to himself. Books he did not read. Sometimes at nights he would sit down to write. He would write for a long time and tear it all up in the morning. More than once he was heard to weep.

In the second half of the sixth year, the prisoner began zealously to study languages, philosophy, and history. He fell on these subjects so hungrily that the banker hardly had time to get books enough for him. In the space of four years about six hundred volumes were bought at his request. It was while that passion lasted that the banker received the following letter from the prisoner: "My dear gaoler, I am writing these lines in six languages. Show them to experts. Let them read them. If they do not find one single mistake, I beg you to give orders to have a gun fired off in the garden. By the noise I shall know that my efforts have not been in vain. The genuises of all ages and countries speak in different languages; but in them all burns the same flame. Oh, if you knew my heavenly happiness now that I can understand them!" The prisoner's desire was fulfilled. Two shots were fired in the garden by the banker's order.

Later on, after the tenth year, the lawyer sat immovable before his table and read only the New Testament. The banker found it strange that a man who in four years had mastered six hundred erudite volumes, should have spent nearly a year in reading one book, easy to understand and by no means thick. The New Testament was then replaced by the history of religions and theology.

During the last two years of his confinement the prisoner read an extraordinary amount, quite haphazard. Now he would apply himself to the natural sciences, then he would read Byron or Shakespeare. Notes used to come from him in which he asked to be sent at the same time a book on chemistry, a textbook of medicine, a novel, and some treatise on philosophy or theology. He read as though he were swimming in the sea among broken pieces of wreckage, and in his desire to save his life was eagerly grasping one piece after another.

II

The banker recalled all this, and thought:

"Tomorrow at twelve o'clock he receives his freedom. Under the agreement, I shall have to pay him two millions. If I pay, it's all over with me. I am ruined forever . . ."

Fifteen years before he had too many millions to count, but now he was afraid to ask himself which he had more of, money or debts. Gambling on the Stock-Exchange, risky speculation, and the recklessness of which he could not rid himself even in old age, had gradually brought his business to decay; and the fearless, self-confident, proud man of business had become an ordinary banker, trembling at every rise and fall in the market.

"That cursed bet," murmured the old man clutching his head in despair. . . . "Why didn't the man die? He's only forty years old. He will take away my last farthing, marry, enjoy life, gamble on the Exchange, and I will look on like an envious beggar and hear the same words from him every day: 'I'm obliged to you for the happiness of my life. Let me help you.' No, it's too much! The only escape from bankruptcy and disgrace—is that the man should die."

The clock had just struck three. The banker was listening. In the house every one was asleep, and one could hear only the frozen trees whining outside the windows. Trying to make no sound, he took out of his safe the key of the door which had not been opened for fifteen years, put on his overcoat, and went out of the house. The garden was dark and cold. It was raining. A damp, penetrating wind howled in the garden and gave the trees no rest. Though he strained his eyes, the banker could see neither the ground, nor the white statues, nor the garden wing, nor the trees. Approaching the garden wing, he called the watchman twice. There was no answer. Evidently the watchman had taken shelter from the bad weather and was now asleep somewhere in the kitchen or the greenhouse.

"If I have the courage to fulfil my intention," thought the old man, "the suspicion will fall on the watchman first of all."

In the darkness he groped for the steps and the door and entered the hall of the garden-wing, then poked his way into a narrow passage and struck a match. Not a soul was there. Some one's bed, with no bedclothes on it, stood there, and an iron stove loomed dark in the corner. The seals on the door that led into the prisoner's room were unbroken.

When the match went out, the old man, trembling from agitation, peeped into the little window.

In the prisoner's room a candle was burning dimly. The prisoner himself sat by the table. Only his back, the hair on his head and his hands were visible. Open books were strewn about on the table, the two chairs, and on the carpet near the table.

Five minutes passed and the prisoner never once stirred. Fifteen years' confinement had taught him to sit motionless. The banker tapped on the window with his finger, but the prisoner made no movement in reply. Then the banker cautiously tore the seals from the door and put the key into the lock. The rusty lock gave a hoarse groan and the door creaked. The banker expected instantly to hear a cry of surprise and the sound of steps. Three minutes passed and it was as quiet inside as it had been before. He made up his mind to enter.

Before the table sat a man, unlike an ordinary human being. It was a skeleton, with tight-drawn skin, with long curly hair like a woman's, and a shaggy beard. The color of his face was yellow, of an earthy shade; the cheeks were sunken, the back long and narrow, and the hand upon which he leaned his hairy head was so lean and skinny that it was painful to look upon. His hair was already silvering with gray, and no one who glanced at the senile emaciation of the face would have believed that he was only forty years old. On the table, before his bended head, lay a sheet of paper on which something was written in a tiny hand.

"Poor devil," thought the banker, "he's asleep and probably seeing millions in his dreams. I have only to take and throw this half-dead thing on the bed, smother him a moment with the pillow, and the most careful examination will find no trace of unnatural death. But, first, let us read what he has written here."

The banker took the sheet from the table and read:

"Tomorrow at twelve o'clock midnight, I shall obtain my freedom and the right to mix with people. But before I leave this room and see the sun I think it necessary to say a few words to you. On my own clear conscience and before God who sees me I declare to you that I despise freedom, life, health, and all that your books call the blessings of the world.

"For fifteen years I have diligently studied earthly life. True, I saw neither the earth nor the people, but in your books I drank fragrant wine, sang songs, hunted deer and wild boar in the forests, loved women. . . . And beautiful women, like clouds ethereal, created by the magic of your poets' genius, visited me by night and whispered to me wonderful tales, which made my head drunken. In your books I climbed the summits of Elburz and Mont Blanc and saw from there how the sun rose in the morning, and in the evening suffused the sky, the ocean, and the mountain ridges with a purple gold. I saw from there how above me lightnings glimmered cleaving the clouds; I saw green forests, fields, rivers, lakes, cities; I heard sirens singing, and the playing of the pipes of Pan; I touched the wings of beautiful devils who came flying to me to speak of God. . . . In your books I cast myself into bottomless abysses, worked miracles, burned cities to the ground, preached new religions, conquered whole countries. . . .

"Your books gave me wisdom. All that unwearying human thought created in the centuries is compressed to a little lump in my skull. I know that I am cleverer than you all.

"And I despise your books, despise all worldly blessings and wisdom. Everything is void, frail, visionary and delusive as a mirage. Though you be proud and wise and beautiful, yet will death wipe you from the face of the earth like the mice underground; and your posterity, your history, and the immortality of your men of genius will be as frozen slag, burnt down together with the terrestrial globe.

"You are mad, and gone the wrong way. You take falsehood for truth and ugliness for beauty. You would marvel if suddenly apple and orange trees should bear frogs and lizards instead of fruit, and if roses should begin to breathe the odor of a sweating horse. So do I marvel at you, who have bartered heaven for earth. I do not want to understand you.

"That I may show you in deed my contempt for that by which you live, I waive the two millions of which I once dreamed as of paradise, and which I now despise. That I may deprive myself of my right to them, I shall come out from here five minutes before the stipulated term, and thus shall violate the agreement."

When he had read, the banker put the sheet on the table, kissed the head of the strange man, and began to weep. He went out of the wing. Never at any other time, not even after his terrible losses on the Exchange, had he felt such contempt for himself as now. Coming home, he lay down on his bed, but agitation and tears kept him a long time from sleeping. . . .

The next morning the poor watchman came running to him and told him that they had seen the man who lived in the wing climb through the window into the garden. He had gone to the gate and disappeared. The banker instantly went with his servants to the wing and established the escape of his prisoner. To avoid unnecessary rumors he took the paper with the renunciation from the table and, on his return, locked it in his safe.

CONRAD AIKEN

Silent Snow, Secret Snow

I

Just why it should have happened, or why it should have happened just when it did, he could not, of course, possibly have said; nor perhaps could it even have occurred to him to ask. The thing was above all a secret, something to be preciously concealed from Mother and Father; and to that very fact it owed an enormous part of its deliciousness. It was like a peculiarly beautiful trinket to be carried unmentioned in one's trouser-pocket—a rare stamp, an old coin, a few tiny gold links found trodden out of shape on the path in the park, a pebble of carnelian, a sea shell distinguishable from all others by an unusual spot or stripe—and, as if it were any one of these, he carried around with him everywhere a warm and persistent and increasingly beautiful sense of possession. Nor was it only a sense of possession—it was also a sense of protection. It was as if, in some delightful way, his secret gave him a fortress, a wall behind which he could retreat into heavenly seclusion. This was almost the first thing he had noticed about it—apart from the oddness of the thing itself—and it was this that now again, for the fiftieth time, occurred to him, as he sat in the little schoolroom. It was the half hour for geography. Miss Buell was revolving with one finger, slowly, a huge terrestrial globe which had been placed on her desk. The green and yellow continents passed and repassed, questions were asked and answered, and now the little girl in front of him, Deirdre, who had a funny little constellation of freckles on the back of her neck, exactly like the Big Dipper, was standing up and telling Miss Buell that the equator was the line that ran round the middle.

Miss Buell's face, which was old and grayish and kindly, with gray stiff curls beside the cheeks, and eyes that swam very brightly, like little minnows, behind thick glasses, wrinkled itself into a complication of amusements.

"Ah! I see. The earth is wearing a belt, or a sash. Or someone drew a line round it!"

"Oh, no—not that—I mean—"

In the general laughter, he did not share, or only a very little. He was thinking about the Arctic and Antarctic regions, which of course, on the globe, were white. Miss Buell was now telling them about the tropics, the jungles, the steamy heat of equatorial swamps, where the birds and butterflies, and even the snakes, were like living jewels. As he listened to these things, he was already, with a pleasant sense of half-effort, putting his secret between himself and the words. Was it really an effort at all? For effort implied something voluntary, and perhaps even something one did not especially want; whereas this was distinctly pleasant, and came almost of its own accord. All he needed to do was to think of that morning, the first one, and then of all the others—

But it was all so absurdly simple! It had amounted to so little. It was nothing, just an idea—and just why it should have become so wonderful, so permanent, was a mystery—a very pleasant one, to be sure, but also, in an amusing way, foolish. However, without ceasing to listen to Miss Buell, who had now moved up to the north temperate zone, he deliberately invited his memory of the first morning. It was only a moment or two after he had waked up—or perhaps the moment itself. But was there, to be exact, an exact moment? Was one awake all at once? Or was it gradual? Anyway, it was after he had stretched a lazy hand up towards the head-rail, and yawned, and then relaxed again among his warm covers, all the more grateful on a December morning, that the thing had happened. Suddenly, for no reason, he had thought of the postman, he remembered the postman. Perhaps there was nothing so odd in that. After all, he heard the postman almost every morning in his life—his heavy boots could be heard clumping round the corner at the top of the little cobbled hill-street, and then, progressively nearer, progressively louder, the double knock at each door, the crossings and re-crossings of the street, till finally the clumsy steps came stumbling across to the very door, and the tremendous knock came which shook the house itself.

(Miss Buell was saying "Vast wheat-growing areas in North America and Siberia."

Deirdre had for the moment placed her left hand across the back of her neck.)

But on this particular morning, the first morning, as he lay there with his eyes closed, he had for some reason *waited* for the postman. He wanted to hear him come round the corner. And that was precisely the joke—he never did. He never came. He never had come—*round the corner*—again. For when at last the steps *were* heard, they had already, he was quite sure, come a little down the hill, to the first house; and even so, the steps were curiously different—they were softer, they had a new secrecy about them, they were muffled and indistinct; and while the rhythm of them was the same, it now said a new thing—it said peace, it said remoteness, it said cold, it said sleep. And he had understood the situation at once—nothing could have seemed simpler—there had been snow in the night, such as all winter he had been longing for; and it was this which had rendered the postman's first footsteps inaudible, and the later ones faint. Of course! How lovely! And even now it must be snowing—it was going to be a snowy day—the long white ragged lines were drifting and sifting across the street, across the faces of the old houses, whispering and hush-ing, making little triangles of white in the corners between cobblestones, seething a little when the wind blew them over the ground to a drifted corner; and so it would be all day, getting deeper and deeper and silenter and silenter.

(Miss Buell was saying "Land of perpetual snow.")

All this time, of course (while he lay in bed), he had kept his eyes closed, listening to the nearer progress of the postman, the muffled footsteps thumping and slipping on the snow-sheathed cobbles; and all the other sounds—the double knocks, a frosty far-off voice or two, a bell ringing thinly and softly as if under a sheet of ice—had the same slightly abstracted quality, as if removed by one degree from actuality—as if everything in the world had been insulated by snow. But when at last, pleased, he opened his eyes, and turned them towards the window, to see for himself this long-desired and now so clearly imagined miracle—what he saw instead was brilliant sunlight on a roof; and when, astonished, he jumped out of bed and stared down into the street, expecting to see the cobbles obliterated by the snow, he saw nothing but the bare bright cobbles themselves.

Queer, the effect this extraordinary surprise had had upon him—all the following morning he had kept with him a sense as of snow falling about him, a secret screen of new snow between himself and the world. If he had not dreamed such a thing—and how could he have dreamed it while awake?—how else could one explain it? In any case, the delusion had been so vivid as to affect his entire behavior. He could not now remember whether it was on the first or the second morning—or was it even the third?—that his mother had drawn attention to some oddness in his manner.

"But my darling"—she had said at the breakfast table —"what has come over you? You don't seem to be listening. . . ."

And how often that very thing had happened since! (Miss Buell was now asking if anyone knew the difference between the North Pole and the Magnetic Pole. Deirdre was holding up her flickering brown hand, and he could see the four white dimples that marked the knuckles.)

Perhaps it hadn't been either the second or third morning—or even the fourth or fifth. How could he be sure? How could he be sure just when the delicious *progress* had become clear? Just when it had really *begun?* The intervals weren't very precise. . . . All he now knew was, that at some point or other—perhaps the second day, perhaps the sixth—he had noticed that the presence of the snow was a little more insistent, the sound of it clearer; and, conversely, the sound of the postman's footsteps more indistinct. Not only could he not hear the steps come round the corner, he could not even hear them at the first house. It was below the first house that he heard them; and then, a few days later, it was below the second house that he heard them; and a few days later again, below the third. Gradually, gradually, the snow was becoming heavier, the sound of its seething louder, the cobblestones more and more muffled. When he found, each morning, on going to the window, after the ritual of listening, that the roofs and cobbles were as bare as ever, it made no difference. This was, after all, only what he had expected. It was even what pleased him, what rewarded him: the thing was his own, belonged to no one else. No one else knew about it, not even his mother and father. There, outside, were the bare cobbles; and here, inside, was the snow. Snow growing heavier each day, muffling the world, hiding the ugly, and deadening increasingly—above all—the steps of the postman.

"But my darling"—she had said at the luncheon table —"what has come over you? You don't seem to listen when people speak to you. That's the third time I've asked you to pass your plate. . . ."

How was one to explain this to Mother? or to Father? There was, of course, nothing to be done about it: nothing. All one could do was to laugh embarrassedly, pretend to be a little ashamed, apologize, and take a sudden and somewhat disingenuous interest in what was being done or said. The cat had stayed out all night. He had a curious swelling on his left cheek—perhaps somebody had kicked him, or a stone had struck him. Mrs. Kempton was or was not coming to tea. The house was going to be house cleaned, or "turned out," on Wednesday instead of Friday. A new lamp was provided for his evening work—perhaps it was eyestrain which accounted for this new and so peculiar vagueness of his—Mother was looking at him with amusement as she said this, but with something else as well. A new lamp? A new lamp. Yes Mother, No Mother, Yes Mother. School is going very well. The geometry is very easy. The history is very dull. The geography is very interesting—particularly when it takes one to the North Pole. Why the North Pole? Oh, well, it would be fun to be an explorer. Another Peary or Scott or Shackleton. And then abruptly he found his interest in the talk at an end, stared at the pudding on his plate, listened, waited, and began once more—ah, how heavenly, too, the first beginnings—to hear or feel—for could he actually hear it?—the silent snow, the secret snow.

(Miss Buell was telling them about the search for the Northwest Passage, about Hendrik Hudson, the *Half Moon.*)

This had been, indeed, the only distressing feature of the new experience: the fact that it so increasingly had brought him into a kind of mute misunderstanding, or even conflict, with his father and mother. It was as if he were trying to lead a double life. On the one hand he had to be Paul Hasleman, and keep up the appearance of being that person—dress, wash, and answer intelligently when spoken to; on the other, he had to explore this new world which had been opened to him. Nor could there be the slightest doubt—not the slightest—that the new world was the profounder and more wonderful of the two. It was irresistible. It was miraculous. Its beauty was simply beyond anything—beyond speech as beyond thought—utterly incommunicable. But how then, between the two worlds, of which he was thus constantly aware, was he to keep a balance? One must get up, one must go to breakfast, one must talk with Mother, go to school, do one's lessons—and, in all this, try not to appear too much of a fool. But if all the while one was also trying to extract the full deliciousness of another and quite separate existence, one which could not easily (if at all) be spoken of—how was one to manage? How was one to explain? Would it be safe to explain? Would it be absurd? Would it merely mean that he would get into some obscure kind of trouble?

These thoughts came and went, came and went, as softly and secretly as the snow; they were not precisely a disturbance, perhaps they were even a pleasure; he liked to have them; their presence was something almost palpable, something he could stroke with his hand, without closing his eyes, and without ceasing to see Miss Buell and the schoolroom and the globe and the freckles on Deirdre's neck; nevertheless he did in a sense cease to see, or to see the obvious external world, and substituted for this vision the vision of snow, the sound of snow, and the slow, almost soundless, approach of the postman. Yesterday, it had been only at the sixth house that the postman had become audible; the snow was much deeper now, it was falling more swiftly and heavily, the sound of its seething was more distinct, more soothing, more persistent. And this morning, it had been—as nearly as he could figure—just above the seventh house—perhaps only a step or two above: at most, he had heard two or three footsteps before the knock had sounded. . . . And with each such narrowing of the sphere, each nearer approach of the limit at which the postman was first audible, it was odd how sharply was increased the amount of illusion which had to be carried into the ordinary business of daily life. Each day it was harder to get out of bed, to go to the window, to look out at the—as always—perfectly empty and snowless street. Each day it was more difficult to go through the perfunctory motions of greeting Mother and Father at breakfast, to reply to their questions, to put his books together and go to school. And at school, how extraordinarily hard to conduct with success simultaneously the public life and the life that was secret. There were times when he longed—positively ached—to tell everyone about it—to burst out with it—only to be checked almost at once by a far-off feeling as of some faint absurdity which was inherent in it—but *was* it absurd?—and more importantly by a sense of mysterious power in his very secrecy. Yes: it must be kept secret. That, more and more, became clear. At whatever cost to himself, whatever pain to others—

(Miss Buell looked straight at him, smiling, and said, "Perhaps we'll ask Paul. I'm sure Paul will come out of his day-dream long enough to be able to tell us. Won't you, Paul?" He rose slowly from his chair, resting one hand on the brightly varnished desk, and deliberately stared through the snow towards the blackboard. It was an effort, but it was amusing to make it. "Yes," he said slowly, "it was what we now call the Hudson River. This he thought to be the Northwest Passage. He was disappointed." He sat down again, and as he did so Deirdre half turned in her chair and gave him a shy smile, of approval and admiration.)

At whatever pain to others.

This part of it was very puzzling, very puzzling. Mother was very nice, and so was Father. Yes, that was all true enough. He wanted to be nice to them, to tell them everything—and yet, was it really wrong of him to want to have a secret place of his own?

At bedtime, the night before, Mother had said, "If this goes on, my lad, we'll have to see a doctor, we will! We can't have our boy—" But what was it she had said? "Live in another world"? "Live so far away"? The word "far" had been in it, he was sure, and then Mother had taken up a magazine again and laughed a little, but with an expression which wasn't mirthful. He had felt sorry for her. . . .

The bell rang for dismissal. The sound came to him through long curved parallels of falling snow. He saw Deirdre rise, and had himself risen almost as soon—but not quite as soon—as she.

II

On the walk homeward, which was timeless, it pleased him to see through the accompaniment, or counterpoint, of snow, the items of mere externality on his way. There were many kinds of bricks in the sidewalks, and laid in many kinds of pattern. The garden walls too were various, some of wooden palings, some of plaster, some of stone. Twigs of bushes leaned over the walls; the little hard green winter-buds of lilac, on gray stems, sheathed and fat; other branches very thin and fine and black and desiccated. Dirty sparrows huddled in the bushes, as dull in color as dead fruit left in leafless trees. A single starling creaked on a weather vane. In the gutter, beside a drain, was a scrap of torn and dirty newspaper, caught in a little delta of filth: the word ECZEMA appeared in large capitals, and below it was a letter from Mrs. Amelia D. Cravath, 2100 Pine Street, Fort Worth, Texas, to the effect that after being a sufferer for years she had been cured by Caley's Ointment. In the little delta, beside the fan-shaped and deeply runneled continent of brown mud, were lost twigs, descended from their parent trees, dead matches, a rusty horse-chestnut burr, a small concentration of sparkling gravel on the lip of the sewer, a fragment of eggshell, a streak of yellow sawdust which had been wet and was now dry and congealed, a brown pebble, and a broken feather. Further on was a cement sidewalk, ruled into geometrical parallelograms, with a brass inlay at one end commemorating the contractors who had laid it, and, halfway across, an irregular and random series of dog-tracks, immortalized in synthetic stone. He knew these well, and always stepped on them; to cover the little hollows with his own foot had always been a queer pleasure; today he did it once more, but perfunctorily and detachedly, all the while thinking of something else. That was a dog, a long time ago, who had made a mistake and walked on the cement while it was still wet. He had probably wagged his tail, but that hadn't been recorded. Now, Paul Hasleman, aged twelve, on his way home from school, crossed the same river, which in the meantime had frozen into rock. Homeward through the snow, the snow falling in bright sunshine. Homeward?

Then came the gateway with the two posts surmounted by egg-shaped stones which had been cunningly balanced on their ends, as if by Columbus, and mortared in the very act of balance: a source of perpetual wonder. On the brick wall just beyond, the letter H had been stenciled, presumably for some purpose. H? H.

The green hydrant, with a little green-painted chain attached to the brass screw-cap.

The elm tree, with the great gray wound in the bark, kidney-shaped, into which he always put his hand—to feel the cold but living wood. The injury, he had been sure, was due to the gnawings of a tethered horse. But now it deserved only a passing palm, a merely tolerant eye. There were more important things. Miracles. Beyond the thoughts of trees, mere elms. Beyond the thoughts of sidewalks, mere stone, mere brick, mere cement. Beyond the thoughts even of his own shoes, which trod these sidewalks obediently, bearing a burden—far above—of elaborate mystery. He watched them. They were not very well polished; he had neglected them, for a very good reason: they were one of the many parts of the increasing difficulty of the daily return to daily life, the morning struggle. To get up, having at last opened one's eyes, to go to the window, and discover no snow, to wash, to dress, to descend the curving stairs to breakfast—

At whatever pain to others, nevertheless, one must persevere in severance, since the incommunicability of the experience demanded it. It was desirable of course to be kind to Mother and Father, especially as they seemed to be worried, but it was also desirable to be resolute. If they should decide—as appeared likely—to consult the doctor, Doctor Howells, and have Paul inspected, his heart listened to through a kind of dictaphone, his lungs, his stomach—well, that was all right. He would go through with it. He would give them answer for question, too—perhaps such answers as they hadn't expected? No. That would never do. For the secret world must, at all costs, be preserved.

The bird-house in the apple-tree was empty—it was the wrong time of year for wrens. The little round black door had lost its pleasure. The wrens were enjoying other houses, other nests, remoter trees. But this too was a notion which he only vaguely and grazingly entertained—as if, for the moment, he merely touched an edge of it; there was something further on, which was already assuming a sharper importance; something which already teased at the corners of his eyes, teasing also at the corner of his mind. It was funny to think that he so wanted this, so awaited it—and yet found himself enjoying this momentary dalliance with the bird-house, as if for a quite deliberate postponement and enhancement of the approaching pleasure. He was aware of his delay, of his smiling and detached and now almost uncomprehending gaze at the little bird-house; he knew what he was going to look at next: it was his own little cobbled hill-street, his own house, the little river at the bottom of the hill, the grocer's shop with the cardboard man in the window—and now, thinking of all this, he turned his head, still smiling, and looking quickly right and left through the snow-laden sunlight.

And the mist of snow, as he had foreseen, was still on it—a ghost of snow falling in the bright sunlight, softly and steadily floating and turning and pausing, soundlessly meeting the snow that covered, as with a transparent mirage, the bare bright cobbles. He loved it—he stood still and loved it. Its beauty was paralyzing—beyond all words, all experience, all dream. No fairy-story he had ever read could be compared with it—none had ever given him this extraordinary combination of ethereal loveliness with a something else, unnameable, which was just faintly and deliciously terrifying. What was this thing? As he thought of it, he looked upward toward his own bedroom window, which was open—and it was as if he looked straight into the room and saw himself lying half awake in his bed. There he was—at this very instant he was still perhaps actually there—more truly there than standing here at the edge of the cobbled hill-street, with one hand lifted to shade his eyes against the snow-sun. Had he indeed ever left his room, in all this time? since that very first morning? Was the whole progress still being enacted there, was it still the same morning, and himself not yet wholly awake? And even now, had the postman not yet come round the corner? . . .

This idea amused him, and automatically, as he

thought of it, he turned his head and looked toward the top of the hill. There was, of course, nothing there—nothing and no one. The street was empty and quiet. And all the more because of its emptiness it occurred to him to count the houses—a thing which, oddly enough, he hadn't before thought of doing. Of course, he had known there weren't many—many, that is, on his own side of the street, which were the ones that figured in the postman's progress—but nevertheless it came to him as something of a shock to find that there were precisely *six*, above his own house—his own house was the seventh.

Six!

Astonished, he looked at his own house—looked at the door, on which was the number thirteen—and then realized that the whole thing was exactly and logically and absurdly what he ought to have known. Just the same, the realization gave him abruptly, and even a little frighteningly, a sense of hurry. He was being hurried—he was being rushed. For—he knit his brows—he couldn't be mistaken—it was just above the *seventh* house, his *own* house, that the postman had first been audible this very morning. But in that case—in that case—did it mean that tomorrow he would hear nothing? The knock he had heard must have been the knock of their own door. Did it mean—and this was an idea which gave him a really extraordinary feeling of surprise—that he would never hear the postman again?—that tomorrow morning the postman would already have passed the house, in a snow by then so deep as to render his footsteps completely inaudible? That he would have made his approach down the snow-filled street so soundlessly, so secretly, that he, Paul Hasleman, there lying in bed, would not have waked in time, or, waking, would have heard nothing?

But how could that be? Unless even the knocker should be muffled in the snow—frozen tight, perhaps? . . . But in that case—

A vague feeling of disappointment came over him; a vague sadness, as if he felt himself deprived of something which he had long looked forward to, something much prized. After all this, all this beautiful progress, the slow delicious advance of the postman through the silent and secret snow, the knock creeping closer each day, and the footsteps nearer, the audible compass of the world thus daily narrowed, narrowed, narrowed, as the snow soothingly and beautifully encroached and deepened, after all this, was he to be defrauded of the one thing he had so wanted—to be able to count, as it were, the last two or three solemn footsteps, as they finally approached his own door? Was it all going to happen, at the end, so suddenly? Or indeed, had it already happened? With no slow and subtle gradations of menace, in which he could luxuriate?

He gazed upward again, toward his own window which flashed in the sun: and this time almost with a feeling that it would be better if he *were* still in bed, in that room; for in that case this must still be the first morning, and there would be six more mornings to come—or, for that matter, seven or eight or nine—how could he be sure?—or even more.

III

After supper, the inquisition began. He stood before the doctor, under the lamp, and submitted silently to the usual thumpings and tappings.

"Now will you please say 'Ah!'?"

"Ah!"

"Now again please, if you don't mind."

"Ah."

"Say it slowly and hold it if you can—"

"Ah-h-h-h-h-h—"

"Good."

How silly all this was. As if it had anything to do with his throat! Or his heart or lungs!

Relaxing his mouth, of which the corners, after all this absurd stretching, felt uncomfortable, he avoided the doctor's eyes, and stared towards the fireplace, past his mother's feet (in gray slippers) which projected from the green chair, and his father's feet (in brown slippers) which stood neatly side by side on the hearth rug.

"Hm. There is certainly nothing wrong there . . ."

He felt the doctor's eyes fixed upon him, and, as if merely to be polite, returned the look, but with a feeling of justifiable evasiveness.

"Now, young man, tell me,—do you feel all right?"

"Yes, sir, quite all right."

"No headaches? No dizziness?"

"No, I don't think so."

"Let me see. Let's get a book, if you don't mind—yes, thank you, that will do splendidly—and now, Paul, if you'll just read it, holding it as you would normally hold it—"

He took the book and read:

"And another praise have I to tell for this the city our mother, the gift of a great god, a glory of the land most high; the might of horses, the might of young horses, the might of the sea. . . . For thou, son of Cronus, our lord Poseidon, hast throned herein this pride, since in these roads first thou didst show forth the curb that cures the rage of steeds. And the shapely oar, apt to men's hands, hath a wonderous speed on the brine, following the hundred-footed Nereids. . . . O land that art praised above all lands, now is it for thee to make those bright praises seen in deeds."

He stopped, tentatively, and lowered the heavy book.

"No—as I thought—there is certainly no superficial sign of eyestrain."

Silence thronged the room, and he was aware of the focused scrutiny of the three people who confronted him. . . .

"We could have his eyes examined—but I believe it is something else."

"What could it be?" This was his father's voice.

"It's only this curious absent-minded—" This was his mother's voice.

In the presence of the doctor, they both seemed irritatingly apologetic.

"I believe it is something else. Now, Paul—I would like very much to ask you a question or two. You will answer them, won't you—you know I'm an old, old friend of yours, eh? That's right! . . ."

His back was thumped twice by the doctor's fat fist—then the doctor was grinning at him with false amiability, while with one finger-nail he was scratching the top button of his waistcoat. Beyond the doctor's shoulder was the fire, the fingers of flame making light prestidigitation against the sooty fireback, the soft sound of their random flutter the only sound.

"I would like to know—is there anything that worries you?"

The doctor was again smiling, his eyelids low against the little black pupils, in each of which was a tiny white bead of light. Why answer him? Why answer him at all? "At whatever pain to others"—but it was all a nuisance, this necessity for resistance, this necessity for attention: it was as if one had been stood up on a brilliantly lighted stage, under a great round blaze of spotlight; as if one were merely a trained seal, or a performing dog, or a fish, dipped out of an aquarium and held up by the tail. It would serve them right if he were merely to bark or growl. And meanwhile, to miss these last few precious hours, these hours of which every minute was more beautiful than the last, more menacing—? He still looked, as if from a great distance, at the beads of light in the doctor's eyes, at the fixed false smile, and then, beyond, once more at his mother's slippers, his father's slippers, the soft flutter of the fire. Even here, even amongst these hostile presences, and in this arranged light, he could see the snow, he could hear it—it was in the corners of the room, where the shadow was deepest, under the sofa, behind the half-opened door which led to the dining room. It was gentler here, softer, its seethe the quietest of whispers, as if, in deference to a drawing room, it had quite deliberately put on its "manners"; it kept itself out of sight, obliterated itself, but distinctly with an air of saying, "Ah, but just wait! Wait till we are alone together! Then I will begin to tell you something new! Something white! something cold! something sleepy! something of cease, and peace, and the long bright curve of space! Tell them to go away. Banish them. Refuse to speak. Leave them, go upstairs to your room, turn out the light and get into bed—I will go with you, I will be waiting for you, I will tell you a better story than Little Kay of the Skates, or The Snow Ghost—I will surround your bed, I will close the windows, pile a deep drift against the door, so that none will ever again be able to enter. Speak to them! . . ." It seemed as if the little hissing voice came from a slow white spiral of falling flakes in the corner by the front window—but he could not be sure. He felt himself smiling, then, and said to the doctor, but without looking at him, looking beyond him still—

"Oh, no, I think not—"

"But are you sure, my boy?"

His father's voice came softly and coldly then—the familiar voice of silken warning. . . .

"You needn't answer at once, Paul—remember we're trying to help you—think it over and be quite sure, won't you?"

He felt himself smiling again, at the notion of being quite sure. What a joke! As if he weren't so sure that reassurance was no longer necessary, and all this cross-examination a ridiculous farce, a grotesque parody! What could they know about it? These gross intelligences, these humdrum minds so bound to the usual, the ordinary? Impossible to tell them about it! Why, even now, even now, with the proof so abundant, so formidable, so imminent, so appallingly present here in this very room, could they believe it?—could even his mother believe it? No—it was only too plain that if anything were said about it, the merest hint given, they would be incredulous—they would laugh—they would say "Absurd!"—think things about him which weren't true. . . .

"Why no, I'm not worried—why should I be?"

He looked then straight at the doctor's low-lidded eyes, looked from one of them to the other, from one bead of light to the other, and gave a little laugh.

The doctor seemed to be disconcerted by this. He drew back in his chair, resting a fat white hand on either knee. The smile faded slowly from his face.

"Well, Paul!" he said, and paused gravely, "I'm afraid you don't take this quite seriously enough. I think you perhaps don't quite realize—don't quite realize—" He took a deep quick breath, and turned, as if helpless, at a loss for words, to the others. But Mother and Father were both silent—no help was forthcoming.

"You must surely know, be aware, that you have not been quite yourself, of late? Don't you know that? . . ."

It was amusing to watch the doctor's renewed attempt at a smile, a queer disorganized look, as of confidential embarrassment.

"I feel all right, sir," he said, and again gave the little laugh.

"And we're trying to help you." The doctor's tone sharpened.

"Yes, sir, I know. But why? I'm all right. I'm just *thinking*, that's all."

His mother made a quick movement forward, resting a hand on the back of the doctor's chair.

"Thinking?" she said. "But my dear, about what?"

This was a direct challenge—and would have to be directly met. But before he met it, he looked again into the corner by the door, as if for reassurance. He smiled again at what he saw, at what he heard. The little spiral was still there, still softly whirling, like the ghost of a white kitten chasing the ghost of a white tail, and making as it did so the faintest of whispers. It was all right! If only he could remain firm, everything was going to be all right.

"Oh, about anything, about nothing—*you* know the way you do!"

"You mean—day-dreaming?"

"Oh, no—thinking!"

"But thinking about *what?*"

"Anything."

He laughed a third time—but this time, happening to glance upward towards his mother's face, he was appalled at the effect his laughter seemed to have upon her. Her mouth had opened in an expression of horror. . . . This was too bad! Unfortunate! He had known it would cause pain, of course—but he hadn't expected it to be quite so bad as this. Perhaps—perhaps if he just gave them a tiny gleaming hint—?

"About the snow," he said.

"What on earth!" This was his father's voice. The brown slippers came a step nearer on the hearth-rug.

"But my dear, what do you mean!" This was his mother's voice.

The doctor merely stared.

"Just *snow*, that's all. I like to think about it."

"Tell us about it, my boy."

"But that's all it is. There's nothing to tell. *You* know what snow is."

This he said almost angrily, for he felt that they were trying to corner him. He turned sideways so as no longer to face the doctor, and the better to see the inch of blackness between the window-sill and the lowered curtains, —the cold inch of beckoning and delicious night. At once he felt better, more assured.

"Mother—can I go to bed, now, please? I've got a headache."

"But I thought you said—"

"It's just come. It's all these questions—! Can I, Mother?"

"You can go as soon as the doctor has finished."

"Don't you think this thing ought to be gone into thoroughly, and *now*?" This was Father's voice. The brown slippers again came a step nearer, the voice was the well-known "punishment" voice, resonant and cruel.

"Oh, what's the use, Norman—"

Quite suddenly, everyone was silent. And without precisely facing them, nevertheless he was aware that all three of them were watching him with an extraordinary intensity—staring hard at him—as if he had done something monstrous, or was himself some kind of monster. He could hear the soft irregular flutter of the flames; the cluck-click-cluck-click of the clock; far and faint, two sudden spurts of laughter from the kitchen, as quickly cut off as begun; a murmur of water in the pipes; and then, the silence seemed to deepen, to spread out, to become worldlong and worldwide, to become timeless and shapeless, and to center inevitably and rightly, with a slow and sleepy but enormous concentration of all power, on the beginning of a new sound. What this new sound was going to be, he knew perfectly well. It might begin with a hiss, but it would end with a roar—there was no time to lose—he must escape. It mustn't happen here—

Without another word, he turned and ran up the stairs.

IV

Not a moment too soon. The darkness was coming in long white waves. A prolonged sibilance filled the night—a great seamless seethe of wild influence went abruptly across it—a cold low humming shook the windows. He shut the door and flung off his clothes in the dark. The bare black floor was like a little raft tossed in waves of snow, almost overwhelmed, washed under whitely, up again, smothered in curled billows of feather. The snow was laughing: it spoke from all sides at once: it pressed closer to him as he ran and jumped exulting into his bed.

"Listen to us!" it said. "Listen! We have come to tell you the story we told you about. You remember? Lie down. Shut your eyes, now—you will no longer see much—in this white darkness who could see, or want to see? We will take the place of everything. . . . Listen—"

A beautiful varying dance of snow began at the front of the room, came forward and then retreated, flattened out toward the floor, then rose fountain-like to the ceiling, swayed, recruited itself from a new stream of flakes which poured laughing in through the humming window, advanced again, lifted long white arms. It said peace, it said remoteness, it said cold—it said—

But then a gash of horrible light fell brutally across the room from the opening door—the snow drew back hissing—something alien had come into the room—something hostile. This thing rushed at him, clutched at him, shook him—and he was not merely horrified, he was filled with such a loathing as he had never known. What was this? this cruel disturbance? this act of anger and hate? It was as if he had to reach up a hand toward another world for any understanding of it—an effort of which he was only barely capable. But of that other world he still remembered just enough to know the exorcising words. They tore themselves from his other life suddenly—

"Mother! Mother! Go away! I hate you!"

And with that effort, everything was solved, everything became all right: the seamless hiss advanced once more, the long white wavering lines rose and fell like enormous whispering sea-waves, the whisper becoming louder, the laughter more numerous.

"Listen!" it said. "We'll tell you the last, the most beautiful and secret story—shut your eyes—it is a very small story—a story that gets smaller and smaller—it comes inward instead of opening like a flower—it is a flower becoming a seed—a little cold seed—do you hear? We are leaning closer to you—"

The hiss was now becoming a roar—the whole world was a vast moving screen of snow—but even now it said peace, it said remoteness, it said cold, it said sleep.

PART *FUN,* PART *SYMBOL*

LOGAN PEARSALL SMITH

Trivia

LONGEVITY

"But when you are as old as I am!" I said to the young lady in pink satin. "But I don't know how old you are," that young lady answered almost archly. We were getting on quite nicely.

"Oh, I'm endlessly old; my memory goes back almost forever. I come out of the Middle Ages. I am the primitive savage we all descended from; I believe in Devil-worship, and the power of the Stars; I dance under the new Moon, naked and tattooed and holy. I am a Cave-dweller, a contemporary of Mastodons and Mammoths; I am pleistocene and neolithic, and full of the lusts and terrors of the great pre-glacial forests. But that's nothing;

I am millions of years older; I am an arboreal Ape, an aged Baboon, with all its instincts; I am a pre-simian quadruped, I have great claws, eyes that see in the dark, and a long prehensile tail."

"Good gracious!" said the terrified young lady in pink satin. Then she turned, and for the rest of the dinner talked in a hushed voice with her other neighbour.

WHISKERS

There was once a young man who thought he saw Life as it really is, who prided himself on looking at it grimly in the face without illusions. And he went on looking at it grimly, as he thought, for a number of years. This was his notion of himself; but one day, meeting some very young people, he saw, reflected as it were in their eyes, a bland old gentleman with a white waistcoat and Victorian whiskers, a lover of souls and sunsets, and noble solutions for all problems——

That was what he saw in the eyes of those atrocious young men.

MARK TWAIN

Baker's Blue Jay Yarn

Editor's Note: In his preface to the following story, Mark Twain claimed to have known "a middle-aged simple-hearted miner," who had the ability to understand the language of the birds and the beasts. His name was Jim Baker, and, according to Twain, Jim told him the following tale.

When I first begun to understand jay language correctly, there was a little incident happened here. Seven years ago, the last man in this region but me moved away. There stands his house—been empty ever since; a log house, with a plank roof—just one big room, and no more; no ceiling—nothing between the rafters and the floor. Well, one Sunday morning I was sitting out here in front of my cabin, with my cat, taking the sun, and looking at the blue hills, and listening to the leaves rustling

From *A Tramp Abroad* by Mark Twain. Reprinted by permission of The Mark Twain Company and Harper & Brothers.

so lonely in the trees, and thinking of the home away yonder in the states, that I hadn't heard from in thirteen years, when a blue jay lit on that house, with an acorn in his mouth, and says, "Hello, I reckon I've struck something." When he spoke, the acorn dropped out of his mouth and rolled down the roof, of course, but he didn't care; his mind was all on the thing he had struck. It was a knot-hole in the roof. He cocked his head to one side, shut one eye and put the other one to the hole, like a 'possum looking down a jug; then he glanced up with his bright eyes, gave a wink or two with his wings—which signifies gratification, you understand—and says, "It looks like a hole, it's located like a hole—blamed if I don't believe it *is* a hole!"

Then he cocked his head down and took another look; he glances up perfectly joyful, this time; winks his wings and his tail both, and says, "Oh, no, this ain't no fat thing, I reckon! If I ain't in luck!—why it's a perfectly elegant hole!" So he flew down and got that acorn, and fetched it up and dropped it in, and was just tilting his head back, with the heavenliest smile on his face, when all of a sudden he was paralyzed into a listening attitude and that smile faded gradually out of his countenance like breath off'n a razor, and the queerest look of surprise took its place. Then he says, "Why, I didn't hear it fall!" He cocked his eye at the hole again, and took a long look; raised up and shook his head; stepped around to the other side of the hole and took another look from that side; shook his head again. He studied awhile, then he just went into the *de*tails—walked round and round the hole and spied into it from every point of the compass. No use. Now he took a thinking attitude on the comb of the roof and scratched the back of his head with his right foot a minute, and finally says, "Well, it's too many for *me*, that's certain; must be a mighty long hole; however, I ain't got no time to fool around here; I got to 'tend to business; I reckon it's all right—chance it, anyway."

So he flew off and fetched another acorn and dropped it in, and tried to flirt his eye to the hole quick enough to see what become of it, but he was too late. He held his eye there as much as a minute; then he raised up and sighed, and says, "Confound it, I don't seem to understand this thing, no way; however, I'll tackle her again." He fetched another acorn, and done his level best to see what become of it, but he couldn't. He says, "Well, *I* never struck no such a hole as this before; I'm of the opinion it's a totally new kind of a hole." Then he begun to get mad. He held in for a spell, walking up and down the comb of the roof and shaking his head and muttering to himself; but his feelings got the upper hand of him, presently, and he broke loose and cussed himself black in the face. I never see a bird take on so about a little thing. When he got through he walks to the hole and looks in again for half a minute; then he says, "Well, you're a long hole, and a deep hole, and a mighty singular hole altogether—but I've started in to fill you, and I'm d—d if I don't fill you, if it takes a hundred years!"

And with that, away he went. You never see a bird work so since you was born. He laid into his work like a nigger and the way he hove acorns into that hole for about two hours and a half was one of the most exciting and astonishing spectacles I ever struck. He never stopped to take a look any more—he just hove 'em in and went for more. Well, at last he could hardly flop his wings, he was so tuckered out. He comes a-drooping down, once more, sweating like an ice-pitcher, drops his acorn in and says, "*Now* I guess I've got the bulge on you by this time!" So he bent down for a look. If you'll believe me, when his head come up again he was just pale with rage. He says, "I've shoveled acorns enough in there to keep the family thirty years, and if I can see a sign of one of 'em I wish I may land in a museum with a bellyful of sawdust in two minutes!"

He just had strength enough to crawl up on the comb and lean his back agin the chimbly, and then he collected his impressions and begun to free his mind. I see in a second that what I had mistook for profanity in the mines was only just the rudiments, as you may say.

Another jay was going by, and heard him doing his devotions, and stops to inquire what was up. The sufferer told him the whole circumstance, and says, "Now yonder's the hole, and if you don't believe me, go and look for yourself." So this fellow went and looked, and comes back and says, "How many did you say you put in there?" "Not any less than two tons," says the sufferer. The other jay went and looked again. He couldn't seem to make it out, so he raised a yell, and three more jays come. They all examined the hole, they all made the sufferer tell it over again, then they all discussed it, and got off as many leather-headed opinions about it as an average crowd of humans could have done.

They called in more jays; then more and more, till pretty soon this whole region 'peared to have a blue flush about it. There must have been five thousand of them; and such another jawing and disputing and ripping and cussing you never heard. Every jay in the whole lot put his eye to the hole and delivered a more chuckle-headed opinion about the mystery than the jay that went there before him. They examined the house all over, too. The door was standing half open, and at last one old jay happened to go and light on it and look in. Of course, that knocked the mystery galley-west in a second. There lay the acorns, scattered all over the floor. He flopped his wings and raised a whoop. "Come here!" he says. "Come here, everybody; hanged if this fool hasn't been trying to fill up a house with acorns!" They all came a-swooping down like a blue cloud, and as each fellow lit on the door and took a glance, the whole absurdity of the contract that that first jay had tackled hit him home and he fell over backwards suffocating with laughter, and the next jay took his place and done the same.

Well, sir, they roosted around here on the housetop and the trees for an hour, and guffawed over that thing like human beings. It ain't any use to tell me a blue jay hasn't got a sense of humor, because I know better. And memory, too. They brought jays here from all over the United States to look down that hole, every summer for three years. Other birds, too. And they could all see the point, except an owl that come from Nova Scotia to visit the Yo Semite, and he took this thing in on his way back. He said he couldn't see anything funny in it. But then he was a good deal disappointed about Yo Semite, too.

JAMES THURBER

The Last Clock

A FABLE FOR THE TIME, SUCH AS IT IS, OF MAN

In a country the other side of tomorrow, an ogre who had eaten a clock and had fallen into the habit of eating clocks was eating a clock in the clockroom of his castle when his ogress and their ilk knocked down the locked door and shook their hairy heads at him.

"Wulsa malla?" gurgled the ogre, for too much clock oil had turned all his "t"s to "l"s.

"Just look at this room!" exclaimed the ogress, and they all looked at the room, the ogre with eyes as fogged as the headlights of an ancient limousine. The stone floor of the room was littered with fragments of dials, oily coils and springs, broken clock hands, and pieces of pendulums. "I've brought a doctor to look at you," the ogress said.

The doctor wore a black beard, carried a black bag, and gave the ogre a black look. "This case is clearly not in my area," he said.

The ogre struck three, and the doctor flushed.

"This is a case for a clockman," the doctor said, "for the problem is not what clocks have done to the ogre but what the ogre has done to clocks."

"Wulsa malla?" the ogre gurgled again.

"Eating clocks has turned all his 't's to 'l's," the ogress said. "That's what clocks have done to him."

"Then your clockman may have to call in consultation a semanticist or a dictionist or an etymologist or a syntaxman," the non-clock doctor said, and he bowed stiffly and left the room.

The next morning, the ogress brought into the clock-room a beardless man with a box of tools under his arm. "I've brought a clockman to see you," she told the ogre.

"No, no, no," said the beardless man with the box of tools. "I'm not a clockman. I thought you said clogman. I'm a clogman. I cannot ethically depart from my area, which is clogged drains and gutters. I get mice out of pipes, and bugs out of tubes, and moles out of tiles, and there my area ends." The clogman bowed and went away.

"Wuld wuzzle?" the ogre wanted to know. He hiccuped, and something went *spong!*

"That was an area man, but the wrong area," the ogress explained. "I'll get a general practitioner." And she went away and came back with a general practitioner.

"This is a waste of time," he said. "As a general practitioner, modern style, I treat only generals. This patient is not even a private. He sounds to me like a public place—a clock tower, perhaps, or a belfry."

"What should I do?" asked the ogress. "Send for a tower man, or a belfry man?"

"I shall not venture an opinion," the general practitioner said. "I am a specialist in generals, one of whom has just lost command of his army and of all his faculties, and doesn't know what time it is. Good day." And the general practitioner went away.

The ogre cracked a small clock, as if it were a large walnut, and began eating it. "Wulsy wul?" the ogre asked.

The ogress, who could now talk clocktalk fluently, even oilily, but wouldn't, left the room to look up specialists in an enormous volume entitled "Who's Who in Areas." She soon became lost in a list of titles: clockmaker, clocksmith, clockwright, clockmonger, clockician, clockometrist, clockologist, and a hundred others dealing with clockness, clockism, clockship, clockdom, clockation, clockition, and clockhood.

The ogress decided to call on an old inspirationalist who had once advised her father not to worry about a giant he was worrying about. The inspirationalist had said to the ogress's father, "Don't pay any attention to it, and it will go away." And the ogress's father had paid no attention to it, and it had gone away, taking him with it, and this had pleased the ogress. The inspirationalist was now a very old man whose inspirationalism had become a jumble of mumble. "The final experience should not be mummum," he mumbled.

The ogress said, "But what is mummum?"

"Mummum," said the inspirationalist, "is what the final experience should not be." And he mumbled to a couch, lay down upon it, and fell asleep.

As the days went on, the ogre ate all the clocks in the town—mantel clocks, grandfather clocks, travelling clocks, stationary clocks, alarm clocks, eight-day clocks, steeple clocks, and tower clocks—sprinkling them with watches, as if the watches were salt and pepper, until there were no more watches. People overslept, and failed to go to work, or to church, or anyplace else where they had to be on time. Factories closed down, shopkeepers shut up their shops, schools did not open, trains no longer ran, and people stayed at home. The town council held an emergency meeting and its members arrived at all hours, and some did not show up at all.

A psychronologist was called to the witness stand to testify as to what should be done. "This would appear to be a clear case of clock-eating, but we should not jump so easily to conclusions," he said. "We have no scientific data whatever on clock-eating, and hence no controlled observation. All things, as we know, are impossible in this most impossible of all impossible worlds. That being the case, no such thing as we think has happened could have happened. Thus the situation does not fall within the frame of my discipline. Good day, gentlemen." The psychronologist glanced at where his wristwatch should have been and, not finding it there, was disturbed. "I have less than no time at all," he said, "which means that I am late for my next appointment." And he hurriedly left the council room.

The Lord Mayor of the town, arriving late to preside over the council meeting, called a clockonomist to the stand. "What we have here," said the clockonomist, "appears on the surface to be a clockonomic crisis. It is the direct opposite of what is known, in my field, as a glut of clocks. That is, instead of there being more clocks than the consumer needs, so that the price of clocks would decrease, the consumer has consumed all the clocks. This should send up the price of clocks sharply, but we are faced with the unique fact that there are no clocks. Now, as a clockonomist, my concern is the economy of clocks, but where there are no clocks there can be no such economy. The area, in short, has disappeared."

"What do you suggest, then?" demanded the Lord Mayor.

"I suggest," said the clockonomist, "that it is now high time I go into some other line of endeavor, or transfer my clockonomy to a town which has clocks. Good day, gentlemen." And the clockonomist left the council room.

A clockosopher next took the witness chair. "If it is high time," he said, "then there is still time. The question is this: How high is high time? It means, if it means anything, which I doubt, that it is time to act. I am not an actor, gentlemen, but a clockosopher, whose osophy is based upon clocks, not necessarily upon their physical existence, but upon clocks as a concept. We still have clocks as a concept, but this meeting is concerned solely with clocks as objects. Thus its deliberations fall well outside my range of interest, and I am simply wasting time here, or would be if there were time to waste. Good day, gentlemen." And the clockosopher left the council room.

The clockmakers of the town, who had been subpoenaed, were then enjoined, in a body, from making more clocks. "You have been supplying the ogre with clocks," the Lord Mayor said severely, "whether intentionally or willy-nilly is irrelevant. You have been working hand in glove, or clock in hand, with the ogre." The clockmakers left, to look for other work.

"I should like to solve this case by deporting the ogre," the Lord Mayor said, "but, as a container of clocks, he would have to be exported, not deported. Unfortunately, the law is clear on this point: Clocks may not be exported in any save regulation containers, and the human body falls outside that legal definition."

Three weeks to the day after the ogre had eaten the last clock, he fell ill and took to his bed, and the ogress sent for the chief diagnostician of the Medical Academy, a diagnostician familiar with so many areas that totality itself had become to him only a part of wholeness. "The trouble is," said the chief diagnostician, "we don't know what the trouble is. Nobody has ever eaten all the clocks before, so it is impossible to tell whether the patient has clockitis, clockosis, clockoma, or clocktheria. We are also faced with the possibility that there may be no such diseases. The patient may have one of the minor clock ailments, if there are any, such as clockets, clockles, clocking cough, ticking pox, or clumps. We shall have to develop area men who will find out about such areas, if such areas exist, which, until we find out that they do, we must assume do not."

"What if he dies?" demanded the ogress eagerly.

"Then," said the chief diagnostician, "we shall bury him." And the chief diagnostician left the ogre's room and the castle.

The case of the town's clocklessness was carried to the Supreme Council, presided over by the Supreme Magistrate. "Who is prosecuting whom?" the Supreme Magistrate demanded.

The Supreme Prosecutor stood up. "Let somebody say something, and I will object," he said. "We have to start somewhere, even if we start nowhere."

A housewife took the witness stand. "Without a clock," she said, "I cannot even boil a three-minute egg."

"Objection," said the Supreme Prosecutor. "One does not *have* to boil a three-minute egg. A three-minute egg, by definition, has already been boiled for three minutes, or it wouldn't be a three-minute egg."

"Objection sustained," droned the Supreme Magistrate.

The Leader of the Opposition then took the stand. "The party in power has caused the mess in the ogre's castle," he said.

"Objection," said the Supreme Prosecutor. "There isn't any party in power. The ogre was the party in power, but he no longer has any power. Furthermore, the mess caused by the party cleaning up the mess caused by the party in power, which is no longer in power, would be worse than the mess left by the party that was in power."

"Objection sustained," droned the Supreme Magistrate.

The Secretary of Status Quo was the next man to take the stand. "We are not getting anywhere," he said, "and therefore we should call a summit conference without agenda. A summit conference without agenda is destined to get even less than nowhere, but its deliberations will impress those who are impressed by deliberations that get less than nowhere. This has unworked in the past, and it will unwork now. If we get less than nowhere fast enough, we shall more than hold our own, for everything is circular and cyclical, and where there are no clocks, clockwise and counterclockwise are the same."

"Objection," said the Supreme Prosecutor. "We are dealing here with a purely internal matter, caused by the consumer's having consumed all the clocks."

"Objection sustained," droned the Supreme Magistrate.

The Man in the Street now took the stand. "Why don't we use sundials?" he demanded.

"I challenge the existence of the witness," said the Supreme Prosecutor. "He says he is the Man in the Street, but he is, in fact, the Man in the Supreme Council Room. Furthermore, sundials work only when the sun is shining, and nobody cares what time it is when the sun is shining."

The Man in the Street left the witness chair, and nobody noticed his going, since the Supreme Prosecutor had established the fact that he had not been there.

There was a long silence in the Supreme Council Room, a silence so deep one could have heard a pin drop, if a pin had been dropped, but nobody dropped a pin. What everybody in the Council Room heard, in the long, deep silence, was the slow tick-tock of a clock, a wall clock, the clock on the wall behind the Supreme Magistrate's bench. The officials and the witnesses and the spectators had grown so used to not hearing clocks it wasn't until the clock struck the hour that they realized there was a wall clock on the wall.

The Supreme Magistrate was the first to speak. "Unless I am mightily mistaken, and I usually am, we have here the solution to all our problems," he said, "namely, a clock. Unless there is an objection and I sustain the objection, which I do not think I shall, we will place this clock in the clock tower of the town, where it can be seen by one and all. Then we shall once again know what time it is. The situation will be cleared up, and the case dismissed."

"One minute," said the Supreme Prosecutor, and everybody waited a minute until he spoke again. "What is to prevent the ogre from eating the clock in the clock tower?"

"If you are asking me," said the Supreme Magistrate, "I do not know, but I do not have to confess my ignorance, since affirmations of this sort do not fall within my jurisdiction."

A bailiff stepped to the bench and handed the Supreme Magistrate a folded note. The Magistrate glanced at it, took off his glasses, and addressed all those present. "The ogre is dead," he announced.

"Objection," said the Supreme Prosecutor.

"Objection overruled," said the Magistrate, "if you are objecting to the fact of the ogre's death."

"I accept the ogre's death as a fact," said the Prosecutor, "but we are moving too fast, and I should like to call a specialist to the stand." And he called a specialist to the stand.

"I am a collector," said the specialist. "The clock on the wall is the only clock there is. This makes it not, in fact, a clock but a collector's item, or museum piece. As such, it must be placed in the town museum. One does not spend the coins in a museum. The wineglasses in a museum do not hold wine. The suits of armor in a museum do not contain knights. The clocks in a museum do not tell time. This clock, the last clock there is, must therefore be allowed to run down, and then placed in the museum, with proper ceremonies, addresses, and the like."

"I move that this be done," the Prosecutor said.

"I should like to continue to know, as much as everybody else, what time it is," pronounced the Supreme Magistrate. "Under the circumstances, however, there is but one thing I can do in conformity with the rule which establishes the inalienable fact that the last clock is a collector's item, or museum piece. I therefore decree that the last clock, the clock here on the wall, be allowed to run down, and then placed in the town museum, with proper ceremonies, addresses and the like."

The next day, at nine minutes of twelve o'clock noon, the last clock ran down and stopped. It was then placed in the town museum, as a collector's item, or museum piece, with proper ceremonies, addresses, and the like. Among those who spoke were the Lord Mayor, the Secretary of Status Quo, and the Supreme Magistrate. They all chose the same subjects, without verbs or predicates, and the subjects were these: glorious past, unlimited opportunity, challenging future, dedication, inspired leadership, enlightened followership, rededication, moral fibre, spiritual values, outer space, inner man, higher ideals, lower taxes, unflagging enthusiasm, unswerving devotion, coördinated efforts, dedicated rededication, and rededicated dedication.

After that, nobody in the town ever knew what time it was. Factories and schools remained closed, church bells no longer rang, because the bell ringers no longer knew when to ring them, dates and engagements were no longer made, because nobody knew when to keep them. Trains no longer ran, so nobody left town and no strangers arrived in town to tell the people what time it was. Eventually, the sands of a nearby desert moved slowly and inexorably toward the timeless town, and in the end it was buried.

Eras, epochs, and aeons passed before a party of explorers from another planet began digging in the sands above the buried town. They were descendants of people from Earth who had reached Venus a thousand years before and intermarried with Venusians. Among them were a young man and a young woman, and it was their fortune to be the first to come upon the ancient library of the old inspirationalist. Among some papers still preserved upon his desk were the last things he had written —bits of poetry from the grand Old Masters and the minor poets. One of these fragments read, "How goes the night, boy? The moomoon is down. I have not heard the clock." And the very last words his wavery pen had put on paper:

> We can make our lives sublime,
> And, departing, leave behind us,
> Mummum in the sands of time.

"What is mummum?" the young woman asked.

"I don't know," the young man said, "but something tells me we shall find a lot of it." They went on digging, and, in the end, came upon the last clock in the town museum, so clogged with sand they could not tell what it had once been used for, and so they marked it "Antique mechanism. Function uncertain. Possibly known to the ancients as mummum." And they took it back to Venus, in a cargo rocket ship, with other mysterious relics of the Time of Man on Earth.

STEPHEN VINCENT BENÉT

The Devil and Daniel Webster

It's a story they tell in the border country, where Massachusetts joins Vermont and New Hampshire.

Yes, Dan'l Webster's dead—or, at least, they buried him. But every time there's a thunderstorm around Marshfield, they say you can hear his rolling voice in the hollows of the sky. And they say that if you go to his grave and speak loud and clear, "Dan'l Webster—Dan'l Webster!" the ground'll begin to shiver and the trees begin to shake. And after a while you'll hear a deep voice saying, "Neighbor, how stands the Union?" Then you better answer the Union stands as she stood, rock bottomed and copper sheathed, one and indivisible, or he's liable to rear right out of the ground. At least, that's what I was told when I was a youngster.

You see, for a while, he was the biggest man in the country. He never got to be President, but he was the biggest man. There were thousands that trusted in him right next to God Almighty, and they told stories about him and all the things that belonged to him that were like the stories of patriarchs and such. They said, when he stood up to speak, stars and stripes came right out in the sky, and once he spoke against a river and made it sink into the ground. They said, when he walked the woods with his fishing rod, Killall, the trout would jump out of the streams right into his pockets, for they knew it was no use putting up a fight against him; and, when he argued a case, he could turn on the harps of the blessed and the shaking of the earth underground. That was the kind of man he was, and his big farm up at Marshfield was suitable to him. The chickens he raised were all white meat down through the drumsticks, the cows were tended like children, and the big ram he called Goliath had horns with a curl like a morning-glory vine and could butt through an iron door. But Dan'l wasn't one of your gentlemen farmers; he knew all the ways of the land, and he'd be up by candlelight to see that the chores got done. A man with a mouth like a mastiff, a brow like a mountain and eyes like burning anthracite—that was Dan'l Webster in his prime. And the biggest case he argued never got written down in the books, for he argued it against the devil, nip and tuck and no holds barred. And this is the way I used to hear it told.

There was a man named Jabez Stone, lived at Cross Corners, New Hampshire. He wasn't a bad man to start with, but he was an unlucky man. If he planted corn, he got borers; if he planted potatoes, he got blight. He had good-enough land, but it didn't prosper him; he had a decent wife and children, but the more children he had, the less there was to feed them. If stones cropped up in his neighbor's field, boulders boiled up in his; if he had a horse with the spavins, he'd trade it for one with the staggers and give something extra. There's some folks bound to be like that, apparently. But one day Jabez Stone got sick of the whole business.

He'd been plowing that morning and he'd just broke the plowshare on a rock that he could have sworn hadn't been there yesterday. And, as he stood looking at the plowshare, the off horse began to cough—that ropy kind of cough that means sickness and horse doctors. There were two children down with the measles, his wife was ailing, and he had a whitlow on his thumb. It was about the last straw for Jabez Stone. "I vow," he said, and he looked around him kind of desperate, "I vow it's enough to make a man want to sell his soul to the devil! And I would, too, for two cents!"

Then he felt a kind of queerness come over him at having said what he'd said; though, naturally, being a New Hampshireman, he wouldn't take it back. But, all the same, when it got to be evening and, as far as he could see, no notice had been taken, he felt relieved in his mind, for he was a religious man. But notice is always taken, sooner or later, just like the Good Book says. And, sure enough, next day, about suppertime, a soft-spoken, dark-dressed stranger drove up in a handsome buggy and asked for Jabez Stone.

Well, Jabez told his family it was a lawyer, come to see him about a legacy. But he knew who it was. He didn't like the looks of the stranger, nor the way he smiled with his teeth. They were white teeth, and plentiful—some say they were filed to a point, but I wouldn't vouch for that. And he didn't like it when the dog took one look at the stranger and ran away howling, with his tail between his legs. But having passed the word, more or less, he stuck to it, and they went out behind the barn and made their bargain. Jabez Stone had to prick his finger to sign, and the stranger lent him a silver pin. The wound healed clean, but it left a little white scar.

After that, all of a sudden, things began to pick up and prosper for Jabez Stone. His cows got fat and his horses sleek, his crops were the envy of the neighborhood, and lightning might strike all over the valley, but it wouldn't strike his barn. Pretty soon he was one of the prosperous people of the county; they asked him to stand for selectman, and he stood for it; there began to be talk of running him for state senate. All in all, you might say the Stone family was as happy and contented as cats in a dairy. And so they were, except for Jabez Stone.

He'd been contented enough the first few years. It's a great thing when bad luck turns; it drives most other things out of your head. True, every now and then, especially in rainy weather, the little white scar on his finger would give him a twinge. And once a year, punctual as clockwork, the stranger with the handsome buggy would come driving by. But the sixth year the stranger lighted, and, after that, his peace was over for Jabez Stone.

The stranger came up through the lower field, switching his boots with a cane—they were handsome black boots, but Jabez Stone never liked the look of them, particularly the toes. And, after he'd passed the time of day, he said, "Well, Mr. Stone, you're a hummer! It's a very pretty property you've got here, Mr. Stone."

"Well, some might favor it and others might not," said Jabez Stone, for he was a New Hampshireman.

"Oh, no need to decry your industry!" said the stranger, very easy, showing his teeth in a smile. "After all, we know what's been done, and it's been according to contract and specifications. So when—ahem—the mortgage falls due next year, you shouldn't have any regrets."

"Speaking of that mortgage, mister," said Jabez Stone, and he looked around for help to the earth and the sky, "I'm beginning to have one or two doubts about it."

"Doubts?" said the stranger not quite so pleasantly.

"Why, yes," said Jabez Stone. "This being the U.S.A. and me always having been a religious man." He cleared his throat and got bolder. "Yes sir," he said, "I'm beginning to have considerable doubts as to that mortgage holding in court."

"There's courts and courts," said the stranger, clicking

his teeth. "Still, we might as well have a look at the original document." And be hauled out a big black pocketbook, full of papers. "Sherwin, Slater, Stevens, Stone," he muttered. " 'I, Jabez Stone, for a term of seven years ——' Oh, it's quite in order, I think."

But Jabez Stone wasn't listening, for he saw something else flutter out of the black pocketbook. It was something that looked like a moth, but it wasn't a moth. And as Jabez Stone stared at it, it seemed to speak to him in a small sort of piping voice, terrible small and thin, but terrible human. "Neighbor Stone!" it squeaked. "Neighbor Stone! Help me! For God's sake, help me!"

But before Jabez Stone could stir hand or foot, the stranger whipped out a big bandanna handkerchief, caught the creature in it, just like a butterfly, and started tying up the end of the bandanna.

"Sorry for the interruption," he said. "As I was saying——"

But Jabez Stone was shaking all over like a scared horse.

"That's Miser Stevens' voice!" he said in a croak. "And you've got him in your handkerchief!"

The stranger looked a little embarrassed.

"Yes, I really should have transferred him to the collecting box," he said with a simper, "but there were some rather unusual specimens there and I don't want them crowded. Well, well, these little contretemps will occur."

"I don't know what you mean by contertan," said Jabez Stone, "but that was Miser Stevens' voice! And he ain't dead! You can't tell me he is! He was just as spry and mean as a woodchuck Tuesday!"

"In the midst of life . . ." said the stranger, kind of pious. "Listen!" Then a bell began to toll in the valley and Jabez Stone listened, with the sweat running down his face. For he knew it was tolled for Miser Stevens and that he was dead.

"These long-standing accounts," said the stranger with a sigh; "one really hates to close them. But business is business."

He still had the bandanna in his hand, and Jabez Stone felt sick as he saw the cloth struggle and flutter.

"Are they all as small as that?" he asked hoarsely.

"Small?" said the stranger. "Oh, I see what you mean. Why, they vary." He measured Jabez Stone with his eyes, and his teeth showed. "Don't worry, Mr. Stone," he said. "You'll go with a very good grade. I wouldn't trust you outside the collecting box. Now, a man like Dan'l Webster, of course—well, we'd have to build a special box for him, and even at that, I imagine the wing spread would astonish you. He'd certainly be a prize. I wish we could see our way clear to him. But, in your case, as I was saying——"

"Put that handkerchief away!" said Jabez Stone, and he began to beg and to pray. But the best he could get at the end was a three years' extension, with conditions.

But till you make a bargain like that, you've got no idea of how fast four years can run. By the last months of those years Jabez Stone's known all over the state and there's talk of running him for governor—and it's dust and ashes in his mouth. For every day, when he gets up, he thinks, "There's one more night gone," and every night, when he lies down, he thinks of the black pocketbook and the soul of Miser Stevens, and it makes him sick at heart. Till, finally, he can't bear it any longer, and, in the last days of the last year, he hitches up his horse and drives off to seek Dan'l Webster. For Dan'l was born in New Hampshire, only a few miles from Cross Corners, and it's well known that he has a particular soft spot for old neighbors.

It was early in the morning when he got to Marshfield, but Dan'l was up already, talking Latin to the farm hands and wrestling with the ram, Goliath, and trying out a new trotter and working up speeches to make against John C. Calhoun. But when he heard a New Hampshireman had come to see him, he dropped everything else he was doing, for that was Dan'l's way. He gave Jabez Stone a breakfast that five men couldn't eat, went into the living history of every man and woman in Cross Corners, and finally asked him how he could serve him.

Jabez Stone allowed that it was a kind of mortgage case.

"Well, I haven't pleaded a mortgage case in a long time, and I don't generally plead now, except before the Supreme Court," said Dan'l, "but if I can, I'll help you."

"Then I've got hope for the first time in ten years," and Jabez Stone told him the details.

Dan'l walked up and down as he listened, hands behind his back, now and then asking a question, now and then plunging his eyes at the floor, as if they'd bore through it like gimlets. When Jabez Stone had finished, Dan'l puffed out his cheeks and blew. Then he turned to Jabez Stone and a smile broke over his face like the sunrise over Monadnock.

"You've certainly given yourself the devil's own row to hoe, Neighbor Stone," he said, "but I'll take your case."

"You'll take it?" said Jabez Stone, hardly daring to believe.

"Yes," said Dan'l Webster. "I've got about seventy-five other things to do and the Missouri Compromise to straighten out, but I'll take your case. For if two New Hampshiremen aren't a match for the devil, we might as well give the country back to the Indians."

Then he shook Jabez Stone by the hand and said, "Did you come down here in a hurry?"

"Well, I admit I made time," said Jabez Stone.

"You'll go back faster," said Dan'l Webster, and he told 'em to hitch up Constitution and Constellation to the carriage. They were matched grays with one white forefoot, and they stepped like greased lightning.

Well, I won't describe how excited and pleased the whole Stone family was to have the great Dan'l Webster for a guest, when they finally got there. Jabez Stone had lost his hat on the way, blown off when they overtook a wind, but he didn't take much account of that. But after supper he sent the family off to bed, for he had most particular business with Mr. Webster. Mrs. Stone wanted him to sit in the front parlor, but Dan'l Webster knew front parlors, and said he preferred the kitchen. So it was there they sat, waiting for the stranger, with a jug on the table between them and a bright fire on the hearth —the stranger being scheduled to show up on the stroke of midnight, according to specification.

Well, most men wouldn't have asked for better company than Dan'l Webster and a jug. But with every tick of the clock Jabez Stone got sadder and sadder. His eyes roved round, and though he sampled the jug you could see he couldn't taste it. Finally, on the stroke of 11:30 he reached over and grabbed Dan'l Webster by the arm.

"Mr. Webster, Mr. Webster!" he said, and his voice was shaking with fear and a desperate courage. "For God's sake, Mr. Webster, harness your horses and get away from this place while you can!"

"You've brought me a long way, neighbor, to tell me you don't like my company," said Dan'l Webster, quite peaceable, pulling at the jug.

"Miserable wretch that I am!" groaned Jabez Stone. "I've brought you a devilish way, and now I see my folly. Let him take me if he wills. I don't hanker after it, I must say, but I can stand it. But you're the Union's stay and New Hampshire's pride! He mustn't get you, Mr. Webster! He mustn't get you!"

Dan'l Webster looked at the distracted man, all gray and shaking in the firelight, and laid a hand on his shoulder.

"I'm obliged to you, Neighbor Stone," he said gently. "It's kindly thought of. But there's a jug on the table and a case in hand. And I never left a jug or a case half finished in my life."

And just at that moment there was a sharp rap on the door.

"Ah," said Dan'l Webster very coolly, "I thought your clock was a trifle slow, Neighbor Stone." He stepped to the door and opened it. "Come in!" he said.

The stranger came in—very dark and tall he looked in the firelight. He was carrying a box under his arm—a black japanned box with little air holes in the lid. At the sight of the box Jabez Stone gave a low cry and shrank into a corner of the room.

"Mr. Webster, I presume," said the stranger, very polite, but with his eyes glowing like a fox's deep in the woods.

"Attorney of record for Jabez Stone," said Dan'l Webster, but his eyes were glowing too. "Might I ask your name?"

"I've gone by a good many," said the stranger carelessly. "Perhaps Scratch will do for the evening. I'm often called that in these regions."

Then he sat down at the table and poured himself a drink from the jug. The liquor was cold in the jug, but it came steaming into the glass.

"And now," said the stranger, smiling and showing his teeth, "I shall call upon you, as a law-abiding citizen, to assist me in taking possession of my property."

Well, with that the argument began—and it went hot and heavy. At first Jabez Stone had a flicker of hope, but when he saw Dan'l Webster being forced back at point after point, he just sat scrunched in his corner, with his eyes on that japanned box. For there wasn't any doubt as to the deed or the signature—that was the worst of it.

Dan'l Webster twisted and turned and thumped his fist on the table, but he couldn't get away from that. He offered to compromise the case; the stranger wouldn't hear of it. He pointed out the property had increased in value, and state senators ought to be worth more; the stranger stuck to the letter of the law. He was a great lawyer, Dan'l Webster, but we know who's the King of Lawyers, as the Good Book tells us, and it seemed as if, for the first time, Dan'l Webster had met his match.

Finally, the stranger yawned a little. "Your spirited efforts on behalf of your client do you credit, Mr. Webster," he said, "but if you have no more arguments to adduce, I'm rather pressed for time . . ." and Jabez Stone shuddered.

Dan'l Webster's brow looked dark as a thundercloud.

"Pressed or not, you shall not have this man!" he thundered. "Mr. Stone is an American citizen, and no American citizen may be forced into the service of a foreign prince. We fought England for that in '12 and we'll fight all hell for it again!"

"Foreign?" said the stranger. "And who calls me a foreigner?"

"Well, I never yet heard of the dev—of your claiming American citizenship," said Dan'l Webster with surprise.

"And who with better right?" said the stranger with one of his terrible smiles. "When the first wrong was done to the first Indian, I was there. When the first slaver put out for the Congo, I stood on her deck. Am I not in your books and stories and beliefs, from the first settlements on? Am I not spoken of still in every church in New England? 'Tis true the North claims me for a Southerner and the South for a Northerner, but I am neither. I am merely an honest American like yourself—and of the best descent—for, to tell the truth, Mr. Webster, though I don't like to boast of it, my name is older in this country than yours."

"Aha!" said Dan'l Webster with the veins standing out in his forehead. "Then I stand on the Constitution! I demand a trial for my client!"

"The case is hardly one for an ordinary court," said the stranger, his eyes flickering. "And, indeed, the lateness of the hour——"

"Let it be any court you choose, so it is an American judge and an American jury!" said Dan'l Webster in his pride. "Let it be the quick or the dead; I'll abide the issue!"

"You have said it," said the stranger, and pointed his finger at the door. And with that, and all of a sudden, there was a rushing of wind outside and a noise of footsteps. They came, clear and distinct, through the night. And yet they were not like the footsteps of living men.

"In God's name, who comes by so late?" cried Jabez Stone in an ague of fear.

"The jury Mr. Webster demands," said the stranger, sipping at his boiling glass. "You must pardon the rough appearance of one or two; they will have come a long way."

And with that the fire burned blue and the door blew open and twelve men entered, one by one.

If Jabez Stone had been sick with terror before, he

was blind with terror now. For there was Walter Butler, the loyalist, who spread fire and horror through the Mohawk Valley in the times of the Revolution; and there was Simon Girty, the renegade, who saw white men burned at the stake and whooped with the Indians to see them burn. His eyes were green, like a catamount's, and the stains on his hunting shirt did not come from the blood of the deer. King Philip was there, wild and proud as he had been in life, with the great gash in his head that gave him his death wound, and cruel Governor Dale, who broke men on the wheel. There was Morton of Merry Mount, who so vexed the Plymouth Colony, with his flushed, loose, handsome face and his hate of the godly. There was Teach, the bloody pirate, with his black beard curling on his breast. The Reverend John Smeet, with his strangler's hands and his Geneva gown, walked as daintily as he had to the gallows. The red print of the rope was still around his neck, but he carried a perfumed handkerchief in one hand. One and all, they came into the room with the fires of hell still upon them, and the stranger named their names and their deeds as they came, till the tale of twelve was told. Yet the stranger had told the truth—they had all played a part in America.

"Are you satisfied with the jury, Mr. Webster?" said the stranger mockingly, when they had taken their places.

The sweat stood upon Dan'l Webster's brow, but his voice was clear.

"Quite satisfied," he said. "Though I miss General Arnold from the company."

"Benedict Arnold is engaged upon other business," said the stranger with a glower. "Ah, you asked for a justice, I believe."

He pointed his finger once more, and a tall man, soberly clad in Puritan garb, with the burning gaze of the fanatic, stalked into the room and took his judge's place.

"Justice Hathorne is a jurist of experience," said the stranger. "He presided at certain witch trials once held in Salem. There were others who repented of the business later, but not he."

"Repent of such notable wonders and undertakings?" said the stern old justice. "Nay, hang them—hang them all!" And he muttered to himself in a way that struck ice into the soul of Jabez Stone.

Then the trial began, and, as you might expect, it didn't look anyways good for the defense. And Jabez Stone didn't make much of a witness in his own behalf. He took one look at Simon Girty and screeched, and they had to put him back in his corner in a kind of swoon.

It didn't halt the trial though; the trial went on, as trials do. Dan'l Webster had faced some hard juries and hanging judges in his time, but this was the hardest he'd ever faced, and he knew it. They sat there with a kind of glitter in their eyes, and the stranger's smooth voice went on and on. Every time he'd raise an objection, it'd be "Objection sustained," but whenever Dan'l objected, it'd be "Objection denied." Well, you couldn't expect fair play from a fellow like this Mr. Scratch.

It got to Dan'l in the end, and he began to heat, like iron in the forge. When he got up to speak he was going to flay that stranger with every trick known to the law, and the judge and jury too. He didn't care if it was contempt of court or what would happen to him for it. He didn't care any more what happened to Jabez Stone. He just got madder and madder, thinking of what he'd say. And yet, curiously enough, the more he thought about it, the less he was able to arrange his speech in his mind.

Till, finally, it was time for him to get up on his feet, and he did so, all ready to bust out with lightnings and denunciations. But before he started he looked over the judge and jury for a moment, such being his custom. And he noticed the glitter in their eyes was twice as strong as before, and they all leaned forward. Like hounds just before they get the fox, they looked, and the blue mist of evil in the room thickened as he watched them. Then he saw what he'd been about to do, and he wiped his forehead, as a man might who's just escaped falling into a pit in the dark.

For it was him they'd come for, not only Jabez Stone. He read it in the glitter of their eyes and in the way the stranger hid his mouth with one hand. And if he fought them with their own weapons, he'd fall into their power; he knew that, though he couldn't have told you how. It was his own anger and horror that burned in their eyes; and he'd have to wipe that out or the case was lost. He stood there for a moment, his black eyes burning like anthracite. And then he began to speak.

He started off in a low voice, though you could hear

every word. They say he could call on the harps of the blessed when he chose. And this was just as simple and easy as a man could talk. But he didn't start out by condemning or reviling. He was talking about the things that make a country a country and a man a man.

And he began with the simple things that everybody's known and felt—the freshness of a fine morning when you're young, and the taste of food when you're hungry, and the new day that's every day when you're a child. He took them up and he turned them in his hands. They were good things for any man. But without freedom they sickened. And when he talked of those enslaved, and the sorrows of slavery, his voice got like a big bell. He talked of the early days of America and the men who had made those days. It wasn't a spread-eagle speech, but he made you see it. He admitted all the wrong that had ever been done. But he showed how, out of the wrong and the right, the suffering and the starvations, something new had come. And everybody had played a part in it, even the traitors.

Then he turned to Jabez Stone and showed him as he was—an ordinary man who'd had hard luck and wanted to change it. And, because he'd wanted to change it, now he was going to be punished for all eternity. And yet there was good in Jabez Stone, and he showed that good. He was hard and mean, in some ways, but he was a man. There was sadness in being a man, but it was a proud thing too. And he showed what the pride of it was till you couldn't help feeling it. Yes, even in hell, if a man was a man, you'd know it. And he wasn't pleading for any one person any more, though his voice rang like an organ. He was telling the story and the failures and the endless journey of mankind. They got tricked and trapped and bamboozled, but it was a great journey. And no demon that was ever foaled could know the inwardness of it—it took a man to do that.

The fire began to die on the hearth and the wind before morning to blow. The light was getting gray in the room when Dan'l Webster finished. And his words came back at the end to New Hampshire ground, and the one spot of land that each man loves and clings to. He painted a picture of that, and to each one of that jury he spoke of things long forgotten. For his voice could search the heart, and that was his gift and his strength. And to one his voice was like the forest and its secrecy, and to another like the sea and the storms of the sea; and one heard the cry of his lost nation in it, and another saw a little harmless scene he hadn't remembered for years. But each saw something. And when Dan'l Webster finished he didn't know whether or not he'd saved Jabez Stone. But he knew he'd done a miracle. For the glitter was gone from the eyes of judge and jury, and, for the moment, they were men again, and knew they were men.

"The defense rests," said Dan'l Webster and stood there like a mountain. His ears were still ringing with his speech, and he didn't hear anything else till he heard Judge Hathorne say, "The jury will retire to consider its verdict."

Walter Butler rose in his place and his face had a dark, gay pride on it.

"The jury has considered its verdict," he said and looked the stranger full in the eye. "We find for the defendant, Jabez Stone."

With that, the smile left the stranger's face, but Walter Butler did not flinch.

"Perhaps 'tis not strictly in accordance with the evidence," he said, "but even the damned may salute the eloquence of Mr. Webster."

With that, the long crow of a rooster split the gray morning sky, and judge and jury were gone from the room like a puff of smoke and as if they had never been there. The stranger returned to Dan'l Webster, smiling wryly.

"Major Butler was always a bold man," he said. "I had not thought him quite so bold. Nevertheless, my congratulations, as between two gentlemen."

"I'll have that paper first, if you please," said Dan'l Webster, and he took it and tore it into four pieces. It was queerly warm to the touch. "And now," he said, "I'll have you!" and his hand came down like a bear trap on the stranger's arm. For he knew that once you bested anybody like Mr. Scratch in fair fight, his power on you was gone. And he could see that Mr. Scratch knew it too.

The stranger twisted and wriggled, but he couldn't get out of that grip. "Come, come, Mr. Webster," he said, smiling palely. "This sort of thing is ridic—ouch!—is ridiculous. If you're worried about the costs of the case, naturally, I'd be glad to pay——"

"And so you shall!" said Dan'l Webster, shaking him till his teeth rattled. "For you'll sit right down at that table and draw up a document, promising never to bother Jabez Stone nor his heirs or assigns nor any other New Hampshireman till doomsday! For any hades we want to raise in this state, we can raise ourselves, without assistance from strangers."

"Ouch!" said the stranger. "Ouch! Well, they never did run very big to the barrel, but—ouch!—I agree!"

So he sat down and drew up the document. But Dan'l Webster kept his hand on his coat collar all the time.

"And now may I go?" said the stranger, quite humble, when Dan'l'd seen the document's in proper and legal form.

"Go?" said Dan'l, giving him another shake. "I'm still trying to figure out what I'll do with you. For you've settled the costs of the case, but you haven't settled with me. I think I'll take you back to Marshfield," he said, kind of reflective. "I've got a ram there named Goliath that can butt through an iron door. I'd kind of like to turn you loose in his field and see what he'd do."

Well, with that the stranger began to beg and to plead. And he begged and he pled so humble that finally Dan'l, who was naturally kindhearted, agreed to let him go. The stranger seemed terrible grateful for that and said, just to show they were friends, he'd tell Dan'l's fortune before leaving. So Dan'l agreed to that, though he didn't take much stock in fortune-tellers ordinarily. But, naturally, the stranger was a little different.

Well, he pried and he peered at the lines in Dan'l's hands. And he told him one thing and another that was quite remarkable. But they were all in the past.

"Yes, all that's true, and it happened," said Dan'l Webster. "But what's to come in the future?"

The stranger grinned, kind of happily, and shook his head.

"The future's not as you think it," he said. "It's dark. You have a great ambition, Mr. Webster."

"I have," said Dan'l firmly, for everybody knew he wanted to be President.

"It seems almost within your grasp," said the stranger, "but you will not attain it. Lesser men will be made President and you will be passed over."

"And, if I am, I'll still be Daniel Webster," said Dan'l. "Say on."

"You have two strong sons," said the stranger, shaking his head. "You look to found a line. But each will die in war and neither reach greatness."

"Live or die, they are still my sons," said Dan'l Webster. "Say on."

"You have made great speeches," said the stranger. "You will make more."

"Ah," said Dan'l Webster.

"But the last great speech you make will turn many of your own against you," said the stranger. "They will call you Ichabod; they will call you by other names. Even in New England some will say you have turned your coat and sold your country, and their voices will be loud against you till you die."

"So it is an honest speech, it does not matter what men say," said Dan'l Webster. Then he looked at the stranger and their glances locked.

"One question," he said. "I have fought for the Union all my life. Will I see that fight won against those who would tear it apart?"

"Not while you live," said the stranger grimly, "but it will be won. And after you are dead, there are thousands who will fight for your cause, because of words that you spoke."

"Why, then, you long-barreled, slab-sided, lantern-jawed, fortune-telling note shaver," said Dan'l Webster with a great roar of laughter, "be off with you to your own place before I put my mark on you! For, by the thirteen original colonies, I'd go to the Pit itself to save the Union!"

And with that he drew back his foot for a kick that would have stunned a horse. It was only the tip of his shoe that caught the stranger, but he went flying out of the door with his collecting box under his arm.

"And now," said Dan'l Webster, seeing Jabez Stone beginning to rouse from his swoon, "let's see what's left in the jug, for it's dry work talking all night. I hope there's pie for breakfast, Neighbor Stone."

But they say that whenever the devil comes near Marshfield, even now, he gives it a wide berth. And he hasn't been seen in the state of New Hampshire from that day to this. I'm not talking about Massachusetts or Vermont.

ROBERT LOUIS STEVENSON

Three Fables

THE TWO MATCHES

One day there was a traveller in the woods in California, in the dry season, when the Trades were blowing strong. He had ridden a long way, and he was tired and hungry, and dismounted from his horse to smoke a pipe. But when he felt in his pocket, he found but two matches. He struck the first, and it would not light.

"Here is a pretty state of things," said the traveller. "Dying for a smoke; only one match left; and that certain to miss fire! Was there ever a creature so unfortunate? And yet," thought the traveller, "suppose I light this match, and smoke my pipe, and shake out the dottle here in the grass—the grass might catch on fire, for it is dry like tinder: and while I snatch out the flames in front, they might evade and run behind me, and seize upon yon bushes of poison oak; before I could reach it, that would have blazed up; over the bush I see a pine tree hung with moss: that too would fly in fire upon the instant to its topmost bough; and the flame of that long torch—how would the trade wind take and brandish that through the inflammable forest! I hear this dell roar in a moment with the joint voice of wind and fire, I see myself gallop for my soul, and the flying conflagration chase and outflank me through the hills; I see this pleasant forest burn for days, and the cattle roasted, and the springs dried up, and the farmer ruined, and his children cast upon the world. What a world hangs upon this moment!"

With that he struck the match, and it missed fire.

"Thank God," said the traveller, and put his pipe in his pocket.

THE DEVIL AND THE INNKEEPER

Once upon a time the devil stayed at an inn, where no one knew him, for they were people whose education had been neglected. He was bent on mischief, and for a time kept everybody by the ears. But at last the innkeeper set a watch upon the devil and took him in the fact.

The innkeeper got a rope's end.

"Now I am going to thrash you," said the innkeeper.

"You have no right to be angry with me," said the devil. "I am only the devil, and it is my nature to do wrong."

"Is that so?" said the innkeeper.

"Fact, I assure you," said the devil.

"You really cannot help doing ill?" asked the innkeeper.

"Not in the smallest," said the devil; "it would be useless cruelty to thrash a thing like me."

"It would indeed," said the innkeeper.

And he made a noose and hanged the devil.

"There," said the innkeeper.

THE PENITENT

A man met a lad weeping. "What do you weep for?" he asked.

"I am weeping for my sins," said the lad.

"You must have little to do," said the man.

The next day they met again. Once more the lad was weeping. "Why do you weep now?" asked the man.

"I am weeping because I have nothing to eat," said the lad.

"I thought it would come to that," said the man.

H. G. WELLS

The Man Who Could Work Miracles

A PANTOUM IN PROSE

It is doubtful whether the gift was innate. For my own part, I think it came to him suddenly. Indeed, until he was thirty he was a sceptic, and did not believe in miraculous powers. And here, since it is the most convenient place, I must mention that he was a little man, and had eyes of a hot brown, very erect red hair, a moustache with ends that he twisted up, and freckles. His name was George McWhirter Fotheringay—not the sort of name by any means to lead to any expectation of miracles—and he was a clerk at Gomshott's. He was greatly addicted to assertive argument. It was while he was asserting the impossibility of miracles that he had his first in-

Reprinted by permission of Willis Kingsley Wing and the Estate of H. G. Wells.
From *Collected Short Stories of H. G. Wells.*

timation of his extraordinary powers. This particular argument was being held in the bar of the Long Dragon, and Toddy Beamish was conducting the opposition by a monotonous but effective "So *you* say," that drove Mr. Fotheringay to the very limit of his patience.

There were present, besides these two, a very dusty cyclist, landlord Cox, and Miss Maybridge, the perfectly respectable and rather portly barmaid of the Dragon. Miss Maybridge was standing with her back to Mr. Fotheringay, washing glasses; the others were watching him, more or less amused by the present ineffectiveness of the assertive method. Goaded by the Torres Vedras tactics of Mr. Beamish, Mr. Fotheringay determined to make an unusual rhetorical effort. "Looky here, Mr. Beamish," said Mr. Fotheringay. "Let us clearly understand what a miracle is. It's something contrariwise to the course of nature done by power or Will, something what couldn't happen without being specially willed."

"So *you* say," said Mr. Beamish, repulsing him.

Mr. Fotheringay appealed to the cyclist, who had hitherto been a silent auditor, and received his assent—given with a hesitating cough and a glance at Mr. Beamish. The landlord would express no opinion, and Mr. Fotheringay, returning to Mr. Beamish, received the unexpected concession of a qualified assent to his definition of a miracle.

"For instance," said Mr. Fotheringay, greatly encouraged. "Here would be a miracle. That lamp, in the natural course of nature, couldn't burn like that upsy-down, could it, Beamish?"

"*You* say it couldn't," said Beamish.

"And you?" said Fotheringay. "You don't mean to say —eh?"

"No," said Beamish reluctantly. "No, it couldn't."

"Very well," said Mr. Fotheringay. "Then here comes someone, as it might be me, along here, and stands as it might be here, and says to that lamp, as I might do, collecting all my will—'Turn upsy-down without breaking, and go on burning steady,' and—— Hullo!"

It was enough to make anyone say "Hullo!" The impossible, the incredible, was visible to them all. The lamp hung inverted in the air, burning quietly with its flame pointing down. It was as solid, as indisputable as ever a lamp was, the prosaic common lamp of the Long Dragon bar.

Mr. Fotheringay stood with an extended forefinger and the knitted brows of one anticipating a catastrophic smash. The cyclist, who was sitting next the lamp, ducked and jumped across the bar. Everybody jumped, more or less. Miss Maybridge turned and screamed. For nearly three seconds the lamp remained still. A faint cry of mental distress came from Mr. Fotheringay. "I can't keep it up," he said, "any longer." He staggered back, and the inverted lamp suddenly flared, fell against the corner of the bar, bounced aside, smashed upon the floor, and went out.

It was lucky it had a metal receiver, or the whole place would have been in a blaze. Mr. Cox was the first to speak, and his remark, shorn of needless excrescences, was to the effect that Fotheringay was a fool. Fotheringay was beyond disputing even so fundamental a proposition as that! He was astonished beyond measure at the thing that had occurred. The subsequent conversation threw absolutely no light on the matter so far as Fotheringay was concerned; the general opinion not only followed Mr. Cox very closely but very vehemently. Everyone accused Fotheringay of a silly trick, and presented him to himself as a foolish destroyer of comfort and security. His mind was in a tornado of perplexity, he was himself inclined to agree with them, and he made a remarkably ineffectual opposition to the proposal of his departure.

He went home flushed and heated, coat-collar crumpled, eyes smarting, and ears red. He watched each of the ten street lamps nervously as he passed it. It was only when he found himself alone in his little bedroom in Church Row that he was able to grapple seriously with his memories of the occurrence, and ask, "What on earth happened?"

He had removed his coat and boots, and was sitting on the bed with his hands in his pockets repeating the text of his defence for the seventeenth time, "*I* didn't want the confounded thing to upset," when it occurred to him that at the precise moment he had said the commanding words he had inadvertently willed the thing he said, and that when he had seen the lamp in the air he had felt that it depended on him to maintain it there without being clear how this was to be done. He had not a particularly complex mind, or he might have stuck for a time at that "inadvertently willed," embracing, as it does, the abstrusest problems of voluntary action; but as it was, the idea came to him with a quite acceptable haziness. And from that, following, as I must admit, no clear logical path, he came to the test of experiment.

He pointed resolutely to his candle and collected his mind, though he felt he did a foolish thing. "Be raised up," he said. But in a second that feeling vanished. The candle was raised, hung in the air one giddy moment, and as Mr. Fotheringay gasped, fell with a smash on his toilet-table, leaving him in darkness save for the expiring glow of its wick.

For a time Mr. Fotheringay sat in the darkness, perfectly still. "It did happen, after all," he said. "And 'ow I'm to explain it I *don't* know." He sighed heavily, and began feeling in his pockets for a match. He could find none, and he rose and groped about the toilet-table. "I wish I had a match," he said. He resorted to his coat, and there were none there, and then it dawned upon him that miracles were possible even with matches. He extended a hand and scowled at it in the dark. "Let there be a match in that hand," he said. He felt some light object fall across his palm, and his fingers closed upon a match.

After several ineffectual attempts to light this, he discovered it was a safety-match. He threw it down, and then it occurred to him that he might have willed it lit. He did, and perceived it burning in the midst of his toilet-table mat. He caught it up hastily, and it went out. His perception of possibilities enlarged, and he felt for and replaced the candle in its candlestick. "Here! *you* be lit," said Mr. Fotheringay, and forthwith the candle was flaring, and he saw a little black hole in the toilet-cover, with a wisp of smoke rising from it. For a time he stared from this to the little flame and back, and then looked up and met his own gaze in the looking-glass. By this help he communed with himself in silence for a time.

"How about miracles now?" said Mr. Fotheringay at last, addressing his reflection.

The subsequent meditations of Mr. Fotheringay were of a severe but confused description. So far as he could see, it was a case of pure willing with him. The nature of his first experiences disinclined him for any further experiments except of the most cautious type. But he lifted a sheet of paper, and turned a glass of water pink and then green, and he created a snail, which he miraculously annihilated, and got himself a miraculous new toothbrush. Somewhere in the small hours he had reached the fact that his will-power must be of a particularly rare and pungent quality, a fact of which he had certainly had inklings before, but no certain assurance. The scare and perplexity of his first discovery were now qualified by pride in this evidence of singularity and by vague intimations of advantage. He became aware that the church clock was striking one, and as it did not occur to him that his daily duties at Gomshott's might be miraculously dispensed with, he resumed undressing, in order to get to bed without further delay. As he struggled to get his shirt over his head he was struck with a brilliant idea. "Let me be in bed," he said, and found himself so. "Undressed," he stipulated; and, finding the sheets cold, added hastily, "and in my nightshirt—no, in a nice soft woollen nightshirt. Ah!" he said with immense enjoyment. "And now let me be comfortably asleep. . . ."

He awoke at his usual hour and was pensive all through breakfast-time, wondering whether his overnight experience might not be a particularly vivid dream. At length his mind turned again to cautious experiments. For instance, he had three eggs for breakfast; two his landlady had supplied, good, but shoppy, and one was a delicious fresh goose-egg, laid, cooked, and served by his extraordinary will. He hurried off to Gomshott's in a state of profound but carefully concealed excitement, and only remembered the shell of the third egg when his landlady spoke of it that night. All day he could do no work because of this astonishing new self-knowledge, but this caused him no inconvenience, because he made up for it miraculously in his last ten minutes.

As the day wore on his state of mind passed from wonder to elation, albeit the circumstances of his dismissal from the Long Dragon were still disagreeable to recall, and a garbled account of the matter that had reached his colleagues led to some badinage. It was evident he must be careful how he lifted frangible articles, but in other ways his gift promised more and more as he turned it over in his mind. He intended among other things to increase his personal property by unostentatious acts of creation. He called into existence a pair of very splendid diamond studs, and hastily annihilated them again as young Gomshott came across the counting-house to his desk. He was afraid young Gomshott might wonder how he had come by them. He saw quite clearly the gift required caution and watchfulness in its exercise, but so far as he could judge the difficulties attending its mastery would be no greater than those he had already faced in the study of cycling. It was that analogy, perhaps, quite as much as the feeling that he would be unwelcome in the Long Dragon, that drove him out after supper into the lane beyond the gas-works, to rehearse a few miracles in private.

There was possibly a certain want of originality in his attempts, for apart from his will-power Mr. Fotheringay was not a very exceptional man. The miracle of Moses' rod came to his mind, but the night was dark and unfavourable to the proper control of large miraculous snakes. Then he recollected the story of "Tannhäuser" that he had read on the back of the Philharmonic programme. That seemed to him singularly attractive and harmless. He stuck his walking-stick—a very nice Poona-Penang lawyer—into the turf that edged the footpath, and commanded the dry wood to blossom. The air was immediately full of the scent of roses, and by means of a match he saw for himself that this beautiful miracle was indeed accomplished. His satisfaction was ended by advancing footsteps. Afraid of a premature discovery of his powers, he addressed the blossoming stick hastily: "Go back." What he meant was "Change back"; but of course he was confused. The stick receded at a considerable velocity, and incontinently came a cry of anger and a bad word from the approaching person. "Who are you throwing brambles at, you fool?" cried a voice. "That got me on the shin."

"I'm sorry, old chap," said Mr. Fotheringay, and then, realising the awkward nature of the explanation, caught nervously at his moustache. He saw Winch, one of the three Immering constables, advancing.

"What d'yer mean by it?" asked the constable. "Hullo! It's you, is it? The gent that broke the lamp at the Long Dragon!"

"I don't mean anything by it," said Mr. Fotheringay. "Nothing at all."

"What d'yer do it for then?"

"Oh, bother!" said Mr. Fotheringay.

"Bother, indeed? D'yer know that stick hurt? What d'yer do it for, eh?"

For the moment Mr. Fotheringay could not think what he had done it for. His silence seemed to irritate Mr. Winch. "You've been assaulting the police, young man, this time. That's what *you* done."

"Look here, Mr. Winch," said Mr. Fotheringay, annoyed and confused, "I'm very sorry. The fact is——"

"Well!"

He could think of no way but the truth. "I was working a miracle." He tried to speak in an off-hand way, but try as he would he couldn't.

"Working a——! 'Ere, don't you talk rot. Working a miracle, indeed! Miracle! Well, that's downright funny! Why, you's the chap that don't believe in miracles. . . .

Fact is, this is another of your silly conjuring tricks—that's what this is. Now, I tell you——"

But Mr. Fotheringay never heard what Mr. Winch was going to tell him. He realised he had given himself away, flung his valuable secret to all the winds of heaven. A violent gust of irritation swept him to action. He turned on the constable swiftly and fiercely. "Here," he said, "I've had enough of this, I have! I'll show you a silly conjuring trick, I will. Go to Hades! Go, now!"

He was alone!

Mr. Fotheringay performed no more miracles that night nor did he trouble to see what had become of his flowering stick. He returned to the town, scared and very quiet, and went to his bedroom. "Lord!" he said, "it's a powerful gift—an extremely powerful gift! I didn't hardly mean as much as that. Not really. . . . I wonder what Hades is like!"

He sat on the bed taking off his boots. Struck by a happy thought he transferred the constable to San Francisco, and without any more interference with normal causation went soberly to bed. In the night he dreamt of the anger of Winch.

The next day Mr. Fotheringay heard two interesting items of news. Someone had planted a most beautiful climbing rose against the elder Mr. Gomshotts' private house in the Lullaborough Road, and the river as far as Rawling's Mill was to be dragged for Constable Winch.

Mr. Fotheringay was abstracted and thoughtful all that day, and performed no miracles except certain provisions for Winch, and the miracle of completing his day's work with punctual perfection in spite of all the bee-swarm of thoughts that hummed through his mind. And the extraordinary abstraction and meekness of his manner was remarked by several people, and made a matter for jesting. For the most part he was thinking of Winch.

On Sunday evening he went to chapel, and oddly enough, Mr. Maydig, who took a certain interest in occult matters, preached about "things that are not lawful." Mr. Fotheringay was not a regular chapel goer, but the system of assertive scepticism, to which I have already alluded, was now very much shaken. The tenor of the sermon threw an entirely new light on these novel gifts, and he suddenly decided to consult Mr. Maydig immediately after the service. So soon as that was determined, he found himself wondering why he had not done so before.

Mr. Maydig, a lean, excitable man with quite remarkably long wrists and neck, was gratified at a request for a private conversation from a young man whose carelessness in religious matters was a subject for general remark in the town. After a few necessary delays, he conducted him to the study of the Manse, which was contiguous to the chapel, seated him comfortably, and, standing in front of a cheerful fire—his legs threw a Rhodian arch of shadow on the opposite wall—requested Mr. Fotheringay to state his business.

At first Mr. Fotheringay was a little abashed, and found some difficulty in opening the matter. "You will scarcely believe me, Mr. Maydig, I am afraid"—and so forth for some time. He tried a question at last, and asked Mr. Maydig his opinion of miracles.

Mr. Maydig was still saying "Well" in an extremely judicial tone, when Mr. Fotheringay interrupted again: "You don't believe, I suppose, that some common sort of person—like myself, for instance—as it might be sitting here now, might have some sort of twist inside him that made him able to do things by his will."

"It's possible," said Mr. Maydig. "Something of the sort, perhaps, is possible."

"If I might make free with something here, I think I might show you by a sort of experiment," said Mr. Fotheringay. "Now, take that tobacco-jar on the table, for instance. What I want to know is whether what I am going to do with it is a miracle or not. Just half a minute, Mr. Maydig, please."

He knitted his brows, pointed to the tobacco-jar and said: "Be a bowl of vi'lets."

The tobacco-jar did as it was ordered.

Mr. Maydig started violently at the change, and stood looking from the thaumaturgist to the bowl of flowers. He said nothing. Presently he ventured to lean over the table and smell the violets; they were fresh-picked and very fine ones. Then he stared at Mr. Fotheringay again.

"How did you do that?" he asked.

Mr. Fotheringay pulled his moustache. "Just told it—and there you are. Is that a miracle, or is it black art, or what is it? And what do you think's the matter with me? That's what I want to ask."

"It's a most extraordinary occurrence."

"And this day last week I knew no more that I could do things like that than you did. It came quite sudden. It's something odd about my will, I suppose, and that's as far as I can see."

"Is *that*—the only thing? Could you do other things besides that?"

"Lord, yes!" said Mr. Fotheringay. "Just anything." He thought, and suddenly recalled a conjuring entertainment he had seen. "Here!" He pointed. "Change into a bowl of fish—no, not that—change into a glass bowl full of water with goldfish swimming in it. That's better! You see that, Mr. Maydig?"

"It's astonishing. It's incredible. You are either a most extraordinary . . . But no——"

"I could change it into anything," said Mr. Fotheringay. "Just anything. Here! be a pigeon, will you?"

In another moment a blue pigeon was fluttering round the room and making Mr. Maydig duck every time it came near him. "Stop there, will you," said Mr. Fotheringay; and the pigeon hung motionless in the air. "I could change it back to a bowl of flowers," he said, and after replacing the pigeon on the table worked that miracle. "I expect you will want your pipe in a bit," he said, and restored the tobacco-jar.

Mr. Maydig had followed all these later changes in a sort of ejaculatory silence. He stared at Mr. Fotheringay and, in a very gingerly manner, picked up the tobacco-jar, examined it, replaced it on the table. "*Well!*" was the only expression of his feelings.

"Now, after that it's easier to explain what I came about," said Mr. Fotheringay; and proceeded to a lengthy and involved narrative of his strange experiences, beginning with the affair of the lamp in the Long Dragon and complicated by persistent allusions to Winch. As he went on, the transient pride Mr. Maydig's consternation had caused passed away; he became the very ordinary Mr. Fotheringay of everyday intercourse again. Mr. Maydig listened intently, the tobacco-jar in his hand, and his bearing changed also with the course of the narrative. Presently, while Mr. Fotheringay was dealing with the miracle of the third egg, the minister interrupted with a fluttering extended hand—

"It is possible," he said, "It is credible. It is amazing, of course, but it reconciles a number of difficulties. The power to work miracles is a gift—a peculiar quality like genius or second sight—hitherto it has come very rarely and to exceptional people. But in this case . . . I have always wondered at the miracles of Mahomet, and at Yogi's miracles, and the miracles of Madame Blavatsky. But, of course! Yes, it is simply a gift! It carries out so beautifully the arguments of that great thinker"—Mr. Maydig's voice sank—"his Grace the Duke of Argyll. Here we plumb some profounder law—deeper than the ordinary laws of nature. Yes—yes. Go on. Go on!"

Mr. Fotheringay proceeded to tell of his misadventure with Winch, and Mr. Maydig, no longer overawed or scared, began to jerk his limbs about and interject astonishment. "It's this what troubled me most," proceeded Mr. Fotheringay; "it's this I'm most mijitly in want of advice for; of course he's at San Francisco—wherever San Francisco may be—but of course it's awkward for both of us, as you'll see, Mr. Maydig. I don't see how he can understand what has happened, and I dare say he's scared and exasperated something tremendous, and trying to get at me. I dare say he keeps on starting off to come here. I send him back, by a miracle, every few hours, when I think of it. And of course, that's a thing he won't be able to understand, and it's bound to annoy him; and, of course, if he takes a ticket every time it will cost him a lot of money. I done the best I could for him, but of course it's difficult for him to put himself in my place. I thought afterwards that his clothes might have got scorched, you know—if Hades is all it's supposed to be—before I shifted him. In that case I suppose they'd have locked him up in San Francisco. Of course I willed him a new suit of clothes on him directly I thought of it. But, you see, I'm already in a deuce of a tangle——"

Mr. Maydig looked serious. "I see you are in a tangle. Yes, it's a difficult position. How you are to end it . . ." He became diffuse and inconclusive.

"However, we'll leave Winch for a little and discuss the larger question. I don't think this is a case of the black art or anything of the sort. I don't think there is any taint of criminality about it at all, Mr. Fotheringay—none whatever, unless you are suppressing material facts. No, it's miracles—pure miracles—miracles, if I may say so, of the very highest class."

He began to pace the hearthrug and gesticulate, while Mr. Fotheringay sat with his arm on the table and his head on his arm, looking worried. "I don't see how I'm to manage about Winch," he said.

"A gift of working miracles—apparently a very powerful gift," said Mr. Maydig, "will find a way about Winch—never fear. My dear sir, you are a most important man—a man of the most astonishing possibilities. As evidence, for example! And in other ways, the things you may do. . . ."

"Yes, *I've* thought of a thing or two," said Mr. Fotheringay. "But—some of the things came a bit twisty. You saw that fish at first? Wrong sort of bowl and wrong sort of fish. And I thought I'd ask someone."

"A proper course," said Mr. Maydig, "a very proper course—altogether the proper course." He stopped and looked at Mr. Fotheringay. "It's practically an unlimited gift. Let us test your powers, for instance. If they really *are* . . . If they really are all they seem to be."

And so, incredible as it may seem, in the study of the little house behind the Congregational Chapel, on the evening of Sunday, Nov. 10, 1896, Mr. Fotheringay, egged on and inspired by Mr. Maydig, began to work miracles. The reader's attention is specially and definitely called to the date. He will object, probably has already objected, that certain points in this story are improbable, that if any things of the sort already described had indeed occurred, they would have been in all the papers a year ago. The details immediately following he will find particularly hard to accept, because among other things they involve the conclusion that he or she, the reader in question, must have been killed in a violent and unprecedented manner more than a year ago. Now a miracle is nothing if not improbable, and as a matter of fact the reader *was* killed in a violent and unprecedented manner a year ago. In the subsequent course of this story that will become perfectly clear and credible, as every right-minded and reasonable reader will admit. But this is not the place for the end of the story, being but little beyond the hither side of the middle. And at first the miracles worked by Mr. Fotheringay were timid little miracles—little things with the cups and parlour fitments, as feeble as the miracles of Theosophists, and, feeble as they were, they were received with awe by his collaborator. He would have preferred to settle the Winch business out of hand, but Mr. Maydig would not let him. But after they had worked a dozen of these domestic trivialities, their sense of power grew, their imagination began to show signs of stimulation, and their ambition enlarged. Their first larger enterprise was due to hunger and the negligence of Mrs. Minchin, Mr. Maydig's housekeeper. The meal to which the minister conducted Mr. Fotheringay was certainly ill-laid and uninviting as refreshment for two industrious miracle-workers; but they were seated, and Mr. Maydig was descanting in sorrow rather than in anger upon his housekeeper's shortcomings, before it occurred to Mr. Fotheringay that an opportunity lay before him. "Don't you think, Mr. Maydig," he said, "if it isn't a liberty, I——"

"My dear Mr. Fotheringay! Of course! No—I didn't think."

Mr. Fotheringay waved his hand. "What shall we

have?" he said, in a large, inclusive spirit, and, at Mr. Maydig's order, revised the supper very thoroughly. "As for me," he said, eyeing Mr. Maydig's selection, "I am always particularly fond of a tankard of stout and a nice Welsh rarebit, and I'll order that. I ain't much given to Burgundy," and forthwith stout and Welsh rarebit promptly appeared at his command. They sat long at their supper, talking like equals, as Mr. Fotheringay presently perceived with a glow of surprise and gratification, of all the miracles they would presently do. "And, by the by, Mr. Maydig," said Mr. Fotheringay, "I might perhaps be able to help you—in a domestic way."

"Don't quite follow," said Mr. Maydig, pouring out a glass of miraculous old Burgundy.

Mr. Fotheringay helped himself to a second Welsh rarebit out of vacancy, and took a mouthful. "I was thinking," he said, "I might be able (*chum, chum*) to work (*chum, chum*) a miracle with Mrs. Minchin (*chum, chum*)—make her a better woman."

Mr. Maydig put down the glass and looked doubtful. "She's—— She strongly objects to interference, you know, Mr. Fotheringay. And—as a matter of fact—it's well past eleven and she's probably in bed and asleep. Do you think, on the whole——"

Mr. Fotheringay considered these objections. "I don't see that it shouldn't be done in her sleep."

For a time Mr. Maydig opposed the idea, and then he yielded. Mr. Fotheringay issued his orders, and a little less at their ease, perhaps, the two gentlemen proceeded with their repast. Mr. Maydig was enlarging on the changes he might expect in his housekeeper next day, with an optimism that seemed even to Mr. Fotheringay's super senses a little forced and hectic, when a series of confused noises from upstairs began. Their eyes exchanged interrogations, and Mr. Maydig left the room hastily. Mr. Fotheringay heard him calling up to his housekeeper and then his footsteps going softly up to her.

In a minute or so the minister returned, his step light, his face radiant. "Wonderful!" he said, "and touching! Most touching!"

He began pacing the hearthrug. "A repentance—a most touching repentance—through the crack of the door. Poor woman! A most wonderful change! She had got up. She must have got up at once. She had got up out of her sleep to smash a private bottle of brandy in her box. And to confess it, too! . . . But this gives us—it opens—a most amazing vista of possibilities. If we can work this miraculous change in *her* . . ."

"The thing's unlimited seemingly," said Mr. Fotheringay. "And about Mr. Winch——"

"Altogether unlimited." And from the hearthrug Mr. Maydig, waving the Winch difficulty aside, unfolded a series of wonderful proposals—proposals he invented as he went along.

Now what those proposals were does not concern the essentials of this story. Suffice it that they were designed in a spirit of infinite benevolence, the sort of benevolence that used to be called post-prandial. Suffice it, too, that the problem of Winch remained unsolved. Nor is it necessary to describe how far that series got to its fulfillment. There were astonishing changes. The small hours found Mr. Maydig and Mr. Fotheringay careering across the chilly market-square under the still moon, in a sort of ecstasy of thaumaturgy, Mr. Maydig all flap and gesture, Mr. Fotheringay short and bristling, and no longer abashed at his greatness. They had reformed every drunkard in the Parliamentary division, changed all the beer and alcohol to water (Mr. Maydig had overruled Mr. Fotheringay on this point), they had, further, greatly improved the railway communication of the place, drained Flinder's swamp, improved the soil of One Tree Hill, and cured the Vicar's wart. And they were going to see what could be done with the injured pier at South Bridge. "The place," gasped Mr. Maydig, "won't be the same place tomorrow. How surprised and thankful everyone will be!" And just at that moment the church clock struck three.

"I say," said Mr. Fotheringay, "that's three o'clock! I must be getting back. I've got to be at business by eight. And besides, Mrs. Wimms——"

"We're only beginning," said Mr. Maydig, full of the sweetness of unlimited power. "We're only beginning. Think of all the good we're doing. When people wake——"

"But——" said Mr. Fotheringay.

Mr. Maydig gripped his arm suddenly. His eyes were bright and wild. "My dear chap," he said, "there's no hurry. Look"—he pointed to the moon at the zenith—"Joshua!"

"Joshua?" said Mr. Fotheringay.

"Joshua," said Mr. Maydig. "Why not? Stop it."

Mr. Fotheringay looked at the moon.

"That's a bit tall," he said after a pause.

"Why not?" said Mr. Maydig. "Of course it doesn't stop. You stop the rotation of the earth, you know. Time stops. It isn't as if we were doing harm."

"H'm!" said Mr. Fotheringay. "Well." He sighed. "I'll try. Here——"

He buttoned up his jacket and addressed himself to the habitable globe, with as good an assumption of confidence as lay in his power. "Jest stop rotating, will you?" said Mr. Fotheringay.

Incontinently he was flying head over heels through the air at the rate of dozens of miles a minute. In spite of the innumerable circles he was describing per second, he thought; for thought is wonderful—sometimes as sluggish as flowing pitch, sometimes as instantaneous as light. He thought in a second, and willed. "Let me come down safe and sound. Whatever else happens, let me down safe and sound."

He willed it only just in time, for his clothes, heated by his rapid flight through the air, were already beginning to singe. He came down with a forcible but by no means injurious bump in what appeared to be a mound of fresh-turned earth. A large mass of metal and masonry, extraordinarily like the clock-tower in the middle of the market-square, hit the earth near him, ricochetted over him, and flew into stonework, bricks, and masonry, like a bursting bomb. A hurtling cow hit one of the larger blocks and smashed like an egg. There was a crash that made all the most violent crashes of his past life seem like the sound of falling dust, and this was followed by a descending series of lesser crashes. A vast wind roared throughout earth and heaven, so that he could scarcely lift his head to look. For a while he was too breathless and astonished even to see where he was or what had happened. And his first movement was to feel his head and reassure himself that his streaming hair was still his own.

"Lord!" gasped Mr. Fotheringay, scarce able to speak for the gale, "I've had a squeak! What's gone wrong? Storms and thunder. And only a minute ago a fine night. It's Maydig set me on to this sort of thing. *What* a wind! If I go on fooling in this way I'm bound to have a thundering accident! . . .

"Where's Maydig?

"What a confounded mess everything's in!"

He looked about him so far as his flapping jacket would permit. The appearance of things was really extremely strange. "The sky's all right anyhow," said Mr. Fotheringay. "And that's about all that is all right. And even there it looks like a terrific gale coming up. But there's the moon overhead. Just as it was just now. Bright as midday. But as for the rest— Where's the village? Where's—where's anything? And what on earth set this wind a-blowing? I didn't order no wind."

Mr. Fotheringay struggled to get to his feet in vain, and after one failure, remained on all fours, holding on. He surveyed the moonlit world to leeward, with the tails of his jacket streaming over his head. "There's something seriously wrong," said Mr. Fotheringay. "And what it is—goodness knows."

Far and wide nothing was visible in the white glare through the haze of dust that drove before a screaming gale but tumbled masses of earth and heaps of inchoate ruins, no trees, no houses, no familiar shapes, only a wilderness of disorder vanishing at last into the darkness beneath the whirling columns and streamers, the lightnings and thunderings of a swiftly rising storm. Near him in the livid glare was something that might once have been an elm-tree, a smashed mass of splinters, shivered from boughs to base, and further a twisted mass of iron girders—only too evidently the viaduct—rose out of the piled confusion.

You see, when Mr. Fotheringay had arrested the rotation of the solid globe, he had made no stipulation concerning the trifling movables upon its surface. And the earth spins so fast that the surface at its equator is travelling at rather more than a thousand miles an hour, and in these latitudes at more than half that pace. So that the village, and Mr. Maydig, and Mr. Fotheringay, and everybody and everything had been jerked violently forward at about nine miles per second—that is to say, much more violently than if they had been fired out of a cannon. And every human being, every living creature, every house, and every tree—all the world as we know it—had been so jerked and smashed and utterly destroyed. That was all.

These things Mr. Fotheringay did not, of course, fully appreciate. But he perceived that his miracle had miscarried, and with that a great disgust of miracles came upon him. He was in darkness now, for the clouds had swept together and blotted out his momentary glimpse of the moon, and the air was full of fitful struggling tortured wraiths of hail. A great roaring of wind and waters filled earth and sky, and, peering under his hand through the dust and sleet to windward, he saw by the play of the lightnings a vast wall of water pouring towards him.

"Maydig!" screamed Mr. Fotheringay's feeble voice amid the elemental uproar. "Here!—Maydig!

"Stop!" cried Mr. Fotheringay to the advancing water. "Oh, for goodness' sake, stop!

"Just a moment," said Mr. Fotheringay to the lightnings and thunder. "Stop just a moment while I collect my thoughts . . . And now what shall I do?" he said. "What *shall* I do? Lord! I wish Maydig was about.

"I know," said Mr. Fotheringay. "And for goodness' sake let's have it right *this* time."

He remained on all fours, leaning against the wind, very intent to have everything right.

"Ah!" he said. "Let nothing what I'm going to order happen until I say 'Off!' . . . Lord! I wish I'd thought of that before!"

He lifted his little voice against the whirlwind, shouting louder and louder in the vain desire to hear himself speak. "Now then!—here goes! Mind about that what I said just now. In the first place, when all I've got to say is done, let me lose my miraculous power, let my will become just like anybody else's will, and all these dangerous miracles be stopped. I don't like them. I'd rather I didn't work 'em. Ever so much. That's the first thing. And the second is—let me be back just before the miracles begin; let everything be just as it was before that blessed lamp turned up. It's a big job, but it's the last. Have you got it? No more miracles, everything as it was—me back in the Long Dragon just before I drank my half-pint. That's it! Yes."

He dug his fingers into the mould, closed his eyes, and said "Off!"

Everything became perfectly still. He perceived that he was standing erect.

"So *you* say," said a voice.

He opened his eyes. He was in the bar of the Long Dragon, arguing about miracles with Toddy Beamish. He had a vague sense of some great thing forgotten that instantaneously passed. You see, except for the loss of his miraculous powers, everything was back as it had been; his mind and memory therefore were now just as they had been at the time when this story began. So that he knew absolutely nothing of all that is told here, knows nothing of all that is told here to this day. And among other things, of course, he still did not believe in miracles.

"I tell you that miracles, properly speaking, can't possibly happen," he said, "whatever you like to hold. And I'm prepared to prove it up to the hilt."

"That's what *you* think," said Toddy Beamish, and "Prove it if you can."

"Looky here, Mr. Beamish," said Mr. Fotheringay. "Let us clearly understand what a miracle is. It's something contrariwise to the course of nature done by power of Will. . . ."

SHIRLEY JACKSON

One Ordinary Day, With Peanuts

Mr. John Philip Johnson shut his front door behind him and came down his front steps into the bright morning with a feeling that all was well with the world on this best of all days, and wasn't the sun warm and good, and didn't his shoes feel comfortable after the resoling, and he knew that he had undoubtedly chosen the precise very tie which belonged with the day and the sun and his comfortable feet, and, after all, wasn't the world just a wonderful place? In spite of the fact that he was a small man, and the tie was perhaps a shade vivid, Mr. Johnson irradiated this feeling of well-being as he came down the steps and onto the dirty sidewalk, and he smiled at people who passed him, and some of them even smiled back. He stopped at the newsstand on the corner and bought

First published in *The Magazine of Fantasy and Science Fiction.*

his paper, saying "*Good* morning" with real conviction to the man who sold him the paper and the two or three other people who were lucky enough to be buying papers when Mr. Johnson skipped up. He remembered to fill his pockets with candy and peanuts, and then he set out to get himself uptown. He stopped in a flower shop and bought a carnation for his buttonhole, and stopped almost immediately afterward to give the carnation to a small child in a carriage, who looked at him dumbly, and then smiled, and Mr. Johnson smiled, and the child's mother looked at Mr. Johnson for a minute and then smiled too.

When he had gone several blocks uptown, Mr. Johnson cut across the avenue and went along a side street, chosen at random; he did not follow the same route every morning, but preferred to pursue his eventful way in wide detours, more like a puppy than a man intent upon business. It happened this morning that halfway down the block a moving van was parked, and the furniture from an upstairs apartment stood half on the sidewalk, half on the steps, while an amused group of people loitered, examining the scratches on the tables and the worn spots on the chairs, and a harassed woman, trying to watch a young child and the movers and the furniture all at the same time, gave the clear impression of endeavoring to shelter her private life from the people staring at her belongings. Mr. Johnson stopped, and for a moment joined the crowd, and then he came forward and, touching his hat civilly, said, "Perhaps I can keep an eye on your little boy for you?"

The woman turned and glared at him distrustfully, and Mr. Johnson added hastily, "We'll sit right here on the steps." He beckoned to the little boy, who hesitated and then responded agreeably to Mr. Johnson's genial smile. Mr. Johnson brought out a handful of peanuts from his pocket and sat on the steps with the boy, who at first refused the peanuts on the grounds that his mother did not allow him to accept food from strangers; Mr. Johnson said that probably his mother had not intended peanuts to be included, since elephants at the circus ate them, and the boy considered, and then agreed solemnly. They sat on the steps cracking peanuts in a comradely fashion, and Mr. Johnson said, "So you're moving?"

"Yep," said the boy.

"Where you going?"

"Vermont."

"Nice place. Plenty of snow there. Maple sugar, too; you like maple sugar?"

"Sure."

"Plenty of maple sugar in Vermont. You going to live on a farm?"

"Going to live with Grandpa."

"Grandpa like peanuts?"

"Sure."

"Ought to take him some," said Mr. Johnson, reaching into his pocket. "Just you and Mommy going?"

"Yep."

"Tell you what," Mr. Johnson said. "You take some peanuts to eat on the train."

The boy's mother, after glancing at them frequently, had seemingly decided that Mr. Johnson was trustworthy, because she had devoted herself wholeheartedly to seeing that the movers did not—what movers rarely do, but every housewife believes they will—crack a leg from her good table, or set a kitchen chair down on a lamp. Most of the furniture was loaded by now, and she was deep in that nervous stage when she knew there was something she had forgotten to pack—hidden away in the back of a closet somewhere, or left at a neighbor's and forgotten, or on the clothesline—and was trying to remember under stress what it was.

"This all, lady?" the chief mover said, completing her dismay.

Uncertainly, she nodded.

"Want to go on the truck with the furniture, sonny?" the mover asked the boy, and laughed. The boy laughed too and said to Mr. Johnson, "I guess I'll have a good time at Vermont."

"Fine time," said Mr. Johnson, and stood up. "Have one more peanut before you go," he said to the boy.

The boy's mother said to Mr. Johnson, "Thank you so much; it was a great help to me."

"Nothing at all," said Mr. Johnson gallantly. "Where in Vermont are you going?"

The mother looked at the little boy accusingly, as though he had given away a secret of some importance, and said unwillingly, "Greenwich."

"Lovely town," said Mr. Johnson. He took out a card, and wrote a name on the back. "Very good friend of mine lives in Greenwich," he said. "Call on him for anything you need. His wife makes the best doughnuts in town," he added soberly to the little boy.

"Swell," said the little boy.

"Goodbye," said Mr. Johnson.

He went on, stepping happily with his new-shod feet, feeling the warm sun on his back and on the top of his head. Halfway down the block he met a stray dog and fed him a peanut.

At the corner, where another wide avenue faced him, Mr. Johnson decided to go on uptown again. Moving with comparative laziness, he was passed on either side by people hurrying and frowning, and people brushed past him going the other way, clattering along to get somewhere quickly. Mr. Johnson stopped on every corner and waited patiently for the light to change, and he stepped out of the way of anyone who seemed to be in any particular hurry, but one young lady came too fast for him, and crashed wildly into him when he stooped to pat a kitten which had run out onto the sidewalk from an apartment house and was now unable to get back through the rushing feet.

"Excuse me," said the young lady, trying frantically to pick up Mr. Johnson and hurry on at the same time, "terribly sorry."

The kitten, regardless now of danger, raced back to its home. "Perfectly all right," said Mr. Johnson, adjusting himself carefully. "You seem to be in a hurry."

"Of course I'm in a hurry," said the young lady. "I'm late."

She was extremely cross and the frown between her eyes seemed well on its way to becoming permanent. She had obviously awakened late, because she had not spent any extra time in making herself look pretty, and her dress was plain and unadorned with collar or brooch, and her lipstick was noticeably crooked. She tried to brush past Mr. Johnson, but, risking her suspicious displeasure, he took her arm and said, "Please wait."

"Look," she said ominously, "I ran into you and your lawyer can see my lawyer and I will gladly pay all damages and all inconveniences suffered therefrom but please this minute let me go because *I am late.*"

"Late for what?" said Mr. Johnson; he tried his winning smile on her but it did no more than keep her, he suspected, from knocking him down again.

"Late for work," she said between her teeth. "Late for my employment. I have a job and if I am late I lose exactly so much an hour and I cannot really afford what your pleasant conversation is costing me, be it *ever* so pleasant."

"I'll pay for it," said Mr. Johnson. Now these were magic words, not necessarily because they were true, or because she seriously expected Mr. Johnson to pay for anything, but because Mr. Johnson's flat statement, obviously innocent of irony, could not be, coming from Mr. Johnson, anything but the statement of a responsible and truthful and respectable man.

"What *do* you mean?" she asked.

"I said that since I am obviously reponsible for your being late I shall certainly pay for it."

"Don't be silly," she said, and for the first time the frown disappeared. "*I* wouldn't expect you to pay for anything—a few minutes ago I was offering to pay *you*. Anyway," she added, almost smiling, "it *was* my fault."

"What happens if you don't go to work?"

She stared. "I don't get paid."

"Precisely," said Mr. Johnson.

"What do you mean, precisely? If I don't show up at the office exactly twenty minutes ago I lose a dollar and twenty cents an hour, or two cents a minute or . . ." She thought. ". . . Almost a dime for the time I've spent talking to you."

Mr. Johnson laughed, and finally she laughed, too. "You're late already," he pointed out. "Will you give me another four cents worth?"

"I don't understand why."

"You'll see," Mr. Johnson promised. He led her over to the side of the walk, next to the buildings, and said, "Stand here," and went out into the rush of people going both ways. Selecting and considering, as one who must make a choice involving perhaps whole years of lives, he estimated the people going by. Once he almost moved, and then at the last minute thought better of it and drew back. Finally, from half a block away, he saw what he wanted, and moved out into the center of the traffic to intercept a young man, who was hurrying, and dressed as though he had awakened late, and frowning.

"Oof," said the young man, because Mr. Johnson had thought of no better way to intercept anyone than the one the young woman had unwittingly used upon him.

"Where do you think you're going?" the young man demanded from the sidewalk.

"I want to speak to you," said Mr. Johnson ominously.

The young man got up nervously, dusting himself and eying Mr. Johnson. "What for?" he said. "What'd *I* do?"

"That's what bothers me most about people nowadays," Mr. Johnson complained broadly to the people passing. "No matter whether they've done anything or not, they always figure someone's after them. About what you're going to do," he told the young man.

"Listen," said the young man, trying to brush past him, "I'm late, and I don't have any time to listen. Here's a dime, now get going."

"Thank you," said Mr. Johnson, pocketing the dime. "Look," he said, "what happens if you stop running?"

"I'm late," said the young man, still trying to get past Mr. Johnson, who was unexpectedly clinging.

"How much you make an hour?" Mr. Johnson demanded.

"A communist, are you?" said the young man. "Now will you please let me—"

"No," said Mr. Johnson insistently, "*how* much?"

"Dollar fifty," said the young man. "And *now* will you—"

"You like adventure?"

The young man stared, and, staring, found himself caught and held by Mr. Johnson's genial smile; he almost smiled back and then repressed it and made an effort to tear away. "I got to *hurry*," he said.

"Mystery? Like surprises? Unusual and exciting events?"

"You selling something?"

"Sure," said Mr. Johnson. "You want to take a chance?"

The young man hesitated, looked longingly up the avenue toward what might have been his destination and then, when Mr. Johnson said "I'll pay for it" with his own peculiar convincing emphasis, turned and said, "Well, okay. But I got to *see* it first, what I'm buying."

Mr. Johnson, breathing hard, led the young man over to the side where the girl was standing; she had been watching with interest Mr. Johnson's capture of the young man and now, smiling timidly, she looked at Mr. Johnson as though prepared to be surprised at nothing.

Mr. Johnson reached into his pocket and took out his wallet. "Here," he said, and handed a bill to the girl. "This about equals your day's pay."

"But no," she said, surprised in spite of herself. "I mean, I *couldn't.*"

"Please do not interrupt," Mr. Johnson told her. "And *here,*" he said to the young man, "this will take care of *you.*" The young man accepted the bill dazedly, but said, "Probably counterfeit" to the young woman out of the side of his mouth. "Now," Mr. Johnson went on, disregarding the young man, "what is your name, miss?"

"Kent," she said helplessly. "Mildred Kent."

"Fine," said Mr. Johnson. "And you, sir?"

"Arthur Adams," said the young man stiffly.

"Splendid," said Mr. Johnson. "Now, Miss Kent, I

would like you to meet Mr. Adams. Mr. Adams, Miss Kent."

Miss Kent stared, wet her lips nervously, made a gesture as though she might run, and said, "How do you do?"

Mr. Adams straightened his shoulders, scowled at Mr. Johnson, made a gesture as though he might run, and said, "How do you do?"

"Now *this,*" said Mr. Johnson, taking several bills from his wallet, "should be enough for the day for both of you. I would suggest, perhaps, Coney Island—although I personally am not fond of the place—or perhaps a nice lunch somewhere, and dancing, or a matinee, or even a movie, although take care to choose a really *good* one; there are *so* many bad movies these days. You might," he said, struck with an inspiration, "visit the Bronx Zoo, or the Planetarium. Anywhere, as a matter of fact," he concluded, "that you would like to go. Have a nice time."

As he started to move away Arthur Adams, breaking from his dumbfounded stare, said, "But see here, mister, you *can't* do this. Why—how do you know—I mean, *we* don't even know—I mean, how do you know we won't just take the money and not do what you said?"

"You've taken the money," Mr. Johnson said. "You don't have to follow any of my suggestions. You may know something you prefer to do—perhaps a museum, or something."

"But suppose I just run away with it and leave her here?"

"I know you won't," said Mr. Johnson gently, "because

you remembered to ask *me* that. Goodbye," he added, and went on.

As he stepped up the street, conscious of the sun on his head and his good shoes, he heard from somewhere behind him the young man saying, "Look, you know you don't *have* to if you don't want to," and the girl saying, "But unless *you* don't want to . . ." Mr. Johnson smiled to himself and then thought that he had better hurry along; when he wanted to he could move very quickly, and before the young woman had gotten around to saying, "Well, *I* will if *you* will," Mr. Johnson was several blocks away and had already stopped twice, once to help a lady lift several large packages into a taxi and once to hand a peanut to a seagull. By this time he was in an area of large stores and many more people and he was buffeted constantly from either side by people hurrying and cross and late and sullen. Once he offered a peanut to a man who asked him for a dime, and once he offered a peanut to a bus driver who had stopped his bus at an intersection and had opened the window next to his seat and put out his head as though longing for fresh air and the comparative quiet of the traffic. The man wanting a dime took the peanut because Mr. Johnson had wrapped a dollar bill around it, but the bus driver took the peanut and asked ironically, "You want a transfer, Jack?"

On a busy corner Mr. Johnson encountered two young people—for one minute he thought they might be Mildred Kent and Arthur Adams—who were eagerly scanning a newspaper, their backs pressed against a storefront to avoid the people passing, their heads bent together. Mr. Johnson, whose curiosity was insatiable, leaned onto the storefront next to them and peeked over the man's shoulder; they were scanning the "Apartments Vacant" columns.

Mr. Johnson remembered the street where the woman and her little boy were going to Vermont and he tapped the man on the shoulder and said amiably, "Try down on West Seventeen. About the middle of the block, people moved out this morning."

"Say, what do you—" said the man, and then, seeing Mr. Johnson clearly, "Well, thanks. Where did you say?"

"West Seventeen," said Mr. Johnson. "About the middle of the block." He smiled again and said, "Good luck."

"Thanks," said the man.

"Thanks," said the girl, as they moved off.

"Goodbye," said Mr. Johnson.

He lunched alone in a pleasant restaurant, where the food was rich, and only Mr. Johnson's excellent digestion could encompass two of their whipped-cream-and-chocolate-and-rum-cake pastries for dessert. He had three cups of coffee, tipped the waiter largely, and went out into the street again into the wonderful sunlight, his shoes still comfortable and fresh on his feet. Outside, he found a beggar staring into the windows of the restaurant he had left and, carefully looking through the money in his pocket, Mr. Johnson approached the beggar and pressed some coins and a couple of bills into his hand. "It's the price of the veal cutlet lunch plus tip," said Mr. Johnson. "Goodbye."

After his lunch he rested; he walked into the nearest park and fed peanuts to the pigeons. It was late afternoon by the time he was ready to start back downtown, and he had refereed two checker games and watched a small boy and girl whose mother had fallen asleep and awakened with surprise and fear which turned to amusement when she saw Mr. Johnson. He had given away almost all of his candy, and had fed all the rest of his peanuts to the pigeons, and it was time to go home. Although the late afternoon sun was pleasant, and his shoes were still entirely comfortable, he decided to take a taxi downtown.

He had a difficult time catching a taxi, because he gave up the first three or four empty ones to people who seemed to need them more; finally, however, he stood alone on the corner and—almost like netting a frisky fish—he hailed desperately until he succeeded in catching a cab which had been proceeding with haste uptown and seemed to draw in toward Mr. Johnson against its own will.

"Mister," the cab driver said as Mr. Johnson climbed in, "I figured you was an omen, like. I wasn't going to pick you up at all."

"Kind of you," said Mr. Johnson ambiguously.

"If I'd of let you go it would of cost me ten bucks," said the driver.

"Really?" said Mr. Johnson.

"Yeah," said the driver. "Guy just got out of the cab, he turned around and give me ten bucks, said take this and bet it in a hurry on a horse named Vulcan, right away."

"Vulcan?" said Mr. Johnson, horrified. "A fire sign on a Wednesday?"

"What?" said the driver. "Anyway, I said to myself if I got no fare between here and there I'd bet the ten, but if anyone looked like they needed the cab I'd take it as a omen and I'd take the ten home to the wife."

"You were very right," said Mr. Johnson heartily. "This is Wednesday, you would have lost your money. Monday, yes, or even Saturday. But never never never a fire sign on a Wednesday. Sunday would have been good, now."

"Vulcan don't run on Sunday," said the driver.

"You wait till another day," said Mr. Johnson. "Down this street, please, driver. I'll get off on the next corner."

"He *told* me Vulcan, though," said the driver.

"I'll tell you," said Mr. Johnson, hesitating with the door of the cab half open. "You take that ten dollars and I'll give you another ten dollars to go with it, and you go right ahead and bet that money on any Thursday on any horse that has a name indicating . . . let me see, Thursday . . . well, grain. Or any growing food."

"Grain?" said the driver. "You mean a horse named, like, Wheat or something?"

"Certainly," said Mr. Johnson. "Or, as a matter of fact, to make it even easier, any horse whose name includes the letters C, R, L. Perfectly simple."

"Tall corn?" said the driver, a light in his eye. "You mean a horse named, like, Tall Corn?"

"Absolutely," said Mr. Johnson. "Here's your money."

"Tall Corn," said the driver. "Thank *you,* mister."

"Goodbye," said Mr. Johnson.

He was on his own corner and went straight ahead up to his apartment. He let himself in and called "Hello?" and Mrs. Johnson answered from the kitchen, "Hello, dear, aren't you early?"

"Took a taxi home," Mr. Johnson said. "I remembered the cheesecake, too. What's for dinner?"

Mrs. Johnson came out of the kitchen and kissed him; she was a comfortable woman, and smiling as Mr. Johnson smiled. "Hard day?" she asked.

"Not very," said Mr. Johnson, hanging his coat in the closet. "How about you?"

"So-so," she said. She stood in the kitchen doorway while he settled into his easy chair and took off his good shoes and took out the paper he had bought that morning. "Here and there," she said.

"I didn't do so badly," Mr. Johnson said. "Couple young people."

"Fine," she said. "I had a little nap this afternoon, took it easy most of the day. Went into a department store this morning and accused the woman next to me of shoplifting, and had the store detective pick her up. Sent three dogs to the pound—*you* know, the usual thing. Oh, and listen," she added remembering.

"What?" asked Mr. Johnson.

"Well," she said, "I got onto a bus and asked the driver for a transfer, and when he helped someone else first I said that he was impertinent, and quarreled with him.

And then I said why wasn't he in the army, and I said it loud enough for everyone to hear, and I took his number and I turned in a complaint. Probably got him fired."

"Fine," said Mr. Johnson. "But you do look tired. Want to change over tomorrow?"

"I *would* like to," she said. "I could do with a change."

"Right," said Mr. Johnson. "What's for dinner?"

"Veal cutlet."

"Had it for lunch," said Mr. Johnson.

FRANK O'CONNOR

First Confession

All the trouble began when my grandfather died and my grandmother—my father's mother—came to live with us. Relations in the one house are a strain at the best of times, but, to make matters worse, my grandmother was a real old countrywoman and quite unsuited to the life in town. She had a fat, wrinkled old face, and, to Mother's great indignation, went round the house in bare feet—the boots had her crippled, she said. For dinner she had a jug of porter and a pot of potatoes with—sometimes—a bit of salt fish, and she poured out the potatoes on the table and ate them slowly, with great relish, using her fingers by way of a fork.

Now, girls are supposed to be fastidious, but I was the one who suffered most from this. Nora, my sister, just sucked up to the old woman for the penny she got every Friday out of the old-age pension, a thing I could not do. I was too honest, that was my trouble; and when I was playing with Bill Connell, the sergeant-major's son, and saw my grandmother steering up the path with the jug of porter sticking out from beneath her shawl I was mortified. I made excuses not to let him come into the house, because I could never be sure what she would be up to when we went in.

When Mother was at work and my grandmother made the dinner I wouldn't touch it. Nora once tried to make me, but I hid under the table from her and took the bread-knife with me for protection. Nora let on to be very indignant (she wasn't, of course, but she knew Mother saw through her, so she sided with Gran) and came after me. I lashed out at her with the bread-knife, and after that she left me alone. I stayed there till Mother came in from work and made my dinner, but when Father came in later Nora said in a shocked voice: "Oh, Dadda, do you know what Jackie did at dinnertime?" Then, of course, it all came out; Father gave me a flaking; Mother interfered, and for days after that he didn't speak to me and Mother barely spoke to Nora. And all because of that old woman! God knows, I was heartscalded.

Then, to crown my misfortunes, I had to make my first confession and communion. It was an old woman called Ryan who prepared us for these. She was about the one age with Gran; she was well-to-do, lived in a big house on Montenotte, wore a black cloak and bonnet, and came every day to school at three o'clock when we should have been going home, and talked to us of hell. She may have mentioned the other place as well, but that could only have been by accident, for hell had the first place in her heart.

She lit a candle, took out a new half-crown, and offered it to the first boy who would hold one finger—only one finger!—in the flame for five minutes by the school clock. Being always very ambitious I was tempted to volunteer, but I thought it might look greedy. Then she asked were we afraid of holding one finger—only one finger!—in a little candle flame for five minutes and not afraid of burning all over in roasting hot furnaces for all eternity. "All eternity! Just think of that! A whole lifetime goes by and it's nothing, not even a drop in the ocean of your sufferings." The woman was really interesting about hell, but my attention was all fixed on the half-crown. At the end of the lesson she put it back in her purse. It was a great disappointment; a religious woman like that, you wouldn't think she'd bother about a thing like a half-crown.

Another day she said she knew a priest who woke one night to find a fellow he didn't recognize leaning over the end of his bed. The priest was a bit frightened—naturally enough—but he asked the fellow what he wanted, and the fellow said in a deep, husky voice that he wanted to go to confession. The priest said it was an awkward time and wouldn't it do in the morning, but the fellow said that last time he went to confession, there was one sin he kept back, being ashamed to mention it, and now it was always on his mind. Then the priest knew it was a bad case, because the fellow was after making a bad confession and committing a mortal sin. He got up to dress, and just then the cock crew in the yard outside, and—lo and behold!—when the priest looked round there was no sign of the fellow, only a smell of burning timber, and when the priest looked at his bed didn't he see the print of two hands burned in it? That was because the fellow had made a bad confession. This story made a shocking impression on me.

But the worst of all was when she showed us how to examine our conscience. Did we take the name of the Lord, our God, in vain? Did we honour our father and our mother? (I asked her did this include grandmothers and she said it did.) Did we love our neighbours as ourselves? Did we covet our neighbour's goods? (I thought of the way I felt about the penny that Nora got every Friday.) I decided that, between one thing and another, I must have broken the whole ten commandments, all on account of that old woman, and so far as I could see, so long as she remained in the house I had no hope of ever doing anything else.

I was scared to death of confession. The day the whole class went I let on to have a toothache, hoping my absence wouldn't be noticed; but at three o'clock, just as I was feeling safe, along comes a chap with a message from Mrs. Ryan that I was to go to confession myself on Saturday and be at the chapel for communion with the rest. To make it worse, Mother couldn't come with me and sent Nora instead.

Now, that girl had ways of tormenting me that Mother never knew of. She held my hand as we went down the hill, smiling sadly and saying how sorry she was for me, as if she were bringing me to the hospital for an operation.

"Oh, God help us!" she moaned. "Isn't it a terrible pity you weren't a good boy? Oh, Jackie, my heart bleeds for you! How will you ever think of all your sins? Don't forget you have to tell him about the time you kicked Gran on the shin."

"Lemme go!" I said, trying to drag myself free of her. "I don't want to go to confession at all."

"But sure, you'll have to go to confession, Jackie," she replied in the same regretful tone. "Sure, if you didn't, the parish priest would be up to the house, looking for you. 'Tisn't, God knows, that I'm not sorry for you. Do you remember the time you tried to kill me with the bread-knife under the table? And the language you used to me? I don't know what he'll do with you at all, Jackie. He might have to send you up to the bishop."

I remember thinking bitterly that she didn't know the half of what I had to tell—if I told it. I knew I couldn't tell it, and understood perfectly why the fellow in Mrs. Ryan's story made a bad confession; it seemed to me a great shame that people wouldn't stop criticizing him. I remember that steep hill down to the church, and the sunlit hillsides beyond the valley of the river, which I saw in the gaps between the houses like Adam's last glimpse of Paradise.

Then, when she had manœuvred me down the long

flight of steps to the chapel yard, Nora suddenly changed her tone. She became the raging malicious devil she really was.

"There you are!" she said with a yelp of triumph, hurling me through the church door. "And I hope he'll give you the penitential psalms, you dirty little caffler."

I knew then I was lost, given up to eternal justice. The door with the coloured-glass panels swung shut behind me, the sunlight went out and gave place to deep shadow, and the wind whistled outside so that the silence within seemed to crackle like ice under my feet. Nora sat in front of me by the confession box. There were a couple of old women ahead of her, and then a miserable-looking poor devil came and wedged me in at the other side, so that I couldn't escape even if I had the courage. He joined his hands and rolled his eyes in the direction of the roof, muttering aspirations in an anguished tone, and I wondered had he a grandmother too. Only a grandmother could account for a fellow behaving in that heartbroken way, but he was better off than I, for he at least could go and confess his sins; while I would make a bad confession and then die in the night and be continually coming back and burning people's furniture.

Nora's turn came, and I heard the sound of something slamming, and then her voice as if butter wouldn't melt in her mouth, and then another slam, and out she came. God, the hypocrisy of women! Her eyes were lowered, her head was bowed, and her hands were joined very low down on her stomach, and she walked up the aisle to the side altar looking like a saint. You never saw such an exhibition of devotion; and I remembered the devilish malice with which she had tormented me all the way from our door, and wondered were all religious people like that, really. It was my turn now. With the fear of damnation in my soul I went in, and the confessional door closed of itself behind me.

It was pitch-dark and I couldn't see priest or anything else. Then I really began to be frightened. In the darkness it was a matter between God and me, and He had all the odds. He knew what my intentions were before I even started; I had no chance. All I had ever been told about confession got mixed up in my mind, and I knelt to one wall and said: "Bless me, father, for I have sinned; this is my first confession." I waited for a few minutes, but nothing happened, so I tried it on the other wall. Nothing happened there either. He had me spotted all right.

It must have been then that I noticed the shelf at about one height with my head. It was really a place for grown-up people to rest their elbows, but in my distracted state I thought it was probably the place you were supposed to kneel. Of course, it was on the high side and not very deep, but I was always good at climbing and managed to get up all right. Staying up was the trouble. There was room only for my knees, and nothing you could get a grip on but a sort of wooden moulding a bit above it. I held on to the moulding and repeated the words a little louder, and this time something happened all right. A slide was slammed back; a little light entered the box, and a man's voice said: "Who's there?"

" 'Tis me, father," I said for fear he mightn't see me and go away again. I couldn't see him at all. The place the voice came from was under the moulding, about level with my knees, so I took a good grip of the moulding and swung myself down till I saw the astonished face of a young priest looking up at me. He had to put his head on one side to see me, and I had to put mine on one side to see him, so we were more or less talking to one another upside-down. It struck me as a queer way of hearing confessions, but I didn't feel it my place to criticize.

"Bless me, father, for I have sinned; this is my first confession," I rattled off all in one breath, and swung myself down the least shade more to make it easier for him.

"What are you doing up there?" he shouted in an angry voice, and the strain the politeness was putting on my hold of the moulding, and the shock of being addressed in such an uncivil tone, were too much for me. I lost my grip, tumbled, and hit the door an unmerciful wallop before I found myself flat on my back in the middle of the aisle. The people who had been waiting stood up with their mouths open. The priest opened the door of the middle box and came out, pushing his biretta back from his forehead; he looked something terrible. Then Nora came scampering down the aisle.

"Oh, you dirty little caffler!" she said. "I might have known you'd do it. I might have known you'd disgrace me. I can't leave you out of my sight for one minute."

Before I could even get to my feet to defend myself she bent down and gave me a clip across the ear. This reminded me that I was so stunned I had even forgotten to cry, so that people might think I wasn't hurt at all, when in fact I was probably maimed for life. I gave a roar out of me.

"What's all this about?" the priest hissed, getting angrier than ever and pushing Nora off me. "How dare you hit the child like that, you little vixen?"

"But I can't do my penance with him, father," Nora cried, cocking an outraged eye up at him.

"Well, go and do it, or I'll give you some more to do," he said, giving me a hand up. "Was it coming to confession you were, my poor man?" he asked me.

" 'Twas, father," said I with a sob.

"Oh," he said respectfully, "a big hefty fellow like you must have terrible sins. Is this your first?"

" 'Tis father," said I.

"Worse and worse," he said gloomily. "The crimes of a lifetime. I don't know will I get rid of you at all today. You'd better wait now till I'm finished with these old ones. You can see by the looks of them they haven't much to tell."

"I will, father," I said with something approaching joy.

The relief of it was really enormous. Nora stuck out her tongue at me from behind his back, but I couldn't even be bothered retorting. I knew from the very moment that man opened his mouth that he was intelligent above the ordinary. When I had time to think, I saw how right I was. It only stood to reason that a fellow confessing after seven years would have more to tell than people that went every week. The crimes of a lifetime, exactly as he said. It was only what he expected, and the rest was the cackle of old women and girls with their talk of hell, the bishop, and the penitential psalms. That was all they knew. I started to make my examination of conscience, and barring the one bad business of my grandmother it didn't seem so bad.

The next time, the priest steered me into the confession box himself and left the shutter back the way I could see him get in and sit down at the further side of the grille from me.

"Well, now," he said, "what do they call you?"

"Jackie, father," said I.

"And what's a-trouble to you, Jackie?"

"Father," I said, feeling I might as well get it over while I had him in good humour, "I had it all arranged to kill my grandmother."

He seemed a bit shaken by that, all right, because he said nothing for quite a while.

"My goodness," he said at last, "that'd be a shocking thing to do. What put that into your head?"

"Father," I said, feeling very sorry for myself, "she's an awful woman."

"Is she?" he asked. "What way is she awful?"

"She takes porter, father," I said, knowing well from the way Mother talked of it that this was a mortal sin, and hoping it would make the priest take a more favourable view of my case.

"Oh, my!" he said, and I could see he was impressed.

"And snuff, father," said I.

"That's a bad case, sure enough, Jackie," he said.

"And she goes round in her bare feet, father," I went on in a rush of self-pity, "and she know I don't like her, and she gives pennies to Nora and none to me, and my da sides with her and flakes me, and one night I was so heart-scalded I made up my mind I'd have to kill her."

"And what would you do with the body?" he asked with great interest.

"I was thinking I could chop that up and carry it away in a barrow I have," I said.

"Begor, Jackie," he said, "do you know you're a terrible child?"

"I know, father," I said, for I was just thinking the same thing myself. "I tried to kill Nora too with a bread-knife under the table, only I missed her."

"Is that the little girl that was beating you just now?" he asked.

" 'Tis, father."

"Someone will go for her with a bread-knife one day, and he won't miss her," he said rather cryptically. "You must have great courage. Between ourselves, there's a lot of people I'd like to do the same to but I'd never have the nerve. Hanging is an awful death."

"Is it, father?" I asked with the deepest interest—I was always very keen on hanging. "Did you ever see a fellow hanged?"

"Dozens of them," he said solemnly. "And they all died roaring."

"Jay!" I said.

"Oh, a horrible death!" he said with great satisfaction.

"Lots of the fellows I saw killed their grandmothers too, but they all said 'twas never worth it."

He had me there for a full ten minutes talking, and then walked out the chapel yard with me. I was genuinely sorry to part with him, because he was the most entertaining character I'd ever met in the religious line. Outside, after the shadow of the church, the sunlight was like the roaring of waves on a beach; it dazzled me; and when the frozen silence melted and I heard the screech of trams on the road my heart soared. I knew now I wouldn't die in the night and come back, leaving marks on my mother's furniture. It would be a great worry to her, and the poor soul had enough.

Nora was sitting on the railing, waiting for me, and she put on a very sour puss when she saw the priest with me. She was mad jealous because a priest had never come out of the church with her.

"Well," she asked coldly, after he left me, "what did he give you?"

"Three Hail Marys," I said.

"Three Hail Marys," she repeated incredulously. "You mustn't have told him anything."

"I told him everything," I said confidently.

"About Gran and all?"

"About Gran and all."

(All she wanted was to be able to go home and say I'd made a bad confession.)

"Did you tell him you went for me with the breadknife?" she asked with a frown.

"I did to be sure."

"And he only gave you three Hail Marys?"

"That's all."

She slowly got down from the railing with a baffled air. Clearly, this was beyond her. As we mounted the steps back to the main road she looked at me suspiciously.

"What are you sucking?" she asked.

"Bullseyes."

"Was it the priest gave them to you?"

" 'Twas."

"Lord God," she wailed bitterly, "some people have all the luck! 'Tis no advantage to anybody trying to be good. I might just as well be a sinner like you."

ABOUT THE AUTHORS

CONRAD POTTER AIKEN was born in 1889 at Savannah, Georgia. In 1930 he received the Pulitzer Prize for poetry. His published works include *Among the Lost People, Blue Voyage, Great Circle,* and *King Coffin.*

ROBERT ARTHUR was born on Corregidor Island, in the Philippines. He graduated from the University of Michigan in 1935 and since that time he has been a writer, combining writing with stints of editing, publicity work, newspaper work, as well as radio production and writing and television writing. He has twice won the annual award given by the Mystery Writers of America, Inc., and has written hundreds of short stories for all types of magazines, and hundreds of radio scripts. He is currently engaged in writing for television.

STEPHEN VINCENT BENÉT (1898-1943) was born at Bethlehem, Pennsylvania. His first book was published in 1915, when he was only seventeen. He wrote many books, plays, long narrative poems, stories, and novels. His most popular work is *John Brown's Body.*

AMBROSE DWINETT BIERCE (1842-1914) was born in Meigs County, Ohio. Although he first achieved fame as a political cartoonist, he eventually turned to writing stories, essays, and a newspaper column. He became a master of the art of writing terse, cold stories of horror, largely as a result of his experience during four years of service in the Civil War. These stories will be found in the collection *In the Midst of Life.*

HEYWOOD CAMPBELL BROUN (1888-1939) began his literary career as editor of his school paper at Horace Mann School, not far from Brooklyn where he was born. All his life he was dedicated to newspaper work, writing baseball stories for the New York *Telegram* and conducting a nationally famous column, "It Seems to Me," for the *Tribune*. Some of his best work is collected in *Seeing Things at Night.*

HENRY CURLER BUNNER (1855-96) was born at Oswego, New York. He spent most of his career in New York City, where, at the age of twenty-two, he became editor of the humorous magazine *Puck.* In this capacity, he wrote hundreds of entertaining poems and stories, achieving national fame for writing short tales with surprising plots. Many of his tales are collected in the book *Short Sixes.*

ANTON PAVLOVICH CHEKHOV (1860-1904) was born in Taganrog, southern Russia, of a family that had once been serfs. He was a doctor during the first part of his career, but gave up medicine for writing. His stories and plays are among the masterpieces of world literature.

ROBERT M. COATES was born in 1896 at New Haven, Connecticut. He has been with *The New Yorker* since 1926, contributing short stories, articles and art criticism.

JOHN COLLIER was born in London in 1901. He has written poems, stories, essays, novels, and informal histories of England.

RICHARD EDWARD CONNELL was born in 1893 in Dutchess County, New York. Collections of his tales include *Apes and Angels, Ironies,* and *The Sin of Monsieur Petipon.*

JULIUS FAST was born in 1919 in New York City. He is best known for his mystery novels and in 1944 won the Mystery Writers of America award for his novel *Watchful at Night.*

MICHAEL FESSIER (1905-), a native of California, has been an editor, a newspaperman, and a screenwriter. His stories have appeared in *Esquire, Harpers,* and *Story* magazine.

SHIRLEY JACKSON was born in 1919 in San Francisco. She has written essays, novels, and short stories, as well as a series of sketches about her children.

STEPHEN BUTLER LEACOCK (1869-1944) was born in England, but moved to Canada early in his life and remained there until his death. He was noted as a humorist, a teacher, and a scientist in economics. His books of humorous essays and stories (*Winsome Winnie, Nonsense Novels, The Iron Man* and *The Tin Woman*) made him as popular in America as Mark Twain.

HECTOR HUGH MUNRO (1870-1916), who wrote humorous short stories under the name "Saki," was born in India, and lived and worked in many European countries. He was killed in action in World War I. Among his books are *Beasts and Super-Beasts, The Toys of Peace,* and *The Chronicles of Clovis.*

FITZ-JAMES O'BRIEN (1826-62) was born in Ireland. His best tales are of weird and uncanny events, which he wrote about in a realistic, conversational style, unlike Edgar Allan Poe.

FRANK O'CONNOR was born in 1903 in Cork, Ireland. His stories—warm, realistic, humorous tales—have been published in many books.

EDGAR ALLAN POE (1809-49) was born in Boston, but spent most of his life in the South. The nature of his famous stories is suggested by the title of his first book: *Tales of the Grotesque and the Arabesque.*

LOGAN PEARSALL SMITH (1865-1946) was born in Millville, New Jersey, but lived most of his life in England. He is one of the few men in literary history who became known for writing imaginative little narratives and essays no longer than one paragraph. Most of his short pieces are collected in the book *Trivia.*

WILBUR DANIEL STEELE (1886-) was born in Greensboro, North Carolina, and now lives in Lyme, Connecticut. A representative collection of his short fiction is *Best Stories 1946.*

ROBERT LOUIS STEVENSON (1850-94) was born in Edinburgh, Scotland. His work includes essays, novels, poetry and short stories. In addition, he wrote a book of short fables, a little-known aspect of his work. Three are included in this collection.

FRANK STOCKTON (1839-1902) was born in Philadelphia. Among his books are *Rudder Grange* and *The Casting Away of Mrs. Lecks and Mrs. Aleshine.* His most famous story, "The Lady or the Tiger?" was once turned into an operetta.

JAMES THURBER (1894-) of Columbus, Ohio, was for many years an editor of *The New Yorker.* Among his best books are *Is Sex Necessary?*, *The Middle-Aged Man on the Flying Trapeze*, and *Fables for Our Time.*

MARK TWAIN [Samuel Langhorne Clemens] (1835-1910), author of *Tom Sawyer* and *Huckleberry Finn,* was born at Florida, Missouri, and is now universally regarded as one of the greatest of all American writers.

H[ERBERT] G[EORGE] WELLS (1866-1946) was born in England. His best-known works include stories of extraordinary imagination like *The War of the Worlds* in which he attempts to prophesy the future.

E. B. WHITE (1899-) was born in Mt. Vernon, New York. The greatest part of his career has been connected with *The New Yorker,* both as editor and free-lance contributor. He has written poetry, essays, and stories. Two of his best-known books are *One Man's Meat,* and *A Sub-Treasury of American Humor.*

OSCAR FINGAL O'FLAHERTIE WILLS WILDE (1854-1900) was born in Dublin, Ireland. He began writing while in college, and later became editor of a popular magazine in London. He wrote fairy tales, a novel, and several very successful plays, among them *The Importance of Being Earnest* and *Lady Windermere's Fan.*

DR. WILLIAM CARLOS WILLIAMS (1883-), a native of Rutherford, New Jersey, has divided his time between writing and practicing medicine, material for the former often deriving from the latter. He is an important modern poet, a novelist, and an essayist. *The Knife of the Times and Other Stories* was published in 1932.

ABOUT THE EDITOR

HART DAY LEAVITT was born in 1909 at Concord, New Hampshire. His great interest, literature, was aroused at Phillips Exeter Academy, and he went on to major in

English at Yale University. After graduating in 1932, he tried a number of odd jobs—selling children's clothes, playing in a jazz band, and writing for a newspaper—but eventually settled on teaching English, and has been an instructor at Phillips Andover Academy for the past twenty-three years. This book is his first work as a professional editor, but as a free-lance photographer and writer, he has contributed to newspapers and magazines. In 1938 he married Caroline Williams Parker of Concord, New Hampshire, and they have three children, Sally, Ned, and Judy.

LOOKING GLASS LIBRARY

The publishers of the Looking Glass Library are Jason Epstein, Clelia Carroll, and Edward Gorey. The consulting editors are W. H. Auden, Phyllis McGinley, and Edmund Wilson.

The following titles are available in the series:

Five Children and It	E. NESBIT
The Phœnix and the Carpet	E. NESBIT
The Story of the Amulet	E. NESBIT
The Book of Dragons	E. NESBIT
The Blue Fairy Book	ANDREW LANG (ED.)
The Red Fairy Book	ANDREW LANG (ED.)
The Green Fairy Book	ANDREW LANG (ED.)
The Princess and the Goblin	GEORGE MAC DONALD
The Princess and Curdie	GEORGE MAC DONALD
Men and Gods	REX WARNER
Wild Animals I Have Known	ERNEST THOMPSON SETON
The Peterkin Papers	LUCRETIA P. HALE
A Book of Nonsense	EDWARD LEAR
The Looking Glass Book of Verse	JANET ADAM SMITH (ED.)
The Looking Glass Book of Stories	HART DAY LEAVITT (ED.)
The Comic Looking Glass	HART DAY LEAVITT (ED.)
The Haunted Looking Glass: Ghost Stories	EDWARD GOREY (ED.)
The Lost World	SIR ARTHUR CONAN DOYLE
The Hound of the Baskervilles	SIR ARTHUR CONAN DOYLE
Otto of the Silver Hand	HOWARD PYLE

The Wizard of Oz & The Land of Oz	L. FRANK BAUM
Countess Kate	CHARLOTTE YONGE
Tarka the Otter	HENRY WILLIAMSON
The War of the Worlds	H. G. WELLS
Buccaneers and Pirates of Our Coasts	FRANK R. STOCKTON
The Spider's Palace	RICHARD HUGHES
The Prisoner of Zenda	ANTHONY HOPE
The Tapestry Room	MRS. MOLESWORTH